ARK
FOUND

AN OMEGA FILES ADVENTURE

RICK CHESLER

10 9 8 7 6 5 4 3 2 1

PROLOGUE

April 15, 1912

North Atlantic Ocean, aboard the R.M.S. Titanic

Chronopoulos Dimitrios wondered why the band was still playing. Clearly, despite all the hoopla proclaiming it "unsinkable," the great liner *Titanic* was sinking. They'd struck an iceberg, he'd heard. From his position above the port side Boat Deck, he watched the seven musicians play as though it was any other late night performance. But the angle of the deck now had a pronounced list to it. Chronopoulos found himself having to reach out with an arm to grab a railing to keep from slipping.

He felt a hand grip him on the shoulder and turned around to see his brother, Apostolos, who'd gone to see if he could get more information from the crew about was going on. His next words unsettled him deeply.

"They're launching the lifeboats."

Chronopoulos made steady eye contact with his brother while he tried to make sense of the uncertainty plaguing his thoughts. A breeze, light but weighted with chill, ruffled his hair.

"Well come on!" his brother pleaded. "We should get in the queue."

Chronopoulos glanced down at the port rail, where he heard a splash over the strains of a waltz. A chorus of shouts erupted as the first boat

1

landed lopsided in the water, nearly tipping over, but then landing upright.

"Third class will be the last to board, anyway," Chronopoulos said, turning back to his brother. Even in steerage class, the trip had been an expensive one for them, but the prospect of a visit to New York City held its own potential monetary reward. "Tell you what: you go down there and get in line. I've got to get my parcel out of the safe."

His brother's eyes widened in fear. "Are you crazy? That part of the ship could be flooded by now!"

"I've got to take a look. It's the whole reason for my trip. I'll be quick about it." Chronopoulos spun on a heel and looked away from the band toward the stairs that led into the ship's common areas.

"Don't be stupid!" Apostolos' voice nagged after him. "It's not worth it. You're risking your life for what, that old scroll?"

At this, Chronopoulos wheeled around. "That *old scroll* as you call it might happen to be the most valuable thing I own. Think about it...the location of Noah's Ark! Invaluable. And there are no copies of it."

Apostolos rolled his eyes. "I respect your career in archaeology, brother, I really do. But honestly, you have no idea if that old paper is genuine or not."

"You know what happened. The papyrus it's printed on was evaluated by a London expert and found to be of proper age, and he recommended I bring it to the collector in New York, who has a network of—" Chronopoulos was interrupted by the sound of a fight breaking out down below on deck. Both siblings turned to look as fisticuffs erupted between two male passengers vying for position in a new line that was forming for a second lifeboat that had not yet been lowered to the water.

"Go then, if it makes you feel better," Apostolos relented. "By the looks of things, we could use Noah's ark right about now, couldn't we?"

Chronopoulos smiled warmly at his brother and gave a slight nod as he turned and ran off toward the entrance to the ship's interior. More people streamed out onto the decks now—both passengers and crew alike—and the young Greek found himself feeling like a salmon swimming upstream as he entered the ship's common area against the flow. He was bumped into more than a few times as he made his way deeper into the ship. Although there was no public address system, no ship-wide announcement that the mighty *Titanic* was going down, people were beginning to suspect that was exactly what was happening. The uncertainty served only to make things worse.

Chronopoulos reached the hallway that led to his quarters and turned left. He didn't need to go to his quarters—he and his brothers had already retrieved all of their belongings, including the key to the safe—but he didn't know how to get to the Purser's Room where the safe was unless he first visited his own room. The ship was that big, and he didn't have time to squander getting lost. Only a few people occupied the space, most of them walking in the opposite direction to get outside. He passed a husband and wife standing in front of an open quarters door arguing fiercely over where their child was last seen.

Strange groaning and creaking noises emanated from places unknown as Chronopoulos forged his way down the hallway. He passed his quarters and peered quickly inside without stopping. The berth's bunk beds, which had housed eight people including Chronopoulos and his brother, were now empty. He noticed the water running in the single communal sink. A shame, he thought, picking up his pace now as he continued down the hall. He really had been having a good time on the voyage. Although he was a third class passenger, he had heard other, more travelled passengers state that the third class accommodations aboard *Titanic* were equivalent to second class room and aboard on most other ocean liners.

He passed the open door to the third class smoking lounge and was surprised to see an old woman inside, seated at a table by herself and smoking a cigarette with a long filter as though she had not a care in the world. She made eye contact with him but said nothing nor changed her expression. Chronopoulos kept moving, by now unconsciously adjusting his gait for the increasingly unsteady movement of the ship. He reached a stairwell and took it up two flights before it opened into another hallway, this one shorter than the last. Near the end of it, he saw a gaggle of three or four people outside the door to the Purser's Room.

They were arguing. Chronopoulos could see and hear that much even before he could make out the details of their faces or hear the individual words being spoken. He wasn't sure about what, but then when he got near enough they all stopped talking and watched him approach. The rowdy group of men, third class passengers by the looks of it, though Chronopoulos realized that he himself might fool some people by the way he dressed up a bit, blocked the doorway. Chronopoulos paused at the double-door entrance and looked past them into the Purser's Room. It appeared no one was inside.

"Excuse me." The archaeologist waited for at least one of them to step aside, but instead they all stopped arguing with each other and stared at him. He could smell alcohol on their breath. One of the men looked as though he was about to object, but one of his companions shot him a look that said, *let him pass.*

Chronopoulos hurried into the room before they could change their mind. The last thing he needed right now was to be involved in some kind of drunken altercation. He fumbled in his pockets for the key to his safe as he walked across the room. By the time he got to the bank of small safes, read the numbers on them, and assured himself he found the correct one, he realized that the passengers outside the room had followed him inside.

The tallest and drunkest of the three, an Irishman of about forty years of age, nodded to the key in Chronopoulos ' hand. "Well go on, open it!"

Chronopoulos hesitated.

"Open it I said!" the drunk man said, taking a step closer. Chronopoulos could smell the cheap whiskey on his breath.

The young archeologist still hesitated, unsure of how to behave in this situation. He had gotten into one fistfight in his life, in Greece, five years ago with a childhood friend. And he had lost, limping home with his tail between his legs and a bloody nose. But now, as he thought about the treasure that lay inside the box—at least he was convinced that's what it was—he was not about to even put himself in a position to truly lose. On the other hand, he thought, it was likely that these drunks would have no interest in an old piece of paper. No doubt they sought jewelry, cash, obvious valuables. He decided that was the route he should take, and made fear-defying eye contact with the lead drunk.

"I have nothing of value in there. Only personal letters and photographs of sentimental value to me and my family."

"He said open it, boy!" One of the other men, to his left, reached out and kicked him in the left leg, a bolt of pain shooting through him as the knee buckled, but held. Chronopoulos was unarmed, untrained in fighting, and outnumbered three to one by men who were not about to listen to reason. He saw no other option than to open the safe and hope they found no interest in his dusty old scroll. He had considered not paying for the safe and instead keeping the parchment in his berth with his general belongings, not wanting to spend the extra money for safekeeping, but the thought of showing up to his meeting in New York empty-handed was enough to get him to pony up the extra funds.

So now he reluctantly held up the key and turned to the safe. "Okay. Fine, you will see there is nothing of interest in there for—"

Suddenly all four men tumbled to the ground as the ship canted sharply to the right. A muffled *crack* was heard at the same time. Chronopoulos winced as his elbow hit the floor. He felt the key leave his grasp and then a tinkling sound as the piece of metal landed out of sight. Then he felt the breath leave his body as a booted foot slammed into his abdomen, knocking the wind out of him. The men untangled from one another and were quicker to rise to their feet than Chronopoulos, but just as they did, the ship rolled again and all of them were back on the floor in a mound.

That's when the water began seeping in from the left, sluicing down the Purser's Room until it jolted them all awake with its icy reality.

Chronopoulos saw an opportunity to get himself out of a losing fight and seized it. "The *Titanic* is sinking! We have to get out of here before it goes down!"

One of the drunkards rose to his feet and moved to kick Chronopoulos in the ribs, but slipped on the water and went down hard, the back of his head striking the floor. The scant millimeters of water cushioned his fall just enough to prevent him from blacking out, but even so he made no move to get to his feet. He lay there on his back, cringing, tears running down the sides of his face. Before anyone could say anything else, the lights in the room blinked on and off three times before remaining off, casting the room in complete darkness. Knowing this was his chance for escape, Chronopoulos slithered across the wet, sloping floor to put some distance between himself and his attackers.

"Power musta cut out!" one of the drunks said. Various crashing noises were heard as unseen furniture rocked around the room and items slid off of shelves and tables. Chronopoulos continued to slide across the floor. He changed directions when he felt he had gone some number of yards from the group of assailants. He had given up all hope of retrieving his map now and wanted only to escape this terrible situation with his life.

Then the lights flickered back on and he saw with a start in the unsteady light that he had gone the wrong way—deeper into the room rather than toward the door as he had hoped he had gone.

"He's trying to get away!" one of the thugs shouted. Chronopoulos managed to stagger to his feet just as the lights stayed on. They were dimmer than before, and the young Greek heard one of the men mutter the word "generator" before he started to run.

"Get him!"

But at that moment, what got him was the wall of the room bursting open as a raging torrent of freezing seawater flooded the room. There was no swimming against it. As water poured into the room with unimaginable force, swift, unrelenting and unbearably cold on contact, Chronopoulos knew that he, nor any of his attackers, would survive this. His mind flashed on his mistake: *you should have listened to Apostolos and not come down here.*

At first, while the icy waters lifted him higher as the room flooded, he told himself that he might be able to swim up to the hallway, but before he had even completed the thought he was being carried as if on a waterfall up and out of the room where the wall used to be and then bashed into the hallway wall, snapping his neck and saving him the torture of holding his breath until he drowned.

His last thought flowed across the neurons in his brain as his body ceased to function forever: *I hope Apostolos made it onto one of the lifeboats.*

#

New York City, one day later

Noted antiquities collector Charles Miller brought a hand to his mouth in slow motion as he reacted to the headline in that morning's *New York Times*: "Titanic Sinks Four Hours After Hitting Iceberg; 866 Rescued By Carpathia, Probably 1,250 Perish; Ismay Safe, Mrs. Astor Maybe, Noted Names Missing."

He spent the next hour wringing his hands over whether his appointment with the young Greek archaeologist, whom he knew had chosen the Titanic's maiden voyage as his means of transportation to New York, would be kept. He re-read the telegraph correspondence he'd had with him to make certain he had the name right: Chronopoulos Dimitrios. So far that name had not shown up on either the survivors or perished lists. Either way, he would miss his appointment with him that day. He knew from the article that the survivors were now en route to New York aboard the rescue ship, *Carpathia*. He could only hope that Mr. Dimitrios would be among them. For if not, Charles, thought, lifting his gaze from the shocking article....

If not, then the ark is truly lost once again.

CHAPTER 1

Present Day
Atlantic Ocean, 370 miles off the coast of Newfoundland

To Carter Hunt's eyes, the dark speck on the horizon was an anomaly that signaled he was almost to his destination. After over two hours of sitting in the Augusta Bell AB-212 helicopter with nothing to look at but endless open ocean, the still indistinct blob was a welcome sight. At the same time, Hunt reflected, it was a sight that filled him with a certain sadness, for it marked the wreck site of the *RMS Titanic,* which had sunk at this very spot over a century ago.

"Hey, can I see the binoculars?" Carter's friend and business partner, Jayden Takada, reached a hand into the cockpit from his seat in the back. Hunt passed him the optics before turning to the pilot of their chartered craft. "Hey Buzz, winds seem pretty light? Should be a good landing?"

The pilot looked over at him and smiled from behind a pair of oversized, mirrored sunglasses. "You know what they say. Any landing you can walk away from is a good one if you ask me. Especially in a 'copter. In a plane, if you lose an engine, you can still glide. Not so in a chopper. You just drop like a stone."

"Thanks for making us feel better," Hunt joked. But he knew the pilot was aware that his two passengers were ex-Navy combat veterans who'd both served with distinction, Carter as an officer and Jayden as a SEAL and submersible pilot. He wasn't telling them anything they didn't already know.

"I only see one ship on site," Jayden informed them from behind the binoculars.

Carter shrugged as he squinted out the window at the distant vessel. "That's good news, unless of course it means whoever's been snooping around on the wreck—I prefer to call it a grave site—already took what they were after and left."

It was Jayden's turn to shrug. "That's our job either way, right? Either to get the map, or else to confirm that someone else already snatched it."

Carter nodded. "There's a third possibility, too."

"What's that?" Jayden handed the binoculars back up front. Carter focused them on the ship as he answered.

"Maybe the safe is buried in the mud somewhere in the wreckage trail and none of us will ever find it." At this Jayden shook his head while exhaling a long breath, and Carter continued. "Or there never was any map to Noah's ark, it was just a hoax, or something that got misconstrued and passed down more and more incorrectly from generation to generation."

"Like that old kids' telephone line game?"

"Exactly. Or, maybe the safe is there but it rusted open, ruining the parchment inside."

"That last possibility would be definitive, at least. It would make our client happy to say for sure what happened."

"True." Carter nodded from behind the glasses. Their client. The only one at the moment, but success with her represented a large payday. Carter was unique in that he insisted his clients pay only half the total fee up front, and the other half only on successful completion of the job. This was both because he wasn't really doing this work for the money. He'd inherited a fortune from his grandfather, and after a ten-year stint in the Navy as a commissioned officer, decided not to re-up as expected. Instead, disillusioned with the wartime looting of priceless historical artifacts he'd seen in the middle east and elsewhere, he opted to started a private company dedicated to the preservation and safekeeping of historical artifacts so that they might be conserved indefinitely for the greater good.

In this case, that meant recovering a scroll supposedly left in one of the safes not already salvaged aboard the *Titanic*, and returning it to the client, one Ashley Miller, great grand-daughter of late antiquities collector, Charles Miller. Ashley had explained to Carter that Chronopoulos Dimitrios' brother, Apostolos, survived in a life boat and met with Miller in New York, to relate that his brother had gone to retrieve the map from the safe as the ship was sinking but never returned. Carter also pointed out to Jayden that providing proof the safe was no longer aboard the wreckage of the famed ocean liner, or nearby on the ocean floor some 12,500 feet down, would also be satisfactory.

The helicopter's radio crackled to life and the pilot spoke into the transmitter, asking if they were clear for approach. A reply came back in the affirmative, and the pilot looked over at Carter. "We're going in."

Five minutes later they hovered over the ship, an immense iron vessel with the name *R/V Deep Pioneer* stenciled in black paint over the white hull. A helipad marked with a yellow circle and letter "H" was situated on a raised platform above the stern. A heavy equipment crane was visible on the aft work deck, while the bridge was about two-thirds of the way towards the bow. The entire ship did not have one large flat deck, but was a complex series of structures with multiple levels, catwalks, machinery, towers, and interior spaces.

Carter and Jayden had spent many a night on vessels of this type, and it wasn't the ship itself that held his interest as he peered out from the helicopter's window. It was the one that lay two and one-third miles below it, the wreck of the *Titanic*. The coordinates of the wreck site were well known, so reaching the general location was not a major problem. But inside the *Deep Pioneer* was an array of sophisticated electronics that allowed the vessel to precisely detect the presence of the fated wreck far below. Side-scan sonar, bottom profiling imagers, magnetometers, pingers, sub-bottom profile data and more. In addition, as requested by Hunt, there was both a deep-dive capable Remotely Operated Vehicle, or ROV, as well as a two-person submersible capable of withstanding the immense pressures at the depths the *Titanic* now inhabited.

Neither Hunt nor Jayden had ever dived on this, quite possibly the most famous shipwreck in the world, and despite the fact that it was here only as the result of a terrible tragedy, he couldn't deny the excitement he now experienced. Besides, he consoled himself, he was attempting to do a service by locating a document that, if genuine, would be beyond priceless and of limitless inspiration for the entire human population.

The location of Noah's Ark...Despite the fact he was about to land in a helicopter on a ship at sea, the notion of what he was really searching for was too intoxicating to set aside. The irony was not lost on him that the *Titanic* itself was once an ark of sorts, a vessel meant to safeguard its passengers, yet one that had failed in that purpose.

An exchange of technical radio chatter snapped Hunt from his thoughts, and then their craft was descending to the ship's helipad. Hunt glanced at the wind sock and was glad to see it hanging limply in the mostly still air. The skids touched down smoothly on the pad and all three of them unbuckled out of their seatbelts. Buzz informed them that he was going to refuel the helicopter before he would be taking off back to Newfoundland.

Carter and Jayden stepped out of the craft into the cool air of the North Atlantic. Behind them was only empty sea, while in front of them stretched the entire research vessel. While it wasn't the busy hive of activity Carter had imagined, it wasn't empty, either. Technology and automation meant that crew sizes could be smaller. Hunt knew, for example, that although the water was far too deep here to anchor, that the ship was kept in position over the wreck site by a GPS-controlled system of thrusters that maintained specific coordinates automatically. But there were people out and about, especially on the aft deck, and one of them came trotting up the helipad stairs to greet them now.

A bearish man looking to be in his mid-fifties with a full white beard, very broad shoulders and carrying two hard hats stepped up onto the pad and extended a hand. "Cliff Jameson, Operations Manager for the *Deep Pioneer*. You must be the specialists hired by Ms. Miller?"

Carter nodded and shook Jameson's hand, noting his vice-like grip. "Carter Hunt, and this is my friend and business partner, Jayden Takada."

Takada and Jameson shook hands. "Nice to meet you both. First off, put these on. You probably know this, but you need to wear them whenever you're not in an inside area of the ship."

Carter and Jayden donned the protective gear and then Jameson continued. "The way I understand it, you have a background in historical artifact preservation, and you..." He turned to Jayden. "Are the submersible and ROV expert."

Jayden nodded. "We can both do a little of everything, but that about sums it up."

Hunt nodded as well and then Jameson pointed down to an area on the aft deck. "Let me talk to your helo pilot for a minute to get him squared away with the refueling process. Meet me down the bottom of those stairs in five, and we'll get you started, okay?"

Hunt and Takada descended the steps from the helipad down to the main aft deck. The sounds of various machinery cranking, men shouting instructions and ropes clinging against metal poles greeted their ears as they walked across the deck to the indicated stairwell. They took it down the equivalent of one floor to a lower deck that was still exposed to the air, but with a metal catwalk above it. Here there were two cranes on either side positioned on the rails, as well as an ROV and a mini-submersible in their respective cradles. Jayden noted aloud to Hunt that an identical ROV berth sat empty.

Behind them, a closed door with tinted glass opened and a man wearing a hard hat emerged from a dark room lit only by the indicator lights and screens of various electronics. "Hey there! You fellas look a little lost!" This man, a skinny individual with long brown hair tied in a ponytail offered a hand, which was shook by first Jayden and then Hunt.

"John Wilcomb, Submersibles and ROV Control Room Supervisor. Call me Johnny."

"Cliff Jameson told us to wait for him here," Hunt said.

Johnny nodded. "In the meantime, come on in. We've got an ROV down now that should be coming up on the wreck any minute." He held the door open and beckoned inside with an extended arm.

"Great, thanks!" Jayden said enthusiastically. The three of them entered the space and Johnny let the door swing shut behind them. The room was occupied with a console of electronic equipment, including a bank of video monitors that now showed different views from the ROV's six cameras. A technician wearing headphones manned the monitors. Johnny introduced him as Bud Grimes, but Bud could not afford to take his eyes or hands off of the screens and controls, and gave only a smile and a quick finger wave. Instead, Johnny pointed to the different screens as he explained what they were seeing.

"They don't look very different now because she's still dropping down through the water, but this one here is front-facing, this one's rear, then we also have Left, Right, Up and Down. Obviously, because it's black down there, it all looks the same, just what the halogens are illuminating. You will see the occasional creature floating by, though."

As if on cue, a squid darted across the field of view of the left camera before appearing again on the front lens until it propelled itself beyond the reach of the lights. The water was not completely clear, owing to bits of particulate matter known as detritus, or "marine snow," that were suspended in the inky liquid. A data readout in the corners of each screen displayed the date and time, water temperature and depth, as well as technical information about the ROV including remaining battery power.

"The wreck should be coming into view in just another minute or so," Johnny said, pointing to the depth readout before adding, "We're not going to take it inside on this dive, we'll leave the penetration dives to you two, but we just wanted to do a general survey and test out the equipment."

"Good idea," Jayden said, eyes flicking back and forth between the different monitors.

"I see it!" Carter exclaimed, unable to keep the excitement out of his voice. The wreck of the *RMS Titanic*. He found it incredible to think he was standing right over it.

"This is the classic bow view." Johnny pointed to the front-facing feed, where the front of the ill-fated liner came into view. The railing was visible, its six bars heavily encrusted with layers of marine growth. "Those are what we call *rusticles*," he said, pointing to the elongated, stalactite-like formations of brownish, oxidized iron. "Very common throughout the ship, inside and out."

Carter and Jayden nodded as they looked on while the ROV propelled itself over the rail and across the bow deck. It was amazing to Carter how intact the ship still was after all these years underwater, not to mention sinking after striking an iceberg. But he knew that the impact had occurred below the waterline—a half dozen lacerations of only about three square feet. From the deck itself, it would have appeared that the ship missed the iceberg, but since most of an iceberg's mass is below the waterline, the ship was unable to completely avoid the obstacle. Hunt found it hard not to visualize the panicking people on board that night, scrambling around to try and fix the damage, and then starting to lose control as they launched the lifeboats.

He was brought back to the present by the door to the control room opening and Cliff Jameson walking in. "Ah, there you are! Good, Johnny found you, or you found Johnny!"

"They found me," Johnny said, without taking his eyes from the monitors.

"So listen, gentlemen," Jameson began as he took a seat in a swivel chair. "As you know, you were retained by Ms. Miller to hopefully recover a very special document from one of the safes aboard the wreck. I do not even know what this document is. What's so special about it, care to tell me?"

Hunt shook his head. "I can't—"

"Excellent! Just testing you. Security is vital to this mission. As it is, we know that someone's been snooping around on the wreck, diving on it not only with ROVs, but with manned submersibles, systematically searching for something."

"Probably the same *something* that Ms. Miller asked us to look for," Carter said. "I can tell you this much: as you said, it's a document, but it's an old one, on parchment or papyrus, and if there was the slightest breach of integrity of the safe, it's likely been totally destroyed by now."

"Someone thinks it might still be intact," Johnny said, still focused on the monitor, where the ROV cruised over the top of the bow deck. Sweat beaded on his brow while Bud Grimes' right hand deftly manipulated a joystick as he sent the robot its instructions.

"You're the only ship on the site," Carter pointed out.

"There was another ship here before we arrived, two days ago. They high-tailed it out of here when they saw us coming," Jameson said with a long face.

"Not only that," Johnny added, "but other ships have reported them in the area during the last few months. Whoever it is, they've been really methodical about hunting for something down there. They're flying in the face of all the treaties too."

"I thought these were international waters?" Jayden asked. "370 miles off the nearest coast?"

Jameson responded to this. "Yeah, but the *Titanic*, and the entire three-by-five mile debris field surrounding the main wreck, are special, registered as a historic grave site. No one is supposed to touch anything on the wreck. After it was first found by Dr. Robert Ballard in 1985, there was a goldrush of sorts to visit the wreck, to commercialize it by taking paying passengers down to it in submersibles. But all that was bad for the wreck, and things—dishes, jewelry, you name it—started to go missing."

Johnny turned toward them from his position in front of the monitors. "But starting in the 2010's, world governments—including Nova Scotia, England, Scotland, and the U.S.--managed to pass legislation aimed at limiting access to the wreck, as well as the ability to profit from items salvaged from it. The upshot of it was that both wanton looting as well properly permitted treasure seekers were reduced in number. Even so, as the deep diving technology gets better and more affordable, there are still those willing to skirt the law in order to steal a piece of history."

Carter nodded slowly, eyes alight with intensity. The discussion was aligning perfectly with his life's work, and he was about to formulate a response when the handheld radio on Jameson's belted crackled.

"Bridge to Cliff, you copy?"

Jameson snatched up the radio and brought it to his lips. "Cliff, here, what's up?"

"Sir, we've got an approaching vessel—a large ship—that has completely ignored our radio requests for identification and purpose. We've been contacting them for over an hour on multiple frequencies—even tried semaphore flags and signal mirrors, just for the hell of it—and we get nothing. Just thought you should know that they'll likely be on site in about ten more minutes. Whether they're just passing through, or they intend to stay, we don't know. Over."

Jameson eyed the other men in the room while voicing his radio reply. "Thanks for the heads up, Bridge. I'll be there shortly. Meanwhile, continue your attempts to make radio contact, over and out." He clipped the radio back to his belt while addressing Carter and Jayden.

"Looks like we've got company. I wanted to give you a full tour of the ship first, but in light of our unexplained visitors, I think it's best if I get up to the bridge right away." He turned to leave until Carter said, "I believe Jayden and I are ready to do a submersible dive." At this Jayden nodded enthusiastically, and Hunt continued. "How about we get the submersible ready? Having some human presence down there in case our mystery guests decide to stay awhile might be an effective preventative move."

Jameson looked to Johnny. "Any objections?"

Johnny shook his head while a sly grin formed on his face. "Not at all!"

CHAPTER 2

Carter and Jayden exchanged concerned glances. Submersible deep diving was not the type of activity that could be safely rushed. Yet at the same time, their purpose for being here revolved around potential confrontation: someone's been snooping around the *Titanic* and it was their job to find the map to Noah's Ark before they did. And now it seemed that confrontation was about to transpire.

They stood on the submersible deck outside the control room, where Bud now piloted the robot back to the surface to keep the site clear for manned submersible operations. Jayden remarked what a blessing it was that the ship featured a "moon pool," which was a rectangular opening farther towards the bow on the same deck. This meant that instead of having to swing the submersible over the side of the ship on a boom arm and lower it down into choppy waters, possibly risking a mishap where it slams into the side of the ship, it could instead be lowered directly into the sea from the safety of the middle of the ship. It also afforded them more privacy as well, since the sub going in and out of the water couldn't be directly observed by prying eyes from other ships or aircraft.

"Tell me again how that giant hole in the ship with the ocean coming up through it doesn't sink us?" Carter asked. He was half-joking since he'd seen them before, but knew that Jayden could explain it technically.

"It's not really a 'hole' in the ship, it's the shape of the ship. The four sides of the pool are sealed as part of the hull. Also, as you can see," Jayden said, pointing down into the rectangular opening where seawater sloshed about below, "there is considerable distance between the surface of the ocean and the top of the pool."

Hunt nodded. It looked like they were about one story, or ten feet above the waves. A waist-high metal railing lined the perimeter of the moon pool, and a retractable cover, now open, could be closed during heavy seas. Above them on one end of the moon pool was a platform deck with a small crane where additional equipment could be lowered into the water as needed.

"Let's make sure the submersible is ready for action," Jayden said, his eagerness evident by the fact that he was already walking toward the multi-million dollar machine. It was positioned on a cradle underneath a split-level deck so that it was shaded and protected from precipitation. "Usually they keep the batteries topped off, but if they used it recently they may not be ready to go yet."

Carter shrugged as he started after Jayden. "If that's the case, then we'll just have to send an ROV back down until the sub's ready."

Jayden agreed and then they were standing next to the craft that would take them down to the *RMS Titanic*. "You can count on one hand the number of privately owned subs in the world that are capable of diving to the *Titanic*. So we know our client must have some deep pockets to spring for this."

Carter nodded, reading the corporate logo painted on the sub's body, with the craft's name stenciled below that: *Deep Voyager*. "She looks like she's up to the task. Hopefully we can do our client justice."

Jayden nodded as he started to walk around the underwater craft. For a sub that held only two persons, it was much larger than Carter expected. Jayden told him it was because such a great depth rating required both crush protection from the immense pressures, as well as large battery banks to power the vehicle for the long periods of time it took to reach miles-deep depths, have some time at depth, and then return to the surface while leaving a margin for error. As with cave-diving, the rules of thirds applied: one-third oxygen and battery power for the actual dive, one-third for the return trip, with one-third remaining in reserve for contingencies. Both Navy men were well aware of this rule and would never willingly break it.

Jayden eyed Carter. "This sub will definitely allow us to have a decent look around the wreck and surrounding site. Whether or not we can find the safe, that's another matter. But we're going to give it a shot. Time for the pre-dive inspection."

Jayden and Carter set about ensuring the craft was ready to dive, running through a diagnostic checklist that took the better part of an hour. They were assisted by a couple of crew members familiar with certain operations including operating the cranes to lower the sub into the moon pool. When Jayden pronounced the sub fit to dive, he and Carter entered the craft, with Jayden occupying the pilot's seat on the left side and Carter on the right, where he would mostly be an observer but also able to operate certain equipment such as the external grab arms and spotlights.

Johnny came back to the work area to supervise the sub deployment, which included not only the crane operation to lower it into the moon pool, but also a dive team of four scuba divers who would inspect the submersible once it was underwater, and then accompany it for the first 100 vertical feet of its dive. Before they closed the hatch, Johnny called up to them from the deck while the sub was still suspended from the crane.

"I'm just back from the bridge. That ship—its name is the *Transoceanic*—it's positioned itself on site, about a hundred yards away from us."

"You have any communication with them?" Carter called down.

Jameson nodded while holding his hands out in a gesture of *what gives*. "Yeah, we told them that we have the legal permits to dive the site and asked them what they were doing here, but they were basically uncooperative, saying only that they also have permits on file, which I know is a crock."

"Does it look like they have manned subs or only ROVs or AUVs?" Carter asked, referring to Autonomous Underwater vehicles, an ROV variant that could be programmed to dive a certain course and therefore be

19

tetherless.

Jameson shrugged. "We observed them with binoculars and it looks like they have both ROVs and AUVs, but we didn't see a manned craft. There could be an indoor moon pool, though. It's a large vessel, only a little smaller than ours. It's a little strange, because they seem to be privately funded—there are no government or institutional markings of any kind on the ship—and yet they're very well equipped. I mean, I realize that we're privately funded, too, but how common is that?"

At this Carter and Jayden exchanged a concerned glance. They had past experience with just such an outfit—private and extremely well-funded—that would stop at nothing to obtain priceless historical artifacts and treasures.

"You'd be surprised who comes out of the woodwork for the lure of historical treasure," Carter said to Jameson.

Then Jayden said to Carter, "Remind you of somebody?"

Hunt slowly shook his head as he recalled a hair-raising race to find the lost city of Atlantis, a quest that ended in success and a reputation that enabled him to launch his treasure hunting and safeguarding business, Omega—so-named because the Greek symbol represented a unit of resistance--the reason they were here today. "It does, but let's not jump to conclusions just yet. We've got a job to do."

Jayden nodded and signaled to Jameson and Johnny that they were ready to dive. A crewman secured the sub's hatch, causing Carter and Jayden to feel a slight pressure in their ears, and then stepped back off of the craft before the crane operator began slowly lowering the *Deep Voyager* toward the water in the moon pool. Jayden peered down below them to make sure their path was obstacle free while Carter gazed up, watching the crew wave as water sloshed over the top of the hatch.

They passed down through the moon pool, enclosed on all sides by the hull of the ship, until they cleared the bottom of the hull into open ocean. When they were safely below the ship, a scuba diver wearing a full face mask asked them over the communications system if they were ready to be released from the cable. Jayden responded via radio that they were, and the diver unhooked them from the crane.

Jayden flipped a switch to release air from the sub's buoyancy tubes. To rise or sink up and down, the sub did not have to rely on its thrusters. In order to conserve power, to sink it released compressed air stored in tanks in the buoyancy tubes, and to rise it either released ballast in the form of lead weights, or added more air to the tubes from the tanks. He informed the support crew of every action over the radio. "Releasing air…" He knew it was of paramount importance to quickly sink below the ship lest a freak upwelling slam them into the hull.

Slowly, the submersible began to drop deeper into the North Atlantic. The four support divers swam around them—one either side, one above and one below—as they began their descent. When they reached a depth of seventy-five feet—safely below the ship—Jayden performed a quick systems check to ensure everything was operational before beginning the long descent to the *Titanic*. A school of silver fish swarmed past them, temporarily obscuring one of the scuba divers before disappearing into the blue.

"All systems go," Jayden intoned into the comm system's microphone. "Commencing descent to the wreck, over." He vented more air from the buoyancy system and the *Deep Voyager* sank at a faster rate toward the bottom of the ocean. Even at this pace, it would take them over three hours to reach the seafloor. When they arrived at the 100-foot mark, the dive team performed a final visual inspection of the sub and reported that all looked well. Jayden also completed one last systems check, also verifying that all systems were operating as they should.

Then the scuba team began their slow ascent to the surface, where they would need to decompress for some time at the twenty-foot level before returning to the ship. Jayden and Carter continued on into the depths alone, plummeting toward the *RMS Titanic*.

CHAPTER 3

Three hours later

"Topside, this is *Deep Voyager,* do you copy, over?" Jayden released the transmitter button on the radio mic while he waited for the reply. He and Carter gazed through the sub's clear acrylic dome at the seafloor below. The wreck was not yet within sight, but the bottom itself was a sight for sore eyes after drifting through literally miles of pitch black water. Even though it was only a flat expanse of grayish-black mud and sand, it was far more interesting than the three dimensional void they had just traversed. And knowing that the *Titanic* lay just out of sight on this abyssal plain made the bottom all the more alluring.

Johnny's voice boomed into their submersible cabin through the radio. "*Deep Voyager,* this is Topside, and we copy you loud and clear. What's your status?"

Jayden replied into the radio mic. "We just reached the bottom. Not yet within sight of the wreck. Going to run a systems check, then adjust our course. We're about twenty feet above the bottom, over."

"Roger that, let me know when you're done with the checks and before you move out, over." Twenty feet was far enough up from the seafloor to avoid stirring up the silt and mud that would ruin the water clarity. Jayden ran through the diagnostic checks, occasionally asking Carter to flip a switch here or read a display there. Battery power, oxygen levels and other parameters came back as they should, and so in a few minutes Jayden was back on the radio informing their support ship that they would now be continuing on with the objective portion of their dive, and heading to the *Titanic.*

"Copy that, *Deep Voyager.* Adjust compass heading to…" He recited the bearing numbers from the ship's navigation equipment, and then Jayden swung the sub around in a slow circle without changing their depth until it pointed in the right direction. "You should come up on the bow section, so watch it, because at your current depth it's going to be towering way above you."

Jayden replied that he understood and then told Carter, "Here we go," before setting the submersible into forward motion toward the historic wreck. A few white crabs skittered along the seafloor as they glided over the bottom. Various other invertebrates including sea stars and sea cucumbers dotted the muddy floor. Carter pointed out a tripod fish, its fins strangely modified to be able to stand on the bottom. The water itself was clear, and their real visibility was limited only by the reach of the sub's lights, both halogen floods for illumination of their immediate surroundings, and LED spotlights for longer-reach targeted light. Carter tested one of the spots now, startling a squid that quickly darted outside of the bright cone of light.

He was sweeping the floodlight along the muddy plains when the far reach of the beam caught something dark and solid above the seafloor. *Far* above the seafloor, Carter noted. Towering, but also absolutely unmoving, so not a large animal. Carter caught his breath as he realized what he was looking at.

The *RMS Titanic,* in its final resting place.

In the narrow cone of the spot light, the famed shipwreck appeared simply as a dark wall, but Carter knew they had reached the bow section and were seeing the hull of the ship, below the oft-pictured bow deck with its iron railings. Carter kept the spot aimed at the hull, moving it around here and there to ensure there weren't other protruding sections they could hit. Jayden slowed the sub's forward progress while keeping it on the same course, aware that bumping into something with the three-ton craft could cause irreparable damage that could leave them stuck down here for eternity, along with the ship they came to investigate.

Carter and Jayden were not merely randomly exploring the wreck. They had spent many an hour poring over images, videos, architectural drawings and builder's plans for the ship and the shipwreck so that they knew not only where the purser's rooms were, but also where the safes in those rooms might have ended up after the ship cracked in two on its way down to the bottom of the Atlantic on that fateful night over a century ago. It was all just calculated guesswork, but they had a game plan, and when you were over two miles deep in the ocean, it didn't pay to be wandering around.

"So like we talked about," Carter said, pointing to their left along the once mighty ship's hull, "our best bet is to take a look first at the gap between the fore and aft sections, which might lead us inside to our Purser's Room."

"Roger that." Jayden eased the submersible to their left, following the gentle curvature of the *Titanic's* hull. Once cruising along, their immediate path illuminated before them as obstacle-free, he radioed Topside to report that they were beginning their course around the wreck. He expected a routine acknowledgement by way of a response, but instead heard Johnny's voice sounding somewhat strained.

"Copy that, *Deep Voyager*. Be advised, this will not affect you for some time, but we have deep operations activity observed on our unknown visitors' ship, the *Transoceanic*."

Jayden eyed Carter briefly before saying into the radio, "What kind of deep ops activity?"

"Manned submersible. So you have about three hours before you're going to have company down there, over."

Carter looked ever at Jayden. "That still gives us time to look around down here. No later than an hour before they get down here, we'll begin our ascent. They won't be able to find us once we're up off the bottom."

Jayden nodded slowly, as if considering this, before replying into the radio. "Copy that, Topside. We're going to proceed with our inspection down here, but we'll make sure to begin our ascent well before their arrival time, over."

Johnny agreed, and then Jayden updated him on their position relative to the wreck. Carter signaled to Jayden that he wanted the radio mic and Jayden handed it to him, glad to be able to focus his full attention on piloting the sub around the hull of the hulking shipwreck.

"Co-pilot here, Topside," Carter began. "Even though they've already deployed their craft, it would be best to keep up the pressure on the rest of their ship's crew. Keep up the requests for radio contact, make sat-phone calls—you can bill them to us—for permit requests, Coast Guard reports, that kind of thing. Don't make them feel welcome, is what I'm saying."

"Copy that, *Deep Voyager*. We'll keep up the pressure. Stay safe down there. Over and out."

Carter replaced the radio mic to the instrument console and then returned his focus to the wreck outside the sub. Using a joystick on the panel in front of him, he swept the powerful spotlight mounted on the bow of the sub along the rust-streaked hull of the *Titanic*. Stalks of sea anemones, sponges and other unknown life forms dotted and encrusted the long-dormant structure.

Unfolding a diagram that showed the Titanic in cutaway form as it lay on the seafloor, Carter tried to reconcile what he was looking at out his window with the drawing in his lap. He used a penlight to illuminate a section of the chart that depicted the bow portion of the ship, before staring out the window and adjusting the spotlight against the massive hull.

"We have a ways to go before we get to the break in the wreck," Carter said, referring to the fact that the ship lay in two major pieces on the seafloor: the larger forward section, including the bow, which they now skimmed past. Then there was a gap of almost a football field of empty seafloor, perhaps with some strewn debris, with the stern portion of the ship lying alone after that, more or less in line with the rest.

Jayden glanced at his instruments before responding. "I'll increase thruster power by ten percent." He grabbed a throttle-like control with his right hand and slowly pushed it up. The whirring noise of the thruster motors increased slightly in pitch and their life-supporting craft propelled them along a little faster at the expense of remaining battery power.

In spite of the fact that he knew he was coasting along next to the *Titanic*, Carter found the view in this part of the dive to be somewhat monotonous, an ever-changing-yet-always-the-same pastiche of encrusted, rust-streaked metal wall. Directing the spotlight above him, at its steepest angle, he could just make out the lip of the deck. They could have taken the sub over the deck, but it was a trickier route, beset with potential obstacles and tangled, twisted wreckage in which to become snagged. The seafloor along the side of the hull would keep them on track while presenting relatively safe passage to their desired entrance point into the shipwreck.

Carter tried to keep the insane amount of pressure, some 377 atmosphere's worth—5,500 pounds per square inch—that their little craft absorbed in order to keep them alive, out of his mind as they glided along over the bottom. Outside of the external lights' radius it was beyond pitch black—a complete and total absence of light save for the sporadic pinpricks of bioluminescent light from unseen creatures. This world was so forbidding, so alien to human life, that they may as well be in deep space. If anything went wrong down here with their equipment, it was a matter of life and death, with death the more likely outcome.

Before long Carter announced they were approaching the great rift between the much larger front section of the wreck and the aft section. He couldn't actually see it yet, but was able to calculate it by using their speed in knots and the length of the forward section from the diagram.

"About thirty more seconds at this velocity," Carter told Jayden, who shot him a doubting sideways glance, but nodded. Twenty-eight seconds later, bare seafloor took the place of the metal hull, and Jayden shook his head as he slowed the sub.

"And to think the best use I ever found for high school math class was to see how long I could hold my breath." Jayden brought the sub around the end of the open wreckage in a wide arc while Carter laughed at the mental image of a young Jayden goofing off in school. Both occupants of the craft held their breath when they saw the open end of the *Titanic's* forward section.

They were looking straight into history.

Carter was not prepared for the wave of emotion that flooded over him at that moment. This wasn't some photograph, or artist's rendering. This was the real thing, witnessed directly with his own eyes. Not much was visible beyond the floodlights, but by aiming the starboard spotlight, they could see some ways into the cavernous maw of the historic wreck. Nothing iconic yet, only unidentifiable debris within the outline of the mega-hull, but it was remarkable, nonetheless.

"You ever think we'd be staring into the freakin' *Titanic*?" Jayden asked, voice laden with reverence. Carter could only shake his head wordlessly, until Jayden tore his gaze from the mesmerizing view and eyed his controls. He made a slight adjustment to the sub's depth, raising it a few feet off of the ocean floor lest they stir up the silt. Then he pivoted the sub to the right while hovering in place so that they were parallel to the open end of the wreck.

"Gonna take us forward now to the middle of the opening," Jayden said, both to Carter and into the radio. It was important to announce each and every step, like how an astronaut relayed his each and every move to the crew during a spacewalk or spacecraft docking maneuver. It gave the opportunity for the crew to remind the pilot of a missing step, for one thing, and kept everyone appraised of exactly what was happening.

"Copy that, *Deep Voyager*," Johnny acknowledged over the comm system. Carter and Jayden each aimed the spotlights on their respective sides of the submersible out in front of them, surveying what lay ahead. Satisfied that to move forward represented a clear path, Jayden activated the forward thrusters and the sub creeped along over the bottom. Carter occasionally swept his spotlight out toward the wreck to get a look at their progress across its open maw and to ensure they were well clear of any protruding obstacles.

Even with their slow and cautious progress, it didn't take long to reach the midpoint of the shipwreck's width. Again, Carter confirmed they were about halfway across the open ship using the diagram in combination with their speed. Jayden eased off the thrusters and brought the sub into a controlled hover before using only the left thruster to pivot the craft around to their right so that the nose pointed toward the open end of the *Titanic's* gargantuan forward piece.

"Here we are," he said to Carter before notifying Topside of their position on the wreck. After another systems evaluation during which everything checked out nominal, Jayden informed Johnny via radio that they were ready to begin the penetration phase of their dive.

"Copy that, *Deep Voyager*. Proceed with extreme caution. Reminder that you have an hour or so before you have company down, there. Over."

Jayden acknowledged the request and turned to Carter. "You ready?"

Hunt glanced ahead of them into the cavernous structure that awaited before nodding.

"Let's go find that safe."

CHAPTER 4

"We'll be entering through the rear cargo holds," Carter said as he looked up from his diagram. Jayden propelled them slowly into the open wreck, about ten feet above the bottom. The ship lay more or less flat and upright, but at a slight angle to the left when looking into it from their vantage point. Carter's diagram showed the Titanic to have five levels in all, including the topmost deck with the funnels, and they were entering on the bottom one.

"Plenty of room to maneuver so far," Jayden said as he steered the sub into the center of the large opening before them.

"So this is where the ship cracked in half as it flooded and sank," Carter pointed out as they passed through the ragged metal outline of the ship's massive, torn hull. "The Purser's Room should be on the third level not far past the Smoking Room."

Jayden laughed. "Even way back then they herded the smokers into one room, huh?"

Carter was more active with the spotlight now, as there was much to see inside the ship, and obstacles in the form of loose cables and random hanging debris could be anywhere and everywhere. "As expected, it's clear up until the end of the cargo hold, then we're going to have to head up and see what it's like."

"Right." Jayden glanced out of the dome to his left and saw piles of what looked like broken wine casks, along with other masses of unidentifiable lumber of some sort, interspersed with twisted metal beams that were part of the ship. Looking ahead, he could see a wall that prevented forward progress. It was mostly solid, but a few small jagged gaps offered glimpses into additional rooms beyond. Carter said that he believed them to be the Engineers Rooms. Jayden gave the thrusters a short burst of reverse as the sub glided toward the wall, the closest thing to brakes that he had at his disposal.

He and Carter looked all around them, carefully checking to ensure they were clear of obstructions on all sides and below. A massive turbine lay off-kilter to their right, but they were far enough from it that it did not present a navigational hazard. Then they turned their attention upward, where a rectangular shaft stretched beyond the reach of their lights.

"Elevator shaft." Carter consulted his diagram before looking upward and back to the drawing again.

"Where's the car?" Jayden wondered, looking around at the chaotic floor, strewn with debris both recognizable and otherwise.

"Probably smashed to bits, or disintegrated if it was mostly wood. You think we can rise vertically through that shaft? Because according to this…" He paused to squint at the diagram again. "…it leads to the hospital on the second level, and then to the restaurant on Level Three, which is not far from the Smoking Room…"

"…Which is not far from the Purser Room," Jayden finished for him.

"Right."

Jayden backed the sub up a bit and then adjusted one of the external halogens, trying to get a better look up into the shaft. "I don't know. It's a small space. I mean, we'd fit, but barely. And I don't need to tell you that if we got snagged on anything in there, like halfway up the shaft…"

"You don't need to tell me," Carter said, trying to push a fate of slow suffocation while they sat trapped in the sub in the pitch dark, counting their breaths until the oxygen ran out, out of his mind.

"We could slip in there and then we'd be able to get a better look straight up the shaft," Jayden said, adjusting one of the spotlight controls before adding, "If it looks too sketchy from the bottom, we can just back right out."

"I'm okay with it," Carter said. "But you're the pilot. I want you to be comfortable. If you're not, then we don't do it, no questions asked, end of story. Your call."

"Let's have a look, then." Jayden brought his hand up to the thruster control and nudged it up, causing the submersible to lurch forward slowly. Carter swept his spot light around, making sure they were free of obstacles as they nosed into the vacant elevator shaft. Jayden let go of the thruster control, allowing the sub's momentum to carry it into the enclosed space.

"Hope you're not claustrophobic, bro," Jayden said as he nudged the left thruster to center their craft in the elevator shaft. Being over two miles deep, inside a wreck and inside what amounted to basically a vertical tunnel inside of that was enough to make even a non-claustrophobic panic. And Carter wasn't about to lie to himself. He felt the beginnings of unease begin to creep around the edges of his consciousness. But he had been in perilous situations involving closed spaces before, such as cave diving and wreck diving with scuba gear, spelunking on land…but this…He warned himself not to think about it too much or his rational brain would tell him to get out of here right now, to do the smart thing and keep yourself alive!

"Snug as a bug in a rug," he said to Jayden, who smiled as he aimed the spotlight on the port side of the craft up into the shaft. Carter did the same with the one on his side, and together they visually appraised what lay straight up above them while Jayden kept the craft stationary at the bottom of the space.

"It looks clear to me," Carter announced after a minute of careful scrutiny. "I'll continue to keep an eye out on the way up, but I don't see any obvious blockages."

"I'm afraid to tell Topside we're taking the elevator up," Jayden said, eyeing the radio.

"They would just tell us not to do it. It's our call."

"They'll know anyway if we find our way in there, won't they?"

Carter shook his head. "We can say there was a break in the wall or something and not even mention the elevator. If we're going to do it, let's go , though. We're burning battery power sand oxygen."

Without another word, Jayden's hands flew over the sub's controls, and the sub began a slow ascent up the shaft. With Jayden's full attention needing to be on the controls, it was up to Carter to operate the lights and identify anything that might represent an obstacle to their upward progress. He called out when they were about halfway up the shaft, and then again at three-quarters.

"Hold up here," he told the pilot. Jayden paused the ascent and maintained their position within the column, hovering. They had perhaps three feet of space on either side of the sub and even less than that off the bow and stern. Carter examined the remaining distance to the top of the shaft with the spotlight.

"Be quick about, would you," Jayden said. "I can't hold this position forever. All it would take is one freak up- or downwelling, and—"

"It's clear, go for it!" Hunt continued to eye the rest of their path as an electronic hum signified the vertical thrusters starting up again. The sub rose slowly through the remaining elevator shaft until the top of the bubble dome was even with the opening in the shaft, where Jayden again held their craft in a tightly controlled hover.

"We've got room to maneuver!" Hunt said, unable to contain the excitement in his voice as he aimed the spot light around. Even the closer range floodlights allowed them to see they had reached an internal area of the ship with considerable space.

"I think…." Hunt began but then paused as he looked around some more with the spotlight. "I think we're in the restaurant." He pointed to an overturned round table, with a chair still mostly intact nearby.

"Yeah, holy crap, I see a bottle of wine on the floor over here! When's happy hour?"

Carter smiled as he imagined using the sub's robotic arm to bring back a bottle of wine from the ship, but in reality he knew better than to disrespect the site like that. They were here for one thing and one thing only. They would leave everything else as undisturbed as possible.

"Which way do we need to go from here?" Jayden asked. "Right, am I right?" He thought he was correct, but knew they had precious little room for error.

Carter was already gazing at his diagram when he answered. "Yes, on the other side of the restaurant to our right we should get to the smoking room, and then after that, the Purser's Room on this same level. It's not all that far from here, really." Yet he knew that conventional terms for distance such as "not that far" down here in the middle of the *Titanic* shipwreck were much different than the same distances on land. The restaurant offered maneuverable space, but neither man was fooled into thinking that hazards did not abound. The water was still and relatively undisturbed inside the inner rooms of the ship. It was possible that the sub's movement alone could move the water around enough to cause a collapse of some sort, like a cave-in.

"Heads up on that big chandelier over there," Hunt said, directing the spotlight until the halogen revealed the glittering of crystals in the pitch dark space, "and there's a smaller one over there."

"Thanks." Jayden now knew not to let the sub be too high in the room, nor too low. He activated the horizontal thrusters and sent them scooting out into the middle of the giant room, about halfway between floor and ceiling. He caught his breath as he saw a flash of white in the floodlights on the floor, realizing it was a human skull, the rest of the skeleton unseen beneath a heavy table top. A none-too-subtle reminder that this was indeed a grave site. He pointed it out to Carter, who asked in a low voice if the video system was recording. Jayden hit a button and then replied in the affirmative. Everything around the sub would be captured in high definition video from six cameras facing every direction including above and below.

The sub made its way through the sunken restaurant, Jayden's brow beaded with sweat despite the chilly temperature inside the specialized vehicle. They came to one area where a mass of furniture was tangled in a heap on the floor, and he had to raise the sub in order to pass over it, before dropping lower again to avoid a mass of cabling or wire of some sort that dangled from the fractured ceiling.

"Got a wall coming up," Carter announced. "This should be the other side of the restaurant. Smoking Room's on the other side."

"We need to find a way through." Jayden cut power to the thrusters and allowed the sub to come to a standstill, hovering about ten feet above the floor, over a pile of dishes and glassware, some of which was still intact.

At that moment the radio crackled with Johnny's voice. "Topside to Voyager: checking in, requesting status, over."

Jayden snatched up the radio mic. "Inside the restaurant now, Topside. We're fine, having a look around, over."

"The restaurant, copy that. Wow, I do believe you two have the dubious honor of being the deepest manned penetration of the *Titanic* ever. Exercise extreme caution and stay in touch. I'll let you get back to concentrating, over."

Jayden signed off the radio and then Carter pointed to the upper right of the restaurant's far wall, where the spotlight illuminated an irregularity. "I think we've got a small break there that we might be able to squeeze through."

Jayden appeared concerned. "*Squeezing* is not really something subs are good at, but okay, let's check it out. I'll move us in for a closer look."

He deftly adjust the thrusters so that the sub rose higher in the room while approaching the spotlighted area of wall, high up towards the ceiling. A startled fish—a large one of some unknown type, dark in color— slithered out of the floodlights along the bottom of the room as the sub neared the wall. Another skeleton made Jayden look away and focus even harder than he needed to on maneuvering the sub. It was creepy down here, he couldn't deny it. Miles down in the freezing, dark ocean, inside a historic tomb…His mind flashed on sunny, tropical beaches and splashing in the ocean with a beautiful woman…

"Watch it, watch, Jayden!" Carter's voice snapped him from his daydream. "Wall coming up!"

"Sorry!" He reversed on the horizontal thrusters and the submersible backed off an instant before it would have collided softly with the wall.

Even at low speeds, however, the sub weighed three tons and had a lot of power behind it once put into motion. As it was, a puff of silt billowed away from the wall, high up near the ceiling. Carter gave a sigh of frustration.

"Visibility's clouded near our opening. We're going to have to wait it out for a couple of minutes. How's our vitals?"

Jayden put the sub into a hover, floating there as if in space, high up near the ceiling. He took a deep breath and exhaled while he eyed the console gauges. "Everything looks good. Time to check in with Topside."

By the time he finished the routine radio check with the support ship, the water had cleared enough for them to be able to see over the top of the wall, where an irregular rift presented itself between the wall and ceiling. "'Man, that is really a tight fit. I'm not sure I can pilot us through that," Jayden said, eyeing the possible passage dubiously.

Carter's gaze lit on one of the sub's controls. "What if we use the grab arm to peel back some of that twisted metal up there—create a bigger opening for ourselves?"

"You crazy? Never mind that, I know you are. But it just might work. Or it could bring the entire ceiling down on us and trap us forever. Your call,"
 he said, turning the tables on Carter from back when he gave him the go-no-go decision on the elevator shaft.

"I'm for it if you are," Carter said without hesitation. "You're the pilot, so you have to be comfortable, though. I don't want to do it if you don't, that's the bottom line."

Jayden considered this for a moment while staring up at the ceiling before replying. "I think it'll work. If it doesn't budge at all after the first grab arm pull, we stop. If too much of the wall or ceiling starts to come down too fast, we stop and hope it's not too late."

"You hold the sub in place while I operate the grab arm, right?" Carter clarified.

"Right." Jayden had confidence in Carter's abilities on a sub. He had seen him operate a grab arm successfully before during a critical mission, and had no qualms about letting him do it now. "Just don't ask to drive this thing."

Carter smiled. "I won't. Let me check the arm before we get up near the ceiling. Carter grabbed the joystick that operated the external grab arm, and tested its controls, first extending the arm, then swiveling it back and forth, rotating the finger-like hand grips. Finally, he closed and opened the hand grips. Satisfied all was in working order and that he was prepared, he nodded to Jayden. "Ready when you are."

Jayden took the sub up to the tear between wall and ceiling and stabilized the craft until it hung motionless, poised next to the jagged window into the next room. Carter operated the spotlight to get a look into the adjacent space. "It's a big room in there," he said. "Not as huge as this one, but definitely big enough to maneuver in. I see a couch, some chairs…Ah, there's an ashtray! It's the Smoking Room."

"Let's give it a go, then," Jayden said.

Carter put his hand on the grab arm control and extended the mechanical arm, which was situated on the right front of the craft, until its claw hand was adjacent to the curl of metal coming down from the wall. He opened the claw and then adjusted its position until it was open in front of the piece of metal.

"How much more room do we need, if I can pull it down some?" Carter asked.

"Two more feet would make me feel a whole lot better about this."

"Here goes." Carter closed the claw around the metal sheeting and tightened the grip all the way down. Then he pressed one of the buttons on the arm's directional pad, and the arm pulled back and downward—three separate joints working together—two arm sections plus the hand.

They couldn't hear anything outside the sub—the acrylic and steel of its construction was too thick—so Carter had to depend on sight alone to gauge whether it was working. At first he saw no movement of the metal, so he gave the arm control a couple more bursts, attempting to pull the metal down with the claw. Still nothing. Then he held the pad down, telling the arm to constantly pull down, and he saw a piece of metal about ten feet long, five on either side of the grab claw, peel back from the ceiling a couple of feet.

"It's working!" he said to Jayden. "We need to move to the left maybe five feet and repeat the process." Jayden adjusted the sub's position accordingly and Carter again utilized the grab arm to pull back the loose wall sheeting until there was a larger opening. Jayden backed the sub away a few feet and examined the newly enlarged opening with a critical pilot's eye.

"I think it's big enough now. You aim the spotlight ahead, I'll drive us through nose first."

Carter complied with his pilot's instruction as the sub crept back toward the enlarged opening, this time at a different angle of approach. "Watch my ceiling clearance," Jayden said. Carter glanced up through the dome above them. "You've got a good couple of feet until we get to the opening, where you'll have to come down about a foot."

"Okay, here goes." Jayden bumped the thruster control and the submersible sliced through the water toward the rift in the wall. Carter inspected the opening with the spotlight, and the area in the new room immediately beyond. Seeing nothing in the way of immediate obstacles, he told Jayden the path was clear for him to proceed.

Jayden's face was a mask of determination as he guided the craft that was keeping them alive through the narrow aperture in the wall and ceiling. Carter swept the spotlight up on the ceiling of the new room.

"As soon as the stern clears you're going to have to angle the nose down so we don't hit the ceiling."

"Got it." Jayden's hands were poised over the controls while his gaze flicked back and forth between the ceiling of the new room and the side of the opening the sub was passing through. The nose of the sub just barely came into contact with the ceiling about ten feet into the Smoking Room when the actions Jayden took a few seconds earlier took effect, sending the sub's nose down at an angle into the center of the watery space. Carter spun around in his seat to watch the tail section of their craft to make sure it would clear the opening.

"You're right on target back there," he told Carter. "Hold it steady."

"That's what she said."

"Seriously?" Carter shook his head but couldn't stifle a laugh. He knew from their experiences in the Navy that Jayden would find a way to crack a joke even during the most stressful times.

"I got this." Jayden continued concentrating until the craft was well clear of the opening. Then he put it into a controlled hover, sat back in his seat and exhaled. The radio crackled.

"Topside to *Deep Voyager*: how we doing down there, over?"

Jayden picked up the radio transmitter. "We're in the Smoking Lounge, taking a break, you know, having a couple of cigars and some coffee, over." Carter shook his head while the radio reply from Johnny came back.

"You're worrying me, Jayden. You are seriously deep inside that wreck. How are your systems, over?"

Jayden's gaze flicked over his controls for a few seconds before replying. "All systems go, Topside. Battery power and oxygen levels where they should be for this point in the dive, over."

"Reminder to exercise extreme caution. We'll let you get back to it. Holler if you need anything, over and out."

Carter pointed forward out into the room. "The good thing about this place is that I think we actually have a straight shot into a hallway, which leads to…"

"The Purser's Room. Let's go." Jayden activated the sub's thrusters and they glided across the Smoking Lounge, passing over furniture that remarkably still had some upholstery on it. Sadly, Carter pointed out another skeleton underneath an upturned circular table in a corner of the room. As they neared the far end of the rectangular room, Carter illuminated the exit, which fortunately was wide enough for the sub to pass through and featured no door.

Carter examined the diagram while Jayden brought the sub up to the room exit. "Once we're in the hallway, it should be the second room on the left."

Jayden allowed the sub to decelerate as it coasted up to the hallway entrance. "Plenty of room over here. How am I for clearance on your side?" he asked, while looking left out of his side.

"Good on this side as well," Carter said. He aimed the spotlight ahead into the hallway. "At least it's not going to be a real tight fit in there. Still, I'm not sure how the turn into a room is going to go."

"Only one way to find out." Jayden brought the sub forward into the hallway. They passed a room on the right with a partially crumbled doorway leading into a room of complete ruin, twisted wreckage everywhere. Then on the left, a room with an open door offering a view of machinery of some sort. "Next one on the left should be it," Carter said.

Jayden continued to push the sub forward until they saw the doorway of what should be the Purser's Room. "Uh-oh," Carter said, "Problem."

"Yeah. How are we going to get in there?" Jayden brought the sub to a hover in front of the room.

The set of double doors was closed.

CHAPTER 5

"Maybe if you nudge into them with the sub's nose they'll just swing open?" Carter suggested.

Jayden considered this, using the spotlight control to highlight the door knob, studying the area where the doors met each other, as well as the frame. The doors looked surprisingly intact. "It looks like they're actually shut, but I can try it. Brace yourself."

"Whoa, I said *nudge*, not *ram*!" Carter said.

"Kidding. I'll just swing the nose into it. Here goes…" He engaged the right horizontal thruster only, sending the sub to the left, which brought the nose of it into light contact with the double doors. Both men felt the small impact as the doors remained shut and did not give way.

"No go," Jayden summarized.

Carter exhaled deeply, studying the ship diagram. "This is the only way into that room, unless there's extensive damage to one of the walls on the other side."

"We could try the door knob," Jayden suggested. Carter looked up from the diagram and stared at the round, brass colored doorknob. "With the grab arm?"

"No, Carter, with your actual arm. Of course with the grab arm!"

"Okay, wise guy. But we'll have to use the arm on your side. Can you keep us in position while you do the arm?"

"I'm going to have to."

Jayden made some adjustments to the ship's thrusters and buoyancy that fine-tuned the hover. Then he turned his attention to the grab-arm controls. He brought the tip of the arm up to the door handle and opened the claw. "Let's hope it's not locked," Carter said, as Jayden closed the claw grabber around the knob.

"This'll be a little tricky, I need to bring the arm kind of up and left at first..." He trailed off as he concentrated on the remote control mechanical task. "It's turning!" Carter said, unable to hide the excitement in his voice. Jayden paused to think about his next move on the remote, then continued, now bringing the claw down and to the left as it turned the knob.

"Try to push them open now," Carter said after the knob had been turned about 180 degrees.

"Cross your fingers," Jayden said as he pushed the arm forward while it still clutched the doorknob. Nothing happened while they sat there staring at the closed set of doors. "Let me try pushing with the sub itself just a little bit..." Jayden engaged the thrusters forward for a quick burst, and for a moment nothing happened. Then suddenly they witnessed a puff of silt around the door frame as the doors were dislodged and swung into the room.

"Behold, the Purser's Room!" Carter said. Jayden checked in with Topside on the radio, telling them they had found the room of interest. Johnny's reply came right away.

"Amazing work, you two! Don't forget to watch your gauges—how are all your systems, over?"

Jayden's gaze roved over the console's various gauges and indicator lights before replying that all systems were go. "We have sufficient clearance through the double door entrance to make it inside the Purser's Room. Doing that now, over."

After Carter declared them to be free of obstacles behind them, Jayden gave the sub small bursts of horizontal acceleration until their craft's nose entered the room at an angle. Then he engaged only the left thruster to swing the craft to the left so that it could then head straight into the room. They scooted inside smoothly without incident, and Jayden kept them in a controlled hover while they examined their new surroundings. This room was small, with not even enough room for the sub to turn around inside due to collections of debris that took up what was once open space.

"We're going to have to back out of here," Jayden noted while Carter swept the spotlight around the floor.

"Except for the major debris piles, it's relatively clean in here," he said. "Looks like-" But then he broke off his own sentence as he saw the skeletons—how many people they belonged to he couldn't tell—piled in a heap in a corner on the floor. But as chilling as the sight was, Jayden's next words made him forget all about it.

"I see two safes!"

Carter looked away from the bones. He eyed the cone of brightness from Jayden's spotlight. In the middle of it was one cube-shaped safe, bronze in color, lying on its side on the floor. Around it was a toppled shelf unit of some sort, now mostly fragmented. Near the edge of the cone of light was a second safe, also lying on its side.

Carter resumed sweeping the rest of the room with the spotlight on his side of the craft. This room was bare compared to the others, with not a lot in the way of furniture, which made it easy to see that there were only the two safes in here and nothing else of real interest.

"Only two safes," Jayden said. "That can't be all they had on the entire ship."

Carter shook his head as he watched a small black fish dart through the cones of light between the two safes. "No, but I have some bad news. I didn't notice this before, but look at that fallen shelf."

Jayden added his own spotlight's beam to the area in question. "Yeah?"

"At first I thought it was laying on the floor, but now I can see that it's actually obscuring a major hole in the floor. See right...there...." He physically pointed through the front of the acrylic dome to a dark patch visible beneath a corner of the overturned shelving unit.

"Oh yeah, I do see it. So that means..."

"Unfortunately, I think it means that there more safes down in that hole there, that broke through the floor. These two over here managed to fall far enough away from the rest that they didn't fall through with the excessive safe weight after who knows how long underwater."

"Let's see if we can get a closer look." Jayden brought the sub over to the break in the floor, hovering a few feet over it so that Carter could aim his spotlight down into it. He shook his head as he peered into the opening.

"It's just a deep black hole, I can't see anything. If safes did fall down there, we're not going to get them on this dive, that's for sure."

Jayden tapped a gauge on console. "It's time for us to head back up, anyway. Let's see if we can grab these two and get them up."

Let's start with the one on my side over here, since we're already facing that way," Carter suggested. Jayden agreed, and nudged the sub a little closer to the target safe. "The claw's not big enough to reach around the whole thing, but fortunately we have those mounting brackets, I guess is what they are, on the back. I should be able to form a sealed grip through one of those."

"Be quick about it," Jayden warned. "Battery power is depleted one-third, so to preserve the rule of thirds we should be heading back right now."

"Just hold her steady then, and here goes…" Carter lowered the arm until the claw hand was next to the mounting bracket on the back of the safe. "Opening the claw." He informed Jayden of each step since the pilot couldn't see what was happening with the starboard side grab arm. "Moving the fingers through the bracket…and…closing the claw….got it!"

"Test it by lifting the arm before I move the sub."

Carter lifted the arm and the claw grip held, but the safe didn't budge. "Looks like it's too much weight for the arm to lift by itself."

"As long as the claw grip holds, the sub itself will lift it. Just make sure the grip is secure."

Carter tested it for a few more seconds and then pronounced it ready to go. "It's closed on there. We'll just have to try it."

"Moving over to the other safe now. You may need to swing the arm without losing the claw grip to avoid obstacles. Definitely will on the way back out, so just get used to the idea."

"Roger that. Let's move."

Jayden expertly sidled the sub across the room to the other safe, where he positioned them over their second target. He rapidly lowered the second mechanical arm, mounted on the port side of the sub, until the claw grabber was next to the back of the safe. Then he paused.

"What's wrong?" Carter asked.

"This one's laying on its back where the mounting brackets are. No easy way to grab it."

"See if you can flip it over with the arm, or just up onto one side."

Jayden adjusted the spotlight and squinted down at the safe. "It does look like there's a small gap between the back of it and floor. I'll see if I can wedge the claw under there and flip it."

"Yeah, try it, but don't take too long, we should probably get—" Carter cut himself off as his concentration was derailed by what appeared to be a flash of light outside of the room—through cracks in the walls—in another part of the ship.

"Probably get what?" Jayden asked, fingers poised over the grab arm controls.

"Get going. Hold on." Carter killed his spotlight, casting the far reaches of the starboard half of the room into darkness. "Do me a favor: turn your spot off, will you?"

"I can't do the work without that, why—"

"I see something. Quick , just do it." With an irritated glance, Jayden pressed the button that turned off the powerful spotlight on his side of the sub. "Floodlights too, hurry," Carter added.

But at this Jayden hesitated. "Carter, what's going on? I need to be able to see in here to keep from hitting stuff."

"I see lights over there, through the walls. Turn it off!"

"Probably bioluminescence." But Jayden complied, dousing the floodlights, casting the room outside the sub into a complete absence of light. Inside the cabin, only the soft glow of the instrument console LEDs and screen readouts illuminated them. Carter pointed to a spot toward the wall in the Purser's Room to Jayden's left. It was pockmarked with small rust-pitted holes and the occasional small tear. A few seconds passed and then, through one these small openings, there came the unmistakable flash of bright, white light.

"That's obviously artificial," Carter said. "Not biological."

Jayden was already reaching for the radio. They continued to watch in the same direction while he keyed the transmitter. The light was visible again, moving sporadically from where Carter first noticed it to their left, very slowly.

"*Deep Voyager* to Topside, come back..." While Jayden waited for the reply, he turned to Carter. "Could it be an ROV from our ship?"

"Why wouldn't they have told us they were deploying one again? More likely, it's an ROV from the mystery newcomer ship." They continued to watch as the lights would disappear from sight behind solid walls, and then reappear. It seemed as though the light was filtering through multiple walls, not just one, where the holes and tears had to line up just right for it to be visible to them in the Purser's Room.

Johnny's voice invaded the stunned silence in the sub cabin. "Topside to *Deep Voyager*, we read you. What's your status? Over."

Jayden kept his eyes on the dark walls, looking for the lights, while he replied into the comm system. "Systems are good, we're about ready to head back out. But we see lights down here. Did you deploy an ROV or AUV? Over."

Johnny's reply was immediate. "That's a negative, *Deep Voyager*. Our vessel, that's R/V *Deep Pioneer* for anyone who might be listening over this frequency, did not, I repeat did *not* deploy a submersible vehicle of any kind after you began your dive, over."

Carter's voice was low but clear in the cabin: "Uh-oh. Well whoever it is, they're heading in our general direction."

"Copy that, Topside. We still can't say for sure, but there sure seems to be some kind of craft down here. We're still seeing the lights, inside the ship coming our way now. They must have deployed something from the

Transoceanic, over."

Carter interjected in the cabin before Johnny's radio reply. "If it's from *Transoceanic,* how'd they get down here so fast? It's only been maybe an hour-and-a-half and it takes about twice that to get down here."

"And they got down inside the *Titanic* already? Johnny's voice was incredulous, while Carter smiled and nodded. "That's what I'm saying!" he told Jayden.

Jayden shrugged as he spoke into the mic. "If they used the thrusters on the way down, at the expense of using more battery power and therefore having a shorter bottom time—"

"That would explain it," Carter said. Then Johnny completed the sentence for him over the radio.

"They might do that if they wanted to get down on the wreck as fast as possible, but why?"

Jayden keyed the mic and asked, "Have you been in contact with that ship yet?"

"*We've* been in contact with *it,*" Johnny said, "but they haven't responded back yet."

Carter motioned for the transmitter and Jayden gave it to him. "Co-pilot here, Topside. Maybe just physically pay them a visit with a tender vessel—send some guys over on one of the inflatable boats with a megaphone and shout up to them, over."

"Not a bad idea, co-pilot. I'll bring it up with Cliff Jameson and we'll take it under advisement. Meanwhile, you better work on getting your butts back outside that wreck. Over and out."

No sooner had they ended the radio call than the mysterious lights were visible again up ahead, but not so far away this time.

"Let's get that other safe and get out of here." Carter flipped the spotlight on his side back on. Jayden activated the floodlights and then his own spotlight, casting the room into temporary unnatural brightness once again.

"So back to this, I'm going to try to flip the safe over so I can grab the bracket on the back." They heard the mechanical whirring noise as Jayden put the external manipulator arm into motion.

"The lights are definitely getting closer," Carter said.

Jayden's response was a sustained hum of the mechanical arm as he kept it engaged while trying to flip the safe. "Here goes…gonna have to bump the whole sub up a foot or so…." He reached a hand over to the vertical thruster control on the console while the other remained on the grab arm joystick. The sub rose slightly in the Purser's Room while remaining in the same position relative to the floor. With it came the grab arm, and then the safe.

"It's off the bottom," Carter said.

"Rotating the arm now." Jayden manipulated the thruster arm until the safe was tipped up on its side. Then he lowered the sub back down a foot until the safe settled onto the floor again in its new orientation. "Now to get the claw grip on the bracket mount." He worked on controlling the arm and claw grabber so that it would grip the safe's bracket, as Carter had done with the other safe. Meanwhile, Carter watched for the mystery craft somewhere nearby in the bowels of the ship. Their own lights made it difficult to see, but he thought he could discern illumination coming through the gaps in the walls. If that's what it was, it was even closer to them now.

"Come on Jayden, not to put the pressure on you, but we really need to get a move on."

"Got it!" The genuine excitement in Jayden's voice was unmistakable. "Let me test it…Okay, now I'm going to pick it up and swing it in closer to the sub. Make sure yours is in all the way in, too. We want to maintain as low a profile as possible on the way back out of the ship."

"Good to go on my side. No desire to make this my final resting place, so, let's make like a tree and leave, shall we?"

Jayden's reply was to turn the back of the sub toward the room exit while hovering in place. Then he did a final systems check, as well as a visual check of the two safes that now hung by one grab arm on each side of the sub. "It's good we have two safes, because they're heavy enough that if there was only one, we'd have uneven weight distribution."

"It also means we're that much heavier and will need to use that much more battery power on the return trip," Carter pointed out.

"Ouch," Jayden said before putting the sub into reverse motion toward the exit with a tap of the horizontal thrusters. When the sub glided to a stop in front of the doorway, they repeated the process they had used to enter the room, but in reverse, with Carter checking for clearance and Jayden adjusting the sub's angle of attack. When they had it right, Jayden tapped on the thruster controls to send the sub out through the doorway in reverse into the hallway.

"Definitely a tighter squeeze this time with the safes sticking out," Jayden said as he worked to align the sub within the relatively tight confines of the hall. He radioed Topside to inform them they were out of the Purser's Room with two "packages" and now on their way out of the *Titanic*. Johnny's reply was a routine confirmation, with no news of the *Transoceanic*.

Everything set, Jayden boosted them down the hallway, back the way they had come, while Carter once again checked their progress against the schematic diagram. "End of the hall we squeeze back into the Smoking Room," he reminded Jayden, who nodded while continuing to take their sub steadily down the hall.

Carter decided that for now the spotlight wasn't necessary and so he turned it off to save battery power. As soon as he did he thought he saw lights up ahead blink off, but it happened so fast he couldn't be sure it wasn't a trick of the light or his eyes adjusting to the sudden lack of the bright spotlight. Jayden bumped one of the safes into the wall and had to reverse once and straighten back on track, but other than that it was smooth going until they reached the end of the hall.

"Back through the Smoking Lounge," Carter said, referencing his diagram for a moment before returning his attention to operating the spotlight. They traversed the lounge without incident, dragging the twin safes across the flooded space. Reaching the double-doored exit they had opened on their way in, they passed through without issue.

When they got to the opposite end of the room, it was time for the tricky maneuvering that had gotten them out of the restaurant. They repeated the process in reverse, jockeying the sub into position so that it could slide through the ragged crevice and back into the restaurant. This time the feat was made trickier by the two protuberances in the grab arms' clutches, and though it took longer than made both submariners comfortable, within a few minutes the *Deep Voyager* was sliding out into the restaurant's open space near the ceiling…

….when suddenly a blinding flash of light erupted below them.

CHAPTER 6

By the time Carter aimed the spotlight under his control straight down toward the source of the new light, he felt the physical impact. First there was a light thud, almost a scraping sound as something came into contact with the sub's grab arm on Carter's side. Immediately following that was a much more forceful impact of something heavy colliding with the *Deep Voyager*'s underbelly.

"What in the—" Jayden began but Carter cut him off as he recognized a discernable shape below them.

"Mini-sub! Manned, two guys inside! Lookout!"

Jayden gunned the horizontal thrusters in the hopes that it would send them darting off into the center of the restaurant space, creating some separation between the two subs. But instead, as soon as he felt the acceleration kick in, *Deep Voyager*'s progress came to a sudden, jolting halt. Jayden knew the thrusters were still turning, his hand was on the control and he could feel the vibrations and hear the hum of the motor. So why did their sub stop? Did he hit something? Looking ahead and up, he saw nothing to get in their way. He was checking left and right when Carter said, "You're not going to believe this."

"Try me," Jayden said, doing his best to keep his voice level.

"Those bastards clamped their grab arm claw onto the other bracket of the safe on my side."

"*What?*"

"They've got it in their own grab arm! Watch it, watch it—their moving the sub now—heading up and away from us."

"Try to radio them on an underwater-to-underwater frequency!" Jayden said, more like yelled, as he grappled with the submersible's controls to try and wrest it from the interlopers. Carter picked up the radio transmitter and did a channel scan, monitoring for activity, while transmitting *"Titanic* sub to *Titanic* sub" on each channel.

Jayden put the sub's thrusters on full and was able to plow the sub slowly out into the spacious room, towing the other sub behind them. But when they reached the middle of the restaurant, the combatant sub applied its own thrusters in the opposite direction, effectively cancelling out the *Deep Voyager*'s forward progress.

"Well this is damned stupid!" Jayden yelled, banging on the console in frustration. "We're both just burning out our batteries! If I stop using our thrusters, we get pulled back that way. What the hell do they want?"

Carter still fiddled with the radio. "They want this safe, that's what they want."

"That's ridiculous! How do they even know what's in it? *We* don't even know what's in it yet!"

"We know what we think is in it," Carter said, reaching out to adjust the radio settings, "and I have a feeling that they do, too." Before Jayden could reply, the radio came to life with a voice that was not Johnny's.

"You must be violating the rule of one-thirds by now. Let go of the safes—we know you have two of them—and you will be able to return to the surface safely." The voice was that of an adult male with a vaguely European accent that Carter couldn't quite place. He turned to Jayden.

"You keep trying to get us away from them and out of this room, back the way we came. "I'll talk to these losers."

Carter held the transmitter up to his mouth. "Who are you and what in the hell do you think you're doing?"

"I told you, we want the safes. Drop them and we let you go. If not, well…let's just say that we're willing to play a little game of chicken with battery supply and oxygen levels." Laughter from the other occupant of the invading sub emanated from the radio speaker. The look on Carter's face said that he was beyond furious. He growled into the transmitter.

"Look: we're both in a very treacherous situation here. Release your grab arm, and we'll be happy to chalk all this up to a happy little accident, okay? Over."

"You release the safes, both of them, and we will consider this little meeting in the same light," came the reply.

Carter became livid as Jayden informed him that he was not having success in freeing them by maneuvering their own sub. The former Naval officer raised the mic to his lips once again. "Listen here, I don't know who you think you are, ignoring all requests for identification, interfering with permitted operations on an internationally regulated historical grave site, but we are authorized to work this site. We have the proper permits to retrieve these safes, and you do not. We know this because no other artifact recovery permits have been issued for this timeframe. So you are the ones who are breaking the law by not having a permit and sabotaging an underwater salvage operation in a manner that equates to reckless endangerment. *Over.*" Radio silence ensued during which Jayden and the pilot of the mystery sub continued their oddly quiet, yet deadly, battle.

"They're smaller than us, and probably a little less powerful, but that also makes them more maneuverable and a little faster," Jayden summed up as he jostled the controls. "Hey, shine your spot to over one O'clock, down low on the floor—what's that?"

Carter illuminated the area of interest as requested. "Looks like a pile of rubble. Something to avoid."

"They're beneath us, grabbing onto us from below, so I was thinking maybe if I can drag them across it, they'll have to let go or else take too much damage." Jayden wrestled some more with the sub's controls, the net result being that their high-tech craft made its way ever so slowly toward the rubble mound. Meanwhile, the radio stayed silent, their subsea foes apparently deciding that communication was not the answer here.

Carter tried out what he thought of as a potential disorientation technique, aiming his powerful spotlight toward the enemy sub and then rapidly moving the beam back and forth in an erratic fashion. He would do that for a few seconds and then stop for a few in an unpredictable cycle. He had no way of knowing if it was working or not, but soon Jayden called out that they were about to go over the rubble mound.

Suddenly, *Deep Voyager* burst forward in a rush of relative speed.

"We're free! They're off of us!" Jayden shouted in spite of the close quarters.

"Did they let go or get knocked off?" Carter wondered aloud.

"Don't know, don't care. Help me locate the exit so we can leave these bastards behind. I don't want them to catch up to us again."

Carter had no argument for that and so, after a last salvo of combative spotlighting, turned the spot toward the front, up high, looking for the tear in the ceiling. The room was big enough that even with the spotlight it was difficult to make out much detail that far away. The sub chugged along toward the wall, and Carter began to truly worry about their battery and oxygen supplies. He didn't dare look at the actual gauges, he was too afraid that would just make him unable to concentrate and send him into panic mode. He scanned the floor and mid-water of the room as well, lest he miss something that could snag them, but found no threats of that type. The next time he swept the beam to the far reaches of the room, in the middle of the wall, he found the top of the elevator shaft from which they had come up.

"I see it, Jayden." He doused the light so as not to give away their destination too early to their opponents. He pointed with his finger in the cabin of the sub, through the acrylic dome. "Head that way."

Jayden altered the direction of their craft, angling it upward at the same time. He furrowed his brow after a glance at his instrument gauges. "We are really burning through battery power. We need to shake these guys and get out of here or we're going to be another stat for *Titanic's* death toll."

"Don't let me stand in your way," Carter said. "Just tell me what to do."

The radio sputtered with Johnny requesting a status report. Jayden nodded to the radio. "You can deal with him while I drag these safes up there with us."

Carter spoke into the mic. "Topside, this is *Deep Voyager*, co-pilot. We are inside the wreck engaged with a combative manned submersible. I repeat: We are engaged with a combative manned submersible. Do you copy, over?"

Johnny's voice came back. "I copy you, *Deep Voyager*. What do you mean by 'combative', over?"

Carter pressed the transmit button and raised his voice. "I mean they've locked onto us with their grab arm claws and didn't let go until we dragged them over a debris pile. We had communications over an underwater sub-to-sub frequency during which they said they want us to drop the two safes we collected. We said no can do, and then they grabbed onto us with their claw arms, we got free, and now they're chasing us around the inside of the wreck. Over!"

"Copy that, we will board their ship now if we have to in order to get them to radio their people and get them to stand down."

"Somehow I don't think that's going to work," Carter said, feeling a bump beneath his feet as something knocked into them from below. "But it can't hurt to try. We're certainly not getting through to them down here, over."

"What part of the wreck are you in now?"

"Restaurant. Trying to head back the same way we came, over."

"Restaurant, copy that. Let me relay this information while you concentrate on getting out of there, but holler if you need anything."

"More battery power would be great."

"Ha ha, *Deep Voyager*. Topside, over and out."

Carter aimed the spotlight back on their adversaries for a little more chaotic flashing. "Wouldn't want them getting too comfy," he told Jayden, who nodded. This time their adversaries returned the action in kind by putting on a light show of their own, casting the cabin of *Deep Voyager* into a kaleidoscope of blinding halogens.

"It's like '70's Nite at my favorite singles bar in here," Jayden muttered under his breath.

"I'd ask you to dance but I'm kinda busy right now," Carter quipped.

"Give me a little light up here now," the Jayden said, fully aware that now was not the time for humor, stress-relieving as it may be. Carter shone the beam up toward where the elevator shaft opening was. They weren't there yet, but they were now close enough to see it in detail with the spotlight. Jayden adjusted their course accordingly, and they began dragging their safes along with them toward their preferred exit.

Suddenly a new barrage of light manifested itself behind them, a searchlight probing in the darkness, passing them by, then sweeping back to hold them in its power.

"They're coming after us," Carter warned.

"Good thing we're a little faster than them," Jayden said.

"Doesn't much matter, because if they get their clutches on us again, literally, we won't even get out of the wreck, much less back to the surface before we run out of oxygen in this tin can."

"Well you're just a ray of sunshine, aren't you, Carter? I mean, if I didn't know any better—"

It suddenly became darker in the large space as the sub in chase behind them doused all its lights.

"Oh good, maybe they lost power," Jayden said gleefully. But Carter shook his head. "They're still moving toward us."

"Yeah, they still have power. They probably decided to save their own battery power by killing their lights and just letting us use ours."

"Hurry, let's get into the elevator shaft, it takes some careful handling and so will take time."

Jayden eyed the approaching vertical shaft that represented their way out. "I've got news for you, though. No way in hell are we going to fit through that with these two safes on the end of the extended grab arms the way we have them now."

"I've got an idea." Carter's voice sounded flat, tentative.

"You don't sound all that sure about it, whatever it is. Give me some enthusiasm, why don't you. I've got an *idea*!"

"Not sure if it'll work, but it's all I got."

"I've heard that before from you and I'm still alive, so I'll take it."

Carter made an adjustment to his spotlight and then continued. "I think we aim ourselves nose first toward the bottom, and head straight down into it, instead of a horizontal orientation like we did on the way up. Should be faster."

He paused as a large squid darted across their field of vision before retreating into a dark corner of the former restaurant. "Looks like calamari's still on the menu here," Jayden said.

Carter shot him a serious look. "We get out of this alive, it's bottomless calamari and brews at Neptune's Net, on me," he said, referencing one of his favorite spots on the coast in southern California.

"I'll remember that," Jayden said, but he couldn't hide his furtive glance at the console's instrument gauges, which gave him increasingly worrying news.

"So let's do it, come on they're going to gain a lot of ground on us while you're maneuvering into the shaft."

Jayden exhaled deeply while shaking his head. "Here goes nothing."

He raised *Deep Voyager*, floating them up to the ceiling, dragging the two safes with them as the spotlight from their foes loomed larger behind them. Then, as planned, he did his best to line them up perpendicular to the opening. But each time he had the right angle, the enemy sub would engage its spotlights, bathing the top of the elevator shaft in a confusing array of photic chaos.

"They might be on to our little plan," Jayden said, fighting the controls to keep the submersible aimed in the right direction.

Hunter moved the spotlight from their target exit to the bothersome sub, at the same time changing the radio frequency to the underwater channel and then yelling into the mic. "Hey hey hey, what is wrong with you, stay back stay the hell back!" He hoped the sudden burst of light and sound would distract them enough to let Jayden make forward progress, and as it turned out, it worked.

"I've got the angle. Here we go, give me the light!" Jayden shouted, the excitement on his face completely unmasked.

"Keep going, full speed ahead. Go, go go!" Carter yelled, before yelling more nonsense into the radio and wavering the spotlight hectically toward their submarine foes.

Jayden brought the nose of the sub over the opening of the elevator shaft, true as could be, and then reversed to stall them over the shaft.

"It's all clear down there," Carter said, aiming his light down into the shaft for a moment. Get us in there."

Jayden hastily lowered the sub into the shaft, and it was all going well until the two extended grab arms reached the top of the shaft walls, halting their downward progress. The port side impacted slightly before the starboard, and so the *Deep Voyager* tipped up to the left before settling back down, where the right safe caught on the edge of the shaft, too. Jayden activated the vertical thrusters, raising the sub higher as it rotated, until the safe in Carter's grab arm was clear of the lip.

"You got it, take us down!" Carter shouted.

Jayden complied, jamming the joystick all the way forward until they could hear the high-pitched whinny of the motors straining against their own design limitations. Carter heard a dull scraping sound as the safe hit something. He turned around in time to be blinded by dual halogen spotlights from the intruder sub that had run dark and silent up from below, until now.

"They're here!" Carter warned his friend, who still wrangled with the controls to angle the *Deep Voyager* down into the shaft.

"I have the angle, thrusters are on, but we're not moving, Carter!"

The Omega founder took a look behind and below them. "That's because the other sub latched onto us again. They've got a hold of the grab arm on your side, with their grab arm. They can't get to mine from this angle, though, but they're trying." Carter's voice rose in volume and intensity. "This is as good as it's going to get. Try and drag them up and over. My hunch is something's gonna break."

Jayden's hands stabbed at buttons on the console as he coaxed the craft down into the elevator shaft, nose first. "Feel like I'm on the Matterhorn at

Disney Land he said as they stared straight down the elevator shaft into the darkness below. Carter swiveled his spotlight so that it shone away from their combatant sub, and straight down into the shaft. "Let's turn off our flood lights and just use the one spot. It'll give them less light to see by."

Jayden agreed and killed the floodlights that provided general light in a short radius out from the entire sub. The latched-on submersible was cast into relative darkness. Carter tried to get a glimpse of the two figures inside, as he had done a couple of times during the dive over here, but could make out only a pair of silhouetted heads-and-shoulders.

"Now just take us down as fast as you can. Vent everything out of the bladders."

"I'm already on full thruster power. I can vent the air, but why?"

"The faster we head down, the more force it's going to put on their little grab arm that's latched onto ours. I'm hoping it'll just snap off."

They heard the shriek of bending and scraping metal. "Something's going to snap off, that's for sure," Jayden said, pressing the button to vent air from the buoyancy tubes. "But we're not moving any further down…seem to be stuck…maybe just—whoa!"

They lurched forward in their bucket seats as the craft suddenly moved straight down after being freed from whatever had been holding it back. Carter aimed his spotlight back up to see if the sub still followed, but it was gone.

"It worked!" he said gleefully. "Snapped it off!"

Jayden looked out the acrylic dome on his side. "Uh, we snapped an arm off, all right, Carter. But guess what? It wasn't their arm, it was ours. We're missing the entire external grab arm assembly on my side of the sub."

Carter swore under his breath as the *Deep Voyager* plunged down the elevator shaft. "That means we lost the safe."

"Wow, you're a sharp one!" Jayden chided. "No arm, no safe that was being held in the claw grabber at the end of the arm. Your analytical abilities are nothing short of amazing." He looked over at Carter to see how he was taking the ribbing, but the historical analyst was facing away from him, looking out his side of the acrylic dome.

"We still have the safe on this side, just don't go too far to the right."

"Want me to take us back up and fight those guys for the other one?" Jayden said, smiling because he knew it was out of the question.

"Not unless you want to die with it down here. Speaking of which," Carter added, "how's our battery life?"

Jayden glanced at his gauges and shook his head. "You don't want to know."

CHAPTER 7

Jayden slowed the sub as they neared the bottom of the elevator shaft. He would need to level the craft out at the bottom and maneuver it into a tight turn to exit the shaft out into the cargo hold area. But the sudden explosion of light from above told them their adversaries were in pursuit and that there would be less time than preferred for the tricky maneuvering.

"They're coming down after us!" Carter said, craning his neck to look straight up. "And they've already got the one safe, I can see it in their grab arm!"

"Greedy bastards," Jayden grunted, putting the one of the sub's thrusters into reverse for a couple of seconds to turn it, then putting both thrusters into forward. Like parallel parking a car into a tight space, he moved forward and back, turning a little more with each pass, until the sub's nose was facing the open side of the shaft.

"They're almost down to us, let's go!" Carter coaxed.

Jayden scooted the sub out of the elevator shaft into the cargo area. Carter swung the spotlight around to the front to aid with navigating the treacherous area with its jumbles of debris piled everywhere in random fashion. "Hopefully they take at least as long as we did to get out of—"

"Nope, here they come, they're already out!" Carter informed Jayden.

"Great. They're sub is smaller, otherwise—"

"This isn't a sub pilot competition, Jayden. These guys are out to take the safe we still have, and no doubt don't care if we live or die in the process. Step on it!"

"Which way?"

"Right, turn right!"

The radio crackled with Johnny's voice requesting a dive status update. "I'll handle it," Carter said, snatching up the transmitter.

"What's up Johnny, we're almost out of the wreck, over."

"Almost out of it? What's your battery situation look like?"

"We're gonna have dead batteries in a few minutes," Jayden said nonchalantly.

Carter continued into the radio, "Almost dead, we've been using a lot of juice for the lights, grab arms and pulling the other sub that latched onto us like a barnacle," Carter said into the microphone.

Johnny sounded flabbergasted. "Jesus, you've absolutely *got* to get outside the wreck before they run out. If you do that, the air system is mechanical and you can use it to inflate the buoyancy tubes to rise to the—"

"We know, Johnny. Listen, that other sub is still in pursuit. If they grab onto us again, we won't make it out of here, and I have a feeling they know that."

"We tried to board their ship, but were repelled by force. We radioed the Canadian Coast Guard, but no telling how long they'll be to get here."

"Okay, listen, I've got to focus here, we'll see you up top in a couple hours, I hope. Over and out."

"This is going to have major ramifications, you guys. Godspeed, over and out."

They reached an obstruction requiring a turn of either left or right. "Which way, you think?" Jayden said before they got to it.

"Left, left—take the left!"

"You got it." Jayden took the sub around the pile of debris and then straightened out on the other side. Both of them were used to looking for daylight when seeking the exit of a wreck or cave, but of course this deep down, it was black everywhere so there was no such advantage. Only the reach of the sub's own lights offered any kind of advance look.

Jayden's eyes lit on the red light that suddenly appeared on the dash. "Battery low warning is on."

"What does that mean exactly?"

"Less than ten percent remaining."

"Great."

Jayden zigged and zagged the sub to thread his way through mounds of debris and twisted wreckage, while behind them, the lights of the attacking sub bobbed and weaved in pursuit.

Carter looked up from his diagram and pointed slightly off center from straight ahead. "Takes us that way as the crow flies and we should be out of the wreck in about three minutes at this speed."

"Crowds don't fly underwater."

"As the fish swims, then. Point is, you might not be able to take us in a straight shot because of all the wreckage in the way, but that's the direction we need to go in."

"Copy that." Jayden made the course correction and proceeded to dart the sub around any obstacles before resuming that course. Once he had to swoop down lower to avoid a series of dangling steel cables, but he kept at it until the irregular yawning maw of the Titanic's opening became recognizable in the floodlights. They opted not to use the spotlights anymore to conserve what little remaining battery power they had.

"Okay, we can start angling up now," Carter said. "I don't recall seeing hanging obstacles on the way in when we used the spotlights."

Jayden reached for the rudder control and the sub slanted gently upward. "Keep a sharp eye out all the same. I don't have a lot of reaction time at this speed using only the floodlights."

"Will do." It was hard for Carter not to keep turning around to check on their pursuer's progress, but he kept his eyes glued to what lay ahead so that they could minimize their chances of hitting any stray wreckage that might be dangling from the shipwreck above or protruding from the bottom.

When they had completely cleared the hulking wreck, Jayden increased the angle of the sub's ascent. No sooner had he finished doing that than the battery warning light began flashing red, instead of steady red, the lights in the cabin dimmed and stayed that way, and an alarm began to bray.

"Time's up Carter. I'd say we have sixty seconds until it's lights off in this bad boy."

Carter reached for the radio. "I'll update Topside." He spoke rapidly into the transmitter, "Topside, this is *Deep Voyager*, we have lost—"

And then the lights in the cabin went dark.

"Crap," Jayden said. After a few seconds a weak field of light appeared in the cabin. Jayden turned in surprise but then saw Carter holding a penlight.

"Never leave home without it."

"Shine it over here so I can activate the switches to add air to the buoyancy tubes." Carter did as asked and Jayden flipped a series of switches. They heard a hiss of escaping compressed air being directed into the buoyancy bladders. Then they slowly began to rise.

"Almost three hours up to the surface. Now it's just a fun game of…Will Our Oxygen Last Long Enough, who wants to play?"

"I think they do." Carter was twisted around in his seat, staring down toward the *Titanic,* which was not visible in the darkness, but the twin stabs of white light aimed up at them were unmistakable.

"You've got to be kidding me," Jayden said.

"Can they catch us?"

"I'm not sure. We have a decent head start and if they're only using buoyancy, which is the norm for ascents, they shouldn't be able to catch us. But if they use buoyancy *and* thrusters…I suppose they could," he finished.

"I've got an idea."

"What?"

Carter flicked off his penlight, casting their sub cabin into total darkness. "They can't catch us if they can't see us."

Jayden nodded in the blackness. "Every five minutes or so I should take a depth reading though. That gauge is a sensor hardwired to the outside, works by pressure, no power needed. Just to make sure we are in fact still rising."

They sat alone in dark silence pondering the hell in which they would find themselves if for some reason the buoyancy system failed and they sank back to the ocean bottom. In a few minutes Carter passed Jayden the penlight. The other sub's lights were still visible far below, now a little more off to one side rather than directly below them. Jayden cupped his hand around the flashlight to avoid giving away their position, and checked the depth gauge. Breathing a sigh of relief, he told Carter, "We're still rising. Long way to go, but we're rising."

"They are too," Carter said, turning around in the dark to watch the lights far below them and to his left. "I wish we could contact Topside and let them know we're on our way. They're going to be freaking out we lost contact."

Jayden settled back in his pilot seat. "Nothing we can do about that. Sit back, relax, and enjoy the trip to the surface."

#

Three hours later

Jayden turned on the mini-flashlight but nothing happened. "Batteries died on the light."

"I don't have any spares," Carter said groggily. The two were tired and cold from sitting for hours in the same position. "Hey, I think it's getting lighter, though." He looked up toward the surface, which was not yet visible.

Jayden's focus was in the opposite direction. "I don't see any lights down there."

"We either outpaced them, or they drifted off course because they couldn't see us."

"Maybe we drifted off course," Jayden posited. "I sure hope we don't come up ten miles from the ship or something." Carter exhaled sharply in response. It wasn't a comforting thought. Adrift in the North Atlantic, bobbing like a cork with no means to control their dead-in-the-water craft. It wouldn't take much to flood and sink them. It wasn't lost on Carter that in that scenario, they would experience much of what the *Titanic* survivors did on that fateful night, freezing to death in the very same patch of North Atlantic.

"Let's just take it one step at a time," Carter said. "In theory, we should be rising straight up, which, since we left from the *Titanic* itself, should have us within visual of our ship when we surface."

"We'll find out soon enough. It is getting lighter, I can see it now." Looking up, the pitch black they had become accustomed to was now more akin to a dark gray.

"Still no sign of them," Carter said, glancing into the depths below.

"Maybe they ran out of battery power after bee-lining down during their descent to catch up to us. We can only hope, right?"

When Carter didn't answer right away, Jayden prompted him. It was still dark, after all, and so they couldn't see each other faces to read expressions. "Right?"

"I've been thinking about who these people are."

"Whoever they are, they basically tried to kill us, and so if they ran out of battery power and got permanently stuck down there, I wouldn't feel bad about it. That's all I'm saying."

At that moment they saw a massive shape above them—moving—and after a few seconds realized it was moving down towards them from above.

"It's way too big to be the sub," Carter said.

And then the humongous form materialized not far above them, arcing down to within a few feet of their bubble dome before gliding upwards again toward the light.

"A whale!" Jayden yelled with genuine glee.

"A Right Whale if I had to guess," Carter added. "They can dive pretty deep, maybe a thousand feet, but still, it means we're definitely getting close to the surface."

The cetacean soared out of view and the *Deep Voyager* continued rocketing towards the surface. Jayden gazed out the window, straining to see slow-moving particles or animals like jellyfish that he could use to gauge their rate of ascent in the absence of functioning gauges. But it was still too dark to discern that kind of detail.

"How fast you think we're ascending?" he wondered aloud.

Carter shrugged in the near darkness. "Beats me. We don't have to worry about the bends, at least."

The pressure inside the submersible never changes, so decompression sickness was not a factor. Nevertheless, as a sub pilot, Jayden knew that it was not wise to ascend too fast. They could strike the bottom of their own ship, for one thing. They could come flying out of the water into the sky and land upside down, jarring loose the various oxygen and electronic systems. He had even heard of a fire starting in a sub that way, once, during his naval training. But since he didn't actually know how fast they were rising, he was too scared to vent any air from the buoyancy tubes, which would slow their rate of ascent. What if they were barely rising as it was, and he let too much air out. He imagined coming to within fifty feet of the surface, the sunlit world above tantalizingly visible, only to begin sinking back down to the depths, slowly at first, then with increasing momentum the deeper they went, knowing that this time it was for keeps…

"Hay Jayden….you fall asleep on me?"

Carter's voice jolted the sub pilot from his unnerving reverie.

"Huh? Nah, I'm with you."

"Good because I'd say we're not more than a couple of hundred feet from the surface. SCUBA depths!"

Compared to where they had just been, 200 feet was like being outside, but still in one's backyard compared to halfway up Mount Everest. They were almost back to the ship.

Jayden stared at the depth gauge and found that he could now read it. The light around them was now dark blue instead of black or gray. A large school of silver fish cascaded past them. They were returning to the familiar world they knew and loved.

"We are going up fast," Carter observed. In just a few seconds they were perhaps half the distance to the surface.

"I don't see the bottom of any ships," Jayden said. "At least we're not going to hit anything."

"Brace," Jayden warned as he gripped onto a handhold above him to the left. They were sometimes used to aid in getting in and out of the sub. This was the first time he'd ever had to use one while underwater, and he wished he didn't have to, but at least it was an option.

Sunlight burst all around them as fractured rays filtered through the ocean's uppermost layers. Carter also held on and they looked upwards into the sun, so blindingly bright after so many hours in darkness. The blue sky appeared wavy and indistinct as they drew near the surface, and then water was washing over the bubble dome as they broke free of the ocean into the world of air once again.

"Hold on," Jayden called out as their craft nearly came completely free of the water. As it levelled out mid-air, he saw two ships, one closer than the other by about a football field.

They landed back into the water with a great splash, both men jarring on impact.

"The good news is we made it back from the deep!" Carter said staring at the seascape in front of them.

"What's the bad news?"

"The bad news is that ship closest to us? That's not our ship, it's the one our submersible friends launched from."

"Great. We're dead in the water," Jayden said.

CHAPTER 8

The throaty roar of a small boat starting up should have been something to instill confidence into the two wayward submariners. Instead, it brought only dread and uncertainty.

"Looks like the support ship of our friends down there launched a little welcoming party for us," Carter said flatly. He eyed the dead radio wistfully. "I'm not sure *Deep Pioneer* can see us, since the *Transoceanic* is blocking their line of sight."

Jayden stared through the dome as the small boat whipped into a turn and began racing toward them, creating a white wake as it moved. He started to feel a little lightheaded and reached up to open the hatch. "Let's pop this sucker and then we can send up a flare. They'll definitely see that."

Jayden undid the latches and then Carter helped him to push the hatch open, tilt it back and secure it in place. In spite of the oncoming threat, the cool, fresh air that washed over them was invigorating and refreshing beyond words after hours in the stale, systems-deprived submersible cabin. But there was no time to revel in the sensation. "Flares, flares, flares…" Jayden was well aware that all seagoing vessels, including submersibles, were required by the Coast Guard to carry distress flares on board. Jayden rummaged underneath the pilot seat and found what he was looking for: an orange plastic case. He hauled it out, unsnapped it and grinned as he eyed the contents.

"Well lookey here: one flare gun and, count 'em…one, two, three, four flares!"

Carter plucked the gun and a flare from the case and loaded one of the red cylinders into the pistol. Standing in his seat, bracing with one hand against the open hatch, he held his firing arm up at an angle toward their support ship and fired. With a soft crack and a loud hiss, the bright orange flare traced a line of fire visible even in the broad daylight.

"No way they can miss that," Jayden said, as the incendiary projectile arced high over both ships, lingered in the sky and then trailed back down toward the sea.

The sound of the oncoming boat's motors was much louder now, racing toward their incapacitated craft. Jayden started to close the flare box but Carter put a hand on it. "Maybe we shouldn't put these things away just yet." He reached down, grabbed another flare and loaded it into the gun. Then he tucked the flare gun into the waistband of his pants, pulling his shirt down over it. "Put the case away," he told Jayden, who snapped the empty container back together and stowed back beneath the seat.

The small boat arced into a turn, pulling up to them without slowing until they were oriented parallel to the sub. The action cause a high wake to nearly turn the sub over, drenching the open cabin and its occupants with icy cold seawater. It was the barest taste of what the *Titanic* survivors experienced, and yet both ex-military men found it to be excruciatingly uncomfortable.

"Don't act adversarial yet," Carter said. "We're just two seamen who need to be rescued. As far as we know, that's all this is."

"Just two seamen in a floating nut?"

"Not the time for jokes, Jayden. Just act like you're grateful for the rescue."

One of the boat's crew, a swarthy-complected man in his late thirties, called out to them. "Your sub lose power?"

"That's right," Carter answered.

"You're lucky to be alive! The man said. Carter thought him to possibly be of Greek heritage, which put him on edge, making him recall a past adversary. Neither Carter nor Jayden said anything beyond nodding, so the crewman continued.

"Hop in and we'll take you the ship."

"What about our sub?" Carter asked.

One of the other crewman held up a bundle of rope. "We can tow it behind us. We'll take it slow."

Jayden couldn't help but look at Carter even though it might seem odd. Who wouldn't want to be towed and rescued from such a situation? But in this case, they were giving up control of their sub—with a safe from the Titanic that might contain a map to a priceless artifact—to an unknown group who had already demonstrated blatant disregard for their safety underwater. Did the boat crew even know what had transpired down below? Chances are they did, Carter mused, since the sub would have a comm system similar to their own in order to stay in touch with their support ship. Carter looked away hastily from Jayden at the boat crew. Everyone here was pretending, yet no one wanted to be the one to start the inevitable confrontation that would likely end badly once the reality of the situation was asserted.

"Sure. Thanks, we really appreciate it."

One of the boat men nodded and held up a coil of rope. "Tie this line off onto your cleat, there." He tossed the coil of rope at Carter, who did as requested. Another line was tossed and fastened to the opposite side, and then Carter stepped off of the sub onto the small boat, where one of the crew grabbed him by the hand and pulled him aboard. Jayden closed and secured the sub's hatch, and then he too climbed aboard the transfer vessel.

Carter shook hands with the man who had helped him aboard. "Thanks a lot for your help, we really appreciate it. As you know, our radio's dead, and I don't think our ship can see us from where we popped up so, many thanks for your help."

The man waved a hand. "Think nothing of it. It's the least we can do."

The boat driver increased their speed, the noise of the motor making normal conversation difficult as they sped toward the *Transoceanic*. At one point the R/V *Deep Pioneer* was visible, but the boat driver quickly corrected course to keep the *Transoceanic* in between them, blocking the line of sight. Carter suspected the maneuvering was purposeful, but didn't want to call attention to it since they would find out shortly.

In another couple of minutes the small boat was pulling up alongside the fantail of the combative sub's support ship. Carter could see the boat driver talking into a handheld marine radio. The noise of the engine prevented Carter from hearing what was said. He tried to read the man's lips, but he kept the radio positioned over his mouth. As one of the ship's crewman stepped down onto the fantail to catch a line thrown from the small boat crew, Carter made eye contact with the driver. "Excuse me, but can you please take us over to our ship first? They're going to be worried since we're without radio contact."

The driver held up the radio. "Do not worry, I took the liberty of hailing them for you to inform them that you are all right, and that we took you and your submersible aboard our ship for a quick tour and some hospitality such as a warm meal and some wine. We are all neighbors here on the *Titanic* site, after all. Please relax and join us!"

Carter and Jayden eyed each other and shrugged. "What the heck, then!" Jayden said. But he and Carter both knew that they had no choice. As they were led single file up the steps to the ship's main deck, Carter glanced down at his waistband to make sure the loaded flare gun was still covered by his shirt. He said under his breath to Jayden, "Dollars to donuts they never notified our ship." Jayden turned around briefly and nodded before stepping up onto the aft deck.

The ship was not unlike their own, but a little smaller. Glancing around without trying to appear overly curious, Carter saw no signs of manned submersible operation, but figured they must have a moon pool. Jayden turned around to look at his sub, paying particular attention to the starboard grab arm and the safe that was still gripped in its clutches. If it were knocked against the ship in the wrong way, it could be jarred loose and sink the miles back down underwater, most likely never to be seen by human eyes again.

As he watched, the boom arm of a stout crane began to swing over toward the *Deep Voyager*. "Don't worry," the small boat pilot said. "We'll take good care of your sub. Forecast indicates the seas are picking up, so it's best if we get her out of the water so she can't bang around."

"Mind the payload in the starboard grab arm," Carter said, his tone not quite icy, but very firm.

"Do not worry, we have the same reverence for the *Titanic* and her artifacts as do you," the boat pilot and crew leader said. "For now, follow me, please, and we'll get you something to eat while your crew comes over to pick you up."

As they walked, Carter felt in his pockets for his cell-phone, hoping he had forgotten to remove it as he usually did before a long submersible dive. No such luck, his pockets were empty of all objects, comfort being the main objective. He deliberately stepped on Jayden's foot as he walked ahead of him, and the sub pilot whirled around.

"Trying to flat tire me, are you?"

Everyone turned to look and Carter rolled his eyes. "We're not in middle school anymore, Jayden." There were a couple of half-hearted laughs and then everyone started walking again. Carter whispered to Jayden, "You got anything in your pockets?" He wasn't sure if he heard and was about to risk repeating the question a little louder when, to his relief, he saw Jayden's hands move to pat down his pants. But then Carter's hopes were dashed he saw him shake his head without turning around. He, too, had brought nothing on his person into the sub. That meant he had the flare gun, loaded with one flare. One shot.

They passed along a series of catwalks and short metal stairwells until they entered a contained portion of the ship, exposed to the air, yet sheltered overhead and partially on each side. A shimmering circle of water occupied the center of this space.

A moon pool.

Carter felt a chill rise along his spine as he eyed it. He suspected they had one, since they had launched a sub without being seen, but now that he knew beyond a shadow of a doubt this was the operation responsible for endangering them underwater, he had all the more reason to fear for his own safety, as well as Jayden's.

"Lunch at the moon pool?" Jayden inquired.

"The boat pilot laughed. "Sure, why not? We thought you'd like to see a little bit about our operations, since we are both in the same line of work."

Jayden shrugged. "Eh, seen one moon pool you seen 'em all. I'd rather have a tour of a ham and cheese sandwich right about now."

The crew leader turned toward Jayden, but before he could reply, his radio blared. He turned away from the moon pool and spoke into the unit, too softly for Carter and Jayden to hear. Carter sidled up to Jayden, aware that they were now loosely surrounded by half a dozen *Transoceanic* crew members. He was about to suggest they ask to visit the bridge, from where they could try to hail their own ship, when the water in the moon pool began to roil.

The pair of treasure seekers couldn't help but walk a little closer to the pool, where water began to slosh over the work deck. As they watched, a shape materialized in the water, blurry, dim and indistinct at first, but becoming clearer and more tangible with each passing second. Of course they knew what it was. But even so they stared at the moon pool, eyes riveted on the spectacle, until the object broke the surface. Sheets of seawater cascaded off the gleaming dome of the submersible that had so callously harassed them inside the wreck of the *Titanic*.

Carter's gaze went to the two men inside it, but for the moment there was still too much water on the dome for their faces to be recognizable. A crane operator lowered a boom arm and several crewman assisted in positioning the steel cables and hook onto the submersible. The sub was lifted out of the moon pool and transferred laterally until it was over a cradle berth on deck. It was lowered onto that, and then a crewman unlatched the hatch and pulled it open. The co-pilot was the first to step out onto the deck. Carter didn't recognize him. But when the pilot's face became visible, a shiver danced up his spine.

Daedalus. The classic Greek face, thick black stubble for a beard, the cocksure way he carried himself. No way it couldn't be him.

Carter shook his head slowly as he watched the sub-pilot shake hands with a couple of crewmen before locking eyes with first Jayden, and then Carter. The stare was hardnosed at first, but after a couple of seconds it morphed into a smile.

"I must say, Carter Hunt, Jayden Tanaka, while it is…scintillating to meet your illustrious acquaintances once again, I was rather hoping we would not cross paths on this particular day."

"I was hoping we'd never cross paths again, period," Carter said.

Jayden gave him a kick in the foot. They were in the lion's den now, and antagonizing their adversaries wouldn't improve their situation. "I don't mind crossing paths as long as there's beer involved," he said.

The crewman hopped into the sub and used the controls to raise the grab arm that held the other safe into a more accessible position. The pilot of this sub looked on and smiled before turning his attention back to Carter and Jayden.

"Perhaps champagne will be more in order. We shall see soon enough. The lost city of Atlantis proved to be a real feather in your caps, did it not?"

Defiance burned in Carter's eyes. "Good will always win out over evil, Daedalus. When your intentions are selfish, you have no hope against those who represent the greater good."

Daedalus exchanged glances with one of his crew and erupted briefly into peals of uproarious laughter. "Greater…good, oh my. Well, 'tis a new day on the *Titanic* and we shall put your little theory to the test. Solomon, release the safe and set it up here." But then he held up a hand. "Actually no, wait. Are you feeling lucky, Carter Hunt?"

Carter said nothing, only stared back at the man.

"I am," Jayden answered.

"I can tell *you* are already," Daedalus glared. "But you two are part of a team, are you not? And a team must work together. So I ask you again, *Carter Hunt*: are you feeling lucky?"

"He must have a thing for Clint Eastwood movies," Jayden answered. A look of annoyance crossed Daedalus' face, and then Carter responded.

"I'm feeling like we're owed an explanation. You could have killed us down there. And for what? Some old trinkets on a shipwreck? That's how little you value human life?"

Daedalus gave Carter a hard stare before replying. "Old trinkets, eh? Well, let's find out, shall we?" He nodded to the crewmen who had just removed the safe from the grab arm of Daedalus' sub.

"Open it."

CHAPTER 9

The crewman gripped the safe handle and tried to pull the door open. After a few futile tries, he looked up at Daedalus. "It's locked, boss."

"Of course it's locked, you idiot. It's a safe! Drill it open. Now!"

A rush of activity ensued as his crew scrambled to put drilling equipment in place next to the safe. In short order a pair of men appeared carrying a large pneumatic drill and set about preparing it for the job.

"What do you think is in there?" Carter asked. "Do you really need a few more jewels for your collection this badly?"

Daedalus shrugged. "Jewels from the *Titanic* are not just any old baubles, Mr. Hunt. But I think you know that's not why I'm here, nor is it why you're here." He locked eyes with Carter, as if waiting for him to say something, but Carter was giving nothing away.

"I'm looking for a map. A rather old one, at that," Daedalus went on.

Carter's heart sank as he tried to remain unreadable, but Jayden slouched visibly, standing next to him.

"What makes you think a map even exists in one of the *Titanic's* safes?"

Daedalus' reply was delivered in a straightforward, matter-of-fact tone. "Your client, Ms. Ashley Miller, was not very private about her attempts to reach out to the deep diving submersible and *Titanic* communities regarding the item her great grandfather told her family may still exist in on board."

At this Carter could only nod. It made sense. While not highly open about it, stopping short of appearing on talk shows and the like, his client did make it known amongst those familiar with deep work submersibles that she wanted a document recovered from the *Titanic*. Those who inquired further were told about the map. It was only after several failed rounds of meetings and negotiations with some of these people that she finally turned to Carter and his fledgling Omega Team.

"Haven't you plundered enough of the world's treasures already?" Carter asked. "Your organization…what's it called, oh yeah: Treasure, Inc., right?"

"Treasure, Stink!" Jayden contributed.

Carter didn't wait for a reaction before continuing. "Whatever you call it, your organization steals priceless antiquities and puts a price on them in the black market, robbing the public at large from ever experiencing them, benefiting only the wealthy collectors who buy them illegally."

Daedalus chuckled softly before speaking. "I will ignore your juvenile assessment of my business for now, since it comes from a place of ignorance. As to my lust for treasure, oh but how I would give up all of my other finds—even the ruins of Atlantis, which you denied me—in exchange for this one…Noah's Ark. If it is real, its value would be beyond compare."

The drill started up and the men had to shout in order to carry on the conversation. Carter was glad to have an excuse to add extra intensity to his voice. "And if the map is real, but the ark is not, you could spend your whole life chasing a wild goose."

"Maybe we should just let him do that," Jayden said. Daedalus ignored him.

"Such is the nature of our business, Mr. Hunt. That is why I asked you if you were feeling lucky, you see?"

The workers shouted to one another as technical adjustments were made on the drilling. "Obviously I'm not feeling very lucky, Daedalus, or I wouldn't have come across the likes of you today."

"Got it, we got it!" came the shout from one of the workers. Daedalus motioned for Carter and Jayden to follow him over to the safe. They all gathered there as the door was swung open, creaking on its hinges. A flashlight was shined in as Daedalus was handed a pair of white latex gloves to put on, presumably to safeguard whatever objects lay inside.

"I see jewelry," one of the crewmen said.

Daedalus knelt, reached inside the safe and pulled out a handful of gold and silver chains. He placed them into a tray held by a worker and immediately put his hand back in the safe. His hand came out again, this time with a roll of silver coins. Three more times he passed his hand in and out of the safe, each time removing valuables that were already over at least one century old, and incredulous in their own right due to where they were recovered. But his face contorted into a mask of disappointment as he stood and turned away from the safe.

"That's it. No map or documents of any kind."

Everyone was silent as they digested this. Jayden was the first to find words. "Gee, I never thought a bunch of people would be so disappointed to bring up a safe full of riches from the *Titanic*. Am I missing something?"

At this, Daedalus seemed to have reached a breaking point, for he whirled around and yelled at Jayden. "Yes, we are missing something! Stop pretending like you don't know what it is—both of you," he added, shifting his gaze to glare at Carter also before continuing. "Never mind. We will check the safe that you brought up now."

At this, Carter stepped forward. "Now wait a minute, Daedalus! That—"

The leader of Treasure, Inc. nodded to one his men, who promptly produced a sound-suppressed pistol. He leveled the barrel at Carter's chest. "You will not interfere," Daedalus said in a low voice. Several of the crew ran back toward the *Deep Voyager,* while Daedalus' goon kept the gun trained on Carter and Jayden. Carter mentally kicked himself for being so gullible, for allowing the Treasure, Inc. crew to take them aboard. But his training and experience taught him that to survive, he would need to remain focused on what lay ahead rather than dwell on events that already occurred, so he pushed his regrets aside and scanned his surroundings in a casual way that did not draw attention. He noticed a bank of green oxygen cylinders that were used for refilling the submersible's onboard oxygen supplies.

The moon pool area they occupied was semi-enclosed, preventing him from viewing the upper deck of the ship, but he could hear footsteps up there so he knew additional crew were nearby. He wondered if all of the crew were Treasure, Inc. employees, or if, like he and Jayden, Daedalus' outfit had chartered the ship along with a crew, adding their own men to the mix as "mission specialists."

A crewmember wheeled a cart into the moon pool area with the still-intact safe Carter and Jayden had recovered. They moved it into position next to the drill.

"That's our safe, Daedalus!" Carter said forcefully.

"You can have the safe," Daedalus laughed, "as soon as we take what's inside it." His hired muscle hooted around them as the drill operator turned on his machine.

"Let's just see what's in it," Jayden reasoned. "Could be nothing for all we know. Or some out-of-fashion necklaces that only Daedalus would wear."

Daedalus scowled but nevertheless extended a hand toward the Asian-American sub-pilot in a gesture of reason. "Listen to the comedian here, Mr. Hunt. Your own pilot." Carter said nothing, only stared at the safe while the drill operator brought the bit to the safe door. The shrill whine of metal on metal trilled the air and then the operator pulled the drill away, the motor slowing as the whine subsided. One of the crew swung the door open and peered inside with a flashlight.

"Got something here!" He rolled an arm rapidly in a "get over here" motion, but Daedalus was already there, shoving the technician aside, leaning in with his own flashlight.

"It's all dry and we've got paper, documents of some kind...." He passed a few small pieces out to a crewman, including a passport, a black and white family portrait..."...and look at this!"

He held up a thick brown envelope, approximately eight-by-ten inches. It was thick enough so that it was either padded, or else very full. While

Daedalus held the envelope up to a rack of work lights, one of the crew began removing the rest of the contents from the safe. A velvet sack was dumped into an open but gloved hand to reveal a pile of gold Krugerrand coins. A diamond broach, a pearl-handled revolver, and a silver cross with chain all came out of the safe and across the years into the hands of Daedalus' employees. But none of these held any interest for the Treasure, Inc. leader. He slowly walked away as the items were extracted, hands turning over the brown, faded envelope.

As his fingers began to pry at the creased edge, Carter admonished, "You need to open that inside, in climate-controlled conditions! You could destroy it by exposing it to the salt air after all these years!"

Daedalus slowly looked up and turned to Carter. "Wouldn't you like to know what's inside?"

"Not if it means ruining the contents."

The Treasure, Inc. leader removed his smartphone from a pocket and handed it off to an assistant. "Take photos." Then he proceeded to rip open the envelope. Carter and Jayden moved toward him. Carter felt a strong grip on his leg and turned to see one of the crew dragging him to the ground. Another man tousled with Jayden while Daedalus sidestepped away without so much as taking his eyes from the envelope while he pulled a piece of parchment from it. The crew member with the phone began taking photos of Daedalus holding the parchment and envelope, and then closeups of the document itself.

"Heavy parchment of some kind," Daedalus said in a detached monotone. "Perhaps papyrus." He started to hold the document up to the light. Carter caught the briefest flash of hand-drawn outlines, foreign words placed in different areas, shading and relief in diverse sectors—enough to see that it was a map—before Daedalus suddenly pulled the document down and shoved it back into the envelope. Then he turned to his men and nodded at Carter and Jayden.

"Tie their hands. Put them in their sub. Leave the hatch open and drop it into the water. Make it look like an accident."

Carter's gaze immediately went to Daedalus' men. Would they actually be willing to carry out such a heinous order? He thought he detected maybe a glimmer of hesitation in one of the goons' eyes, but his answer came a lot sooner than he would have liked. He felt thin plastic flex-cuffs start to close around his wrist. The same thing was happening to Jayden a few feet away. He cursed himself for letting his situational awareness slip, but after the hours-long ordeal in the mini-sub, his reflexes and perception were dulled. He knew he had to act fast, right now, or the situation would only get more difficult to extricate himself from as the seconds unfolded.

He slammed the heel of his right foot down on the toes of the crewman's foot. He heard the rush of the man's exhalation and then was able to slam his right elbow into his assailant's gut as he doubled over in pain from the foot stomp. This incapacitated the crewman and Carter was able to knock him down with a simple kick to the side. Knowing he had mere seconds to act before he would be overwhelmed by the entire crew, Carter withdrew the loaded flare pistol from his waistband and fired it at the group of oxygen tanks that were in the process of being filled. Through his peripheral vision he could see pistols being drawn at him by Daedalus' goons, but he kept his focus as he aimed the flare gun. He pointed it at the valve of one of the green oxygen tanks twenty-five feet away and fired the flare. A satisfying whooshing noise escaped from the gun as a streak of reddish orange rocketed out of it.

While everyone else either stared dumbly at the oxygen tanks or dove for cover, Carter hurled the now empty pistol at Daedalus ' head, and without waiting to see if his aim was true, he spun around and bashed Jayden's attacker in the side of the head with a two-fisted hammer blow. Stunned, that crewman slumped to the deck and Jayden was able to slip out of the zip-tie cuffs, which hadn't yet been cinched all the way tight.

"This way," Carter muttered to Jayden as he ran for a metal stairwell about twenty feet away leading up. Jayden wasted no time running for it, and was faster than Carter who still had both hands tied behind his back. The shouts of the crew and trammel of footsteps told them without having to look back that they were being pursued by multiple men. Walkie-talkies blared while they bolted for the steps....

….until the sound of the explosion overrode it all.

Jayden reached the steps first and his stomach leapt to his throat when he saw a burly crewman thundering down the steps. Behind them, billows of black smoke erupted from the fire started from the flare gun oxygen tank explosion. Carter was only a couple of steps behind, but now preoccupied with monitoring the extent of the damage dealt by the explosion, Jayden would have to do the fighting. He put one hand on each rail and pushed off the deck with both feet, swinging them up into the chest of the crewman as he ran down. The attacker's eyes rolled back in his head as he was knocked backwards. The back of his skull bashed into the edge of one of the metal steps, rendering him unconscious. Jayden swiped the walkie-talkie from his belt, along with a heavy-duty Maglite-style flashlight that could be used as a club, and kept moving up the stairs. Carter caught up to him and turned around.

The shouts of their pursers grew louder while Carter checked the fallen foe's pulse, which was there, but faint. "He'll be okay," he told Jayden.

They scanned their new surroundings, heads on swivels as they looked for signs of crew other than the herd pounding up after them from below. They could hear them over the spraying of fire extinguishers, even louder now, and knew it would be only a matter of seconds before they caught up with them.

"Which way?" Jayden asked. They stood in the center of a veritable maze of catwalks, passageways and overhead platforms. Jayden's answer was the sharp *ping* of a bullet ricocheting off the stairway railing and hitting something else above them and to their right.

"Any way but here, come on." Carter took off to their left, now able to move unencumbered, down a mesh catwalk that opened up into a wider platform about fifty feet later.

"I see sky, that way." Jayden pointed ahead, to where another stairway led up.

"That goes to the aft deck," Carter said, already moving toward it.

As they ran, Jayden eyeballed the radio and recognized it as a standard marine VHF unit. He changed the channel to the common maritime emergency frequency, knowing it would be monitored by their ship, floating only a hundred yards away.

He keyed the transmit button and yelled into the radio as they sprinted across the vessel toward the stairs. "*Research Vessel Deep Pioneer*, this is Jayden and Carter from *Deep Voyager*. Mayday, Mayday, Mayday! We surfaced safely in the sub but were taken hostage on the surface by the crew of the *Transoceanic*. Mayday, Mayday, Mayday..." He repeated the message three or four times as they ran. When they reached the stairs, he released the transmitter to listen for incoming transmissions.

More gunfire sounded behind them and they hauled themselves up the stairs by the railing. No one came from the opposite direction, but they could hear radio chatter on deck up above. Jayden considered changing channels back to the one it was on before he made the distress call, so that he could monitor the enemy crew, but the radio blared before he could change it.

"Copy, Jayden. We're sending a boat crew now, over."

But Carter tapped Jayden's shoulder before he could reply and pointed to a tender vessel—a small inflatable boat with outboard motor—suspended by a crane. "Must be a second one because the other one they picked us up in is back there by the moon pool. Tell 'em to forget the tender—they'll just get shot at, anyway. We'll take that one. Meanwhile, have them call for our chopper."

Jayden spoke into the radio and relayed the information while they continued running.

"Your chopper isn't scheduled to be here until tomorrow afternoon."

"Buzz will come out early for us. He knows we take care of him and that if we're asking for a major change in plans it's critical, not on a whim. Just let him know that he needs to leave right now, out!"

"Copy that." The radioman from the *Deep Voyager's* bridge signed off and the pair of ex-Navy men continued negotiating the ship's challenging obstacles at high speed. Down a short flight of metal grated steps here, along a solid deck for a stretch where they caught a crewman unaware on watch duty. He paid the price with an unscheduled nap on the deck after a swift blow to the back of the head with Jayden's newfound Mag-light.

More gunfire erupted behind them at the same time they heard a walkie-talkie blare from somewhere up ahead. Carter grabbed Jayden by the shoulder. "Let's split up and meet at the boat. It'll make us harder to track." Well aware of this fact, Jayden agreed. "Last one there's a rotten egg," he said, before leapfrogging over a metal railing and dropping down to a catwalk, parkour style.

Carter chose to sprint straight ahead, knowing he was heading toward a direct confrontation with at least one unknown crewman. Better to face an opponent who might not know he was coming than one already shooting at him. He winced in pain as his left shoulder slammed into a stairway railing when he reached the landing and tried to make the turn too sharply. It was good he did, though, since a bullet pinged off of a metal bar mere feet away. Carter took the bottom half-flight of stairs in one leap, hit the landing with a loud clang, and then bolted across a short catwalk until it opened up onto the expansive deck.

He could see the tender vessel suspended over the side of the ship about a hundred feet away. Although tempted to rush straight for it, he curbed the instinct. Being out in the open increased the likelihood of being spotted and shot. Also on his mind was Jayden. He pivoted in place, looking for him, but saw no one except for a single crewperson, handheld radio raised to his mouth but apparently weaponless.

Good as it's going to get, Carter thought. He knew this unarmed individual was no threat to him, no match for his military training and high level of physical prowess. Still, the old adage about not being able to outrun a radio flashed through his mind as he crept toward the adversary while sticking to the shadows. Carter ducked behind a stack of life rafts and observed the crewman. This was as close as he could get to the man without walking straight out onto the wide open deck.

Suddenly the individual turned his head sharply toward the other side of the deck, where the boat was hanging. A noise was heard from that direction, and the man's head turned, tracking it. Jayden tossing something, Carter thought, glad for the distraction. Not wanting his friend's good thinking to go to waste, Carter silently dashed across the deck and took the crewman down with a flying tackle, cupping a hand over his mouth while simultaneously knocking the radio away. A measured knee to the throat ensured the treasure-looting thug wouldn't be calling for help in the next minute or so, but without being fatal.

Carter left him there writhing and sputtering to join Jayden beneath the tender vessel. The boat was uncovered but still needed to be lowered into the water. Carter pointed into the boat. "You get in and get ready to start it while I get the winch."

Jayden jumped and hauled himself into the boat, a twelve-foot inflatable with an outboard motor controlled from a steering console. "Where's all the empty beer cans and bait wrappers? Doesn't anybody have any fun on this thing?" Jayden wondered aloud. Carter shook his head as he moved toward the winch control station while keeping an eye out for the oncoming pursuers. His friend's capacity for levity never ceased to amaze him.

"Something tells me these guys don't have all that much fun," Carter said, pressing a green button on a metal pole at the same time as a shower of orange sparks erupted six inches over his head, the result of a near-miss 9mm round. He ducked down to the deck, arms over his head, as the boat began to lower toward the water, accompanied by a mechanical hum.

"I'll unhitch us, you just get in here without getting shot!" Jayden yelled from his hunkering position behind the boat's steering console. But although it was the gunmen Carter worried most about, he heard pounding feet and turned in time to see a bear of a man barreling toward him with a large dive knife held out at the ready in his right hand. Stealth not being his mode of operation, the combatant uttered a hoarse war cry he lumbered toward Carter and the tender. Carter quickly looked left and right, searching for anything that might be used as a weapon of opportunity—something to throw, a loose piece of metal or cable to trip him up with, anything—but he could find nothing in the two seconds he had available before his opponent reached him.

Carter was about to stand and fight when his ears locked onto the sound of the boat lowering on the winch, and a new idea occurred to him. A split second before the fighter got to him, he turned and ran toward the tender, now out of sight below the ship's rail, having been lowered nearly to the waterline.

"Uuuuuugh!" came the yell from Carter's pursuer as both of them ran toward the ship's rail. Who is this guy? Carter couldn't help but think, even as he ran or his life. Ships' crew weren't exactly the upper crust of society in his experience, but this guy was a real knuckle-dragger. To make matters worse, a bullet struck the deck a few feet to his right, ricocheted, and Carter felt it lodge into the sole of his rubber boot.

From down below, Jayden called, "I'm unhooking us, let's go!"

"On my way—bringing a friend!" Carter answered as he launched himself up and over the rail without looking back. He could feel the brute's thundering footsteps right behind him. He heard metal clunking followed by a booming splash as Jayden untethered the tender vessel from the crane and it dropped into the water from a few feet up. Carter didn't have the luxury of choosing the best place to land in the boat—he would simply have to hope he landed in it at all, for that matter, and pray for the best.

As he expected, the brute followed him right over the rail, intent on capturing his prey. The landing was not a pretty one, and had Jayden not had the presence of mind to kick a life jacket underneath Carter as he landed on the forward portion of the steering console, he would have broken his knee for certain. As it was, the knee screamed in pain anyway, and the right side of his face smashed into the deck hard enough for him to see an entire galaxy of stars. All this was made worse when the brute landed on top of him, limbs flailing and mouth drooling warm spit onto Carter's neck.

Jayden was unable to help Carter with the actual fight, since getting the boat underway beneath the impending onslaught of bullets was priority number one. He was on his own with the beefy gladiator while Jayden fired up the motor, took up position behind the wheel in an awkward ducking stance to partially shield him from enemy fire, and put the tender vessel into gear. Luckily for Carter, when Jayden jammed the throttle all the way up, the sudden momentum and burst of speed caused him and his attacker to roll over one another such that Carter ended up on top, a few feet away from where they landed.

Even with bullets flying overhead, Carter wasted no time in taking advantage of the small upper hand he'd been given. He racked his left elbow into the bigger man's ribcage, taking great satisfaction in the resulting grunt and exhalation of air. His opponent came back with a powerhouse fist meant for Carter's temple that he ducked, sending the opponent's knuckles into the boat's deck. As an inflatable boat, it was a soft deck, though, granting him a bit of the luck Carter had been given earlier. He used the same balled fist to spring himself up from the deck, intending to fall back down on Carter in some kind of pseudo-pro wrestling move.

But Jayden, having cleared the vicinity of the ship where they were in imminent danger of being shot at, now came to Carter's aid. He grabbed a nearby bungee cord that had been securing a small fire extinguisher, and used it to lash the steering wheel into position so that the boat would continue on a straight path unaided. On a whim, he picked up the extinguisher, too. Then he stepped around the console the long way to both shield himself from any further gunfire and to hide from the opponent's view when he came in for his attack.

As he rounded the console he was distracted by a streak of white in the water—the other small boat rounding the ship's bow and coming after them. First things first, he thought, as Carter grappled with the much bigger individual a few feet away on what little deck space there was available. Jayden pulled the pin on the extinguisher and aimed it at the head of Carter's rival.

"Get away from him, Carter. I got this!"

Both men looked over and then Jayden blasted the brute in the face with the pressurized chemical powder from about six feet away. Not lethal, by any means, but more than enough to give the fighter pause for a few seconds, which was all Carter needed to regain his feet and kick his foe in the face. Blood splatter suddenly appeared on the boat's PVC tubes, and then the burly crewman slumped onto the deck in an uncoordinated heap.

"Take the wheel, I got him!" Carter shouted. While Jayden retreated back around the console, Carter grabbed a life vest and strapped it on the semi-conscious man, whose eyes were open and was mumbling incoherently. Carter hefted him by the shoulders, dragged him up onto one of the boat's buoyancy tubes, and then tossed him off into the sea. He watched to make sure the man was floating face up, and then moved to the console, where he picked up the radio. Broadcasting on an emergency channel he informed the *Transoceanic* that they had a crewman in the water. Then, recalling Daedalus ' ruthlessness, he radioed his own ship as well, knowing that they would actually pick up a seaman overboard no matter what was at stake. He wasn't so sure Daedalus would even bother to stop to pick up his own crewman.

"Pick him up first if you have to," Carter told the *Deep Pioneer's* bridge, "and then catch up to us."

CHAPTER 10

Daedalus paced back and forth in the bridge of the *Transoceanic*. "Yes, pick up our man on the way to taking down the other tender. We don't need to leave him to be rescued by *Deep Pioneer* and draw more attention to ourselves. But those two treasure hunters must not be allowed to escape."

"Why not?" one of the bridge crew who sailed the ship asked. "We have the map. Why not just let them go rather than risk an international incident?"

Daedalus shook his head while continuing to pace. "Believe me, while what you say seems reasonable on the surface of it, I know from past experience that these two are quite capable of becoming serious thorns in our side. The implications of the discovery the map leads to are far too profound to assume that anyone privy to its existence will simply walk—or boat—away. They must be neutralized."

The bridge officer nodded and stepped aside as he brought a radio to his mouth.

To the captain, Daedalus said, "I want the helicopter pilot on standby."

The captain nodded and barked into an intercom. Then he turned to Daedalus. "He'll be ready to lift off in five minutes. Really, we can call the boat off after it picks up the man overboard. The chopper will catch up to the boat and we can have a gunner on board to shoot it down."

"As much as I would like to see that," Daedalus said, "it will not come to pass."

"Why not?" The captain appeared perplexed.

"Because the helicopter is to carry me and my new map to Newfoundland, so that I can begin the search for Noah's Ark."

CHAPTER 11

Jayden turned around from his position at the steering console. How close were their pursuers? The two boats were identical makes and models, including the outboard motors, so there was no inherent speed advantage to either vessel. Jayden and Carter had a head start, and as a skilled small boat pilot, Jayden didn't intend to squander that lead.

"I'd say we've got half a football field on them," Carter estimated from his sitting position on the starboard side pontoon behind Jayden. Black smoke still filtered into the sky from the fire in the moon pool.

Carter eyed their own ship, the *R/V Deep Pioneer*, looming not far away, still in position over the wreck site. "Try to board our ship?"

Carter eyed the vessel dubiously. "If we do, we'll just bring the fight to them because Daedalus' ship will follow. Advise them to get underway and they'll catch up to us later, unless our chopper reaches us first."

Jayden nodded and shouted the plan into the radio transmitter while steering the boat out into the open sea. Carter kept watch on their pursuers as well as the enemy ship. When he saw something moving on the *Transoceanic*, he stared intently at the area until he could make sense of it in the bouncing craft. The realization of what he was looking at sent a chill up his spine. "Helicopter!"

Jayden whipped his head around to get a look at it. The black body with a white logo wrapped around the fuselage blended in somewhat with the smoke that still rose from the oxygen tank fire, but the steady vertical lift was a dead giveaway.

"We can't outrun that!" Jayden said, stating the obvious.

"Head for our ship!" Carter shouted. Jayden course corrected toward the *Deep Pioneer*, shaking his head as he mentally calculated how far they would make it before the aircraft overtook them. Not even halfway, he thought. But as the 'copter levelled out onto a steady course, it became apparent that it was not coming their way.

"What's it doing?" Jayden wondered aloud as he continued rocketing full throttle toward their ship.

Carter cupped a hand to his mouth to be heard over the racket. "Looks like he's making a beeline for the mainland."

"Not complaining," Jayden shouted over the engine. "But why would he do that?"

Carter stared up at the chopper as it levelled out and accelerated toward the distant North American continent. "Because he's got the map."

"Our friends in the other tender are slowing down," Jayden observed, without slowing their own inflatable boat. Radio chatter erupted at that moment, confirming that the Treasure, Inc. crew had picked up their own overboard crewman.

"Good on them for that, at least," Carter said a split second before the pursuing Zodiac ramped up speed once again.

"They don't seem intent on bringing the guy back to the ship right away," Jayden said, craning his neck to look back past their wake. "I was hoping the chase was over but it doesn't look like it."

Carter waved an arm out in front of them. "Keep going, don't stop!"

Jayden sped past their own ship, waving at their own crew, some of whom were lined up against the rails on deck as they motored past. Jayden picked up the radio after hearing it crackle. "What's our chopper status?"

"You're in luck," *Deep Voyager*'s radioman came back. "Buzz says he happened to be at a fueling station for a non-critical assignment, and so he's in the air right now on his way out here.

At that moment a bullet ricocheted off the console after passing inches from Jayden's head. As he moved down and to the right, a second shot smashed into the radio, darkening the display and ending communication. "We lost comm!" he shouted to Carter, who was already down on deck.

"Keep going," Carter waved him on. "If we stop to board, they'll shoot us to pieces."

"They're shooting us to pieces anyway!"

"Keep zig-zagging—you got it!" Indeed, Jayden had begun to almost subconsciously weave the spry little boat back and forth in an erratic, unpredictable pattern, making them a more difficult moving target. Carter scrambled over to the console and sneaked a peek at the compass mounted on top in a clear bubble. He gave Jayden a heading number from memory. "That'll take us straight to St. John's, Newfoundland. Just head that way until we see our chopper."

"Be a couple hours at least," Jayden said.

Carter jerked a thumb back toward the shooters in the chase boat. "Hopefully those guys will give up before then when they realize we're just leading them out to the middle of nowhere." Jayden instinctively ducked as he heard another gunshot. The bullet didn't hit the boat. "Hopefully," he said, but there was a lack of conviction in his voice.

"Our ship has instructions to follow us back," Carter said, undaunted. "Even though we're out of comm, they should still do that. Their work on the wreck site is done, and there's no physical anchor to pull, so it shouldn't take them long to get underway."

Jayden looked back to the Treasure, Inc. ship. "They have our freakin' sub! How could our work be done?"

Carter shrugged. "I didn't say it was pretty, but the mission objective has been completed. We recovered the map from the safe. It's not our fault it was stolen from us afterwards, along with our sub."

"I hope our client sees it that way," Jayden said, turning his attention back to eluding their pursuers. They had gained some distance when the Treasure, Inc. tender vessel stopped to pick up their man overboard, putting them physically farther back, but they were still within shooting range. Jayden kept the boat ramped up to full throttle, weaving this way and that but always centering back on the heading to the faraway Newfoundland port.

"How are we on gas?" he asked.

Carter crawled to the back to stay beneath the line of fire and shoved the gas can. "Good. This one's still half full, and the spare is full, too. That's one thing we don't have to worry about right away."

"Hopefully those guys are almost empty," Jayden said, but their pursuers showed no signs of slowing even as both tender vessels left their support ships in their wakes.

"Just keep going."

CHAPTER 12

Carter shook his head as he spied the enemy craft from a prone position at the back of the inflatable boat. "Looks like they kept that one gassed up the same as ours."

"They don't seem to have an ammo shortage, either," Jayden said, as another gunshot boomed from behind them. The round was lost to the sea, but that didn't make him feel any safer. For the past two hours, the Treasure, Inc. attackers had kept up a regular volley of shots, intended more to keep Carter and Jayden on edge than to have any real hope of hitting them. The tactic was successful, though, and while Jayden had done a good job of maintaining their lead, the weather had taken a turn for the worse. The squall that was promised on the *Titanic* site was finally materializing here in the middle of the North Atlantic. Whitecaps dotted the increasing swells, and the motorized rafts rode up and over each wave like rollercoaster cars over hilly tracks. At the peak of each roller was when they were most vulnerable to enemy gunfire.

"Carter, where's our chopper? Where's our ship?"

Hunt's gaze scanned the skies, but the rain that had begun to fall made sighting anything up there problematic at best. Their ship had been out of sight since they left it behind, its top speed being slower than that of the inflatable, although sustainable for a much longer period. As Carter nudged the remaining gas can, after running the first one dry over an hour ago, he knew that they didn't have long before the ship would catch up to them much quicker indeed. But so would their pursuers. Carter glanced back at them. One of them wore a headlamp, which made them easy to pick out against the rapidly darkening sky.

And then it happened. They heard the faint boom of a shot being fired—still audible at this distance but the meat of the percussive blast was lost to the howling wind and motor noise. But the truly frightening sound was the soft *pffft* that came immediately after. As they took a sled-ride down the face of another big swell, Carter felt the tube on the left side of the Zodiac begin to soften beneath his arm.

"Bad news, Jayden: they hit our port side pontoon. We're losing air."

"Wonderful!" Jayden yelled as he struggled to keep the frail craft headed into the oncoming swells, lest they turn broadside and be swamped with onrushing water. "This wasn't difficult enough already, I really needed more of a challenge!"

Another gunshot was the reply to Jayden's sarcasm, but fortunately this round found only the ocean. Making matters doubly worse, water began to flood into the inflatable raft while the deflated side sagged and was unable to keep out the roiling seawater. Both of the experienced mariners knew that an inflatable boat wouldn't actually sink, even with all tubes deflated, it would remain floating, but would become an unnavigable piece of drifting debris, offering no control of any kind. It wouldn't take much for them to be swept off of it by a passing wave.

But their mercenary attackers kept coming, now rapidly closing the gap between the two boats as Jayden and Carter's craft limped along, flooded with water. Carter began to look around for items with which to mount a last resort defense. "Flares, where's the flares?" He scrounged around through the console cubbies, and then looked inside the small anchor hold, but found none.

"Figures, these guys don't follow any laws, including those pertaining to maritime safety," Carter muttered. Then, out of desperation as the enemy tender neared, he removed the small anchor from the hold. About the size of a large grappling hook, it was connected to a short length of chain which was in turn tied to a long length of manila rope.

He told Jayden to cut the motor. "It's pointless to keep going, might as well try and mount a defense. Actually, try waving a white flag first. Let them take us alive if they're willing."

Regretfully, Jayden stripped off his white T-shirt, with a logo from Sloppy Joe's, a well-known watering hole in Key West, Florida, and began to swing it around above his head. "All right, I'm waving the white flag of surrender."

But the act seemed to make no difference, for another gunshot rang out and then the other pontoon began to hiss out the air that was keeping them afloat. Carter was in the process of looping the anchor rope around his arm while gripping the anchor in his other hand, when he realized it was hopeless. The enemy Zodiac pulled up alongside them, manned by four men, three of which pointed pistols straight at them. The boat pilot held a megaphone to his lips and addressed them:

"Nice day for a boat ride, eh?" He laughed along with the rest of his motley crew as a large wave steamrolled over the now deflated dinghy of Carter and Jayden while Treasure, Inc.'s air-filled craft was lifted harmlessly up and over the passing water. Then the sky split open with a crack of lightning, a booming explosion of thunder, and a torrential downpour began to fall.

The motor of Carter and Jayden's boat sank beneath the waves, no longer supported by the airless tube. The two men now floated in water as if in a bathtub. They were able to support their weight on the submerged mass of rubber, but they were no longer dry. The boat pilot waved an arm at his crew.

"Cease fire, men. There is no need to waste any more bullets on these two. Shooting them would be too kind. Let them finish their boat trip out here in these friendly seas!" He looked up at the darkening sky as the rain drenched his face while another peal of thunder boomed around them.

"No, do not let them go or their ship could pick them up!" one of the crew protested.

"Our own ship is doing battle with them at this very moment! On our way back, we will distract them as well. Let these two scum drown, and it will look like an accident. All the better for us. Let's go!"

He shot Carter a cold stare before putting the boat into gear and turning away from them, throwing a wake that flooded the stricken vessel even more, drenching Carter's face with icy ocean water.

"Awesome," Jayden said, legs floating out in front of him while his elbows rested on the bunched up mass of rubber that used to be their pontoon, as if he were relaxing in a hot tub. No longer wearing a shirt only added to the picture. "This is just great. Real pickle we're in, Carter. Any ideas?"

The treasure seeker slowly shook his head while he searched his mind in vain for a plan. But the cold water made it difficult to concentrate. "It'll be dark before too long..." he began, when he was interrupted by a faint sound to the east. He turned that way, coaxing his ears to magnify the noise, but it was lost to the wind and sea spray before returning a few seconds later, a tiny bit louder this time. And more identifiable.

"Helo!" he yelled.

"Hopefully that's not Daedalus," Jayden said.

"I have a feeling he's checked into St. John's premiere luxury hotel by now," Carter said. "It's got to be Buzz. It's got to be..." He turned to silent prayer as they drifted in the freezing water while the sound of the rotors drew nearer. The running lights of the aircraft were the only distinguishable feature in the dim light, but when the spotlight brightened a circle of dark sea beneath the 'copter, Jayden let out a whoop.

"It's Buzz. He's looking for us!"

"He sees us," Carter confirmed, as the aircraft slowed and began to descend toward the ocean surface.

"And our friends over there see him, too," Jayden pointed out. Near the edge of their visibility into the wind-whipped, salty gloom, the small boat made a wide turn back toward them.

"So much for leaving us to the elements," Carter said.

"Well, to be fair, an Augusta Bell AB-212 helo is not exactly 'the elements', is it?"

"Do we have a light, anything to warn the pilot with?"

Jayden scrounged around the console for a bit before coming up empty-handed while shaking his head. "'fraid not. Maybe now's the time for your anchor trick. Buzz might not know these guys are willing to shoot first and cover things up later."

Carter nodded. "I'll do what I can. You maintain eye contact with Buzz and guide him in."

As the chopper neared the rotor wash stirred up the water to the point that their swamped raft was nearly impossible to stay with. "He's waving us over!" Jayden said, and then a second later, the pilot's voice was heard through a loud-hailer: "I can't get any closer without blowing you away in the raft. Get out and swim to me, I'll lower a ladder. Give me a hand signal if you understand."

Jayden immediately held up his hand in the universal "okay" signal, thumb and forefinger held in a circle. "Ready, Carter?"

The Treasure, Inc. Zodiac was a stone's throw away now and not slowing down as it approached them. It was obvious they meant to pass Carter and Jayden and assault the helicopter.

Carter responded with, "Jump in three, two, one…Go!" He stood in the deflated raft as best he could, and from his wobbly stance he wound the anchor at the end of the chain around in a loop like a cowboy getting ready to lasso a bull. He watched as the enemy craft cruised past their port side. When he heard the splash signaling that Jayden had launched himself into the open sea, Carter began the mental process of timing his anchor swings while watching the assailant's boat speed past.

One of the crew fired the first shot at the helicopter as it hovered, waiting for Carter and Jayden to swim beneath it. Carter let go of the chain with the anchor near the apex of its loop and aimed far ahead of the speeding raft. Carter knew he should start swimming as soon as he let the anchor fly, but it would only take a couple more seconds to see the results of his offensive move and the curiosity was overwhelming. He was rewarded with the sight of the boat's driver suddenly being ripped off of the craft into the water behind it. The Zodiac then spun wildly to the left in an out-of-control turn.

Having seen enough to know that his stunt had proven as effective as he could have hoped for, Carter dove off of his crippled raft, knifing underwater in a dive so as to remain unseen on the surface for as long as possible. He found the relative quiet beneath the waves to be peaceful, a serenity that was shattered the moment he surfaced for air. His ears were greeted with the din of a helicopter motor and a boat engine, against a backdrop of thunder, howling wind, and a heavy rain splattering on the waves. He could see the chopper hovering about thirty feet away, but the seas were too chaotic to permit him a decent view of the water itself, so he couldn't see Jayden or even the rival boat.

Carter began to swim as fast and hard as he could. He could feel the pull of a strong current and knew that he would need all his strength to make progress against it for even the short distance to the helicopter. Kicking with everything he had, he reached the peak of a swell and used to the opportunity to check the water around him. He spotted Jayden's black-haired head beneath the chopper. Carter's heart sank as he realized just how precarious their situation was. This helicopter was not some coast guard chopper equipped with a winch and rescue basket, much less a crew separate crew to handle those things. It was fast and light, designed for transport over relatively long distances for a 'copter. But this meant the pilot would face the Herculean task of lowering the chopper close enough to the water for them to be able to grab hold of the skids, while avoiding the unpredictable rogue swells that cropped up all around them. And the enemy gunfire.

Carter bodysurfed down the face of the swell he was on and kicked hard until he felt himself rising up the next one. At its crest, he used the viewpoint to look back toward their abandoned and ruined inflatable boat. He was beyond surprised to see a man swimming only ten feet behind him, coming right towards him with a powerful crawl stroke. At first he thought his adrenaline-riddled mind might be playing tricks on him, that it was Jayden and that he had somehow gotten disoriented and turned everything around in his mind. But a quick 180 and visual check of the helicopter, where Jayden's arm was swiping unsuccessfully for the skid, told him that no, it was someone else.

He realized with a start that it was the pilot of the Zodiac he had grappled overboard with the anchor. Coming after him in the water to exact his revenge? It seemed absurd, but Carter knew he didn't have time to tread water and think about it. He kicked off toward the helicopter once again, hoping that at least Jayden would be aboard before he got there so he would be able to help pull him up and in.

But when he felt the rotor-driven spray on his face, he looked up to see that Jayden was, in fact, still in the water. The problem was that the chopper pilot was too scared get low enough for a person treading water to grab hold of the skids. Carter couldn't blame him. It was possible for the entire aircraft to be engulfed and pulled underwater once the skids were submerged. But meanwhile the savage in the water behind him was gaining, and to make matters even worse, Carter spotted the lights of his boat drawing nearer.

The pilot lowered the helicopter once again, doing his best to time the swells. He lowered the craft into a trough, but had to pull up as a swell approached before Jayden was able to grab the skid. It was close, though, and Jayden gave him a hand signal that indicated he should try the maneuver again.

Carter called over to Jayden to let him know he was here. "Keep trying to get in, I'll fight this guy off." The enemy combatant swimmer reached them too, and the battle was on. Carter made a mental note to find out more about Daedalus ' employee motivation program, because he couldn't help but think that these guys were non-stop go-getters. Surely, they could have driven back to the ship after picking up their man overboard, and the boat chase, and no one would have said anything about a lack of effort. But here this killer was, swimming through a tempest beneath a helicopter to get at an ex-Navy man who had ripped him off of a boat after being shot at.

Was it the power of the ark? The strange thought sprouted in Carter's historian brain even as his primal systems readied themselves to brawl.

Carter wasn't worried too much about the fight. Though Jayden had been the SEAL and not him, he was still extremely comfortable in the water and a trained fighter as well. He took a deep breath as the peak of a swell was about to reach him and ducked below the water. Opening his eyes despite the cold sting, he locked onto the blurry form of his adversary and angled up toward him from below. Like a shark, Carter thought. *From below and behind. Take him out...*

But as Carter's right hand reached out to drag his opponent beneath the waves, the foe was suddenly yanked up and out of the water. No way could he propel himself like that, Carter thought. So, what....he surfaced in time to see the undercarriage of their helicopter—its engine roaring in his ears with the close proximity—lifting away...

...with Jayden gripping onto the skid with both hands—and Daedalus ' thug holding onto his ankles, also being lifted into the stormy sky.

"Jayden, kick! It's not me!" Carter screamed, in case Jayden wasn't aware who it was that was holding onto him. He saw the former Naval warrior glance down, and a bolt of lightning illuminating his shocked face told Carter that his message had not been in vain. In a feat of sheer strength befitting an ex-SEAL, Jayden raised his knees until the adversary latched onto his ankles was within striking distance. Holding onto the skid with only his left hand, Jayden clocked the thug in the jaw with a powerful right, knocking him back into the water. He landed right next to Carter, nearly on top of him.

In a lucky break for the hired goon, his Zodiac pulled up next to him at that moment. Carter had been listening to Jayden scream something at the helicopter pilot, but the engine droned out the words, as well as the sound of the small boat's motor, which was why he didn't hear it approach. Carter felt his stomach leap into his heart as he turned around and saw the rubber tubes of the inflatable mere feet from his face. The attacker who had just fallen from the helo was being dragged aboard by his associates--the two, that is, who were not either driving the boat or pointing the gun at Carter.

He whirled right, knowing his movements were slowed in water but needing to get out of the gun's sights. He barely heard the pop of the pistol over the chopper engine noise, which grew louder as the 'copter lowered itself over the boat. Carter saw his chance and took it. He was a sitting duck in the water. He ducked underwater to cloak himself while moving to another part of the boat, forward of where his adversary was being pulled back in following his ordeal. He scissor-kicked up to launch himself from the water and took hold the grab line that was strung around the boat's sides. Using this he was able to swing his right leg up and over the tube and roll into the boat even before his adversary was helped aboard.

Even so, he knew he had all of about a single second in which to act before he was gunned down and tossed back overboard. The chopper was so close he instinctively brought up an elbow to shield his face when he looked at it, but then he realized this was Jayden's doing. His friend was now standing on the skid, one hand gripping the door frame, waving Carter up, mouthing the word *Jump!*

Carter took the not-so-subtle-suggestion and, with a running start, bounded off the pontoons at the bow of the small craft, basically trampolining himself up toward the hovering helicopter. His jump was a good one, and he was able to wrap both hands around the skid. As soon as he did that, he looked up and saw Jayden, head turned toward the pilot, waving at him to move.

In the boat, his takes-a-licking-but-keeps-on-ticking attacker was somehow back on his feet and rampaging toward Carter once more. Carter saw him by looking down through his legs, but was much more concerned about the crewman standing in the rear of the boat aiming the gun at him. There wasn't much he could do about that, and he now felt terribly exposed due to his elevation above the other people on the raft. But a rolling wave crested beneath the boat at that moment, and as luck would have it, tipped the boat enough to throw off the shooter's aim, causing him to miss all three rapid-fire shots.

At the same time, the chopper lifted off in earnest, with Jayden yelling at the pilot to go, go, go. By the time Carter began to lift himself into the chopper, he was out of realistic range of the guns. Still, the boat pursued them for a short distance, and more shots were fired as evidenced by the tiny orange muzzle blasts visible against the dark sea in the distance, but they had eluded their pursuers.

For now, Carter thought, kneeling at the edge of the open door while Jayden steadied him with a hand on his shoulder. He knew Daedalus wouldn't be satisfied until all threats to his illicit enterprises were neutralized. He watched the heavy rain fall while the angry sea surface faded into obscurity until Jayden pulled the door closed.

For now.

CHAPTER 13

St. John's, Newfoundland, Canada, next day

Carter and Jayden clinked frosty mugs of cold Canadian lager over their table inside a waterfront pub. "Here's to being alive," Jayden toasted. They soaked up the brew in silence for a while, savoring this simple but extravagant fact. The remainder of the helicopter ride back to the coast had been non-eventful, save being nearly out of fuel when they made the heliport in St. John's.

The easternmost city in North America, St. John's was originally a fishing village established by European colonists. The small city reminded Carter of San Francisco with its steep hills, but also of Caribbean architecture with its bright wooden houses. The climate, however, was definitely not Caribbean, and was even cooler on average than San Francisco, with the current temperature being in the mid-forties, Fahrenheit.

Carter looked around at the pub, sparsely populated at this early hour of the day. Later, when the fisherman arrived back to the docks, it would fill up with boisterous men unwinding after a hard day's work. But for now, Carter and Jayden had time to reflect on how this port was the closest to where the *Titanic* had sunk. And they were lucky to be drinking here. Jayden set down his empty mug and requested another round from a passing server.

"I can understand trying to kill us when we still had the map, but I can't for the life of me figure out why they wanted to kill us so bad *after* Daedalus already had the map." He shook his head slowly as he finished his sentence. Carter swilled the last of his brew and set the empty mug on the worn, wooden table with a soft clack.

"We're a threat to his livelihood, to his illicit antiquities business."

"I guess we kind of proved that in Atlantis, didn't we?" He grinned at the memory of their epic sojourn into the legendary city, culminating in a standoff against Daedalus and Treasure, Inc.

"I'd say we did," Carter agreed. The server returned with their second round and he paused until after she had left before continuing. "But as usual, it's Daedalus for himself first, leaving his people to handle the dirty work for him. He left early in their helo for a reason, not because he didn't want to take us out."

Jayden nodded. "Right, they could have strafed us from their chopper when we were in the Zodiac and this fledgling bar tab here never would have happened." He took another long pull from his mug. "He just wanted out of there with the map."

"No question about that," Carter agreed. "The question is, where did he take it?"

Jayden looked outside at the waterfront, at the gulls wheeling in the sky, the row of fishing boats at the dock, at the smattering of pedestrians passing by. "He left in a helo, and since most helo's don't have much range, I'm guessing he would have landed in the nearest port, which is right here." He waved an arm at the view outside and then stared intently in that direction, as though Daedalus could walk by at any second.

"I'm sure he landed here, too. But I mean, what's his next move with the map? Where does he go based on the info it provides?"

"I don't know. Too bad we didn't get a picture of it so that we know what it is that he's going by," Jayden lamented.

"I only got the barest glimpse of it for all of two seconds, and while it appeared old and possibly authentic, and it did look like a map of some kind, I can't say for sure it was a map that depicts the final resting place of Noah's Ark."

"So you didn't see a picture somewhere on there of a big boat with a bunch of animals on it?"

Carter laughed in the negative until a new group of patrons, all of them male and middle-aged, entered the pub. Carter scrutinized them carefully. It wouldn't take a great leap of logic for Daedalus' team to figure out that they must have landed in St. John's from the 'copter, as they had, and that a local watering hole would be their preferred hangout while they recovered from their at-sea ordeal. But after observing them, he concluded that all of them were locals and therefore highly unlikely to be affiliated with Treasure, Inc.'s European-based operations.

"But you can't say for sure that it's not a map to the ark, either," Jayden said after sufficient time to observe the newcomers had elapsed.

"Right. So let's assume for a moment that it's the real deal." Carter swilled some more Canadian flavor as he considered this. "Where would Daedalus take the map *after* landing here? What would his next move be?"

Jayden shrugged. "Guy like that, lots of resources…could be almost anywhere, I suppose. But he really wants to find Noah's Ark, so if he's going to go right after it without letting things cool off…"

"I think that's the Daedalus we all know and hate."

Jayden continued. "Then I'd say his first move might be to have images of the map sent to his history and authentication experts, in Europe, I guess, and see what they say as far as where it points to."

Carter gave Jayden a long stare. "That's what I was thinking. But let's say that process takes about a day given his resources and…motivational acumen…a timeframe which has already transpired, since he landed here yesterday a few hours before us. Where would he be going based on that?"

Jayden made a gesture of futility, tossing his hands wildly. "Look, Carter, if I knew where Noah's Ark was—"

"We don't have to know where the ark is. That's the beauty of it. We just have to know where Daedalus thinks it is. The general vicinity. Because if we can find Daedalus, then we can take the map back from him."

"I can think of a way that is simpler, in theory." Jayden appeared pleased with himself. Again, a server appeared, this time with a tray of scallops with pork hock, and they halted the conversation until she had left.

"I'd love to hear it," Carter said, before taking a bite of the fresh seafood.

"If we could hack into whatever systems Daedalus used to send those scans of the map to his people—I mean really, how many Wi-Fi routers and cable Internet providers could there be in this Podunk little town-- then we could just steal the images from there and be looking at the map ourselves."

Carter nearly choked on his shrimp. "I'm a historian, Jayden, and you're a SEAL. We're not computer experts. Especially you."

Jayden let the jab slide. "Yeah, but you've got the money to hire one." That point was true enough. The fortune Carter had inherited from his grandfather that had enabled him to start Omega Team would enable him to do that.

"In theory," Carter said, "that could work. I give you that. But it's got issues. One: it would take time to vet someone and hire them, then wait for their results. Time during which we could be doing some real boots-on-the-ground treasure hunting. Two: it creates an additional security risk. The more people we have over here poking around, the more noticeable we are, and the more likely it is that someone will hear about our activities sooner or later. Our computer expert would always know what we did; they would probably always have a copy of the map. I don't like it."

Jayden threw his hands up in a gesture of surrender. "I'll be honest with you, Carter. I was hoping we could speed-dial some Russian babe with serious technical skills who would drop through the ceiling in a catsuit and... well, you get the idea."

"Yeah, I get it." Carter swilled some more of his beer while his eyes took on a faraway look.

"What is it? You're warming to the idea, aren't you? I knew it!" Jayden sounded excited.

"Well no, the hacker thing is too crazy for the reasons I mentioned. But there is someone we can call who might be able to help us."

"Oh, and who's that?"

"Maddy."

Jayden brightened. "Good idea! But, she's your woman, so I still want my Russian hacker."

"Tell you what. We find Noah's Ark, and I'll see to it that we add a hacker to Omega's payroll, okay?"

Jayden raised his glass in a toast. "Deal. So does Maddy know where Noah's Ark is or what?"

"If anyone knows where to look, it's her. She'll know all the history behind the searches for it that have already been done, so that should save us some time."

Dr. Madison Chambers, a professor of archaeology at a major American university, was an on-again, off-again girlfriend for Carter. She had also helped them in the search for Atlantis.

"I'll send her an email," Carter said. "But in the meantime, we should check out of our hotel and get to the airport."

"What for? I thought you said we need to consult Maddy?"

"We do, but that's more for the micro-details once we're there. Besides, like you said, it might not be all that hard to hack into our emails here—not than many servers in this little town, right? And I'd have to use an Internet café since I don't have my laptop or phone with me. We don't want to be tracked like that."

"Okay, I get it. So what's up?"

"I know a little bit about Noah's Ark myself. I've always been interested in the stories of expeditions that went looking for it in real life. I did a little research of my own before we left for the *Titanic*, just to brush up on it…"

"And?"

"And one of the most well-known hunting grounds for the ark is Mt. Ararat, Turkey."

Jayden stared at him over his now ignored plate of seafood. "So we're going to Turkey just based on that?"

"Yeah. Leaving today, hopefully. Let's get to the airport."

Jayden still didn't look convinced. "Seriously?"

"Yeah. First of all, almost all of the places reputed to possibly be the final resting place of Noah's Ark are on that continent, so we might as well get over there. And second, hanging around here for much longer is probably not advisable since I think one of those dudes who walked in with that group not too long ago has been scoping us out. Don't turn around. Act normal."

Jayden's eyes widened as he remained facing toward Carter. "Are you sure?"

"Pretty sure. I think we need to make a little bit of a show here of you walking up to the bar. Complain that the server is taking too long for our next round. Order a shot and ask for the check and a cab ride to our hotel. Give them the name of some other hotel, and say the name loudly. Then when we get in the cab, we'll have the driver take us to the airport."

"Did I mention I love this job? Good thing we visited the embassy this morning for temporary passports."

"Good and bad. Good, obviously, in that it allows to travel, but bad in that it's an easy place to keep tabs on."

"Here we go." Jayden nodded, took a deep breath while looking at Carter, and then he slammed a fist on the table loud enough to make the plates and silverware clatter.

"Damn, how long does it take to get a beer around this hellhole!"

Carter played along, raising his arms in an exaggerated gesture of rhetorical uncertainty, while Jayden stood up and shoved his chair backwards, tipping it over onto the concrete floor. "If you want something done right, man…" He swiped his not-quite-empty beer mug from the table and staggered over toward the bar, chugging down the remaining beer dregs as he went. The group of men who had drawn their attention all turned to look at him, as did their server from four tables over.

"Hey, hey what's the problem, Sir?" the bartender, a man pushing sixty with a bald dome and gray hair on the sides, asked from behind his drink station. "Rachel?" He called over to the server and she apologized to the young couple at her current table before hurrying toward the bar. The bartender finished pouring a mixed drink for another customer already seated at the bar and then walked over to Jayden, who pulled a barstool out of the way to stand there. He plunked his empty mug on the bar.

"Ridiculous! Just get me a shot, would you, and cash us the hell out! We'll head somewhere that knows how to sling drinks." Inwardly, Jayden intensely disliked playing the part of a boisterous, drunken lout, since he was aware of the reputation American tourists had in many foreign countries, but he placed mission success ahead of all else.

The bartender frowned at him in disgust. "Sir, I don't understand the problem. First of all, you're seated at a table, not the bar, and you were served drinks." The server arrived and bounced her concerned gaze between Jayden and the bartender. "I'm sorry, I didn't realize you wanted another round already," she offered.

"Never mind, it's too late now. This place killed my buzz," Jayden growled, tossing some bills on the bar top. "Where's that shot? Maybe you have some whiskey worth a damn in this country? And call me a freakin' cab, can you do that or is it too much to ask of a drinking establishment?" The stunned employees could only gawk at the wild-eyed Jayden in disbelief, and he took advantage of the silence to step up his act a notch. He raised his voice to a full-on yell.

"Are you deaf or something? I said, CALL US A CAB! WATERSTONE HOTEL—RIGHT NOW! And where's my stupid shot?"

The bartender's eyes narrowed and he turned to the server. "Give me their ticket and I'll handle this, dear. See to your tables." She nodded and handed him a piece of paper. He promptly picked up a phone and placed a call.

"Yeah, Robby, listen, we need a cab over here as soon as you can. Heads up: guy is pretty drunk, kind of an asshole, but he only wants to go to the Waterstone. Yeah, let me know." He hung up and turned to Jayden. "Your cab's on the way pal. But here's the deal: you want that shot? You drink it right here and then you and your buddy get out of my bar right now. Wait for your cab on the street, and never come back. Do we have a deal?"

Jayden felt terrible inside but kept up the act. He made a mental note to make it up to them somehow whenever he could. He met the man's steely gaze with one of his own. "You got it, pal. Serve it up."

The bartender poured Jayden a shot of what he recognized as the cheap, house whiskey and plopped it down in front of him. "Better hold your liquor, buddy. Around here it doesn't take much to draw the attention of the Mounties. You might not like our bar, but I guarantee you it beats spending the rest of your vacation in the clink."

Meanwhile, Carter was making a show of wolfing down the rest of his meal and drink while surreptitiously keeping an eye on the party of men seated a few tables away. He noted that they followed Jayden's confrontation with interest, and watched two of them confer in hushed tones after the name of the hotel was announced.

At the bar, Jayden threw his head back and poured the entire shot of whiskey into his mouth by dumping the glass held at arm's length over his head. He tossed the shot glass to the bartender, who stepped back and caught it before promptly pointing to the door. "Out of here now before I call the police! Your cab is on the way." Then he looked over to Carter. "I'd get your buddy out of here right now, pal, if I were you."

Carter nodded and rose slowly, as if he was used to it. "Come on, Eric, let's hit our hotel bar. You know, that place where everybody knows our name."

The bartender gave a sarcastic laugh. "Yeah, please do that. And don't let the door hit you on the ass on your way out."

The party of locals watched Carter and Jayden stagger out of the bar, with Jayden kicking the front door open and stumbling out. "Thanks for everything!" he yelled back before it swung shut. He and Carter stood directly in front of the door so that everyone inside could see they were indeed waiting for the called taxi. "How was I?" Jayden asked under his breath.

"Oscar consideration is in your future. Here's our ride." A classic yellow and black taxi rolled up to the curb. The driver spoke to them through the open window. "Waterstone?"

They got in and the cab pulled out into the light traffic.

CHAPTER 14

"Have a few too many in there, did ya?" the cabbie asked over his shoulder as he drove along.

"Yeah well, that's what bars are for, right?" Jayden deliberately over-slurred from the back seat next to Carter, who was scanning their surroundings out the windows.

The cabbie took his hands off the wheel for a moment in order to momentarily throw his hands up. "Hey, I don't judge. A big part of my business is making sure drunk people get to where they're going safely, and without hurting anyone else. Your decision to call a cab is commendable. Waterstone Hotel is only fifteen minutes away, but if you're three sheets to the wind…"

Carter and Jayden exchanged glances and then Carter spoke. "Actually, can you just take us to the airport instead?"

The cabbie glanced at him via his rearview mirror. "St. John's International?"

"Yes. I know it's further, but here…" Carter dug some cash out of his pocket and handed it over the seat to the driver. Apparently it was more than enough, because he saw the man's eyes widen just slightly for a moment and then he picked up his radio and told his dispatcher, "Change of plans, cancel Waterstone, heading to SJI, fare pre-paid." Carter heard the dispatcher acknowledge the call and then the cabbie hung up the radio transmitter.

That was it, Carter thought. Their escape plan was in action. Daedalus' hired local goons, if in fact that's who they were, would be going to the Waterstone Hotel, while he and Jayden would be heading in the completely opposite direction to the airport. But something nagged at his mind, something not quite right. Daedalus and his outfit ran a tight ship, Carter knew. He didn't leave a lot of things to chance. And what was the safest thing to do here, if they really wanted to stay with their quarry? To head to the Waterstone in a few minutes after the cab left? Or to simply follow the cab, just in case plans changed or were never honest in the first place? Carter had heard rumors that Daedalus employed a couple of ex-Mossad agents in his organization, to keep all of his field agents on their toes, and this was exactly the kind of scenario where that kind of preparation might play out in Treasure, Inc.'s favor.

Carter did his best to turn around and glance out the back window without it appearing unusual. Only a half dozen cars plied the lanes behind them, and one of them was a silver sedan with local plates that he thought he'd seen parked at the curb in front of them when they'd gotten into the cab. But he couldn't be positive. He mentally kicked himself for not paying more attention. He turned back around and faced forward. Traffic was becoming slightly more congested up ahead, but still not serious like anyone from a big city would be used to.

"Just relax, we'll be there in under twenty minutes," the driver said as he changed into the left lane. Carter found he was able to get a glimpse of the vehicles behind them by looking at the mirror on the driver's side. He was dismayed to see the silver sedan ease into the left lane also.

"Any chance we could hear a local radio station?" he said to the driver. "I like to hear radio in different countries."

"Sure thing." The driver put on some classic rock that could be heard basically anywhere in the western world, but Carter only wanted it for the noise cover. He leaned a little closer to Jayden and told him he thought they were being followed by the silver sedan. "Don't look back. I've already looked once, and you can see them in the left mirror now."

Jayden eyed the mirror and then said, "Yeah, they were at the bar. That grill is kind of distinctive."

Carter shook his head. "Not good at all. If they see us even take the airport exit, they'll know we're leaving the country even if they don't manage to tail us on foot all the way to our gate."

"You have any more cash on you?" Jayden pulled a rumpled bill from his pocket. This is all I have on me. Might not be enough to convince this guy to lose 'em."

Carter considered the implications of Jayden's question. If they did convince the cabbie to pull evasive maneuvers in order to leave their tail behind, it would also tip them off that they were right about who they were following and what they were doing. If they were unsure as it was.

"It might be better to have him drop us off early, in a crowded place, and try and lose them on foot. Then make our way to the airport after that."

Jayden called over to the driver. "Excuse me, but are there any more areas with shops, maybe liquor stores, that we could stop at on the way to the airport?"

The driver turned down the music and asked him to repeat the question, which Jayden did.

"No sir, I'd have to loop all the way back. I'll do it, if you want, but you'd really be going out of your way. If I were you I'd just hit the airport bars and duty-free shops once you get into St. Johns International."

Carter eyed Jayden and shook his head. Casually changing their destination was not going to be an option. Time for Plan B. He figured they didn't have much to lose by trying, so he took Jayden's cash, added what he had to it, and held it out to the cabbie.

"You see that silver car back there?"

The driver appeared confused, then concerned, as he consulted his rear view mirror. "Yes? Something wrong?"

"Not really, but those are friends of ours who have been getting on our nerves. They came here on vacation with us, but we're leaving early. I think they're trying to talk us out of it, and I'd rather just avoid them, so if you can do us a favor and lose them, this cash is all yours."

He glanced at the bills and then into his rearview mirror. "That silver sedan four cars back, same lane as us?" he clarified.

"That's the one," Carter answered.

The driver looked back at them with a wide grin. "Put on your lap belts, please." Carter and Jayden did so and then the driver accelerated smoothly, passing three cars in the next lane before changing into that lane. He continued the same process, changing into the next lane over after passing a few more cars. He was speeding in order to do it, but not recklessly so. One car even passed him. But their tail was out of sight, at least for now. The driver pointed out the sign for the airport.

"Sure you don't want me to take it? I don't see your friends."

Carter saw a public bus pulled over at a stop on the right. "Does one of those go to the airport?"

"Yes, that one does, in fact. Takes the long way around."

"Sounds perfect," Carter said. "Can you gain a little more distance from our friends and then drop us off at the next bus stop?"

"Yes, sir." The cabbie sped up again, passing the bus and several cars in the right-most lane. Looking back, Carter still couldn't see their tail. He knew that didn't necessarily mean they weren't back there, but it did make him feel better that they hadn't gained on them. He watched the scenery of a country he'd never visited prior to this day whiz by, and he couldn't help but feel how he wished they could slow down and enjoy their stay. But this was a business trip of sorts, and he knew that he had to stay focused. One day, he would return here on vacation, he told himself. After Noah's Ark had been found.

For now, he stared nervously behind them and felt his guts clench up when the silver car came into view two lanes over. It was still far back, but accelerating. Clearly, they knew they had been evaded. Up ahead two big rig trucks blocked the two righthand lanes, and Carter could see the next bus stop not far ahead of them. "If you can pass these trucks, you could drop us off at the next stop," he told the driver, who immediately stepped on the gas and switched into the leftmost lane in order to pass the eighteen wheelers.

But this lane change did no go smoothly, for just as he switched into the new lane, the driver of the car in that lane ahead of them braked suddenly, and the car rammed into the back of it. Carter and Jayden braced for the impact, now thankful to be wearing seatbelts, as the small SUV ahead of them was pushed left until it spun out and tipped on two wheels. For one horrifying second, Carter thought it was going to tip over, but it plopped back onto all four wheels amidst a screech of rubber that left deep black skid marks. But the incident started a chain reaction. The cab was rear-ended by the car behind them, not terribly hard, but just hard enough for Carter to wonder if they were going to have whiplash. Another car careened into their front right quarter panel, sending a column of steam up from the hood.

The cabbie uttered a curse as he lifted his hands from the wheel in a gesture of futility. He turned around to address his passengers as all traffic slowed to a stop behind them, in all lanes. "If you want to catch that bus, go now. This is not your fault, it was mine. But my company will pay for it. You do not need to stay, you have done your part," he said, patting his shirt breast pocket which was full of their cash.

"Thank you," both of them said. "We're sorry for the damage," Carter added. He pushed open the right-side door and he and Jayden exited the cab, closing the door after them. He looked around, mostly behind them, but also ahead and laterally, but couldn't see the silver car. He thought it might be about ten cars back, but couldn't be certain. He pointed to the bus stop. "Let's get to it before the bus does or we'll be sitting ducks on the side of the road."

For right now, the bus had pulled over to the shoulder of the right lane, but most of the pileup was in the left-most lane, and already other vehicles in the right lane were starting to ease back into traffic. This opportunity to reach the stop before the bus wouldn't last long. He and Jayden ran toward the stop, which featured a simple open bench with a sign on a pole next to it. No other people waited there.

Jayden threaded his way through traffic with the grace of an NFL running back, while Carter, a tad slower, took an alternate route that was more in his comfort zone. After enduring a few choice gestures and horn honks from frazzled drivers, along with one person who asked them if they were all right and were they in the accident, the pair of treasure-seekers reached the other side of the road in front of the bus stop.

"Nothing like a real life game of Frogger to wake you up!" Jayden exclaimed, resting with his hands on his knees.

"I like being able to put another quarter in if I die," Carter huffed. He eyed the traffic to their left and saw that the bus was almost to them. He raised a hand to indicate to the driver they wanted to board.

"Any sign of our tail?" he asked Jayden, who also stared in that direction. He replied in the negative.

"Then let's get on."

"Only one problem with that," Jayden said. "I'm out of cash. You got any?"

Carter shook his head. "Gave it all to the cabbie."

Jayden shrugged. "When I was a kid going to school on the public bus in Seattle, sometimes I'd spend my bus fare on candy bars at the 7-11 and then have to talk my way onto the bus."

"How'd you do that?" Carter asked as the bus air brakes belched and the doors opened. "Just kind of pretend like I'm digging around in my pockets for the fare and then, if the bus was crowded enough, sort of shuffle off down the aisle and hope the driver didn't notice."

Carter laughed. "And if he did notice?"

"Usually some adult would take pity on me and give me the fare."

"Somehow I'm not so sure that'll work for you these days. But let's hope it does, because don't look now, but I see the silver sedan coming up back there. Let's get on before they see us!"

He and Jayden waited for an elderly couple to disembark at a painfully slow rate, the man helping the woman down step by step, steadying her when she was on the ground before hobbling off together. Jayden boarded the bus first, while Carter was close behind, glancing back behind the bus at the silver sedan as it switched from the same lane the bus was in to the middle lane.

"You go to the airport, right?" Jayden asked the driver, an older woman with curly silver hair.

"Just like the sign says," she said, pointing to the electronic sign inside the bus that read, AIRPORT.

"Perfect, thanks!" Turning to Carter, he said, "Yep, it goes to the airport!"

"Great." He and Jayden took a couple of steps away from the driver toward the back of the bus, hoping she would start to drive away, but she only sat there, looking at them expectantly. The bus was not crowded, with plenty of empty seats stretching all the way to the back. "So much for your childhood ways," Carter muttered to Jayden under his breath.

"I need your fares, gentlemen," the driver said loudly in an exasperated tone.

"Uh, right, hold on," Jayden said before beginning a show of looking through his pockets, then his small backpack he had purchased at the hotel gift shop. Carter did the same. "I'm flat broke," he grumbled to Jayden. "Turn around!" He could see the silver sedan approaching the bus in the next lane. He and Jayden faced the sidewalk, hunching over a little.

"Listen, you two, if you don't have the fare ready, you'll have to get it ready while you wait for the next bus. There'll be another one coming along in twenty minutes."

"We could ask if anyone has it, just straight up beg," Jayden said in a low voice.

But Carter shook his head. "Probably it would work, and it's not that I'm beneath it, but I don't like the idea of calling that much attention to ourselves. Bus isn't that crowded, but there's still like twenty people back there. I'd rather just make a deal with the driver directly, that way only one person will remember us."

"Okay, you got anything to trade for fares?" Jayden looked his body up and down, lingering on his Omega dive watch, a gift from Carter's grandfather upon graduating naval officer school worth thousands of dollars.

"Not that," Carter said shaking his head.

Jayden nodded and instead glanced at his own wristwatch, a relatively cheap Casio digital with high-tech bells and whistles such as a barometer, compass, and elevation readout. He unstrapped the gadget from his wrist. "I don't know how I'll know what time the moonrise and low tide is anymore without this thing, but I suppose it's the price I'll have to pay."

He held out the watch and stepped up to the driver. "Look, this thing's all I got. It's worth a couple hundred American. We can't wait for another bus or we'll miss our flight. It's not refundable and we'd be out thousands of dollars."

The driver examined the watch with a begrudging look before snatching it from Jayden's hand and closing the bus door. "Welcome aboard!"

Carter and Jayden took seats in the middle of the bus and hunkered down, Carter at the window seat where he scoped out the passing vehicles, looking for signs of the silver sedan. "I think it worked."

"Let's hope so, because my wrist feels awfully naked."

"Sorry. I'll make it up to you. Let's focus right now on getting out of here." Before long they saw signs for St. John's International and entered a curving roadway with a sign warning, AIRPORT ONLY—DEPARTURES / ARRIVALS. They were glad to see the bus take the fork leading to departures, with each stop representing a different collection of airlines.

"Let's just get off at the first one," Carter suggested, "since we don't know which one we need yet."

With no arguments from Jayden, the pair of treasure hunters walked to the back door of the bus in anticipation of the stop. Jayden pressed the button to request a stop while Carter eyed the scene outside the door windows. He saw no signs of any pursuers or tails, so when the door opened the two stepped out onto the sidewalk bordering the air terminal.

"Let's get inside," Carter said, still worried their adversaries might know to troll the airport looking for them. With each only carrying a small backpack, they were able to thread their way quickly through the crowds without attracting much attention. "Turkey, Turkey, Turkey..." Carter said under his breath as they scanned the departure boards.

"Is that Europe or what?" Jayden wondered.

"A small part of it is in Europe, but most of it is in Asia. This way, come on." They fast-walked until they reached an Air Canada terminal with service to the Turkish capital of Ankara.

Staring at the departure times, they saw that the next flight left in just under two hours. "Let's see if we can get on." Carter stepped up to the ticket counter, eyeing the flag with red and white sickle and star with both trepidation and hope.

CHAPTER 15

Doğubayazıt, Turkey

Carter and Jayden stood in the middle of a crowded, dirt street lined on both sides with ramshackle vendors and simple storefronts of all sorts, fruit stands, cell-phones, curios and trinkets, rugs, incense, candles, spices, fresh fish and clothing. Musicians played doumbek hand drums, sitars, and flutes, their middle-eastern rhythms permeating the air and mingling with pungent hookah smoke. After travelling for nearly twenty-four straight hours, Carter and Jayden were exhausted, having slept only on the plane and then on the long bus ride from the airport in Ankara to the country's eastern border with Iran. The town of Doğubayazıt was the jumping-off point for expeditions to climb the mighty Mt. Ararat, which loomed in the distance like an otherworldly symbol of mystery and enchantment. The mountain was actually comprised of two distinct peaks, known as Greater and Lesser Ararat, with the Lesser having an elevation 12,782 feet, and Greater thrusting 16,854 feet into the heavens.

Despite the extraordinary view of a snow-capped volcano rising over three miles into the air only a few miles away, the place had an air of poverty about it characteristic of undeveloped nations. To Carter, it contrasted sharply with the majesty he associated with the region due to its rich and almost mythological history. Noah's Ark was thought to be buried somewhere in this land.

It was cold, too, with a light snow falling, and dirty, sooty snow lining the ground. He and Jayden had picked up parkas, knit caps and wool pants at an outfitter store catering to mountaineers, so they weren't uncomfortable, but the low temperatures only added to the austerity of the town.

"Think about how cold it is up there!" Jayden said, pointing to the snow covered peak in the distance.

"I'd rather think about finding out where Daedalus went. What do you say we do some leg work?"

Jayden nodded. They'd told everyone they'd encountered so far, on the day-long bus ride here, at the backpacker's hostel where they booked a room, and to the shopkeeps where they purchased mountaineering gear, that they were tourists from America here to climb Mt. Ararat, as many thousands do each year. It wasn't known for being a particularly difficult or technical climb, and was not high enough to require bottled oxygen for most people. Anyone capable of a strenuous hike a high altitudes for several days in a row could do it, like backpacking the Sierra Nevada mountains in California, or parts of the Rockies in Colorado. The upper portion was mired in snow 365 days a year, which made it cold, however, but so was any mountain over 10,000 feet.

"Seeing as the sit-on-our-butts work didn't pan out, looks like we've got no choice." Jayden was referring to their time the day before in the bustling, modern capital city of Ankara, where they'd sat in an Internet café for a couple of hours, searching for signs of archaeological permitting activity that might be associated with Daedalus. Naturally, they found none.

"It's not like we were expecting Treasure, Inc. to file for a permit, but it can't hurt to see if anyone has. It might draw Daedalus to them like flies to a jar of spilled honey." But no recently applied for archaeological digs had turned up, and none of the ongoing operations were noted as having activity right now. Mt. Ararat—for the moment, at least—was free from diggers and those who would plunder its past.

RICK CHESLER

But Carter was under no illusions that locating Noah's Ark could be as simple as wandering up a single mountain—snow-covered or not—and digging it up. If it was, it would have been found by now. And there are those, he was aware, who claimed that it already has been. One of the more well-known cases occurred in 1959, when a private individual discovered an object that was roughly boat-shaped, with dimensions that could fit those of Noah's Ark. The Turkish government at that time prevented his work from continuing and mounted their own investigation. It wasn't until 1987 that Turkey officially recognized the discovery, and at that time credited the individual with the find. Still, it was not definitive and many historians claimed that that the fossilized timbers located could have come from numerous other sources besides Noah's Ark, if in fact the ark was something other than a fictional creation in the first place.

Also, in 1978, an earthquake exposed rib timbers that were 515 feet in length, or 300 royal Egyptian cubits. The measurement units were a significant point, since the Egyptian cubit, rather than feet or meters, was used in the ancient world. Using these units made the timbers the approximate dimensions of the ark. Could they be from a petrified ship? But again, the world was not convinced. Still, Carter thought it a good bet that perhaps the map led to either this discovery or the previous one upheld by the Turkish government. He had made up his mind that, in the absence of more concrete leads, to head for these two sites first and see if anyone else might be hanging around.

It occurred to Carter that any time after the Bible was written, anyone could have built an ark of their own to recreate the story, and that, if found in modern times, could easily be confused with the "real" thing. He wasn't sure what it would take, exactly, to convince the world that the authentic, biblical Ark of Noah had been found, but a wooden boat dated to the proper age and of the proper dimensions would be a start. And he knew of a map that supposedly led right to it.

Daedalus ...He felt the anger begin to seethe inside him and willed himself to redirect it by concentrating on the immediate task in front of him—hooking up with a local guide outfit that could inform him about

124

recent expeditionary activity. He knew full well that Daedalus or anyone working on his behalf would skirt the established legal permitting channels for acceptable archaeological work. They would be posing as backpackers, like Carter himself was, and would attempt to follow the map to wherever it led under that guise.

Carter intended to find him. However, as he looked around, away from the mountain toward the vast expanses of rolling hills in either direction away from it, he was aware that Mt. Ararat itself need not be the resting place of the ark.

"Let's go, Carter, before I decide to lay around in some hookah bar for the rest of the month." As usual, Jayden was impatient to get moving even though he wasn't exactly sure where they were going. Carter consulted a local guidebook he'd picked up at the airport and had studied some on the bus ride over. Around them, people passed by wheeling carts, guiding livestock such as goats and sheep, and riding all manner of wheeled vehicles from bicycles to small trucks.

"The largest guide company is Ararat Trekking, and they have an office in the center of town. I say we check in there and see if there's anyone we can chat with. Then from there, see if we can arrange a guide to take us to the two sites associated already with Noah's Ark finds."

Jayden signified his agreement with a shrug and the two waited for a man pulling a cart laden with caged roosters to pass, and then set off on foot down the street. As they moved the snow stopped falling, the light wind died out and the sun shone a little through the clouds. Carter unzipped his parka and began to enjoy the experience. Although he and Jayden had been to the Middle East many times on deployment, Turkey was a first for both of them, and they soaked up the experience like any first-time traveler to the country.

"Here's what I don't get, though," Jayden said as he walked, deliberately looking away from a woman approximately his same age. It was difficult for him, but he avoided eye contact with the women they passed, most of whom were covered from head to toe including face scarves. He knew that they had strict customs here and that he could not afford to ruffle any feathers on their current agenda.

"What don't you get?" Carter asked.

"If this map was made back in the pre-Titanic days, then how could it point to the discoveries that were found in the 20th century?"

Carter shrugged. "Maybe they found them first and the modern people re-discovered them independently? I don't know but I figure it's worth a shot."

The walked along in silence for a while. "You know, Carter," Jayden said after a spell, "I've got to tell you, this is by far the best job I've ever had. Especially if I live through it."

Carter smiled and shook his head. "Omega's first official case is turning out to be a doozey, I'll give you that. But hey, we go the extra mile for our clients."

"Extra fifteen thousand miles or whatever it took to go halfway around the world."

"Whatever it takes. If Noah's Ark does exist, no one wants it to fall into the hands of a black market collector who only cares about himself."

"No one except that black market collector and his obviously well-paid minions, you mean."

"I stand corrected." Carter held his guide book up to his nose, then looked down the street. An elderly man with a long white beard was walking by and he held the book up to him. The man stopped, smiled and looked at the open page. Carter knew not a lick of Turkish, so simply pointed to the photo of the tour company's storefront, then looked around at the street and shrugged.

"Ah!" the man exclaimed before turning and pointing down the road.

"He says we take a left down there," Jayden guessed. They both thanked the man by nodding and smiling before continuing down the street. They turned left onto a busier street that was paved, although the traffic seemed to be of the same chaotically mixed variety as the last street. Carter recognized the sign for the place from half a block away, since it was one of the few two-story buildings on the street. As they continued down the road, Carter made it a point to keep his situational awareness up, keeping his head on the proverbial swivel. He wasn't looking for a repeat of being accosted as they were in Newfoundland, and certainly didn't want to end up back in the clutches of Treasure, Inc., as they were aboard the ship.

"Hey, did you ever contact Maddy?" Jayden wanted to know. "Not that I don't think you know what you're doing, mind you, but you know—"

"Yeah, yeah she's an archaeology expert, I get it. No offense taken. I sent her an email yesterday from our room. I'll check it tonight. I doubt she'll have anything at this stage for us, but once we get into a situation where we need more detail about something specific, she'll come in handy."

"Oh I bet she'll come in handy all right," Jayden said, a mischievous tone to his voice.

"Seriously, bro?"

"Seriously, when are you two going to tie the knot? Not that I'm looking forward to losing one of my drinking buddies, but you know, you two are good together."

Carter moved along in silence, sidestepping a gaggle of running children until they were in the clear again. He saw the mountain tours outfit up ahead on their left and began gravitating toward it. "We'll see. I asked her to officially join Omega, full time, but she declined, so... Getting her to consult with us is the next best thing."

"That's just work, though," Jayden persisted. Most guys don't work with their wives, it's not necessary is it?"

"Nope. But we both do a lot of travelling for our careers. Okay, so here we are. Remember—I'm sure I don't need to tell you this, but no mention of you know what."

"Your future wife?"

"The A-R-K, Jayden."

"Oh, thaaaat! Gotcha. Mum's the word. I just want to climb that big ole volcano just for that fun of it, yep, that's me!"

"Good." Carter reached the front door of the place and found a set of dusty glass doors with pull bars. He pulled one open and they walked inside to a small, bare floor with only a stairway leading up, a sign next to it on a stand reading: "Mt. Ararat Climbing Tours Upstairs."

They looked around for second, seeing absolutely nothing else of interest on this bottom floor except for a single closed door on the far wall. From upstairs they could hear the chatter of people conducting business, phones ringing, quiet music playing. Reaching the second floor, Carter was relieved to see a normal-looking place of business, with a help desk of some sort, a waiting area with a couple of chairs and then a cubicle area behind the desk staffed with half-a-dozen workers.

A middle-aged, bearded man eyed the two westerners with interest and walked out from around the counter to greet them. He introduced himself in English, saying his name was Ayaz. Carter and Jayden introduced themselves as well, using the same fake names they'd used to make the initial contact by calling from the hostel.

"Oh yes, I remember, you said you would be coming by. Welcome to Doğubayazıt. Are you enjoying your stay thus far?"

Both Americans nodded vigorously, aware that they were being watched by some of the other locals in the place, although they weren't the only westerners here. A group of European tourists was seated in the adjacent room, planning their trip with an employee.

"Unbelievable!" Jayden said with over-the-top enthusiasm. "Never seen anything like it. So authentic!" Carter stepped on his foot.

"What my friend, here, means is that you have a unique way of living here, all in the shadow of Mt. Ararat, and that we look forward to our climb."

The tour operator beamed. "Yes, well most of those who trek Ararat come away as a changed person. Our mountain is a special place indeed."

Jayden helped himself to a cup of tea brewing in a pot meant for customers. "Indeed," he echoed before taking a sip of the steaming aromatic liquid.

"So we have a group leaving tomorrow morning for a trek to the summit, would you like to join us?" Ayaz asked with enthusiasm that seemed genuine.

"While we would like to visit the summit someday," Carter answered, "right now we're trying to catch up with some friends of ours who we think may already be on the mountain. Can you tell me, do you know of any well-outfitted expeditions that have left recently—in the last couple of days?"

"Well-outfitted..." Ayaz pondered this while eyeing Carter and Jayden in turn before settling his gaze back on Carter. "As a matter of fact, one of our groups that left yesterday—we stay in contact via radio in order to provide a safe experience for all of our participants—did report passing a small group that was not known to be affiliated with any of our local trekking groups."

Carter held up a finger. "Did this group, by chance, happen to be on a route that would take them to one of the known Noah's Ark sites?"

At this Ayaz paused to watch Jayden slurp down the rest of his tea and refill his mug. "They were on a route that could lead to one of those sites, but they were still far from it. We also offer tours of the Noah's Ark sites, as opposed to the summit treks. Is that something you would be interested in?" Naturally, the tour operator wanted to keep the focus on discovering whether these two Americans represented any potential business for his company. Carter recognized that once he found out they were not potential clients, the flow of information would be quickly shut off.

"We wouldn't mind going up there with you, but we also want the flexibility to do our own thing. Is there a one-way option where we can go part way with your group, but then split off on our own?"

At this, Ayaz turned around and beckoned one of his co-workers, an older woman wearing a full-length dress and a head scarf. He spoke to her in rapid-fire Turkish while she gave the pair of Americans an appraising stare.

Jayden leaned in closer to Carter and said in a low voice, "Aren't we raising a little suspicion here, Carter? Not exactly blending in by saying we want to go it on our own."

Carter answered quickly in a low voice. "If we're seen leaving with a group, that should help us blend in. But when we get to the first ark site, we'll need to stay a while without prying eyes. I haven't heard from Maddy yet, and so these people could lead us to those sites. Also, one of their groups saw another outfit that could be Treasure, Inc., so I'd like to stay with them if possible."

Before Jayden could reply, the woman nodded and then Ayaz addressed the Americans. "I believe we have a group tour option that will meet your needs for flexibility. Are you able to leave tomorrow at first light?"

CHAPTER 16

Slopes of Mt. Ararat

Daedalus paced back and forth around the small campsite he and his two associates had cleared in the snow. Three white pup tents, a color chosen deliberately in order to blend in with the high-altitude surroundings, formed a rough triangle around the camp's perimeter. The ground was only a slight slope here, but to ascend any higher up the mountain meant to begin a steeper trek. The Treasure, Inc. leader watched his breath dissipate into the freezing atmosphere while a scowl formed across his features.

"I am not convinced," he said to the man nearest him, also a Greek, his brother, Phillipo. "The map is vague enough that it could even be referring to Lesser Ararat." He gazed distastefully in the direction of the sister peak, a little over seven miles away, connected to Greater Ararat by a lower elevation "saddle" of land. At the crux of his frustration was the fact that no timbers had been found here. "This map is a hoax!" He crumpled up his paper facsimile of the map, whose parchment his paid experts had authenticated as being "about 600 years old, " placing it in the fifteenth century, the age of Da Vinci.

Phillipo put a hand out to stop bis brother as he went pacing by. "Daedalus, we must consider that this mountain range has experienced numerous volcanic eruptions and seismic activity in the millennia following the supposed landing of Noah's Ark. The land itself may now be geographically different than it was even since the map was made."

"*Supposed* landing?" Daedalus spat. "That's where it landed. The Bible says so."

Phillipo shrugged. "It's the Bible, brother. Do not forget that many people today consider it to be nothing more than the greatest piece of fiction ever written. A creative work by a collaboration of great minds, cobbled together from numerous translations, transcriptions and re-tellings across the centuries. Even finding wooden timbers or a boat matching the physical dimensions of the ark does not mean that the story itself is real. Anyone, after all, could have built a replica at any point in time after the Bible was created."

Daedalus suddenly whirled around and eyed his brother angrily. "What is real, Phillipo? Are stocks and bonds real? Is money itself real? No, they are simply constructs of the human mind, meant to symbolize value and ideas. If enough people believe in them, they become real. That is all that matters. Show me a boat made from acacia timbers about 4,800 years old, and of the same dimensions as those described in the bib—excuse me, in the bestselling work of fiction the world has ever known—and the world will want to believe that it *is* Noah's Ark. They will clamor for it, they will lust after it, and dare I say, they will even kill for it."

Phillipo stared at him doubtfully. "Are you sure it is not yourself which you describe, dear brother?"

One of the other two expedition members—an Italian man in his mid-thirties, started to approach the two brothers, but upon seeing the angry and uneasy looks on their faces, turned away without speaking. Daedalus turned to his brother.

"The only thing I am sure of is that when you lash out it me it's because you're questioning the direction of our company."

Phillipo extended an arm and gestured at their snow-covered surroundings, somehow bleak and majestic at the same time. "And why would I ever do that? Because you have led us to this mountain, at great time and expense, on a wild goose chase based on a map purporting to lead to something out of a fairy tale? If the map is anything genuine, we could simply sell that without leaving home in Athens, and then look for treasures that actually exist. Why would I ever question our direction?" His words dripped with sarcasm that echoed off the volcanic rock beneath their feet.

Daedalus pointed his finger at his brother's chest in a stabbing motion. "Great accomplishments come with great pain. It seems you have never learned this lesson, instead wanting everything handed to you. If you want a safe office job in my company, it is waiting for you in Athens. You can be a manager, work for a reasonable set salary keeping normal business hours and spend every weekend with your lovely wife."

"You leave my wife out of this, Daedalus."

"Well I did, dear brother. I left her, as you recall, even though she desired me. I left her so that you could have her. I basically gave you your wife, gave you your job, and now you complain that the job is too demanding."

"Daedalus, Phillipo—over here! We found something!"

Both brothers turned to look up the mountain to where their expedition mate beckoned by waving frantically. When he had their attention, he pointed off to his right, down the mountain slope.

CHAPTER 17

Foot of Mount Ararat, elevation 2200 meters

The ground surrounding Carter and Jayden was strewn with boulders that were interspersed with short green grass. After riding in a Suburban most of the entire morning, they had been dropped off here for the trek on foot up the volcano. Had they not been part of the tour, Carter reasoned, they would have had to rent a vehicle, leaving a paper trail, and then leave it out in the open. He wondered how Daedalus had managed it, if in fact he was up on the mountain somewhere. It bothered Carter that "Ararat" could also mean Little Ararat, or even another part of Turkey, possibly even Armenia or Iran, since the modern day political lines were different from five thousand years ago.

"Steve. I said *Steve*," Jayden repeated, nudging Carter with a light body slam.

Carter was wrested from his thoughts and said, "Sorry, Brad, my mind got lost in that spectacular view." He turned away from the volcanic peak and faced Jayden. They had decided to use bogus names when interacting with the group, including the tour outfitters, which they had paid in cash. Carter was certain Daedalus knew their real names.

The group itself was both boisterous and varied, a crazy assortment of people from all walks of life, totaling fifteen altogether including the three guides. There were Armenians, Turks, Americans, Europeans, and Japanese. The oldest was a man of 68, and the youngest a girl of 11. One couple even brought their dog along. Almost everyone had more than one camera, usually a Canon or Nikon DSLR, and then maybe a GoPro or cell-phone camera, even though there would be no cellular service after the first day of trekking up into the mountain. On the drive over, the guides had gone over the routines to expect, and now the group was ready to begin its ascent. For those heading to the summit, at an altitude of over 16,000 feet, it would be a six-day adventure all told. Carter and Jayden, who had made it clear with the guides that they would be going their separate ways when they reached the lowest elevation ark site, were warned by the guides not to attempt going too high on the mountain without acclimating for at least a day at designated lower altitudes, as the rest of the group would be.

They began hiking, with the guides passing out ski-poles to use as walking sticks. Both Carter and Jayden declined the poles, wanting to keep hands free and knowing they could make the climb unaided. Even all the way to the summit, the climb was not a technical one that required ropes or specialized gear. One could simply walk all the way up, if they were able-bodied and took it slow enough, allowing time to acclimatize. Carter had climbed California's Mt. Whitney as a teenager, an elevation of 14,500 feet, and Jayden had ascended McKinley in Alaska, an elevation of 20,000, so neither were unaccustomed to the effects of altitude on exertion. Time passed quickly as they traipsed through the new scenery, the brisk mountain air invigorating to their lungs. In the distance were herds of cattle or perhaps oxen, and apart from their own group, they saw no other people.

They marched up a dirt track etched out of the side of the mountain, which still had the same boulders and grass, except now the ground was steeper and the boulders were covered with moss and lichens. The first day of hiking passed quickly with casual conversation, although most of the groups who had come together, especially the couples, stayed together. One guide took point, as Carter and Jayden thought of it, while another brought up the rear and a third roved around the middle, having brief conversation with each group to make sure everyone was happy. Any doubts that the trekking guides had done this same journey many, many times before were quickly dispelled when Carter saw how efficiently they set up camp. The first drifts of snow were on the ground, and the incline just a bit steeper when they reached the site where they would spend the first night on the mountain, at an altitude of 3,200 meters. A large mess tent was erected for the kitchen, complete with a wooden sign reading, MT. ARARAT CAFÉ. Each group set up their individual sleeping tents, including Carter and Jayden.

"Glad we sprung for the four-man," Jayden said, pounding in a tent stake with a rock. "Don't get me wrong—I like you, man—but not in a two-man tent kind of way, you get what I'm saying?"

"Feeling's mutual," Carter said, hammering in a stake on the opposite side. Dinner consisted of *Harissa*, a filling chicken porridge, prepared quickly with camp stoves as well as a small open cook fire inside a circle of stones. After dinner, there was even Armenian cognac to go around, and then the group stayed up long enough to watch the moon rise, its pale light glinting off the snow. They retired to their tents, exhausted after a busy day of travel and hiking. The guides pointed out that tomorrow would be a long, full day of hiking, and that they should get as much rest and sleep as possible.

Carter and Jayden had no problem with this, and retired to their tent, zipping up the flap for not only protection against insects and wind, but also added privacy for conversation. Jayden lay on his side of the tent in his sleeping bag, staring up without saying much.

"You think we're on a fool's errand up here?" Carter put out into the open.

"Could be. Seems too easy. Waltz up here and find Daedalus at a well-known Noah's Ark site? It could happen, though, who knows?"

"I'm more concerned about the map," Carter said. They could hear soft laughter coming from one of the other tents nearby, murmured prayers of the Armenian couple, still outside, for whom this trek was a pilgrimage to a holy site as part of their faith, and a light wind rustling the tent fabric. "I'd really like to recover it, since it's an artifact itself, and our client retained us to deliver it to her."

"I wonder if we would have had better luck figuring out where Daedalus was staying in Doğubayazıt, and just sneaking into his place and taking the map while he's up here! Because you know he wouldn't actually bring along the original. What's the point of that? He'd just use a copy or the photos."

"Finding out where he's staying might not be so easy though, and breaking and entering is not a crime you want to be convicted of in Turkey."

"True," Jayden considered, turning over onto his side. "I rather like my head where it is—on my neck."

"Yeah, same here. Even letting the government get wind that we're looking for you know what is not in our best interest. Remember, we have no permits because everything happened so fast."

"We don't need no stinking permits!"

#

The next morning saw them in the breakfast tent and nursing steaming mugs of Turkish tea around the cook fire before first light. By the time camp was broken down and packed up and they had hit the trail again, the first pink hues of daylight streaked across the sky. The team dog was out front, rooting around here and there, and hikers wondered aloud if it would get too tired to make it the full day since it was running three times the linear distance. Its owners assured them that it would not, and a comfortable enough silence fell over the group as they trekked up increasingly steeper ground through the early morning. A Pair of oxen blocked the path at one point, but the dog came in handy, barking wildly until the hefty beasts lumbered off the path and downhill.

As they trekked, Carter and Jayden kept their gazes peeled, especially up mountain, for signs of other climbing parties, but so far had seen none. Despite the chilly air and patches of snow on the ground, the exercise created enough warmth that Carter unzipped his parka. He sipped water through the hydration bladder tube coming through his pack and clipped to his shoulder strap, and he wondered why so many in the group used water bottles, meaning they had to stop, set down their packs, pull out the bottle, drink, and put it away again and re-don the pack. Still, Carter reminded himself, these were not paramilitary operators, or even ex-military, they were outdoor recreational enthusiasts, and so he told himself not to let his and Jayden's efficiency mark them for something other than what they represented themselves as. *We're just regular Americans on vacation, climbing a mountain for the thrill of it, that's all....*

Even so, by the time they broke for lunch, Carter had to admit that he was feeling the workout. He asked himself if his time away from the service, almost a year now, had made him softer. The dog slurped up water from its bowl while the Turkish couple faced the peak of Ararat and knelt on a prayer rug. The others took photos and videos, or made brief satellite-phone calls to friends and loved ones back home. Glancing around at the vistas below, Carter was taken aback by how vast the region was. All of it qualified as "Ararat," and so the ark could have come to rest anywhere up here, according to the Bible. It only had to be high enough elevation to make sense with the great flood waters subsiding and the ark coming to rest on what would likely be part of a mountain. He considered that the ground would be damp from the flood, and that possibly it would have sunk into a bed of mud, possibly submerged all the way beneath it. By now the wood would likely be petrified. Carter wished they could have brought a drone to obtain aerial views, but none were for sale in Doğubayazıt, and being on the run had not afforded them time to plan ahead. He reminded himself to try calling Maddy again, at camp tonight.

The group eased back onto the trail and continued up the volcano. Much of the time there was silence and Carter and Jayden dared not have conversation that involved their agenda, but when others in the group did strike up a conversation, or when the dog barked and everyone told it to be quiet, they would seize the opportunity to discuss what might lay ahead for them. "Do you think Daedalus will be armed?" Jayden asked.

"Don't know," Carter replied in a low voice, "but we have to assume that he could be. A man like Daedalus—with both means and a lack of moral scruples—would be able to get almost anything he wanted. It just depends how important he thought being armed was compared to the hassles it would involve, if any."

Other than the knives, multitools and hatchets they carried that would not look out of place with camping or outdoors gear, Carter and Jayden were unarmed.

"Hopefully we can do a stealth infiltration of his camp," Jayden said. Carter agreed, and then they trudged on in silence. The air became chillier as the elevation increased, and the parkas were zipped back up. After a while, Carter and Jayden found themselves having to deliberately hold back their pace in order to stay with the group, and they were glad to think that tomorrow they would strike out on their own. At base camp they had joked with the guides about the possibility of getting lost, saying that if all else failed, down was the way back, right? But they knew it wasn't that simple. Besides Turkey, Mt. Ararat shared borders with Iran, Azerbaijan, and Armenia. Traipsing down without knowledge of where they were going meant that they could end up in an unforgiving nation with no travel visa. A very serious matter were they to be detained, the trekking operation had warned them.

When the sun was visibly lower in the sky, the guides announced they had reached their campsite for the night, a craggy, snow-strewn plateau with a steep drop-off on one side, and a long, gradual slope on the other, while the summit of Mt. Ararat lorded over them above a steep incline. While they set up camp, Carter took out a pair of binoculars (he told he group he was an avid bird watcher) and scanned the territory below the steep drop-off, looking for any signs of backpackers. But he saw none; he scanned the other directions as well, but they were just as free of human presence.

After dinner, the lead guide took Carter and Jayden aside and asked them if they were ready to go off on their own in the morning. "The ark site is down there," he said, pointing down the steep incline, "and then that way for probably ten kilometers uphill," he finished, pointing out of sight.

Carter and Jayden nodded enthusiastically, playing the part of gung-ho adventure travelers. "Game on!" Jayden gushed.

"We'll miss you guys," Carter said. "You're a great group, but we'd rather see the ark than the summit, and unfortunately we don't have time for both."

"I understand," the guide said. "I just wanted to confirm that you are leaving us in the morning—I assume you will dine with us for breakfast?"

Carter nodded. "That's right, then we'll pack up with you, but when you guys head up there..." He looked up at the snowy summit. "...we'll be going down there." He looked down the steep incline.

"Do you think we'll meet any other climbers at the ark site?" Jayden asked the guide. He was fishing for information on whether the guide knew of other climbing parties there, and of course whether they might be Treasure, Inc., but he thought it was a reasonable enough question to ask without raising suspicion.

"Probably not," the guide answered. "There's not much to see, really, just the vague outline of something that might be a ship. Every now and then people come digging for timbers, but most people who come up here just want to go to the summit."

"Well, we better enjoy the company of other humans while we can!" Jayden said to Carter, before adding to the guide, "Hopefully we won't get too sick of each other!"

The guide laughed. "Yes, well that's another reason why group travel is recommended. Good company!"

#

That night in the tent, Carter used his satellite-phone to check his messages. "Got something from Maddy!" He told Jayden. He listened to the message, disconnected, and then recapped it for Jayden. "She says she's still on a dig in Kyrgyzstan. Wants to meet up when we're done if possible."

"I'm sure she does," Jayden said with a suggestive lilt to his voice. Carter pressed the button on his phone to call Maddy. "I'm going to tell her where we are—just approximately, not exactly-- and what we know so far about the map and our search, to see if she has anything that might help us." But the call went straight to voice-mail. Carter left her a message.

Outside it was dead quiet, with none of the group having the energy to stay up after the day's uphill trek, knowing they faced another day of it tomorrow.

CHAPTER 18

The next morning played out as planned, with Carter and Jayden parting ways with the trekking group after breakfast and camp breakdown. Both groups wished each other luck, with the tour leader asking Carter to phone a message to the trekking operation when they returned, to let them know they had made it down off the mountain safely. Carter agreed to this, and after a final warning about not ascending too rapidly without acclimating, he and Jayden watched the tour group continue up the trail that switchbacked further up the volcano.

"I will miss those guys," Jayden said.

"Good group of people," Carter said. "The kind of people who would respect a treasure like Noah's Ark. Makes me want to stop Treasure, Inc. even more."

"True. If Daedalus gets his way, he'd have the ark in his living room and no one would ever see it again."

"Probably the centerpiece of his home bar."

Jayden appeared thoughtful. "Hm, now that would be cool, I have to admit. Probably too cool for a low-life like him."

"Speaking of," Carter said as he shouldered his pack, "what do you say we head down there?"

He and Jayden eyed the precipitous slope down to a snow-filled ravine or gully of sorts. Jayden took a last look through a pair of binoculars. "No signs of anyone. Let's do it."

The two set out off the beaten path down the steep slope. The going was much slower than walking up the established track, since they needed to test each snow-covered step to make sure their footing was secure before putting their full weight down, unless they wanted to tumble down the rock-strewn face with its boulders hidden beneath the snow drifts. It also became colder the further down into the ravine they ventured, especially when the direct sunlight was blocked by the mountain itself overhead. Carter eyed the freshly fallen snow carefully for footprints, but it was all unbroken as far as he could see.

It took them the better part of three hours to reach the bottom of the ravine. When they did, they decided to break for lunch. "After we eat we'll round that bend there," Carter said, pointing to the bottom of another side of the mountain section, around which it sloped up sharply again.

"I'm ready for some more uphill after this morning," Jayden said, shrugging off his pack onto a dry boulder.

"It's a lot harder on the knees going down," Carter said.

Jayden laughed. "That's what she said."

"Really, wow, that would have been funny maybe ten years—"

They heard a loud noise somewhere up above them, out of sight around the mountain. A sharp hissing sound. Both became silent as they froze in place and looked around while listening for more. After hunching in place for another two minutes without detecting further signs of activity, Carter pointed ahead of them, the signal to move out. The pair of ex-military men crept silently through the snow toward the mountain bend. To their left, about a hundred feet away, was the opposite wall of the gulley which rose steeply to the grand face of the mountain. After every few feet they would stop and listen again. On the fourth such auditory check, they heard what sounded like a human voice, distant and carried as an echo down through the ravine, the words, if any, indistinguishable. They continued following the contour of the ravine's base until they could just see around an outcropping of rock into a new area of the ravine. Here, the trench between two walls increased in slope as well as becoming narrower. It went up for a long ways, Carter estimated perhaps a thousand yards, before it opened up onto the main volcanic slope, rejoining the mountain.

And there, toward the left side of that confluence, Carter picked out a splash of color. Any type of color stood out against a natural background that was all shades of green, brown and white, and so the splotch of blue stood out easily. Jayden saw it too. "Parka, or maybe a hat."

Carter nodded and pointed to the opposite side of the ravine, up a little higher in the narrower section. "Let's make our way up on that side." Jayden moved up ahead as point man while Carter stayed back to observe. He removed the field binoculars from his pack—a small, inexpensive pair of 10 x 25s—and wished they were more powerful. Still, they were much better than the naked eye, so he brought them to his eyes while Jayden ran across the open ravine section to the wall on the other side. Focusing on the patch of blue up top, Carter waited for his eyes to adjust to the view. A couple of seconds later he saw the figure of a person—still too far away to distinguish facial features, but he could definitely make out the outline of a human body wearing cold weather gear—carrying or hefting a piece of equipment of some type. Whatever it was gleamed in the sunlight, so Carter figured it must have at least some metal on it.

He lowered the binoculars in time to see Jayden make the opposite ravine wall and look back at Carter, no doubt wanting confirmation from his scout that he wasn't being observed by their unknown quarry up above. Carter gave him a hand signal that indicated he was clear to move forward, and Jayden set off up the ravine. While the point man progressed up the slope, Carter again raised the binoculars to his eyes. This time he saw two people, one of them grabbing the metallic object from the first and carrying it out of sight. Some kind of operation is going on up there, he thought. He lowered the glasses and monitored Jayden's progress. When he turned around again to check in, Carter gave him the halt signal. With a last glance up the mountain to be sure no one was watching or moving toward them, Carter ran across the ravine to where Jayden's first stop was, so that the two of them were now on the same side of the ravine, with Jayden a little further up.

Hugging the side of the craggy, snow-flecked wall, the pair of ex-Navy sailors eased their way up the ravine, stopping frequently to assess their surroundings and listen for changes in activity. They were able to progress with a quiet rapidity due to their former training and good physical conditioning. Three-quarters of the way up, Jayden waited for Carter to catch all the way up to him. They needed to communicate well to plot their approach out of the ravine. Neither was even breathing particularly hard, though they also had to slow their pace somewhat the nearer the top they reached, so as not to be heard by whoever was up there.

Carter whispered, "As soon as we make sure it's not Treasure, Inc., we should back down without being detected. We don't want to scare the crap out of someone by sneaking up on them."

"Right, and possibly get shot at," Jayden added. "Unless it actually *is* Treasure, Inc., in which case we'll definitely get shot at."

They heard another sharp hissing noise from above, louder this time because they were closer. Then they heard spoken words. They were still indistinguishable even though they were clear, and it took Carter a moment to figure out that it was because they were speaking a foreign language. Not Turkish or Armenian, which he could recognize enough of from being in Turkey the past few days, but....*what was it?* He strained to listen in, but instead of more talking they heard a loud, motorized buzzing start up. Carter and Jayden eyed one another with quizzical expressions.

"Chainsaw?" Jayden posited.

"Could be."

"They found the ark and they're cutting it down?" Jayden's eyes opened wide.

"That would be a monumental no-no, permit or not. They must be using it to build something, would be my guess."

"Enough guessing," Jayden said. "Let's go have a look-see."

They low-crawled side-by-side up the remaining slope, moving very slowly so as to remain noiseless. A couple of times on the way up they heard the strange hissing of air again, as well as the chainsaw, if that's what it is. And the voices. Carter heard them more clearly now—two different adult males, from the sound of it—but more importantly, he could identify their language, and it caused his adrenaline to spike: Greek.

Carter reached out and tugged on Jayden's foot to get his attention. "It's them." Jayden nodded and patted his hunting knife, sheathed on his belt, as was Carter's. He reached down and undid the retaining snap so that he would be able to withdraw it quick if need be. He glimpsed up at the ravine wall next to them. It was only a few feet above their heads, while they were lying on the ground, which meant they had almost reached the top. Down at the bottom, before they had started low-crawling, the wall as a good fifty feet high or more. The idea of randomly popping out in the open over the wall was unappealing, since they had no way of seeing who or what was up there right now. Was there a campsite, or was this a work site they "commuted" to from wherever their camp was? It made a difference because his goal was to obtain the map, or a copy of it. It was doubtful Daedalus would have brought the original with him, for fear of it being destroyed or lost…or was it?

Perhaps he simply hadn't had time to put it anywhere else for safekeeping other than keep it on his person. He'd only had a few hours head-start over Carter and Jayden, after all. Copy or original, something had brought them here, one way or the other, and Carter was determined to find it, and then either steal it or copy it by taking a photo of it. He patted one of the cargo pockets in his pants to make sure the camera was still there. Check. He had already gone into the device's settings the previous night and disabled all beeps and shutter sounds, to ensure silent operation. This phase of the mission was as about as planned in advance as it could be, Carter thought, trying to calm himself against the uncertainty that now represented his immediate future.

He eyed Jayden and dared not even whisper at this point, simply mouthing the words: *straight up and stop at the edge.* Then he pointed to his own eyes with two fingers, meaning *take a look.* So the plan was to low-crawl the last few feet, which would expose them to Treasure, Inc.'s line of sight for at least a few seconds, but during that time they would get to see what they were dealing with.

Another hiss of air made him jump and he took a couple of deep breaths to calm his nerves. He thought the sound seemed familiar to him now, and yet it made no sense in this context. *Can't be…* He probably would have recognized it if he'd had a few more seconds to think, but Jayden was tugging at his sleeve with urgency while he began to slither up out of the ravine onto the mountainside.

Taking a deep breath, Carter did the same.

CHAPTER 19

"Are the tanks set up yet, Phillipo?" Daedalus bellowed.

His brother's reply echoed from off the ice below but was perfectly audible. "That should be the last one. Four rigs ready to go. Just need some more hot tea."

"We can have tea after we do the dive."

"Oh c'mon, brother, we've waited 5,000 years to recover the ark, what's five more minutes?"

"It's that much more time for the Turkish government to find out we are excavating archaeological ruins without a license, that's what it is, Phillipo. Then you will be drinking your tea in a Turkish jail."

"You have a way of looking on the bright side, Daedalus."

"As did Noah. He knew the world would soon be flooded, and yet he had a plan for it, a plan that would not only save him and his family, but the animals of the world as well. Are the drysuits and the rest of the gear down by the lake?"

Daedalus stared down at the object of their new attention, a small lake—some might call it a large pond—partially iced over. It had been difficult to detect at first because fresh powder covered the intact ice, but on closer inspection, but the team member had noticed water sloshing against the shore while Daedalus and his brother had been arguing.

Daedalus picked up his binoculars and stared down at the lake. *Was it possible?* Then, for probably the tenth time that day, he took out the map from his pack, the original map from the *Titanic*. He very much regretted having to bring the original on the expedition and risk something happening to it, since he was aware of its intrinsic value even though he already had copies of it, but the timeline of recent events had necessitated that he keep it with him. He unfolded it now and looked at it again. He could have viewed a photo on his tablet, but he felt like for some reason he was missing something when he did that. He liked the feel of connecting more intimately with the past, and so he risked the old document to the elements in the pursuit of inspiration.

He stared yet again at the X—literally a small black X-marks-the-spot—that had been the focus of his recent obsession. He was confident about the general location, eastern Turkey, and even as far as Mt. Ararat, which was clearly indicated on the map. Not Lesser Ararat, he was sure, but the main, Greater Ararat on which they now found themselves. But more specifically than that is where things became increasingly subject to interpretation. After staring at the map for hours at night by lantern light in his tent, he was still unable to determine if the cartographic rendering had been accurately drawn to scale, or if it was simply meant to be a symbolic representation of roughly where the ark lay. Also, the X was disturbingly close to an already discovered ark site—discovered in modern times well after the map was made. It ate Daedalus up inside to think that what he had thought of as a priceless treasure map, dredged up from the bottom of the sea—and the ages—could in reality lead to something that had already been discovered without its aid.

As he stared down at the lake while his team readied the SCUBA gear, Daedalus considered the route they had taken up the mountain, based both on a known ark site, and on the graphical depiction on the map. At first he had thought the X to be distressingly close to the known site—a grouping of timbers of appropriate age and in the shape of the storied ark with the proper dimensions, but which has already been discovered and dismissed by professional archaeologists as definitively being Noah's Ark. But when his team member had pointed out the semi-frozen lake below the known ark site, Daedalus had pored over the map again. There were no elevation contours or other cartographic methods employed that would be considered sophisticated by modern standards. So although on paper the X-marks-the-spot appeared to be very close to the known "ark" site, a scant millimeter's positioning of the X's cross point could well make a difference in real life that translated to a completely separate location, miles away. It was, Daedalus reflected, like a crude form of geocaching—hunting down planted treasures with the aid of modern GPS gadgets. And even in that scenario, arriving at a specific set of GPS coordinates where treasure is located, further hunting was still required much of the time. There could be a tree at that location, for example, and rather than being buried in the ground, the treasure is up in the tree.

Or a lake, with the treasure down in the lake. The fact that the lake was partially frozen and oftentimes covered with snow meant that it would obscure whatever was down below. And, as the illicit treasure hunter brought binoculars to his eyes once again, there did appear to be something down there. He could pick out the dark, linear forms of what appeared to be timbers of some sort. It excited him to think that if they were from the ark, or a replica of the ark old enough to be considered "real" to most believers, that the cold water might have preserved them to the point that they are not even petrified wood, but still wood. How amazing that would be!

He stared back down at the map again while the sound of a chainsaw cutting through ice rent the frigid air. Daedalus had not relied solely upon this old piece of paper. He had also used modern technological aids, such as Google Earth to examine satellite photography of the region. In this imagery he had noticed the lake that was superficially "next to," but also physically far *below* the X-marks-the-spot on the map, which appeared close to the already-discovered ark artifacts site. This prior knowledge of the area was why he had insisted on lugging hundreds of extra pounds of SCUBA gear up the mountain, along with the chainsaw and gas cans to run it. But when they had first gotten up here and looked around, the lake was nowhere to be found, and he worried that the image was outdated, or that an earthquake or avalanche had since covered it over. They had located the known "wreckage" and then worked from there to where the lake should be. He had been about to give up when they came across it.

Now it was a matter of the technical SCUBA dive to get down to the timber-like objects they could see at the bottom of the lake. Ice diving combine with high altitude in an extremely remote area did not for an easy or safe dive make. Add to that the fact that he was deliberately operating with a skeleton crew of four people including himself, both to expedite things so that they could get up here as quickly as possible as soon as he had the map, and also because loose lips sink ships, as he was fond of saying. The less people who knew where the ark was, should they find it, the better.

Daedalus spoke into a two-way radio to his team members working to get the scuba gear down to the lake. They had already rigged a system of ropes from the side of the slope down to the basin the lake occupied, and now they were attaching the gear to the ropes and pulling it down to the lake on a pulley system. At least that was how it was supposed to work. He was well aware that there were a lot of things to go wrong with the system such as losing gear on the way down, the rope and pulley system itself failing, his personnel slipping down the mountain and falling into the icy lake, things like that. Preoccupied with thinking of every little detail that could go wrong with the execution of his dive plan, Daedalus failed to notice the small movements to his left, barely within his peripheral vision.

Two men crawled up out of the ravine behind him and paused, looking around. They saw Daedalus standing there, binoculars to his eyes, and then looked ahead and to their left at the rope and pulley system that ran out of sight down the slope to the lake, which they could not see from their current position. Further distracting Daedalus was his radio crackling with Phillipo's voice, speaking in Greek.

"Copy, Daedalus. Three sets of gear down at the lake shore, one set on its way. You can make your way down to us whenever you're ready. All your gear will be waiting for you, including the underwater video system."

"Copy, see you soon." Daedalus clipped his radio back onto his belt and walked to the edge of the slope. He looked down at the lake, gazing into its icy blue depths and wondering what he would find there. Time to find out, he thought, but first...

He unzipped his trousers and urinated into the snow.

CHAPTER 20

Jayden had to lay his face flat into the snow to stifle a laugh despite the seriousness of the situation. Carter remained stock still but kept his head up to watch Daedalus. As best he could tell, the rest of his team was down the slope off to his left, leaving him up here alone. Even better, although he couldn't understand the radio conversation in Greek, he could see that Daedalus was preparing to join his team down the slope. Whatever was down there, they were very interested in it, because they had set up some kind of rope system that led out of sight down the slope.

Carter tensed as Daedalus zipped up his fly. If he turned this direction, he would probably see them. If that happened, Carter thought, they'd have no choice but to fight. At least it would be two-on-one until his team heard the struggle and scrambled up from down the slope, however long that took. It sounded like they were far down below, so that was something. But then, to his relief, that entire line of thought became a moot point as Daedalus walked straight over to the rope system, and without looking over at them, gripped the rope and walked out of sight down the slope.

Jayden picked his head up out of the snow and looked at Carter, who now found it was his turn to try not to laugh while looking at his friend's snow-caked face. He pointed down the slope. Jayden's response was to crane his neck and look around behind them, meaning, *Is anyone else up here?*

Carter shook his head in the negative. Off to their right, maybe a hundred feet away, he thought he saw evidence of a campsite—some packs on the ground, maybe a tent set up. Down the hill they could hear some walkie-talkie chatter and the occasional yelled command to facilitate some kind of operation. Carter's curiosity as to what they were doing down there was overwhelming, but he wasn't about to stick his neck out over the slope and risk being seen. First things first, he thought.

The map. Whether original or copy, some version of it had to be up here somewhere, unless Daedalus had the only copy on his person. But Carter doubted that, and he knew there was only one way to find out. He and Jayden crawled a little farther away from the slope to ensure they couldn't be seen when they stood up. When they regained their feet, they tip-toed over to the camp gear they'd seen.

An additional problem now presented itself. Carter held out a hand to signal Jayden to stop as they neared what looked like a mess tent, as well as a small cook fire still smoldering. They didn't see any other people, but what if someone was inside the tent, sleeping, or working on kitchen detail, something like that? No doubt he and Jayden would be able to take him or her out, even silently, but they were using radios, and it would only take two seconds of frantic warning to send the reinforcements up to camp.

They stayed put for a full minute and observed the tent carefully, watching for shadows inside, and listening for any sign of human activity. But there was none, and so they crept over to the tent, whose flaps hung loosely open. Carter peered inside and saw that it was clear. Quickly he pulled Jayden inside and they did a more through sweep to make sure someone wasn't actively hiding beneath folding table or the tarp on the ground. They found the space to be unoccupied.

"Jayden, you go back to the slope and act as lookout. I'll look for the map."

Jayden wasted no time slipping out of the tent and creeping across the campsite back toward the slope. Carter turned his mind to the map search. He didn't know how long Daedalus and team planned to be down there, but all it would take is for one of them to come back up and they'd likely be gunned down like animals. Out here in the wilderness, no one would ever know. The trekking group would report them missing a few days after he didn't check back in at the appointed time, but nothing would likely come of that in the way of an investigation—they'd be presumed lost in the mountains, and it would be too late for them, anyway.

Carter quickly rummaged through a couple of stuff sacks on the ground, and moved a couple of tarps around, but quickly came to the realization that this was only a mess tent and he wasn't likely to find the map in here. His time was best spend searching elsewhere in the camp, so he left the tent and began moving around.

Glancing to his left he saw Jayden in a prone position to the right of the rope and pulley system, with a fallen branch strategically positioned in front of his head for concealment as he observed the activities down by the lake. This left Carter free to roam about the campsite. He went looking for backpacks, those personal items that would represent a likely place for something valuable one wanted to keep close at hand.

#

Daedalus stood on the edge of the lake and zipped up his dry suit, a diving suit that, unlike a wetsuit, did not allow any water at all to come into contact with the skin.

"Ready when you are, Daedalus." Phillipo fastened the strap on his scuba rig's BC, or buoyancy compensator. Of their other two team members, one would be also diving with them, while the fourth would be remaining on shores as both surface support—ready to aid the divers in and out of the water, enter the water to help if necessary--and to act as general site lookout. Daedalus' main concern was that he had not filed any permit paperwork for archaeological operations here, so should they be seen by any type of Turkish authority, or even a local guiding operation who might report the activity to authorities, it could mean trouble.

"It's cold," Phillippo said with a grin as he stepped into the water, fins in hand. The underwater topography of the lake was such that there was a very shallow lip around the edge of the shore before it dropped off sharply down to depths that exceeded 100 feet. The trio of divers entered the water and hugged the shoreline while they adjusted their gear and tested it to make sure it was working properly, including the underwater video and photography equipment. With the drysuits on, the could still feel the chill of the iced water, but it was tolerable rather than life-threatening, like wearing a jacket in cold weather. The full suits restricted movement somewhat, especially with the SCUBA gear on over that, but there was no other way to explore places like this.

"Let's make it quick," Daedalus said to his dive team, and with that, he stepped off the shallow edge of the lake and into deep water. He placed his regulator mouthpiece between his teeth and pressed the button on his BC inflator hose to let the air out of his vest. He maintained a vertical posture as he began sinking beneath the surface of the lake. His brother and their other team member followed suit, and a minute later all three of them were descending into the lake.

#

The campsite was not as organized as Carter had hoped for. There was no central location other than the mess tent where he could find all the gear piled together. He found one backpack leaned against a tree by itself, and searched through it exhaustively, but found no paper maps, and zero electronic devices such as a laptop, phone, camera or flash drive. Looking around some more, he located a second pack. The only difference between this one and the first was that it contained a smartphone. Carter frowned as he started at the modern device. A photo of the map could be on a phone, he thought, and yet this presented a new problem, since most phones were locked by default for security purposes. He powered it on, and sure enough, was met with a passcode screen.

He clenched his teeth and powered down the phone while considering available options. He could steal the phone and try to electronically unlock it later—hack into it, basically—or else he could see if it had a removable memory card and take that out of it. But for now he put the phone back in the pack where it was and decided to keep looking for something more definitive. He was pretty sure that only Daedalus himself would have a copy of the map, after all, so the chances that this one phone would have anything were one out of four. At least he thought their team consisted of four.

Carter moved around the site some more until he found another backpack, this one simply lying on the ground on a light snow drift. They must have been in a hurry to unload and get the operations set up, he thought. He rummaged through this pack, which he noted was a top name brand, moderately used. He felt something flat and slim right away and removed it to reveal an iPad. Again, it could have useful info on it, but it was likely passworded. He kept looking through the pack. He recognized a slim compartment on the back of the pack as being for firearm concealed carry, and paused. It felt like something was in there…he unzipped it and pulled out a 1911 pistol. Checking the magazine, he saw that it was full.

Carter got up from his kneeling position and checked his surroundings as he popped the magazine back in. This was an interesting turn of events, he thought. But now he had a major decision to face. He saw three options: One, keep it. Could come in handy if they were discovered by Treasure, Inc. He could discard it once they got near the bottom of the mountain so as not to risk being seen with it in town and detained. Two, hide it, toss it down the mountain into a snow bank so that Daedalus—he was pretty sure that's whose pack this was—would never find it. Or three, just put it back like nothing ever happened.

He heard footsteps treading lightly and reflexively raised the loaded gun, pointing it in that general direction, but then lowered it when he saw that it was Jayden. Carter lowered the gun and saw Jayden's gaze travel right to it.

"Bonus!" he said in an exaggerated whisper. "The map?"

Carter shook his head. "Not yet."

"You gonna keep it? I think you should keep it, and find one for me if you can. Toss theirs." Carter nodded. "I'm inclined to agree. What are they up to down there?"

"That's what I came to tell you while I have a little time. Three out of four of them just went for a dive in the lake!"

"Dive?" Carter was confused. "You mean, like they took a swim?"

"No, SCUBA dive! They dragged a bunch of tanks down there with those ropes, used a chainsaw to cut an opening in the ice, and now three of them are underwater."

Carter pondered this for a moment. "Wow. And what's the fourth guy doing?"

Jayden glanced back to the edge of the slope as if that man might appear at any moment. "He's the posted lookout, I guess. When I left my post he was just standing on the shore where the divers entered, and looking around a bit, but not too much. He never looked up in my direction."

"All right. Sounds like I have some time to work with. You re-take your post." He turned back to the pack and began unzipping one of the small "admin pouches" on the front, which usually contained smaller non-weapon or survival items such as flashlights, documentation, keys, perhaps a multitool, pens, notepads, extra batteries and the like. This compartment contained a pair of fleece gloves and a ski mask, as well as a small penlight and a candy bar. He continued to rummage through the backpack, tossing items obviously not of interest out of the pack, then putting them back in after the space they had occupied had been "cleared." He was about to declare the entire pack as having been searched when he shoved some items of clothing back down into the bottom of the main compartment—and felt it shift. He thought maybe it had a zipper or tie on the bottom that had come undone to allow the pack to be accessed from both ends, but a quick glance at the outer bottom of the pack told him this was not the case. Which left only one explanation.

The backpack had a false bottom!

Carter snaked his fingers down inside the pack and felt for the edges of it. He was able to slip a finger against the side and then pry it up, removing the black canvas-covered piece of fiberboard from the pack. His heart rate sped up as he felt a layer of thin plastic at the very bottom—the true bottom—of the bag. He pulled the item out and immediately held his breath as he recognized the map he and Jayden had so painstakingly brought up from the *Titanic*. It had been placed inside clear plastic cover to protect it somewhat against the rigors of travel.

Carter eyed the document ravenously, drinking in its details as if it could be snatched away from him again at any moment. Which is not far from the truth, he thought, taking his phone from his pocket and powering it on in order to use the camera. He placed the map on the ground and snapped off a few close-up photographs of it. After checking to see that the resulting images were in fact readable, he then powered his phone off and pocketed it.

He glanced over toward the edge of the slope and saw Jayden hunched down low, monitoring the lake divers, his back to him. Carter put the rest of the items back in the backpack, and did his best to organize it the way it was, minus the gun and the map, of course, and then to leave the pack in the same position on the snow-packed ground as he had found it. He had a major decision to make now: should he steal the original map back from Daedalus or put it back in his pack so that he never knew they were here. If he put the map back, though, he'd really need to put the gun back, too. Unless….perhaps he would blame the missing items on one of his own expedition mates and think they did it? That could cause a nice row between them, Carter mused. But on the other hand, the map itself was valuable and technically belonged to his client. He saw himself as duty-bound to bring it to her.

There was something else, too, he was aware as he stood. The lake. What was down there? Treasure, Inc. had obviously gone to great lengths to probe its depths, with an extensive, tricky dive operation. They must have either seen something compelling down there or else the map told them where to look…

The map! He held it up again and began to study it, but then realized he hadn't even told Jayden the news yet. He should let him know, before—*but wait, what's that?* His gaze bored into the map where a solid black "X" seemed to indicate something important. Literally an X-marks-the-spot? Carter wondered. He mentally pictured the satellite photos and modern maps of the Mt. Ararat region he had briefly perused before beginning the trek. As far as he could tell from his hurried examination of the map, which indicated clearly the mountains of Ararat, though not the country of Turkey or any nation by name, it could be their current location. So this map is what led them here, Carter thought. And so close to the known ark site. Then he had the same thought process as Daedalus had, that maybe the old map pointed to the timber wreckage that had been discovered in the latter 20th century...

But wait, what's this? It happened by accident, a trick of the light. Carter was holding the map with two hands, turning to orient it to the sunlight that was filtering through a stand of sparsely-leaved trees, when a shaft of light reflected off of a small pool of melted snow directly beneath the map. The effect was to light the map from beneath, which revealed faint lines he hadn't noticed before. They led from the X to another part of the map. To make sure he wasn't imagining things, Carter stepped away from the reflecting light, still eyeing the map. No more lines. He then turned away from the sunlight filtering through the trees, viewing the map in solid shade, and still no lines appeared. Then he positioned the map back over the light reflecting up from the ground, and there they were again: hidden lines on the map revealed.

Carter furrowed his brow as he inspected the map further. One interesting thing about it was that it was oriented vertically rather than horizontally, as most maps are. By tracing the lines from where they were— at the X—to where they went...which seemed to be...some part of Africa?...his finger went from the top down towards the bottom of the map. And yet, there was no X or similar marking there. Again, he moved the map so that it was not bottom lit, and scrutinized it again. The X was definitely there, but the lines were gone, and the spot to which they led— somewhere in east Africa, Carter guessed—was otherwise unmarked or designated in any special way. *Or was it?*

Eyeing the map even more closely while a few birds chirped and squawked around him in the otherwise quiet mountain ecosystem, Carter could see that the region of east Africa where the invisible lines led was extremely detailed. He hadn't noticed it before, but the Ararat region of the map had a similar level of pronounced detail, while the rest of the map, depicting part of Europe, the Middle East, some of Asia and almost all of Africa, had reasonable detailing but not as much as those two areas. That in itself was a clue of sorts, wasn't it, Carter reasoned.

He wondered if Daedalus and his team had picked up on that yet. No doubt he had archaeological and antiquities experts inspecting and analyzing copies of the map at this very moment to try and elucidate its secrets. Ah, but that was his mistake, Carter now realized. For no digital copy or even physical reproduction or facsimile of any kind would be able to duplicate the hidden physical content in this document. That was Daedalus' mistake, his fatal flaw, if you will, Carter thought. He kept the best of everything for himself, relying only upon himself, thinking that others could do what they needed to with less.

And that will be your downfall, Daedalus, Carter decided. But the puzzle the map presented tugged at his intellect. Why the two parts? The X—that was clear enough. But why the lines that led to Africa? Was it saying the ark was in Africa? Was Daedalus and his team diving the lake for nothing?

His thought train was interrupted by a yell from far below, and then, much closer, he heard Jayden's footfalls, running toward him.

CHAPTER 21

"Are they done with the dive already?" Carter asked Jayden as he came running up.

"Yeah! They got something out of the water—a timber, it looks like. Small enough for one person to carry."

"Probably for analysis."

"Yeah, but listen: the lookout guy is running up here right now! They've got the log on shore and they're rigging it up to the rope system they set up, but I guess something needs to be done up here to pull it up, so he's on his way." Jayden now noticed the map in Carter's hands.

"Is that...?

"Yes, I found it in Daedalus' pack there."

"Holy crap! That's the map, we got it back!"

Carter glanced toward the slope where the team could be heard preparing to climb back up from the lake. "For now, anyway."

"We've got to get out of here. Even with one gun, it's still two against four and who knows what other tricks Daedalus has up his long, dirty sleeves. But wait—is that it?" He looked back toward the lake. "Is that where it says Noah's Ark is?"

Carter glanced at the map. "I think so, but it's more complicated than that. I'll tell you later. But you said they brought up a timber?"

"Yeah, two of them, actually, but they're just loading one of them right now."

Carter looked down at the map.

"So is this it—this is Noah's Ark?" Jayden asked again. Carter had no choice but to explain about the hidden lines leading to east Africa, even though time was extremely short. Jayden had to know what was going on.

"Africa?" Jayden pondered. "But there's no mention of what's there?"

"Not a single notation, other than it looks like the region is more detailed than usual. We'll have to check it out in more detail when we have time."

"Which is not now," Jayden agreed. "Should we hightail it out of here?"

Carter considered this for a moment while they listened to the sounds of the expedition beginning to ascend the slope.

"I think we should take a page from Treasure Inc.'s own book, and let them do the dirty work of finding and bringing up the artifact…"

"Then we take it?" Jayden guessed. "But how?"

"I don't know, but what would you rather do, grab a piece of the timbers they already brought up, or come back again with SCUBA gear, hope they don't find out what we're up to…"

"I see your point, but Carter, c'mon! There's no way they won't see us."

"Let's take a look. We should see where they are now, anyway."

They jogged back over to the slope, sliding into crouch positions as they neared the edge. The rope and pulley system was in motion now. Carter raised his head just enough to be able to see down to the lake, to see if one or both logs was coming up yet, but he was stunned and shocked to see the lookout man nearly three-quarters of the way to them.

He shrunk back down, shivering with the sudden, massive jolt of adrenaline at almost being seen.

"The rest of the team is on the way up too," Jayden said, also having seen the lookout.

"We have to do something," Carter said, looking around. "We need to not be seen, but we also need those logs."

"We could leave and come back with our own dive gear and dive in peace," Jayden suggested. But Carter shook his head.

"What, and risk our every move being tracked, and if Treasure, Inc. doesn't kill us when we're sleeping, the Turkish government will throw us prison for not obtaining a permit? We just need a small sample of what they already brought up. Break off a chip, and then we're out of here."

"How the hell are we going to do that?" Jayden hissed. He sounded uncharacteristically strained. "That guy is almost to us, and the rest of them are not far behind!"

Carter's gaze was already roving around their immediate surroundings. He spotted a SCUBA rig at the very top of the drop-off to the lake, beneath the rope rig. Then he belly-crawled to the edge and looked down. A smile crept across his face as he looked back to Jayden and waved him over. "I have an idea."

"Uh-oh."

"Hey, sometimes they work."

"No, I mean uh-oh, my pack is over there." He pointed to a spot about a hundred feet away, where his backpack lay out in the open on a rock.

"Get it!" Carter whispered. "Then come back here and we should be ready."

Jayden didn't ask for details, just backed up and set himself into motion to go get his backpack.

Carter slinked forward on the ground to a spare SCUBA tank that was already rigged with a regulator, complete with "octopus" or second breathing mouthpiece in case of emergencies where the primary regulator failed. He looked down the lake slope and saw the lookout thankfully facing the other way down toward the lake, watching his three dive team members hook one of the timbers up to the pulley and rope system. He shouted something down to them in Greek, while pointing up to the top of the pulley system that Carter now lay directly underneath. He didn't think he'd been seen, but that the non-diver of the group who was almost to the top of the lake basin was telling his team that he was going to operate the pulley system to pull up the logs, Carter guessed. He sure hoped so, anyway.

He knew the next minute or so was critical to the success of his hastily formed plan. He reached out and swiped an arm around the SCUBA tank, knocking it over. Then he dragged it toward him by the regulator hose. He knew this wasn't a good thing to do as it could possibly break the regulator or dislodge the seal where the regulator attaches to the tank's valve. With seconds to act, he had to take that chance; there was no time to employ proper tank carry methods. He also had to try and be as quiet as possible with the Treasure, Inc. man almost to the top of the lake basin, but hopefully his own footsteps and labored breathing as he hiked up the steep grade, near-vertical at the top, would prevent him from noticing the dragging noise.

Carter dragged the tank until it was close enough to him to get his hand around the K-valve and then pull it by that. When he had it next to his body he looked back down the slope from his prone position, hunched into a copse of weed-like brambles. *What if he comes straight up this way?* The drop-off at the lip of the lake basin was steep here, almost vertical for about six feet, so Carter had assumed he'd take a different way up. But he was almost to it and still heading straight for it. *What if they'd rigged a rope ladder or something like that?* But then he heard footsteps leading away from him, out of sight and below, and he knew that the lookout was going to walk laterally along the lip of the lake basin for some distance, probably until he was beneath the rope rig, and then climb out.

Jayden jogged over, wearing his backpack with both straps on, and slid on the ground up to Carter, pulling himself along on his elbows to make sure he stayed low. Carter tapped him on the shoulder, mouthed the words, "He's right down there," and pointed toward the rope rig setup at the top of the slope. Jayden turned his head that way and nodded that he understood. Carter pointed down over the edge of the lip, meaning, *Let's go.* He started worming his way over there, belly on the ground, dragging the SCUBA tank with him.

Jayden tugged on his leg. The lookout was scrabbling up the final few feet of lip now, just beneath the rope rig.

Carter snapped his head around and repeated his gesture, pointing down below the lip. It was apparent to him that Jayden was confused. Why would they drop over the side into the lake basin when the other three Treasure, Inc. divers were about halfway up now, and would be able to see them. But Carter had a plan, and he had to trust that. He'd done it before and had lived to tell the tale.

But this was not looking good. The lookout man appeared up on the top of the slope, only about twenty feet to their right as they slid as silently as possible, while dragging a SCUB A rig, over the side of the precipice, sort of a cornice at the very top. In Carter's mind, this was the riskiest part of his whole plan. There was no cover to be found on this vertical section, and meanwhile the other three members of the dive team, including Daedalus himself, were about halfway up from the lake. Carter could see them as a blurry rush as he fell down the cornice, dragged even faster by the weight of the SCUBA apparatus, Jayden close behind.

He also registered in that blurry rush his immediate objective. A comforting flash of white, comforting because he hoped it would be their cover. A thick snow bank that persisted in a groove or ravine all the way down to the lake. He hoped it was well-packed and wasn't only a superficial layer that would collapse too much on contact. But other aggregations of snow he'd seen, such as in the much larger ravine they'd worked their way up in order to reach the top of the slope where the rope rig was set up, had snow banks he'd walked though and found them to be tightly packed. The kind that you wouldn't want to fall into if they were very deep, because it was impossible to breathe inside them for long. People have been known to die of asphyxia after being covered in snow, not only children in collapsing snow forts, but also seasoned skiers after an avalanche where they survived the initial impact, but later suffocated because the snow wouldn't support their weight enough to reach the air, nor was it sparse enough to have sufficient air spaces.

Carter wasn't sure exactly how deep this snow bank was. It could be deeper than they would easily be able to get out of before they suffocated, he knew. But that's why he'd brought along the SCUBA rig. He dragged it into position now and tapped Jayden on the ankle to get his attention. Then he handed him the "octopus," the extra second stage regulator, or breathing mouthpiece, with an extra-long hose that was used in out-of-air emergencies to share air with another diver, or as a backup to the diver's primary regulator. If Jayden had questions, he wisely refrained from asking them as he shoved the octopus between his teeth and plowed straight ahead and down next to Carter into the snowbank. From this place of concealment, they would be hidden from line-of-sight to Daedalus and his associates.

Carter took his first breath beneath the snow. He hadn't had time to test the regulator. He tried to take a breath but nothing happened. Meanwhile, he and Jayden began sliding down the lake basin, deeper into the snow as they went. He tried pulling a breath again but with the same lack of results. He pictured the SCUBA rig standing there, already set up at the basin. Could it be an empty tank they'd already used and that's why it was up there? The thought chilled him to the bone more thoroughly than did the snow that surrounded him. He stuck his feet down and could feel the rocky surface. It was there within reach, but he and Jayden were bouncing along too fast to be able to get purchase long enough to stop in one place and assess the situation. Or possibly to break their heads through the surface of the snow to snatch a quick breath if need be, risk of being spotted aside.

He pulled the regulator out of his mouth and tried a test breath in the snow itself, using his hands to clear away a pocket of air right in front of his mouth. It didn't work. He got maybe the barest gulp of air, but that was followed by a slushee of ice down his throat that made him choke and cough as gravity jostled him along. He knew Jayden must be going through the same thing next to him, probably wondering why he had put them in this situation.

He forced his mind to think through the problem of why the tank wasn't delivering air rather than on the risks and hopelessness of their predicament. He went back to his previous line of reasoning on the matter: *what if the tank he'd grabbed was used and therefore empty?* But as an experienced diver he knew that it was highly unusual for a diver—especially an experienced one, as this group must be in order to successfully recover heavy objects from the bottom of a semi-frozen high altitude lake—to breathe a tank completely dry. Leaving a reserve was a cardinal rule imprinted into every diver from their Basic Certification class onward. When the air pressure gauge reads 500 PSI (out of an initial 3,000), it was definitely time to begin your ascent, sometimes closer to 1,000 PSI if it was a deep dive or if a decompression stop was needed to avoid the dreaded "bends."

The answer hit him with blinding suddenness. *Of course!* He flashed on snagging the tank up under the pulley rig. In his haste to get it, put it on and then get over the precipice without being detected, he'd neglected to do the most basic of SCUBA pre-dive tasks: turn the air on! A simple turn of the K-valve—the black knob at the top of the tank to which the regulator was attached—was something he hadn't done. If the valve was already open, well then. It was game over. He knew that. But at least they now had a real chance.

He tried to reach back behind his head for the valve as he tumbled down the snowy chute. Being able to do this underwater was a skill that was practiced in SCUBA classes. Doing it while tumbling down a snowy whiteout was another matter altogether. He brought his right arm up and back behind his head, where the valve was. His arm nearly broke when the ground beneath him dropped out and he flipped over, landing on his bent elbow that he was holding behind his head. He thought he may have at least dislocated his shoulder. He expelled most of his last remaining breath with another hard impact where his own knee doubled up and rammed him in the solar plexus, knocking the wind right out of him. As soon as he recovered from that, he started to try again. He reached out for the valve—and to his surprise—brushed across Jayden's hand already on it. He tried to take a breath, expecting to be met with empty resistance, but instead was pleasantly surprised with the familiar metallic-tinged pull of air through a regulator.

He immediately reached out and tapped on Jayden's arm. There was no way they could actually see one another in the zero visibility whiteout soup, but he wanted to let him know somehow that things had changed, he was breathing, and Jayden should be, too. They continued their slide down the slushy, snowy channel. He wished he had a facemask on, that would keep the snow out of his eyes and maybe even help him to see a little bit, but he knew that he was lucky to have made it this far. The closer to the bottom they got, the less steep the incline became, so that their speed and tumbling gradually decreased the further they went along. A couple of times Carter could see enough light peeking through the snow over their heads that he thought maybe they would be exposed, but it never actually happened. They remained concealed beneath the snowpack as they effectively SCUBA-dived through the snow down the side of the lake basin. *SCUBA diving through snow!* Carter almost had to suppress a laugh through his mouthpiece even though he knew they were far from out of the woods yet.

After an indeterminate period of time during which they were tossed about like ragdolls on a wagon train, Carter and Jayden came to rest with a painful thud against a cluster of rocks. The white shroud of snow still covered them completely. Carter listened for signs of any activity around them but could hear nothing save the raspy draws of air through their regulators. He tried push some snow out of the way of his face, but again, it simply collapsed back into place around him. He felt for the SCUBA rig's gauge console so that he could see how much air remained in the tank. He felt the rubber hose attached to the gauge, traced it down to the console, and brought it all the way up to his eyes. Plenty of air remaining, even after two of them had been breathing on it and exerting themselves heavily. This was because their depth was zero, he knew, which is what the depth gauge read.

It was time to see where they had ended up. Carter tapped Jayden on the arm and began shifting his body to get into a standing position. He felt Jayden begin to do the same next to him, both still breathing from the rig. He could hear nothing from the outside world. When he felt like he had a secure stance on the uneven, but no longer steep, ground, Carter flexed his knees and slowly rose until his head broke through the snow.

CHAPTER 22

The first thing that met Carter's gaze was the shimmering, blue surface of the lake. They had slid, tumbled and SCUBA-dived all the way down to the body of water through the snow. Jayden's head of black hair popped up next to Carter as he looked around for signs of Daedalus and his divers. He saw none of them down here by the lake, and looking up at the slope where the rope and pulley rig was set up, he found he could not see anyone there, either. They were all up at the camp site, he supposed.

After scanning their surroundings himself, Jayden shot Carter a wide-eyed stare. "I guess we're certified snow divers now! Remind me to let the Professional Association of Diving Instructors know that I earned my specialty badge." He was grinning from ear to ear.

Carter could only shake his head in wonderment. He slowly flexed all of his limbs and joints, feeling for anything that might be broken. Although he was certain he'd be black and blue all over tomorrow, it seemed like he was still able to move unhindered, though not without pain in most joints. Jayden went through the same process, and with the same results. Now that they were no longer moving, both shivered from their time immersed in the snow. Carter looked for a good spot to move to, and spotted a stand of brush closer to the water's edge, not too far away. He got no arguments from Jayden about leaving their place of powdery concealment.

After a last glance up top to make sure they were unobserved, the two treasure seekers emerged from the snowbank. They ran across the rocky, snow-spotted ground to the vegetation, and ensconced themselves inside it. They found this to be an ideal hiding spot since it was dry and offered concealment, but also allowed them to peek out at both the lake as well as up at the slope and pulley system.

"I can see the timber," Carter pointed through the brush to a dark brown, almost black log about four feet long and at least a foot in diameter. Jayden nodded while eyeing the top of the slope.

"They've got the other one up there already so it won't be long before they come back for this one. We should make our move."

Carter felt for the dive knife he had strapped to the inside of his left calf in preparation for the snow dive, but was appalled to feel only smooth pant leg. When he looked down at it, he saw that the knife and sheath were gone, no doubt ripped away during the tumultuous ride down here. He supposed he shouldn't complain since he still had his backpack on, although one of the straps had broken. He wished he would have put the knife inside the pack, but couldn't have known how bad the trip down would be.

"My knife is gone, do you have one?"

"Uh-oh." Jayden swatted at his back. "I just realized my entire pack is gone. I was so happy to be alive I didn't even notice!" He and Carter peered out of the brambles to see if it was visible on the ground. That would not be good as it would give away their presence. But it was nowhere to be seen.

"Look on the bright side. You'll be a lot lighter on your feet now," Carter said.

"Yeah, but I had my best knife in there, my Benchmade folder." Jayden reached a hand into his front jeans pocket and pulled out a Swiss Army Knife. "This is all I've got. Had it since my Boy Scout days, since my Grandfather gave it to me. But you know what they say. The best knife or tool is the one you actually have with you when you need it."

Carter nodded. "True that. It'll have to do. We don't need a big chunk of it, anyway, just enough of a sample to be able to do lab work on it to date it and verify its composition."

"Oh good, because I thought we were going to lug that whole log down off of Mt. Ararat like those guys are."

Carter suppressed a laugh. "Those guys are planning to lug *two* of them off the mountain."

"Coast looks clear up there," Jayden said, eyeing the top of the slope. "Let's do this."

They parted the foliage and then bolted across the open space to the salvaged timber, careful not to turn an ankle among the uneven cobblestones and snow pockets. The timber was situated such that it lay only a few feet from the water's edge, roughly parallel to shore. They walked around it and hunkered down so that its bulk mostly shielded them from view if anyone from up top were to glance down at it.

Jayden took out his Swiss Army Knife and went to work on removing a sample from the timber. He found the log to be remarkably solid for a piece of wood that had been waterlogged for who knows how long, probably about five thousand years, if it was in fact from the days of Noah's Ark. It wasn't waterlogged at all. It would take some doing for Jayden to whittle it apart, not a quick process with such a small tool, so while he worked on the timber sample, Carter turned to his pack, now the only stash of gear that the two of them had in this vast wilderness area while being confronted by a hostile group. Except for the broken strap, which meant that he would have to sling it over one shoulder like a college student for the rest of their trek, it appeared to be intact. It was soaking wet on the outside from the snow, but the material was heavy denier and he thought the inside would be mostly dry. The map was what he worried about the most, but it was in a plastic bag. Still, what if the bag had ruptured during all the jostling?

He glanced up at the slope while Jayden whittled away at the log, and then after finding it clear, he unzipped the pack and took out the map. Still in its sealed plastic bag and none the worse for wear. He put it back in the bag and then stowed it away in his pack. He briefly checked his other gear and found it all to have survived the ordeal and be still serviceable.

Feeling satisfied with his inventory management, Carter glanced back up to the rope and pulley system at the top of the slope and saw a man standing there.

#

"We got what we came for. Let's get that other timber and prepare to move out," Daedalus called out to his expedition team as he walked toward his pack. He was pleased with the dive, and his mind was still flooded with what he had seen at depth in the lake. Noah's Ark. There can be no doubt! His team had collected two solid timbers that had been loose in a pile on the bottom inside the large wooden boat shape. He'd taken a lot of high definition video and now wanted to secure the invaluable footage by placing the memory card safely inside its case in his pack.

While the other two divers broke down their SCUBA equipment, the lookout man went to retrieve the SCUBA rig that had been on standby in case it was needed, but ended up going unused.

"You got it," he called out to his boss, feeling satisfied that things were going well. He hoped to be promoted within the organization following this most important expedition. But when he reached the rope and pulley rig, he looked around but didn't see the extra tank. He leaned over the edge of the slope and eyeballed the steep terrain on the way down to the lake to see if it had somehow fallen over the side, but didn't see it. Again he searched the camp area briefly without success. The tank must have been knocked over the side when the first timber was hauled up on the pulley rig, he thought. Deciding they would probably find it when they went back down to haul up the second timber, he began to focus on that instead. Besides, he reasoned, it would be a bitch as it is transporting those two timbers all the way down the mountain. If they couldn't find the SCUBA rig, it was just one less thing to carry. As long as it wasn't found anytime soon by Turkish authorities— that was the only reason Daedalus would care about it. They didn't want to give away the location of Noah's Ark, after all, or be hounded after more than they already were for looting historical artifacts.

The lookout man turned to the pulley system and began readying it for the next timber haul. He re-rigged the harness for the timber and activated the pulley to send it back down to the lake shore. As he looked down the rope line to make sure it was operating smoothly, his vision registered an anomaly down on the lake shore—something that hadn't been there before. Was that the missing SCUBA rig? He reached for a pair of binoculars in his jacket in order to investigate.

Meanwhile, Daedalus reached his backpack and opened it to put the camera memory card inside it. He noticed right away that something was off: the zipper pulls were in different positions than how he normally left them. He'd had the same pack for a while now and was very familiar with it. He always left the different zipper pulls for each compartment in the same position, which he found made it easier to keep track of which compartment they opened. So to see them set differently made him wonder if someone other than him had gotten into his pack. He quickly turned around to see if any of his team was observing him, but the other three men were going about their business of breaking down the dive gear and readying the harness for the remaining timber.

Opening his pack, he went immediately to where he'd stashed the map, in a semi-hidden zippered compartment inside the main compartment, so as to be both well-hidden and protected deep inside the pack. He felt the breath leave his body.

The map! Gone!

He had to get down on his knees or risk falling over. He told himself to make certain he hadn't somehow misplaced it inside the pack—it had a lot of compartments, after all, and at first he had occasionally "lost" things inside it after not being able to remember which section of the pack he'd put them in. But no, this was different. He was absolutely positive he'd put that map right there. Nothing else inside the pack seemed to be out of place. Only the—*wait a minute.* His hands went to the concealed carry firearm compartment and immediately found it to be feel distressingly flat.

My pistol! Gone. Daedalus seethed, for this brazen theft meant one of two things. Either he had a very serious traitor in his own expedition, or the Omega Team was proving itself more effective than he would have given them credit for. He stood up from his ransacked pack and was about to approach the nearest of his expedition mates when the lookout man called his name, over by the rope and pulley rig on the edge of the slope.

#

"Almost got it." Jayden was cutting away on the timber with his Swiss army knife. No sooner did he complete his sentence than a gunshot echoed into the lake basin and a bullet thudded into the log, sending a shower of splinters up into his face. He and Carter immediately lay prone behind the log, waiting to see if more gunfire was coming. Another shot rang out and a bullet thudded into the ground near Jayden's feet.

"Do you have the sample?" Carter asked. "And not a piece with lead in it."

"Almost."

"I guess I don't need to tell you to hurry up." As if to underscore his point, another round embedded itself into the old timber, splintering more of it off.

Jayden reached his hand up holding the knife and stuck it into the section of wood he'd been working on. He pried at the lumber for a few seconds while they heard shouts from the men above.

"They're mobilizing to come down here," Carter said, an edge to his voice. "We've got to go."

"Got it!" Jayden pulled his hand back down with a foot-long sliver of wood just as bullet smacked into the log where his hand had been. Carter had been mulling over their options while Jayden was cutting the sample free. Climbing back up through the snow was not an option—the tank air would probably run dry even if they could climb their way up, which he seriously doubted. Not only that, but now that they were getting shot at, going to the camp would be like entering the dragon's lair. Obviously, they had learned that map and gun were missing.

Carter had removed Daedalus' gun from his pack while waiting for Jayden. It was loaded with a full magazine. He eyed the escape route he had identified as giving them the most chance of success. The opposite shore of the lake from where they had come out of the snow featured a gentler incline up to the main mountain slope. It lay a decent distance away from the Treasure, Inc. camp, although he was sure that Daedalus would be breaking camp now that he had his timber samples (one of them, anyway), and that the map had been discovered missing. Carter was hoping that having discovered the ark, if that's what this was, would make him care less about no longer having the map. But that didn't seem to be the case, and he knew that even if he didn't care about the map, Daedalus preferred that he and Jayden disappeared off the face of the Earth rather than having people walking around who knew where the Noah's Ark find was.

This was life or death, Carter knew. And life was up that slope. It didn't have much snow, but it had enough vegetation to offer some concealment for part of the way.

"That way." Carter cocked his head toward the opposite slope. He didn't want to point and risk telegraphing their plans to their adversaries, who could be observing them with binoculars. "You start running, I'll provide cover." He waggled the pistol. Jayden nodded and moved to a crouching position from which he could spring into a sprint like a track runner.

"Go!" Carter fired off a shot at a man visible beneath the pulley system. It was an accident, but he smiled in satisfaction nonetheless as he watched the structure fall over as his bullet severed the rope, a very lucky shot. Jayden was springing and bounding across the open shore of the lake, zigging and zagging to make an erratic course while still moving very fast. Carter blasted off two more rounds, aiming at the same general area even though he could no longer see any human targets. They had wisely moved behind cover, he decided, since he didn't register any movement coming down the slope. Yet he knew they probably would mount an offensive soon when they saw their foes absconding with the map.

Carter maintained his post at the timber until he saw Jayden disappear into a copse of scrubby reeds at the lake's edge, beyond which the basin sloped upward. Firing a last shot up at the downed pulley rig, he dashed across the open space as Jayden had done. He was nearly to the same vegetation Jayden had disappeared into when he saw the dirt kick up in front of him and felt something sharp slice his right cheek. He didn't stop moving, and a few seconds later had made the plant cover where he dove to the ground and crawled forward, looking for Jayden.

"Over here!" he heard his friend snarl. Carter felt his cheek and his fingers came away warm and sticky. He figured he'd been hit with a fragmented piece of rock the bullet had struck when it hit the ground in front of him. Close call. It seemed like the longer he chased after the ark, the closer and more frequent those calls got. *Was it really worth it?* He knew he had done his job and then some. He could easily have reported back to the client what had happened on the *Titanic* site and walked away on good terms, with the job no doubt satisfactorily completed. But that would be taking the easy way out, and that's not what Carter Hunt did. Noah's Ark, if it was real, and certainly the map salvaged from the *Titanic*, belonged in the public eye for all to see, not under the auspices of some private collector like Daedalus to sell to the highest bidder, never to be seen again. No, that was simply unacceptable if he had anything to say about it.

Carter resolved to see this assignment through as he belly-crawled through the brush toward Jayden's voice. He heard and felt another bullet smack into the ground somewhere off to his right, but it was pretty far away and it was clear that they were shooting blind into the vegetation. Still, blind or not, being shot at was not something to take lightly, and so Carter picked up his wormy pace, slithering along even faster.

"This way!" Jayden called out to him through the tall reeds just as Carter saw him, higher up and to the left. He low-crawled the rest of the way to him, careful not to bend the reeds too much and give away their position. Carter pushed his way through. A little bit farther on and the ground started to slope up so that it was no longer flat, but not as steep as the path they'd taken on the way down.

They reached the edge of the reeds where there was a small clearing, maybe twenty feet across to where the next stand of vegetation began. From their current position they could not see through the plants that concealed them to monitor what was happening at Daedalus' camp.

"How you holding up?" Jayden asked Carter, noting the blood on his face and Daedalus' gun still in his hand. "We're going to have to move really quick across the open space here, but if we can get across that, we've got pretty solid vegetation cover most of the way up."

"I'm ready. As soon as we think it's clear." Carter dared to stick his head out of the reeds and look to the right. "Can't see around this bush."

"You want to both go at once or one at a time?"

"I think both at once, because if we go one a time, they could see the first one with not enough time to shoot, but then have a heads up on where to aim by the time the next guy goes."

"Okay, so I'll go first!" Jayden grinned, his infectious humor an attempt at lightening the mood in what was otherwise a serious situation for them. Being pursued by killers, lightly wounded, with a bare minimum of gear between the two of them in a snow-covered mountain wilderness, sometimes called for a mood-lifter.

"Let's both go at once, fast as we can, straight shot, no zig-zagging. Should take less than five seconds."

"Yeah but remember, we don't want to go smashing into the bushes on the other side, because if the tops of them move too much, they might see it."

"Right. Ease in gently."

"That's what she s—"

"Jayden, seriously. Is there ever a time—never mind. Let's do this." He and Jayden crept to the very edge of the reeds and then listened for any sign of their pursuers. A steady wind began to blow, making it more difficult to hear over the rustling reeds, but also making their own movements less noticeable. Hearing no human activity, Carter gave a countdown from three. On *one*, they raced across the small clearing to the scrubby vegetation on the other side, both of them reaching it at the same moment. Carter planted a foot down hard right before reaching the tall plants, turned himself sideways, and sort of fell into the plant growth on his side, landing on the ground in between woody stalks. Jayden performed a different set of maneuvers that were equally as effective, and in a minute the two of them were on their feet, able to stand at only a slight stoop while still being surrounded by plant life.

Jayden pointed up and to their left. "I eyeballed it just before we went in. That's our course."

Carter unslung the remaining strap off his pack and set it on the ground. "Hold on. I have something that'll help." He dug around in the pack for a few seconds. "Things got a little jostled around in here, but here it is…"

"A little?" Jayden said. "More like put to the shake test."

Carter pulled out a simple plastic compass. He opted for plastic because of its light weight compared to metal, with the durability not all that far behind. "Let's take an actual bearing. We can't afford to head in the wrong direction. We need to get out of this engagement zone ASAP."

"Couldn't agree more," Jayden concurred. Carter took a compass heading and then pocketed the instrument. Then they set out in that direction, walking as fast as possible though the plants without bending them too much so as to draw attention. They kept up a steady pace but would stop periodically for a few seconds at a time to listen. On one of these stops, Carter could barely make out voices, too faint to tell what was going on or where they were coming from. Somehow, he doubted Daedalus would be just sitting around, though. Something told him they should keep moving, that they needed to get back to town in Turkey and leave the country as soon as possible.

But first they had to get off this holy mountain.

CHAPTER 23

Jayden was first to reach the lip of the lake basin, which was windswept and barren compared to the lake below. Carter, encumbered by the backpack and not willing to take the gun out of his right hand, was a little behind him. Again, they faced a situation where they had reached the edge of their concealment and now faced an open run. With no signs of their pursuers, they scrambled up the open face with its thin layer of snow. It led to a smooth, wide mountain slope, similar to the one on the other side. From this vantage point they could look out across the entire lake basin to the Treasure, Inc. camp on the other side. Both men dropped to a prone position. Carter handed Jayden the gun while he removed the small pair of binoculars from his pack.

He focused in on the destroyed rope pulley station. Nobody there. He scanned the surrounding camp area, but also saw not only no people, but no sign of them at all—no backpacks, tents, gear, anything. It was as if they had already broken down the site and moved out. While Carter watched through the optics, Jayden kept a naked eye out while holding the pistol, monitoring their nearby surroundings.

"They're coming up." His voice was so calm that it belied the import of the words.

"What?" Carter looked away from his binoculars, where'd been scoping the far side of the lake basin, near the snow tunnel to see if he could detect traces of their passage. He could not.

"Where?"

Jayden pointed down at a sharp angle.

"Whoa!" Carter didn't know what he had been expecting—some sort of tactical approach, he guessed. This might involve Daedalus splitting his team member into two squads of two, perhaps, or even retreating back to town to resupply and come back with more technology with which to track them down, maybe even a helicopter. What he was not expecting was for all four of them to have beelined single file down to the lake basin, and all the way across the bottom of it to climb the far slope at the top of which Carter and Jayden now lay. He eyed them carefully and noticed they carried minimal gear.

"They must have hidden their campsite gear up top, carried it somewhere off site, before moving out to find us."

"Well, I give them an A for effort," Jayden said as he turned to look back in the other direction, plotting a potential egress route. "But I don't want to do it in person. Let's blow this popsicle stand, shall we?"

Carter stuffed his binoculars back into his pack. "Where to? See any good routes?" He eyeballed the direction Carter had just looked in.

"We're just going to have to go that way and wing it."

They could hear the signs of human passage below, as Daedalus and his men trekked their way up the slope. The efficiency with which they had moved this far this fast was frightening, and so Carter and Jayden lit out onto the broad slope, where hopefully they would have sufficient space in which to get lost. The area was a broad one once again, no longer a confined lake basin.

"If we get far enough out in front of them," Carter said as they started to walk, softly so as not to give away their position, "we can break into a run and then hopefully get far enough away where they won't be able to tell which way we went."

"Try not to leave footprints or bend the tall grass," Jayden said, stepping around a stand of scrub brush as he looked back to see if he could spot their pursuers. Not yet.

Looking ahead, Carter saw only a wide open area sloping gently up, with a few plants over two feet high that struggled to eke out an existence between small boulders and rocks amidst a patchy crust of snow. Once they got farther up the slope....

"I don't see how we're going to be safe up here," Carter said, slowing down. "Once they get to where we are, they'll be able to see us, even if we're all the way up there." He pointed far up the gentle slope, to where the mountain leveled off for some distance before the much steeper peak began its majestic rise.

"Got to make the best of it," Jayden said.

Carter looked around for some way to set a booby-trap, or to build an impromptu shelter of some sort—anything to temporarily buy them a little more time. But he could see or think of nothing constructive, and he recognized the beginnings of panic beginning to wrap around the edges of his mind. A decent amount of his military training, and he knew that of the SEALs, of which Jayden had been one, dealt with how to recognize and forestall panic. It seemed just as he was about to come up with something, the wind would blow stronger and ruffle his hair in some distracting way, or knock a small stick into him or some trivial thing that normally he could ignore.

"Let's go this way," Jayden suggested, pointing out a course that was parallel, around the broad mountain face, rather than straight up it. "Wind's blowing with us if we go this way, we'll go a little faster."

Carter knew they needed every edge they could get. He could hear the Treasure, Inc. killers forcing their way through the uppermost basin foliage now. They were reasonably quiet for four men moving quickly through the brush, but not Navy SEAL silent as Carter and Jayden had been. But now that no longer mattered. They knew they were here, and it had come down to a footrace. A race with the wind, Jayden was telling him. Carter tried adjusting his pack to balance it as best he could with only one remaining strap for the run ahead, and that's when he thought of it.

The wind! It was really howling now, exposed on the open face like this, and he thought he knew how to take advantage of it. He flung his pack back on the ground and knelt to open it. "Jayden, I need you to cover me while I set something up."

Jayden looked wide-eyed at his friend. "Now's not the time for experimental stuff, Carter. I can see the first guy coming up now." He lined the gun sight up and stared down it at the oncoming foe.

"One minute…"

"Are you kidding, me? They'll be here by then. What've you got?"

Carter didn't answer with words, but removed their tent's nylon ground cover from the pack. He unfolded it rapidly, spreading it out to its full length. "Need you to stand on one end to hold it down," he told Jayden, who begrudgingly did as he was asked.

"This thing doesn't exactly blend in with the ground, Carter, if your plan is to hide under it," Jayden said, frowning at the dark green tarp, which contrasted sharply against the white snow and light brown rocks and soil.

"Bear with me while I get this going…." They heard voices now, able to recognize the Greek language. Carter unspooled a length of rope and threaded one end through one of the grommets on the ground cover.

"Bear with you?" Jayden's voice betrayed his exasperation now. "Carter, you're not giving a PowerPoint presentation at a conference, you know that? There are four armed men coming through those bushes to kill us right now."

Carter didn't look up from what he was doing with the ground tarp, but continued threading the rope through the grommets. "You still got that Swiss Army Knife handy?"

Jayden frowned while aiming the pistol toward the oncoming threat. The wind had picked up to the point it was impossible to tell if the plants were moving due to wind or because people were moving through them.

"Here. But that thing and one pistol against whatever they have, I'm guessing three pistols and—"

Carter made several quick cuts into the tarp with the knife and handed it back to Jayden. Then he threaded the rope through the new cuts he'd made. The entire assembly he'd just worked on almost blew away when he tried to shake it out and open it up. But he had it by both ends of the rope, which pulled it together sort of like a jellyfish bell.

And then the first gunshot rang out.

"Times up, Carter, what's our move?" Jayden answered the round with one of his own fired into the foliage, where the Treasure, Inc. team was just now emerging.

Carter tossed the nylon sheet up into the air and let the wind fill it out, expanding it to a full form that was constrained by the ropes Carter had woven into it. He held the trailing end of the rope while the tarp started to take off into the air.

"Go fly a kite! That's your response?" Jayden said angrily.

"Here, take this, wind it around your left hand so you can still shoot. Don't let go of it or you'll be left behind and there won't be anything I can do. Here it goes!"

Jayden knew from past experience that when Carter had a plan, it didn't always seem to make sense but that it was usually best to go with it. Now, facing a gun battle against three angry black market antiquities dealers who would prefer he had never existed, Jayden took the end of the rope and wrapped it around his left wrist a few times, then gripped the end with his left hand, so that he could let it unravel if he needed to but it couldn't accidentally slip out. Then he aimed the gun toward the oncoming adversaries while Carter finished grappling with his odd construction.

Carter tossed the material into the air as another Treasure, Inc. gun blast went off. This time the wind caught the expanded surface area of the contained tarpaulin and lifted Carter a little into the air, allowing the bullet to smash into the rock he had had his right foot on only a moment earlier.

"Whoa!" Jayden wasn't expecting the sudden acceleration as the wind filled the tarp and began pushing it along like a sail. Unlike sailing, though, he was being dragged along the ground, ankles bashing into raised boulders which he couldn't look out for since he was still aiming the gun at the oncoming pursuers. "We're sailing, Carter, but you forgot the boat, and the bikini babes and the margaritas. This cruise really leaves a lot to be desired!"

He fired a round as Daedalus came out of the bushes, the only one of his team wearing a woodland camo pattern jacket. "Smug jackass!" he yelled as he was dragged up the hill. It was uncomfortable going, but he had to admit that it was saving his life at this point, as they were moving along at a good clip, faster than a human could run on the uneven, sloped ground.

Whether Carter could control where they were going was another matter, but right now neither of them cared as long as they were being taken away from their assailants. Daedalus' crew shot more bullets at them, but they were out of range and landed harmlessly into the dirt behind them.

They were being blown in the same direction as the wind, which was sideways along the face of the mountain. But Carter found that by pulling the rope in his left hand (he had another in his right) that he could somewhat steer the jerry-rigged parachute. He pulled the 'chute down to the left and the wind filled it at an angle, blowing them slightly up slope as well as laterally. He faced the direction in which they travelled, while Jayden faced the rear so as to monitor and defend from their aggressors.

The wind kept up its blustery force, whipping them along the mountain while their pursuers fell more and more behind. Jayden would kick off the ground when he got solid footing, and this would temporarily increase their speed slightly while he was airborne. After a while Carter started doing it too, and when they were both airborne at the same time, their speed increased dramatically for those few seconds. Carter continued "steering" the parachute, and after a while they found that they had made their way significantly up the mountain. Jayden looked down on the Treasure, Inc. group, and saw them as small dots on the barren slope, hopelessly far away now. They could still see them with binoculars, but there was no way they could catch up.

And still they raced along the ground with the wind. Jayden even let out a little whoop, like a surfer catching an awesome wave, so caught up was he in the exhilaration of not just being alive, but of having fun doing it. But even as he was dragged up the face of the holy volcanic mountain, Carter couldn't help but think of the sacred document stashed away in the backpack that was still slung over one shoulder.

The hidden lines, the fact that it had led to a seemingly unknown artifact site with timbers that appeared at least superficially as though they could belong to a boat as old as the fabled Noah's Ark. It was all so heady, so enrapturing, that as he stumble-dragged along the ground, pushed by a fierce high-altitude wind, he considered that if he were to die, if a rogue round from Daedalus' gun were to find his skull, or if the winds became too unpredictable and he was carried aloft in the chute and dashed apart on the side of the mountain somewhere, that he would still be happy with his life and, indeed, with this Omega Team mission. He felt that he was doing what he was born to do and that calmed his demeanor, made his outlook more open and accepting of different possibilities and outcomes...

"Hey Carter, really you run a great parasailing operation, but I feel like I've more than got my money's worth at this point and I'd like to come down now, okay? Don't worry, you'll get my five stars on Yelp all the way!"

Carter bounced out of his introspective thoughts and scanned the mountain ahead. They had reached a plateau of sorts, snow and even ice-covered by the looks of it. The terrain changed here, and the mountain became to Carter's eyes more mountain-like and less giant sloping hill, which could describe much of Mount Ararat. But this section appeared to have an edge they were headed straight for that for all he knew could be a steep drop-off. He lacked confidence in his spur-of-the-moment constructed parasail that he would be able to stop them in time if he waited much longer so he pulled hard left on the cord to send them into a hard right turn, up the mountain. This took them further into the middle of the plateau, which was very rocky and spotted with ice patches.

Carter eyed the landscape up ahead and saw that it was pocked with large rock outcroppings, some of them as tall as he was, and made a decision.

"Okay Jayden, you're right, we've had enough fun for one day. On count of three I want you to let go of your rope, so start unwinding it off your wrist now, copy?"

"What?" Most of what Carter said had been lost to the formidable winds.

"On three, let go of the chute!" Carter bellowed as loud as he could in

Jayden's direction.

At this Jayden nodded with vigor, eyeing with apprehension a crag of rock coming up.

"One!...T—" An exhalation of air replaced the rest of the word as Carter was body-slammed into a boulder, but he continued the count. "Two! And, Three—release!"

Carter let go of his rope smoothly and tumbled away on a relatively level patch of icy ground. Jayden, who had to be a bit more careful, as he was still carrying the handgun, also let go of the rope without incident. He opted for a different, more difficult landing, which was to literally hit the ground running. His legs pedaled fast, pumping high to avoid rocks while maintaining enough speed to keep upright after disembarking at what he guessed to be around twenty miles per hour. Somehow he managed to stay on his feet, gun in his right hand. The only snafu was when Carter's pack was knocked loose from his shoulder and Jayden nearly tripped over it. He saw it coming, though, and high-stepped over it like a track star, smoothly dodging a cluster of snow-covered rocks after that before coming to a stop, still on two feet, where Carter lay sprawled on a thin sheet of hard-packed snow.

Jayden looked down on Carter, whose sunglasses prevented him from seeing if his eyes were open or not. "You okay?"

"Think so." Jayden reached out a hand and pulled his friend to his feet. Then he pointed to the edge of the plateau, some twenty feet away, where their parachute was blowing over the side of a sheer drop.

"Hate to see it go. It served us well," Carter said, watching it blow away.

Jayden nodded, watching until he could no longer see the green tarp as it drifted away in the winds and out of sight over the side of the precipice. "Not to mention we'll have to set up our tent directly on the cold, wet ground tonight. But Carter, your knack for incredible escapes never ceases to amaze me. I seriously thought we were goners back there, and I'm super-glad to be alive. But right now I've got one question."

"What's that?" Carter said, picking up his pack and dusting the snow off of it. Jayden looked around the wind-blasted plateau, at the steep drop-ff to their left, the long slope behind them back down to the Treasure, Inc. team, and the edge of the plateau straight ahead, with what appeared to be a sizable gap before the mighty Mount Ararat rose again, this time straight to the summit.

"What now?"

CHAPTER 24

"So what now?" Phillipo asked his brother, a cold wind whipping his hair. Daedalus threw up his hands. He carried a fixed blade knife in one of them because he no longer had his gun and he hated to be or appear weaponless. He wished he had gotten the chance to use it on Carter Hunt, and maybe even his Asian sidekick, too, but for now it seemed they had eluded him once again.

He levelled an icy gaze at his brother, and his two expedition members in turn. "Now we split up. I will be going back into Dogu. My first order of business will be to have the timbers tested to vouch for their authenticity as to whether they could be from the ark. Assuming they are, I will then begin arranging a clandestine full-scale archaeological salvage operation—the first of its kind—of the true and genuine Noah's Ark. All of that is a lot of work to do, and so I will be departing shortly."

Phillipo appeared gut punched. "And the rest of us?"

"Like me, you also have much to do, and in two parts. First, you will hunt down the men who stole our map and get it back. Killing them would be worth an appreciable bonus to all three of you. Conversely, not getting the map would mean a serious demotion within our esteemed organization."

The two expedition members who were not blood related to Daedalus appeared upset, but said nothing. Phillipo, on the other hand, could not contain his emotions. "But what difference does it make that they have the map, when we have the timbers? We have the *ark*!" He made a grand sweeping gesture with his arm back down the mountain toward the lake basin.

Daedalus was not swayed. "They know where the timbers and the ark are, you idiot! If they get down off of this godforsaken mountain, they will be able to tell everyone about where it is and what they have seen."

Phillipo gasped while the other two men flinched at his use of the Lord's name in conjunction with such a holy site. But Daedalus steamrolled on.

"And the map itself is valuable. It came from the *Titanic*. Have you already forgotten what we went through to get it?"

"Actually they got it, sir," one of the team members said. "We took it from them, remember?"

Daedalus shot him a dagger stare. "And was that easy?"

The man shook his head. "I didn't say that."

"He also has my gun. Get it back if you can—there will be a handsome bonus for that as well. It is not traceable, but it has killed people before and could be used to match ballistics reports the world over. Let's get going. You three will hunt down that map, and kill those two thieves if at all possible. I will head back to our campsite, take a small sample from each timber that I can easily carry by myself, and make sure the timber and our gear is still well hidden. Then I will head back to Dogubeyazıt, first, and then Ankara, to do as I said. We can stay in touch by satellite phone. Check in every four hours."

His three team members stood there, looking dejected at the prospect of traipsing up the snow-covered mountain after two armed and resourceful men.

"Don't just stand there, let's move! Your jobs will be easier the sooner you catch up to those thorns in our side. Now go!"

With that, Daedalus turned and stomped down the mountain into the wind.

#

Carter lost track of how long they'd been trekking. He knew he could find out by looking at his trusty Omega dive watch, but he thought it best at this point to be blissfully unaware. They'd marched straight to the end of the plateau. Looking down from there, it was a rocky slide to another slope. They had opted to take the somewhat perilous route rather than hike back down the mountain toward Daedalus' outfit. They didn't know if they were still coming after them, but knowing Daedalus, they wouldn't give up. The best thing to do, Carter decided, was to take a circuitous route back into town by walking all the way around the mountain and not returning the same way they came.

Jayden pointed up at a sheer rock wall. "I'm pretty sure we're not going to be able to make it back up to the main slope by going that way."

Carter actually laughed out loud. "Pretty sure? There's no way whatsoever we're going to make it up that, even with the incredibly extensive array of climbing equipment we have at our disposal, which includes all of two ropes and one carabiner."

"Yeah, my solo free-climbing is a little rusty these days."

They eyed the craggy, near-vertical ice-covered wall in silence. This style of formation was rare on Mt. Ararat, but they had ventured onto a less-travelled route. At length, Carter spoke. "We're just going to have to go down this way, then walk around the long way until we can cut back across."

"Walking sounds good. As opposed to ice-climbing, or running to dodge bullets. I'd kill for a nice stroll in the park right about now."

"Not the best choice of words, Jayden, because we might just have to. Kill, that is. But let's take your stroll and hope for the best, shall we?"

They headed down the relatively gentle slope that led away from Doğubayazıt, taking the path of least resistance, knowing it also led farther away from where Daedalus' team was last sighted. They took turns shouldering the backpack with the single remaining strap, since it was their only bag. "I guess there's no need for you to literally shoulder that burden alone," Jayden quipped. But Carter was thankful that he had offered without being asked. He was a good friend to have and hoped that the two of them would make it out of this okay, although right now he wouldn't have put much of a bet on that.

They settled into a monotonous rhythm, hiking downhill overall, but encountering flat or even slightly uphill stretches here and there before leading down again. He would gladly take the physical drudgery over the excitement of being shot at, that was for sure, and he knew Jayden, as just about any rational human, would as well. As the day wore on into late afternoon, their elevation gradually decreased. Even so, snow and even patches of ice still coated the ground here and there, requiring them to maintain a good watch on the ground ahead or risk a slip-and-fall or maybe twisting an ankle.

When they reached a ledge overhanging a dry patch of flat, smooth rock, Carter suggested they make camp for the night, since they wouldn't be making it all the way back to town before nightfall anyway. Hiking at night was unsafe, and even if they used lights, that could attract a lot of attention.

"Well if it wasn't for that, I'd be ready to go all night," Jayden joked. And that was the other thing, Carter said. "We need to rest, so we might as well pick a decent spot for it, get a good night's sleep and be on the trail before daybreak."

"Yeah, okay, I guess I can go along with that," Jayden said, persisting with the humor as he shrugged off the backpack and shone a flashlight around the campsite, checking it out. "Might even be enough dry wood around here to start a fire, if we get lucky. How about you set up the tent and I'll see if I can get a fire going."

"Sure, but we're going to have to make do with no ground cover since we put it to good use already."

"Yeah, it's probably been blown halfway to Istanbul by now. 'Put it go good use' is an understatement if there ever was one, though. Thing saved our life!"

They set about the work of establishing a workable campsite, with

Carter putting up the tent beneath the overhang, which would keep most of the direct wind off of it as well as any precipitation, while Jayden gathered rocks for a firepit outside the overhang, including a couple of small boulders suitable for sitting on. With most of his extra clothing lost with his pack in the snow tunnel, Jayden did his utmost to get a fire going, gathering wood, using his Swiss Army Knife to shave off bark to use for kindling, and his hand to shield his lighter from the wind. After multiple failed attempts, he let out a whoop of joy as a lick of orange sprang from the bottom of the pit.

"*Fire!*" he fake-roared in a low voice, since he knew a full-voice yell could carry a long way from their elevated, shielded position. Since he didn't know where the Treasure, Inc. team was, he didn't want to take any chances on giving them a clue as to their position.

"Good work. Got the tent set up." Carter exited the small shelter and brought the mess kit over to the fire. "Hungry?"

"Yeah, what's on the menu tonight, maybe a rack of lamb with a side of potatoes and some red wine to wash it down?"

Carter laughed. "Unless you see a mountain goat and you're a pretty good shot with that pistol, we're looking at freeze-dried beef stew and water."

Jayden gave a slow nod as he watched his budding cook fire. "You know me, I never met an MRE I didn't like." Carter recalled that it was true. While most enlisted men had their favorites, Jayden had been known for being willing to eat any of them, and would even trade the more popular ones for two or more of the least popular so as to build up a stockpile of extra rations.

"I figured it would. Let's not get complacent. There's still a little daylight left. You act as lookout while I prepare the food, so we don't have any surprises from uninvited guests."

Jayden agreed and walked to the edge of their cleared area, which afforded an excellent view of an extensive, brown, sandy desert in the distance. Scanning the area from left to right, up and down, then back again right to left, he spotted no threats.

It wasn't long before Carter called out that it was chow time, and the two ate their no-frills dinner over the fire as night blanketed Mount Ararat. After they had eaten, Carter rummaged through his pack. He produced a small bottle of liquor. "Got it in the airport in Ankara. I was saving it as a souvenir gift for someone back home, but I think we could use our spirits lifted."

"I wholeheartedly agree. What is it, not that it matters?"

"*Raki.*" The brandy-like liquor was a Turkish staple made from grapes.

"Ah, the after-dinner liqueur to complement our meal," Jayden said while Carter uncapped the bottle. He poured some into his canteen cup and passed the bottle to Jayden.

Talk soon turned to the map. "Does this mean we're going to Africa?" Jayden asked. "Seems like we're going to Africa."

Carter took out the map from his backpack and smoothed it out in his lap. Holding it up to the fire, he found he could easily see the hidden lines that ran from the Mr. Ararat lake to a location in east Africa. "Africa's a big place. We've got to know where to go."

Jayden took a swig from his cup. "What part of east Africa is it? Does it have countries labelled?"

Carter shook his head. "It has outlines of what look like countries, but no names. But this map was made before the *Titanic* sank, so ..."

"African countries change names more often than a stripper changes outfits."

"Right. But if I had to guess—"

"And you do!"

Carter nodded. "And I do, indeed--I'd say it's about where modern day Ethiopia is, but I'm pretty sure that wasn't the name of it way back when."

"Ethiopia, huh? Never been."

"Me neither. It's not exactly a tourist hotspot, I don't think. Hold on. I downloaded a modern day map of Africa to my phone when we were at the Internet café in Dogu." Carter retrieved his smartphone from his pack and powered it on. He brought up the modern political map image of the African continent and showed it to Jayden. "That's Ethiopia."

"Ethiopia, huh? Never been. There must be some cool stuff there," Jayden said, savoring the *raki* while eyeballing the map on the screen.

"There must be. But what? If Noah's Ark is here on Mount Ararat, then why would the map want us to consider Africa? Why draw those invisible lines that can only be seen under certain backlit conditions, that connect the Ararat lake site to a vague destination in east Africa?"

"Maybe there were really two Noah's Arks?" Jayden ventured. He looked up at the brilliant display of night stars. There was no moon in the sky which made them stand out all the more.

"Two arks?"

Jayden shrugged. "Yeah, like maybe Noah realized after the first ark was full, 'Hey, no way are we going to fit all these animals. We're gonna need a bigger boat!' But instead of building the first ark bigger, they built a whole second ark."

"I guess that's testable. If we found timbers in the Ethiopian location—wherever that may be—and they did happen to be of the exact same stock as the ones here..."

"Two arks!" Jayden beamed.

Carter raised his eyebrows while shifting his gaze from the electronic map to the paper document. "There has to be something to these lines."

"Well they point to Ethiopia. Which part? Is there a town?"

Carter shook his head. "Not on the old map, but let's see if the modern one has one where the lines end up." He held the phone with the map on the screen up over the paper map, next to the Ethiopia region. "Yeah, town of Axum."

"Never heard of it."

"Me neither. But I have a feeling we're going to get to know it a whole lot better."

Jayden took a deep breath. "What, we're going to go to this town and wander around looking for a *second* Noah's Ark? That doesn't seem a little weird to you? Kind of wild goose chase-y?"

Carter didn't answer but stared down at the map some more, before handing the phone over to Jayden. Then he held the map up over the fire light and stared at the "invisible" lines again.

"I agree with you that we need something more specific. There's also something else I don't understand."

"What's that?"

"Why are there three lines that all converge on the single point in the town of Axum?"

Jayden looked over at the paper map. "Let me see. Okay, so there's three lines but only two of them actually end up in Axum, isn't that right? One goes from the Ararat lake to….Israel?"

"Jerusalem, looks like," Carter said, eyeing the phone map.

Jayden continued. "And then the third line is actually from Israel to Axum, Ethiopia. All very Biblical places—Ararat, Jerusalem, and…well I don't know about Axum, but Ethiopia, if I recall my Sunday School days correctly… Wasn't that where King Solomon went? Also, that line—the one from Israel to Ethiopia—crosses through the Red Sea, which is what Moses parted."

Carter stared at the map in deep thought. "We're going to have to think on this some more. There's something missing. I'm sure that Axum, Ethiopia is the place to be, though, but like you said, exactly where is another matter."

Jayden handed Carter his phone back. "Axum might be the place to be, but we still have the little detail of getting down off of this volcano without being pumped full of lead or freezing to death."

Carter powered down the phone. "You're right. We should call it a night, get out here at first light. We've got a long hike tomorrow."

CHAPTER 25

"We'll take a break while I check in on the sat-phone." As expected, Phillipo received no arguments from his two expedition team members. After they had lugged the heavy timbers an appreciable distance to a spot where he thought they would be well hidden enough, they turned their attention to tracking the Omega Team pair. So far, however, they had turned up no trace of them. He had thought he had an edge over them since he had a walkie-talkie with which he could communicate with local trekking guides, and he hoped one of them might report a sighting. He had asked about a pair of hikers who had become separated from their group, hoping that putting out the word might bring in a report of a sighting. But nothing came in.

Visually, they had strategically set up concealed nests in key places offering good visibility for long distances, monitoring huge tracts of land with binoculars that most hikers used to get up and down from the mountain, and still nothing. His brother would not be pleased, he knew. And yet, it was past time to phone in a report. He lit up his sat-phone and dialed Daedalus, who answered on the first ring.

"Tell me." His tone gave away nothing as to his mood.

"We moved the timbers closer and hid them in a safe spot. Then—"

"Of course. But do you have the map back?"

"We haven't found them yet."

"*What?*" Phillippo could hear his brother's anger through the phone. "How is that possible? There aren't that many routes up and down the mountain! There are three of you!"

"I know. And we have looked, believe me, we have stationed ourselves strategically, separating when necessary to cover more ground. I have been in communication with local guides, requesting to be notified if they are sighted, and we have used binoculars, all to no avail."

"You must not be trying hard enough!"

Phillippo gritted his teeth and told himself to stand up to his brother for once in his life. "I can assure you, it is not that."

"Well then what is it?"

"They must have taken an alternate route back down. Either that, or they went even higher up. But they don't have supplies to last long up there, and they're not acclimated for that, so I doubt that is a real option for them."

"There are no other routes down!" Daedalus screamed.

"Well if they continued down the eastern flank…."

"Eastern flank! Don't be ridiculous. If they did that they would end up in…Iran!"

#

"Where are we, anyway?" Jayden asked. "I don't remember any of this."

Carter stopped moving, shrugged off his pack and took out the binoculars. He held them to his eyes and focused on the flat expanse of brown sand he could see far below and out as far as their naked eyes could see. "It's just a lot of desert."

"Yeah, I'm getting thirsty just looking at it. I'm glad we left the snow behind, though."

"I'm glad we left the guys with guns behind who would kill us for the old piece of paper in my pack. Staring out at the view isn't going to get us down there, so we might as well keep putting one foot in front of the other."

"I guess we need to get down anyway, wherever it is. Straight up and over this thing is no longer an option." He glanced up at the snow-capped peak far in the distance.

"Got that right," Carter said, sipping some water from a canteen. He shared it with Jayden and then pulled his pack back on.

The two set off down the mountain, the climate growing more arid as they descended. Despite a paranoid sense that they were being tracked, they detected no trace whatsoever of Daedalus or his cronies. "Maybe they gave up on us in order to get those logs down off the mountain and into town where they can start analyzing them," Carter theorized aloud. "That can't be an easy task."

"Yeah, maybe they figured that we're not worth it, for once. The only thing that makes me question it is that we have the original map from the *Titanic*. Somehow I doubt Daedalus would let that pass him by so easily."

Carter shrugged and they wore on in silence, the crunch of their boots on the rock and dirt mountainside the only sounds as the morning wore on. He marveled at how peaceful it was, yet for a natural setting, how little wildlife they saw. Only a few birds, and on the way up, some goats, sheep and head of cattle. He supposed that there was life here if one knew where to look, but that without dense forests, it was more difficult to come across. By the time Carter handed the backpack off to Jayden for his turn to shoulder the gear, they were nearly to the bottom of the mountain, and working up a good sweat as the air became progressively warmer.

"Last chance to do a little survey," Carter said, reaching for the binoculars.

"Yep, flat ground for miles once we get down there." Jayden's voice had an edge of concern to it. "Say Carter, can I take a look at that map you have on your phone?"

"Sure." Carter handed him the phone before going back to his binoculars. He scanned the flat terrain again, noting the featureless sand, while Jayden brought up the digital map and adjusted it to show the Mt. Ararat region.

"Looks like in the distance a little sandstorm is kicking up," Carter noted.

Jayden continued squinting at the phone screen. "Hey Carter, do you have the compass?"

"Yeah." He opened one of the zipper pockets and took out the simple magnetic compass.

"I'd say we've come about ten miles since yesterday. Which way are we facing?"

"Southeast."

Jayden's only reply was a very deep breath that made Carter look over at him. "What's up?"

"I really hope I'm wrong, but...." He hesitated while looking up from the phone map and out across the dusty landscape that stretched seemingly to infinity ahead.

"Out with it, Jayden. You hope you're wrong, but what?"

"I think that's Iran."

A weighty silence settled over the duo as they considered the land before them. The implications were both many and deep. Carter let the binoculars hang by the strap around his neck while he wiped the sweat from his forehead.

"Are you sure? Maybe it's Armenia? That'd be better."

But Jayden was staring at the phone map again, this time while shaking his head. "No, it's the northwesternmost tip of Iran, I'm sure of it. Look, here's the peak of Mount Ararat, there's Turkey and the town of Dogu, where we left from, and here's how we must have picked our way around...."

"No wonder we haven't seen those guys," Carter said, referencing Daedalus and his disciples.

"Yeah, even they aren't crazy or stupid enough to just waltz into Iran."

Carter eyed his friend. "We've got to go back. We've got no visa to be here. You know what would happen."

"Yeah I'm not looking forward to letting people know that my new address is some impossible-to-write name of an Iranian prison, either. But on the other hand, I'm not looking forward to receiving a bunch of lead slugs."

Both Jayden and Carter had been to Iran before, on deployment with the US Navy. But serving the largest military force in the world and wandering into a hostile nation alone and unaffiliated with any official purpose, with no travel papers, permits or visas of any kind, were completely different stories.

"We're Westerners, Jayden. Americans, even. We will stand out like sore thumbs if anyone sees us."

But Jayden already seemed to have made up his mind as he pulled a bandana from his pocket and wrapped it around his face, sunglasses over that, hat pulled down tight. "We can't go all the way back the long way, Carter. Never mind the threat from Treasure, Inc. We don't have the *supplies*—food, water." He checked the phone map again. "We just need to skirt the edge of Iran for fifteen miles or so, then we can duck back into Turkey and head back to Dogu."

Carter brought the binoculars to his eyes again. "I don't see anybody or anything, anywhere."

"That's good. Maybe we should get going before that changes."

They each ate a Power Bar and drank some more water before setting out into Iran, Carter shouldering the pack, Jayden with the binoculars around his neck in case they needed to see what lay ahead. Walking northeast, they hiked down all the way off the mountain until the land was flat, at first with hard-packed dirt, but then they found themselves trudging through a layer of loose, brown sand; not as much as a classic Sahara type landscape, for they could feel hard dirt beneath the sand, but there was enough loose sand to be blown about by the formidable wind that persisted here.

Carter kept a close eye on the compass as they trekked, knowing that they could not afford to veer off course and wander deeper into the anti-Western nation. Not only that, but their water supply was perilously low to be travelling on foot in such a hostile environment. He mentally kicked himself as they walked along for getting them into such a dicey situation.

The only consolation was the heft of his backpack, which he knew contained the enigmatic map from the *Titanic*. By the time the sun was nearly straight overhead, its heat pushing down on them like a physical force, Jayden stopped moving forward to check something with the binoculars. Not realizing he had stopped, Carter kept walking. When he turned around after not hearing the shuffling footfalls he'd become accustomed to somewhere behind him, he saw Jayden staring into the binoculars.

"See something?"

Carter looked in that direction but saw only the same unbroken expanse of blowing sand and brown, hard-packed dirt.

"I think so, yeah. Weird."

"What is it?" Carter didn't want to walk all the way back to him if he could help it. But at the same time he could tell that Jayden was definitely transfixed by whatever he was looking at through the lenses. Could it be just a trick of the optics? He was certain it was too soon for them to begin experiencing hallucinations due lack of water.

"I think I see a road."

Carter looked in the same direction Jayden still focused on with the glasses. He couldn't see anything, not even a break or anomaly in the blowing sand.

"You positive?"

"Not positive, but I see shimmering heat waves, and for just a second I thought I saw a flat strip..." He trailed off as he continued staring through the binoculars.

Carter reflected on what this would mean if it were in fact true. A road was both good and bad. Good because it offered a landmark, something to orient themselves by, perhaps an easier means of travel at least for some distance, as well as possible encounters with people who might be of assistance. They could hitch a ride, for example. On the other, darker, hand, a thoroughfare represented potential interactions with authorities, including military, or militia groups, bandits, the possibility of stepping on an Improvised Explosive Device; he and Jayden were only too familiar with the dangers of IEDs from their time serving in the middle east.

All of these thoughts were swirling around in his brain when Jayden said, "It's a road. Positive. Just saw a truck drive past." He pointed off to their left, indicating that the road led away from them on a perpendicular path.

Jayden checked his compass, very glad now that he had gotten into the habit of never going into the wilderness without a real, physical compass, not an electronic app. "The road, if it does actually lead off the way you're pointing, is not heading in the direction we need to go in."

"Figures," Jayden said, letting the binoculars drop around his neck. "Water?"

Carter took the single remaining canteen from his pack, shook it so that they could hear the low volume of water remaining that sloshed around inside, and handed it to his friend. "Just a sip," Jayden said, aware for the need to conserve. He took one, handed it back to Carter, who did the same before putting the canteen away in his pack.

"Looks like we have no choice but to cross the road to follow our course back into Turkey," Carter said as they began to hike again. "It must be a pretty small road, though, since we didn't see any major highway or anything like that when we were camped out up the hill last night."

"No, it's just a little dirt road," Jayden said.

"We'll find out soon enough." But as they walked through the sand, the wind continued to pick up to the point that visibility was reduced to only 100 feet or so ahead of them in any direction. They tightened their clothing, pulled down their hats and bandanas, but Carter could still feel the sand chafing his skin. He had to recheck the compass frequently to make sure they still headed toward the road. He began to worry about how difficult they would be to see now—what if they wandered out onto the road and were hit by a passing truck that couldn't see them? With the howling wind and scraping of sand, it was hard to hear much, either.

Walking on, they glanced periodically in all directions but still saw nothing but a disorienting world of shifting sands and muted brown hues. Both found it tiring to be sandblasted as they walked, hunched over into the wind and stinging particles. Conversation became impractical and they struggled on in silence, with Carter keeping a close eye on the compass. After a while, when he confirmed they were still heading in the intended direction, he grabbed Jayden's shoulder.

"We must have passed it by now."

"We probably crossed right over it," Jayden agreed. "Let's just keep moving, then."

They set out once more, toughing it out against the elements as they forged across the wind-blasted desert, heads hunched over against the blowing sand. Conditions deteriorated to the point that Carter was about to suggest that they simply hunker down in the sand and wait for it to clear, when the wind began to let up. Not a whole lot, but enough to make the pelting grains more bearable and to lessen resistance as they trudged forward. They continued travelling until the sandstorm abated and Jayden was able to use his binoculars again.

They stopped for a water break—getting very low now—while Carter checked the compass heading and Jayden scoped out their environs through the optics.

"Okay, I definitely see something now," Jayden said. "Wow!"

CHAPTER 26

Jayden kept looking through the binoculars as he answered Carter. "People. Animals. Some kind of caravan, by the looks of it. I don't see any motor vehicles, don't see any road. Just a group of people wandering the shifting sands, like us. I guess we should meet up."

"You make it sound like we're going to a festival or something. What if they're bandits, or insurgents?"

"What if they're not?"

The two stood there in the waning winds, sand still kicking up in small flurries around them, but nothing like it had been only an hour before. "I'd take another look at them, but I'm afraid they might see the sun reflecting off the lenses," Jayden held the binoculars at the ready while glancing up at the merciless sun, now high in the sky at an angle.

"Let me take a look." Jayden passed Carter the binoculars and he held them up to his eyes. "Yeah, probably a Kurdish tribe." He handed the binoculars back Jayden. "Thing is, I doubt we can pass by them without them seeing us, anyway. It might seem weird to try and slip by like that, so maybe we should seek contact."

"We may not be able to communicate anyway, since neither of us speaks any kind of Kurdish dialect or Farsi or whatever, but if they do have someone who speaks English, how do we explain our presence here?"

Carter considered this for a moment while taking a sip of the last ounce or so their remaining water while handing the rest to Jayden, who promptly finished it off. "I guess we could just say we're Mt. Ararat trekkers who got separated from our group coming back down from the peak, and ended up on this side by mistake. Closest thing to the truth."

Jayden agreed that's the story they would use and they set out toward the caravan. Estimating distances in the flat, featureless terrain that shimmered with heat waves and blowing sand was difficult, but he estimated the group to be about a quarter-mile away at this point. Carter checked the pistol. He had kept it stashed in the pack to prevent it from being exposed to the dust storm, which would increase the likelihood of a jam.

"How many rounds left?" Jayden asked while Carter checked the chamber and the magazine.

"Six."

Jayden shrugged. "Okay." To them it was a ridiculously paltry amount of firepower compared to what they were used to toting in this part of the world. But at the same time, they were all too aware that it was all they had and that they would have to make the best of it. In fact, simply having it at all could get them in a world of trouble, and Carter stuck the gun in the cargo pocket of his pants in recognition of this fact.

"The caravan is likely armed too," Jayden said.

"Right. Well, live by the code, right?"

Jayden nodded. The code: their simple traveler's version of, treat others how you would want to be treated, had served them well during their travels all across the planet. Now they simply had to hope that they had a little bit of luck on their side.

"Tell you what," Jayden said. "We need to get some water from these people, Carter. I'm not sure I can make it another ten miles or whatever it is back into Turkey like this. Sun is killing me."

"I hear you. Try not to think about it too much. What do you think Daedalus is up to right about now?"

Jayden laughed. "Probably ordering room service and hookers at some swanky hotel while waiting for his antiquities experts to analyze the timber samples from the lake. Oh, why did you have to bring that up, Carter."

"Hey, I'm sure he'd welcome you over to the dark side if you wanted to go."

"What and trade all this?" Jayden swept an arm at the desert. "No, I like my morals intact, thank you very much. We'll get out of this pickle, Carter. The one after this, I have no idea, but we can make it ten miles, come on."

But even as he said the words, his feet plodded more slowly through the thin sands. "Any more food?"

Carter shook his head and also trod in a more labored fashion. "We're out."

"I hope this tribe doesn't just take all our stuff, Carter I really do. After all we've been through to hold onto this map…"

"Don't mention the map or the ark. I took a page from Daedalus' book and created a false compartment in my backpack if they do force a search. But hopefully it won't come to that."

Then they saw a flashing of light about an eighth of a miles away. "They see us," Jayden said. "Signal mirror."

"Yep." Carter stopped walking and put the binoculars up to his face. "Clansman on a camel, waving a piece of metal to catch the sun. They see us all right. I don't see them using any binoculars. Let's see if we can signal them back." He tilted the binoculars so that the lenses caught the fierce sunlight and reflected it toward the tribe.

"He signaled back," Jayden said. Carter sent another flash from the optics, and again they received a flash in response.

"Okay, so we know about each other." Carter dropped the binoculars. "Let's go meet up."

Energized by the impending confrontation, they summoned reserves of energy they didn't know they had in order to walk the remaining distance to the nomad camp. Carter scoped them out one more time through binoculars before making the final approach. He saw old men, young men, women and children—a complete mini-society, which made him feel somewhat more secure in the knowledge that they were not likely to be a band of insurgent rebels who would be prone to kill them for the publicity of lashing out against the West. Still, his senses were on edge as they approached the camp, hungry, thirsty, tired and harboring a valuable map that likely led to a secret of biblical proportions.

"You know the drill, Jayden. Let's walk slow, keep our hands in plain sight."

"Got it." He held both hands up as they approached the camp, where a few tent-like structures had been set up, and a few camels were sitting on the ground. A dozen or so people of all ages and sexes milled about in plain sight, and Carter supposed there were more inside or behind the tents.

When they got close, an old man with a white, flowing beard, and a younger man of indeterminate middle age stepped forward to greet the two travelers. The concern in their eyes registered that they knew these two vagabond souls were not experienced desert travelers, but almost surely to be people in need. The old man held out a leather bladder, ostensibly filled with water. He held it out to them and said a word in his native language which neither westerner understood.

Carter nodded his thanks, not ready to reveal to them that they spoke English, and took the bladder. He tipped it to his mouth and tasted the liquid, tentatively at first, then upon tasting that it was clean water, gulping more down before handing it off to Jayden. While Jayden drank, Carter slowly pointed off in the direction they were travelling in, and said the word, "Turkey," hoping that it would be recognizable. Immediately the two Kurds exchanged knowing glances.

Carter didn't know if they thought he was implying he and Jayden were from Turkey, and asking if the gypsy-like band of desert dwellers was from Turkey, but it was a start to communication. Jayden finished with the bladder and offered it back to the old man, who nodded and took it. Then he extended a hand toward the camp, presumably inviting them to stay. Carter and Jayden nodded and they walked with the two men to the largest tent, where the others now gathered to witness these strange people who had been walking the desert sands alone with almost no provisions.

The old man—Carter thought he looked like some sort of Sultan, draped in robes, long beard—spoke in his dialect to his people. Carter was glad to see him point in the same direction he had pointed—toward Turkey—during this introduction. The reactions of the people were appropriate for a story about two lost men in the desert, which Carter was also grateful for, since it meant that these people seemed to have understood Carter's story the way he intended.

Another man of the tribe stepped up, this one younger, perhaps in his twenties, and he spoke what Carter recognized as the same Istanbul Turkish they had been hearing since being in Turkey. So it was all the more embarrassing when, after that man stopped speaking and waited expectantly for their reply, that they were unable to do so in the same language. Carter saw no other alternative than to speak English, although he knew this would open a can of worms.

"We need to get back into Turkey," Carter said clearly and in English. Sure enough, the reaction was unfortunately as expected. He heard small gasps from a couple of the nomads, and the eyes of the man who had asked the question widened in surprise. Several of the gypsies began talking to one another at once, no doubt now openly speculating as to who exactly these travelers were. Carter was still thinking of how to play this, of what he should say or do next, when two or three of them began pointing to one of the smaller tents off to the side of the makeshift camp. A child ran to the tent and ducked inside, emerging a few seconds later with a middle-aged woman in tow, who carried with her some fabric in the process of being hand woven.

She looked confused until she followed the little girl's point over to the gathering of people surrounding the two newcomers. She stood still for a second, as if assessing a possible threat, and then walked over to the group. She ignored Carter and Jayden, who nodded to her, and instead looked to the elderly man who had escorted them into the camp. This person walked up to her and spoke softly to her for a few seconds, until she nodded her head and stepped forward to the newcomers.

"Hello, English?"

Carter and Jayden turned to one another in surprise. "Let me go first,"

Carter said.

"What, you think I'm gonna tell her my dirty jokes or something?" Jayden said in a soft voice.

"Just let me do the talking at first, okay?"

"Fine. You've gotten us this far." Jayden smiled as he looked up at the woman. Her age was hard to guess since she was draped in robes and scarves, with only part of her face visible, but she did not appear to be elderly; she moved well and the skin that was visible around her eyes and mouth was taut and smooth.

"Yes, we speak English," Carter said, making eye contact with the woman, whose role it was now clear was to serve as the group's translator.

"You come from Turkey?" she asked, pointing toward the bordering country. Carter and Jayden nodded, and she continued her questioning. "You lose way?"

It was clear that her English was not fluent, but it was more than enough to get the point across, and Carter knew full well that it was far better than any middle-eastern language he or Jayden could speak. "Yes, we are lost," Carter answered. "Need to get back to Turkey." He pointed in the same direction as had the woman.

"You no from Turkey? No speak Turk?" the translator asked, her gaze alternating between Carter and Jayden. At this the elder men asked her something in their native language—presumably what she had just asked them—and she translated the question for them.

"No," Carter said, while Jayden also shook his head. "Canadians. From Canada." He thought that maybe Canada would inspire slightly less animosity than the United States, if these people even cared about such matters. He hoped that they were so divorced from everyday news cycles that they had no idea conflicts with their country (if they even thought of Iran as being theirs) and the western nations existed. He considered that perhaps they were truly a nomadic desert tribe who plied the remote sands of multiple middle east countries without even knowing which nation they were in, just as Carter and Jayden hadn't realized they were no longer in Turkey.

Yet the reactions of the translator and the two men who had initially met them and guided them here told Carter otherwise. *We have Westerners in our midst*, they seemed to be saying. Complete outsiders, so foreign as to be exotic and dangerous at the same time.

Not good.

The translator addressed Carter once again. "You climb Ararat?"

Carter and Jayden nodded vigorously.

"Only with that?" she pointed to his single damaged backpack.

Carter explained, "We had more gear but lost some of it on the way down."

The woman translated this for the old man, whose reaction was unreadable to Carter. Then the woman said, "We help you. You have trade for us?" She eyed the backpack. The hair on Carter's arms stood on end beneath the long sleeves of his thermal underwear, the last layer he had to peel down to in the desert heat, one which also shielded him from the blistering UV rays.

"Trade what?" Jayden said softly to Carter, who shrugged off the pack. "I'm sure we have something they can use that we can live without in return for their services."

"Not my Swiss Army Knife, okay? If we can help it. It's from my Granddad."

"How about these?" Carter said, pulling out the case for the binoculars.

"Sure."

He removed the binoculars from his neck, held them up to the nomads, then put the binoculars in the case, closed and opened it to show how it worked. Then he handed the binoculars to the old man, who took them without breaking eye contact with Carter.

"Binoculars, let you see things far away," he said to the translator, who repeated what he said to the old man in their language. The old man took them and, after removing them from the case, held them up to his eyes, aiming them at some faraway spot on the desert floor. He nodded and handed them off to one of the other men who were eager to try them out. It was clear to Carter that they had seen binoculars before, but that owning a pair was not normal for them, hence a good offering. Carter only hoped he and Jayden wouldn't need them again on this trip themselves. Time to seal the deal, he told himself. He cleared his throat and looked at the translator while smiling.

"You like them?" he asked, nodding to one of the nomadic tribesman now looking the wrong way through the binoculars.

To Carter and Jayden's relief, she nodded right away.

"You stay here for night."

Jayden glanced at Carter. "And then?"

"Tomorrow we take you Turkey." She pointed toward the border. "Tomorrow."

At this, Carter held up a finger and said, "Hold on, please." Then he huddled with Jayden in conference. Jayden looked up at the sky. "Stay the night? We still have two or maybe three hours of daylight left. Now that we know for sure which direction it's in, all we really need is some water, maybe a bite to eat before we leave."

Carter nodded. "I agree." He turned back to the translator. "We go tonight for Turkey." He pointed to the country before continuing while Jayden nodded his agreement. "You keep those." He pointed to the binoculars, still being ogled by different members of the tribe. "Give us more water?" He simulated drinking from the bladder.

At this the translator's expression remained unchanged as she turned and spoke to the old man, who seemed to be the leader of the group. He put an arm around her shoulder, spun her away from Carter and Jayden, and said something else to her before walking away toward the tents and the gathering of others. The woman addressed Carter and Jayden.

"He say sandstorm coming. No good you leave now. Tomorrow."

Carter and Jayden eyed the atmosphere, where all seemed blue and calm. Even the wind had died completely down. Jayden said to Carter, "Look, this is ridiculous, let's just ask them for a sip of water now and we'll go. In this weather we can make it, it's only a few miles. I'd rather do that than risk sleeping overnight in Iran with no visa, no ID, nothing. We'd be really screwed, Carter. It's best to get out of here."

Carter nodded and spoke again to the translator. "I'm sorry, but we really must get going. May we trouble you for some water first?" Again he mimicked using the hydration bladder, and again she looked back to the old man, who now was nowhere to be seen. One of the side tents opened, though, and from it emerged a corpulent male, late teens or early twenties, who Carter would not have guessed could fit in that tent. His bulk was not the thing that caught his attention. Jayden saw it, too.

"Uh, Carter? I think that's a scimitar."

CHAPTER 27

The fat nomad wielded the trademark curved machete like someone who knew how to use it. Though he was laying eyes on the foreigners for the first time, since he had not emerged from his tent at any point up to now, he showed no interest in conversing with them, or about them, in any way. Carter guessed that he had already been given his orders by the tribal elders, and now he was going to carry them out, bar nothing.

The brandisher of the scimitar did not run at them full flail, rather he executed what Jayden would later recount as a "controlled power-walk" with the weapon held at the ready until he stood four feet away from them.

"You will stay here for the night," the translator said when their security force was in position. While cautious, Carter and Jayden were not scared of this man. Little did he know that he faced an ex-SEAL and a very fit ex-Navy man with a concealed firearm in the backpack that hung from his shoulder. Carter had no doubt they could fight their way out of this and live to tell the tale. But the truth of the matter was that things were more complex than that. They didn't just need to escape this place. They *needed* supplies, particularly water. He was still incredibly thirsty, having had only a few sips of water since his arrival here. Jayden was nudging his leg with his foot, the signal: *should we fight?*

"Stand down," Carter told him in a low voice. "We'll stay."

Jayden took a deep breath. "Darn, I was really looking forward to a good scimitar brawl, you know? It's been a while."

"Yeah well, don't feel too bad. You might get your chance yet." He leaned in closer, aware that the translator was watching his lips move. "Act friendly, we'll make our move in the morning if they won't let us go then. For now, let's try to cooperate enough so that they feed us."

"Gotcha." Jayden slowly put his hands over his head in the universal gesture of surrender, and Carter did the same. At this the scimitar man-boy smiled ever so slightly, while the old man returned to the fore.

"Okay," Carter said with as genuine a smile as he could muster, "It's all right. We will stay for the night. We don't want to cause any trouble, and you know the area far better than we do." The translator converted this to the old man's language and he nodded in return without smiling.

Although they were not allowed to leave, after an awkward few moments, the gypsy camp returned to normal as a couple of women stoked a cook fire while the men went about their business of tending to the goats and camels while keeping a wary eye on the visitors. Carter scrutinized them as they worked. Most of them had deeply weathered faces and dark skin, the kind of look that suggested a largely outdoor life for many decades. These were truly a wandering, nomadic people, Carter thought, perfectly at home in the middle of nowhere. Glancing off to the Ararat mountains, he now wished they had toughed it out and kept going past this tribe, but it was easy to say that now with water and food close at hand.

A water gourd was lifted from one of the camels, which were draped with rugs, blankets and various hanging baskets full of fruits, vegetables and grains. Some of the camels were unladen, however, suggesting that these were for carrying human riders, while the rest were beasts of burden used for carrying heavy loads. The gourd was passed around and both Carter and Jayden drank until their thirst was completely quenched. A boy played a soothing melody on a Persian flute called a *ney* while pans of food began to simmer over the campfire.

"Don't know what it is," Jayden said, eyeing the cooking dinner, "but I'm more than ready to eat it."

"Some kind of stew," Carter surmised. "Looks like chicken, but who knows." Presently a small girl approached them with both hands joined in front of her. She walked up to them and opened her hands, palms up to reveal six dates. She smiled at them and Crater and Jayden each took three, saying "Thank you." Carter looked over at the translator who nodded at them without smiling.

"Nice," Jayden said, popping one of the fruits into his mouth. "This'll keep us going."

"Kinda makes me think of the date scene with the monkey in that famous relic hunter movie," Carter said ominously. Jayden shrugged and popped another of the middle eastern delicacies.

"Chance I'm willing to take at this point. Besides, they're eating them." He nodded toward a group of adults who were also snacking on dates being passed out by the girl.

They watched the sun set until it melted into the desert sands. It became cool surprisingly fast, and the wind picked up a touch, nothing like the sandstorm of earlier that day, but adding to the chill. The boy stopped playing the flute when dinner was ready, announced by the banging of a simple hand drum called a *doumbek*, with either a sharp, piercing *tek* sound, or else a dull *boom*.

Jayden was beside the fire before the beating of the drum had ended, while Carter took a more laid-back, sauntering approach. It felt odd to him, this being forcibly detained yet free to interact with the group as though they were invited, if not honored guests. The food was satisfying, though, served on battered metal plates, and there was no shortage of it. Jayden had his plate refilled three times while washing it down with copious amounts of water. There was even a jug of some kind of weak wine that went around, which Carter and Jayden sampled liberally. It was certainly a simple, itinerant existence these people led, Carter reflected, yet they were not wanting for the basics.

By the time an incredibly thick blanket of stars lit the evening sky, the camp was beginning to turn in for the night. Carter observed them watering the camels, goats and sheep, and then adding more wood to the fire, which they apparently kept burning all night. They added a lot of wood, Carter noticed, converting the burn from a cook fire to a small bonfire, sending up a thick column of smoke. Probably helped ward off pests, he thought.

It also became clear that two guards were posted while everyone else slept. Carter wondered if they normally kept guards at all or if they maybe posted two instead of one tonight. They might assume that no Westerner in their right mind would dare to venture out on their own at night. Perhaps they really were only worried about their safety?

Carter's thoughts were interrupted when the translator walked over to them and informed them that they were to occupy one of the small lean-to shelters—open on one side facing the camp—to sleep for the night. "Works for me," Jayden said, even more jovial than usual considering the situation, now that his belly was full.

After a last 360 degree look around outside, where they sighted absolutely zero human activity outside the camp, Carter and Jayden retired to the lean-to. The inside was surprisingly comfortable, there being a Persian rug lining the ground and with the three heavy canvas sides serving to block any breezes. The air inside was warmer than out, and they soon realized it would be all too easy to fall asleep for the night. They could hear very low murmurs of conversation from the neighboring tents, but save for that and the occasional noise from one of the pack or farm animals, it was quieter than they were used to, and even quieter than it had been camping with the trekking group on Mt. Ararat.

They lay back as if preparing to sleep. Carter placed his backpack in the corner next to his head. The clan had never searched his pack, as if they didn't care about weapons. Maybe they figured that they were too intimidating for two lost tourists to try and fight? He didn't know, but he was glad they weren't completely locked down. Seeing his pack made him realize that he had never checked his sat-phone messages. He pulled the device from it and powered it on, glad that he had previously set all notifications to silent so that he could use it confidently in covert situations such as this.

"Gotta renew your Netflix subscription?" Jayden asked, head propped up on his jacket as a pillow while staring out the open door at one of the guards walking by in the distance.

"Haven't had a chance to check back with Maddy. I'm just going to call her. Pretty sure she's still in Kyrgyzstan on a dig…" There was a pause for almost thirty seconds and then a female voice answered. Carter held a finger up to Jayden, since the phone was not in speaker mode and he couldn't hear. "It's her, keep watch!" Jayden nodded while Carter concentrated on the phone call. He wasn't sure if this tribe would care about a satellite phone or not, but he couldn't afford to find out in the negative.

"Maddy, it's Carter. You get my message?" He spoke in the lowest possible voice without having to whisper.

"I did, but I'm sorry, I didn't have time to hear it yet. Hey, so how was the *Titanic*? You dove it, right?"

"It went pretty well. I'll have to tell you about it sometime. But listen, things have changed since I left you that message. Here's an update: We came down the wrong side of Mt. Ararat into Iran, and are now being held in the desert by Kurdish nomads…" He went on to supply her with a few more details about how they had come to be here and how they had thus far been treated by their "hosts."

Maddy's voice was laden with concern when she replied. "Carter, listen to me. You have to get out of there."

"Well we are, first thing in the morning…"

"No, I mean right now, as soon as you possibly can. Even if you have to cross the desert at night."

"What, why? It's not *that*, bad they—"

"Carter, I've done a lot of work in that part of the world. What they do is try to hold Westerners—or anyone who might be of value, like a fugitive—long enough until they come into contact with authorities."

"How can they do that, we're in the middle of nowhere?"

"A lot of them have sat-phones, Carter, or regular radios. Like one for the entire group, not each person, but that's all they need. Even smoke signals are sometimes used." Carter eyed the fire outside, with its thick column of black smoke issuing into the clear night sky. It must be visible for dozens of miles. He had wondered why they put on the extra logs to make it smoke, thinking perhaps it was to keep insects at bay.

"I'm actually in Kyrgyzstan now," Maddy went on, "excavating an ancient Roman fort, of all things, found somewhere it's not supposed to be. I'll have to tell you about it sometime. Anyway, if I were closer I'd come help you, but I won't be able to help with the Iranian government if they take you into custody, if it's even on the books at all. These people will sell you to the highest bidder, Carter. To an Al-Qaida type radical group, to the Iranian government, whoever! They collect a cash reward for turning in illegal aliens who happen to be Westerners, and they'll be on their merry way while your and Jayden's experience will be most assuredly unpleasant."

"Why would anyone want a couple of shmucks like us? We're not wanted in this part of the world."

"Carter, you and Jayden are Americans. That makes you useful as political bartering chips. If you don't want to end up in one of those videos reciting some prepared statement with a weird flag in the background and some masked guy holding a machete to your throat, I'd get the heck out of there *right away*!"

The fear that crept into her voice disturbed Carter. Then he felt kind of silly, what with his military experience, and here a civilian had to tell him what was going on. But that was just it—outside of the actual war zone, he felt safe, too safe, and he had let his guard down.

He felt Jayden's fist rapping on his arm. He looked up and saw him pointing outside the tent, where one of the guards approached the opening to their shelter. Carter quickly made sure the light of the phone screen faced away from the opening. "Hold on, Maddy," he said into the phone while he watched the guard to make certain he wasn't going to interrupt. He did stop outside and look into the shelter, but didn't linger, and before long was on his way again making slow rounds around the camp.

"Okay, Maddy, so listen. I don't want you to worry if I can't get back to you, so here's our plan..." He told her how they intended to make their way back into Turkey and from there catch a flight to Ethiopia in order to follow clues as to the whereabouts of Noah's Ark.

"Wait a minute, did you say, *Axum*, Ethiopia?"

"Yeah, Axum. Why, been there?" It was definitely not a normal place for anyone to have been, but as a professional archaeologist, Maddy had travelled the globe to out of the way spots on various digs.

"Never been to Ethiopia at all, but the town of Axum is well known as an ark hotspot."

"Really, that's funny, because—"

"Not Noah's Ark, though, Carter. The Ark of the Covenant."

Her words made their way through the lobes of his brain as he processed them while the sounds of camp life outside—the crackling fire, the guards' footsteps-- faded to nothing. *Not Noah's Ark...The Ark of the Covenant.*

"Carter? You still there?" Maddy's voice brought him back to the moment.

"Yeah I'm here." But he had nothing to add, he was still in shock at something that was beginning to gel in his mind. *Noah's Ark, The Ark of the Covenant...*

"You okay?"

"I'm fine. Listen, Maddy, you say Axum is a hotspot for Ark of the Covenant hunters?"

"That's right, definitely. Just like Mount Ararat is for Noah's Ark seekers, that's Axum for the Covenant. There's a church in Axum that's famous for claiming to have the real Ark—that's the gilded, wooden box from the Bible in which Moses placed the stone tablets inscribed with the Ten Commandments—thou shalt not kill, and all that—"

"Or lust," he couldn't help but add.

"Or lust," she said, with a coyness to her voice that even thousands of miles worth of distance and a signal bounced around multiple satellites before reaching Carter's ears couldn't hide. "There's a church that supposedly takes it upon itself to guard the original ark."

Jayden leaned over and spoke to Carter. "Hey, I'm glad you two lovebirds are having a nice chat, but really, we're pushing it here. They might be able to hear you, and the one guy is about to walk in front of us and probably peek in here again."

Carter, realizing that in addition to what Jayden said, the phone's remaining battery power was also a concern, nodded and returned to the call. "Maddy, we've got some things going on here. I'm going to have to end this call. Thanks for all your help."

"You'll get out of there tonight, right? Because believe me, Carter, however hard you think it'll be to escape the nomad camp, it'll be a hundred times harder from prison or an insurgent labor camp."

Carter glanced out the door to the lean-to, where two guards conferred with each other. He saw both of them look into the lean-to for a second, before walking off in opposite directions. Into the phone, he said in a quiet voice, "Understood Maddy. Thanks again for all your help. See you soon."

He disconnected the call and powered down the sat-phone.

"What, no 'I love you'?" Jayden asked.

"Conserving battery power," Carter said as he stuffed the phone back into his backpack. In addition to the fire smoke, they could now detect a new odor wafting throughout the camp, a sweet, fragrant scent, kind of like incense.

"Maybe those guards are smoking some good stuff and we should go join them out there," Jayden suggested, no doubt only half-joking.

"You might change your mind after you hear this," Carter said. Then he recapped the call for Jayden, emphasizing Maddy's warning about what the tribe might have in store for them.

"There goes my plans for a relaxing night of Z's on the desert sands."

"Yeah, we need to get out of here. Here's what I have in mind."

CHAPTER 28

Two hours passed while Carter and Jayden waited for everyone in camp except the guards to fall soundly asleep. Two men they felt they could handle, but the entire tribe? The time did not pass as slowly as they might have expected, since their minds were occupied with a heady mix of trepidation, excitement, critical planning, and a general fear of the unknown that would have made sleep difficult even had they allowed it. Even after the day's exhausting activities, they were able to stay alert while at least resting by laying down in their lean-to and pretending to sleep. But in curt, whispered phrases, they lay the plans for their escape from Camp Nomad, as Jayden had dubbed it.

At first, Jayden was openly doubtful about their odds of a successful getaway. He questioned that the nomads would really be turning them in to anyone. But Carter laid out the facts: if Maddy was right, and they were planning on turning them in, it would absolutely be easier to escape now than later. Also, even if the nomads weren't planning to turn them in—they needed to get to Africa as soon as possible to continue their search for the ark. Which ark, Carter was no longer exactly sure, but he hadn't had time to think further on that issue; he only knew that the longer they stayed here, the longer they were giving Treasure, Inc. to make their next move, while making no move themselves. Finally, Carter pointed out that the nomads had already threatened them with violence and were in fact holding them captive against their will, decent treatment or not. Jayden reluctantly agreed that in light of all this, they would have to undertake what he termed the most "hairbrained jailbreak plan ever in the history of the world."

Everything was ready: the gear they anticipated needing, such as the compass, flashlights, and pistol, placed in accessible places such as pockets or clipped to the outside of the pack, which still safely concealed the precious map and the satellite-phone. Boots on, clothing on, a second backpack strap improvised out of strips of cloth torn from the tent blankets so that it would stay securely on Carter's body while in rapid motion. They were ready.

One at a time, they reoriented themselves in the lean-to so that their heads faced the exit. The guards had lapsed into less of a walk-the-perimeter routine, and more of a stand-around-and-talk, then patrol-a-little-bit-every-twenty-minutes-or-so routine. Carter couldn't blame them, and was actually surprised they were as attentive as they were, given the circumstances.

"Next time they look in here, we go," Carter whispered. Jayden nodded. Every twenty minutes or so one of them had taken a look into their lean-to, and not from very close. They lay there, peeking out from beneath their blankets, fully dressed and kitted out, waiting to move. Somewhat frustrating was that they could hear the guards talking, not about anything important by the tone of it, and the occasional quiet laughter, but just shooting the breeze. Carter had just begun to wonder if they'd be here all night simply waiting for them to stop talking when the sound of their voices started to come from a different direction. They were moving again.

Carter tapped Jayden on the shoulder. *Almost time.* When the plan was conceived the guards had mostly been apart, talking only in passing. But for the last hour or so, after everyone was fully asleep, Carter guessed, they had spent more time together, conversing, possibly smoking and sharing the wine. He preferred them to be apart, since it made for a clean one-on-one takedown for him and Jayden, very stealthy. Two men sneaking up to the same place was inherently less stealthy than two going to physically separated targets. But either way, they both knew they were capable of getting the job done.

Sure enough, they could hear the guards chatting to one another as they walked behind the rear wall of the lean-to. Carter quietly threw the blanket off of him and pointed out of the lean-to's entrance and to their left. Jayden nodded before shedding his own blanket. No moon lit the night sky, but the campfire, which the guards periodically kept going strong by adding more wood, provided a decent amount of light throughout the camp.

Carter looked to their right, to make certain no one else besides the guards happened to be up. Seeing no one in that direction, he crept to a kneeling position and stuck his head out of the lean-to entrance. Looking left, he also saw no one, and could still hear the guards taking their leisurely stroll around the shelter.

He and Jayden exited the lean-to at the same time, Carter on Jayden's left. He wanted to get around the corner of the shelter to be shielded from view by most of the rest of the camp, should someone happen to look out of their shelter or get up for some reason. They crept around the side of the lean-to and crouched, waiting for the pair of patrols to walk around the structure.

They were laughing softly when they walked around the side of it, one man with his head thrown back, looking up to the sky, while the other looked at him. Carter tapped Jayden on the shoulder as he sprung, the signal that it was go-time. Both ex-warriors moved fluidly and as an efficient, single unit. Jayden took the guard on the right, while Carter was responsible for the other. They had the guards in headlocks so fast the men hardly realized anything was wrong until they were having trouble breathing.

Carter knew it would only take a minor slip for their breathy gasps to turn into an audible scream, and so he looked at Jayden and nodded. It was obvious to them what they had to do. They had no desire to kill or even seriously hurt these people, they only wanted to temporarily incapacitate them so that they could be on their way. Still, there was no way to avoid some pain, and both treasure hunters were okay with that.

Simultaneously, Carter and Jayden pushed the heads of the guards into one another in swift, decisive motions that cracked their two skulls together with an audible thud. Both nomads fell to the sandy dirt like dropped laundry bags. Carter immediately put two fingers to his eyes, then pointed to Jayden and then pointed to the main camp in front of their shelter: *go check to make sure no one heard that and is coming out of the tents.* Jayden silently complied, and while he was creeping around the front of the lean-to, Carter dragged the first unconscious guard into their shelter. He eyed Jayden, who gave him the okay sign. No one had been alerted, at least not yet.

Carter returned for the second body. Unfortunately this man was beginning to stir, moaning softly and so Carter gave him a medium punch to the face which knocked him out cold. Then he dragged this guard into the lean-to and lay him down next to his comrade. He checked their pulses to make sure they were steady, which they were. Then he covered each with a blanket and left the shelter to join Jayden outside. Jayden looked at him expectantly and again he gave the okay sign, indicating that they were ready to proceed to Phase 2 of their hastily contrived plan.

They snuck past the far side of the camp fire, which still burned strong, sending a thick column of dark smoke high into the clear night sky. Past the visual cover of the bright fire, since while they were behind it shielded them from the view of anyone happening to peer out from the tents, they dropped to their bellies and low-crawled the rest of the way. It offered a much lower profile and was quiet. When they were behind the shelters and no longer in direct view of anyone, they stood and moved to the area behind the camp where the animals were tied for the night.

With the shelters blocking the fire light, the darkness in this area made it difficult to see the animals' hulked forms as they sat or lay on the ground, dozing. Carter activated the red LED mode of the headlamp he wore in order to give them some light without sacrificing their night vision or alerting others to their presence with a bright light. In the red cast they could see there were a total of three camels, although only one was outfitted as a riding camel. It was a dromedary, the single-humped variety, and was outfitted with a saddle behind the hump.

"You good at riding these things?" Jayden whispered.

Carter shook his head. "Same as you, basically. Camel novice."

"Now camel toes, that's another—"

"Jayden, come on!" Carter whispered sharply. Was there ever a time his friend could be serious?

"Okay, so I guess one of us gets the saddle and the other the hump." Although outfitted with only one saddle, the camel was a large one and appeared to be able to support the weight of two men. The other camels, they had noticed, were smaller in size and yet draped with hundreds of pounds of goods.

"You take the saddle, I'll get up front. But let me get up front first. Keep watch." Carter stepped up to the camel, which had its eyes closed while snoring lightly, its lips flapping with each breath. "Okay buddy," he whispered. Time for a ride." He pushed off the ground and swung a leg over the animal's neck, glad he had improvised a new strap for his backpack, which stayed firmly in place as he mounted the beast. The dromedary stirred slightly and made a loud snorting sound, but that was the extent of its reaction.

"Okay, get on before it stands up," Carter told Jayden, who moved next to the saddle. He jumped up on to the beast, grabbing hold of a leather handle on the saddle to secure his position atop the beast of burden. He tapped Carter on the shoulder in front of him. "Ready. How do we get it to stand up?"

"Kick it in the sides."

"Why do I have to kick it? You want it to be mad at me?"

"Just do it, you're over the part where they kick it."

Jayden dug both booted heels into the animal's ribs at once and braced himself for a lurch. No reaction. He tried again. "He doesn't seem to care."

"Harder!"

"I don't want to break his ribs!"

"You won't. C'mon, before somebody wakes up."

"Okay, gonna kick him hard. Here goes…" Jayden slammed both heels into the camel's sides, and this time it brayed loudly, an ugly sound, sort of a cross between a cow and a horse. But it didn't get up.

Carter jumped off the camel. "Stay put. Let me try something else." He'd seen camel drivers walk behind the dromedary before and swat them, so he tried that, wary of being kicked.

He looked around for a switch and found one hanging from the saddle assembly. He grabbed it and used it to swat the camel's hindquarters hard, with a clicking sound from his tongue. That did it, and the camel lurched to its feet.

"Carter we never untied it!" The animals were tied to a packing crate of some sort that had been set in the sand. Carter found the end of the rope lead and untethered it. He pulled the camel by the lead to the crate, which he was able to stand on to raise his height enough to be able to jump onto its neck.

Suddenly they heard a shout followed by pounding footsteps. "They see us, let's go!" Jayden kicked the camel again while Carter made the clicking sound as he yanked on the lead. The dromedary finally started to move forward. Not at a trot, though, but at least it was walking.

"Carter, we can run faster than this, maybe we should just—"

"No, this will be faster over the long haul. Here, you shoot if you have to, I'll steer." Carter handed him the pistol, but right at that moment the camel decided to break into a trot, and the resulting jolts caused Jayden to drop the gun. He flailed for it but saw it cartwheel across the desert floor until it was lost in their quadruped's wake.

"Sorry, I lost the gun."

"What!" Carter called back as he tried to read the compass in his headlamp's red glow while bouncing up and down.

"Should I take us back for it?"

But that question was answered for them by the sound of a gunshot from the nomad camp. Carter saw a patch of sand kick up about twenty feet off to their left. "No! Keep going, we only had six rounds left for it, anyway."

Carter switched off his headlamp so as not to provide a shining beacon in the night to target shoot at. Then he began zig-zagging the camel, jerking the reins right and then right again before going back left, in an attempt to make for a more difficult moving target.

Another shot was fired but he didn't see—or feel, luckily—where it ended up. He kept up the zig-zagging, with the camel cooperating and keeping up a good trot. It was not as fast as a horse, but Carter thought the ride was somehow smoother, which was a good thing, because now he needed to pass the compass back to Jayden, and that was something they could afford to lose even less than the gun.

"Jayden, put your hand out in front of you and I'm going to hand you the compass."

"What?"

Carter repeated himself, yelling loudly since they were now out of hearing range of the campsite.

"Okay." Jayden stuck his hand out by Carter's right side, palm outstretched.

"Hurry up, I need two hands to hold onto this ship of the desert!"

Carter pressed the compass into Jayden's palm and held it there until he felt his fingers curl around it. "Got it?"

"Got it." Jayden withdrew his hand and held onto the saddle to steady himself.

They heard another gunshot and this time Carter turned around to look. What he saw shook him to his core. Another camel and rider silhouetted in the darkness behind them, but not all that far. He had no doubt that the nomads were expert riders and would catch up to them in short order. Deciding that all the zig-zagging was making it easier for the wanderers to catch up to them, Carter clicked his tongue at the camel and kicked it once with his feet to spur it on. It did, galloping a little faster across the cracked dirt.

"We going the right way?" Carter called back. He gave him a heading.

"I need the light to read the compass."

"Here." Carter swiped the headlamp from his forehead and held his hand behind him until he felt Jayden take the lamp from it. Another gun blast punctuated the desert night. Jayden slipped the headlamp over his forehead and aimed the beam at the compass held flat in his hand. It took a while to get a confident reading while bouncing around on the dromedary, but after a bit he tapped Carter's shoulder and pointed at about a forty-five degree angle off to their right.

Carter immediately corrected their steed's course, pulling the reins to the right and letting go once its head was pointed in the indicated direction. They rode on at full gallop, and after a while it dawned on Carter that no more shots had been fired. He glanced behind them and saw the solitary camel rider, but farther back now. Maybe they had given up, Carter thought, or run out of ammo.

They had made reasonably good progress during the camel chase, too, Carter thought, now able to see real detail of Mount Ararat once again. Turkey lay ahead; they were getting there. Still, he knew the nomads were a crafty people and that they might be trying to lull them into a sense of complacency, so he deliberately kept the pack animal running along at full trot for longer than he wanted to. He didn't know how long camels could keep up this pace, if they would keep running until they had a heart attack, or would just stop and lay down when they had had enough, but he hoped the latter.

"Definitely faster than walking," Carter told Jayden.

"Yeah, easier on the feet, too. Our feet, at least. Sorry buddy." He patted the camel's back.

"I don't think it's very hard for them. Let's take another heading."

Jayden read the compass again and this time Carter made only a slight adjustment to their course. "Won't be too long now," Carter estimated. Still, he dared not ease back on the camel's speed. "Just sit back and enjoy the ride."

They rode on under the dark night sky, lit only by a thick blanket of stars, constellations so vivid it seemed to Carter like he could reach out and pluck them out of the heavens like jewels. He thought of the phone conversation with Maddy. *Not Noah's Ark, the Ark of the Covenant*...As he stared at the cracked desert floor sliding by beneath the camel's feet, he let it morph in his mind into an image of the old map, of the three invisible ink lines he had found there…

He was still thinking about it when something began to invade his thought process, something piercing, not in a loud way—the dromedary's hoofs were still brashest sound in the vicinity—but piercing in a different way. Illumination…He was on the verge of making a connection with the map, of what it all meant, when his mind registered light—artificial light. He had just ripped himself from his silent analysis of the map's possible meanings when Jayden's voice finalized the intrusion and made it very real.

"Big trouble, Carter. Those are headlights behind us."

CHAPTER 29

At the mention of headlights, Carter whirled around on the camel and looked behind him. Sure enough, twin artificial lights that cast a bluish wide beam, most likely newer style xenon bulbs. The naval historian's blood ran very, very cold.

"Not good, Jayden. It means Maddy was probably right, and that tribe contacted someone about us, either the Iranian government or some insurgent group."

"Those desert hermits were going to sell us into slavery?"

"For political pawns, probably, but listen," Carter said, kicking the camel hard now and urging it on with clicking sounds, "our only chance is to make it into the wooded area at the foothills of Ararat, there."

"Pretty sure that's Turkey."

"Yeah. But who knows, they might not be scared of driving a few feet into Turkey, I don't know. Or shooting at us while they stay on their side of the border."

"I get it. We need to get into the cover of those trees."

"Right, and from there work our way deeper into Turkey."

Jayden spurred the camel with his boots, but the animal was already giving its all, running at top speed, which seemed woefully lacking as the vehicle raced along the hard-packed dirt behind them. Carter couldn't make out any details about it because the lights in the front were too blinding. But the way he saw it, they were only about a hundred yards from the Turkish border now, with the plant life cover perhaps another hundred beyond that. He only hoped it wasn't a "technical," a type of vehicle he and Jayden had become acquainted with during their deployments in Iraq and other middle eastern Gulf states. Basically consisting of a modern pickup truck with a mounted machine gun such as a 50-cal in the bed, they were typically used by insurgent groups where one man would drive, another man the machine gun and another would ride shotgun to shoot an AK-47 or similar out the passenger side, or perhaps even lob grenades.

In this case, the motive would likely be to take them alive to use as hostages for money from relatives or companies they work for, perhaps, or else political pawns, so Carter hoped they wouldn't be mowed down right away. Still, when they saw their meal tickets disappearing into Turkey, they might try to cut them down in a hail of lead even if they didn't get to see the results, a sort of "if we can't have you nobody can" attitude.

As the vehicle neared—the ground in front of the camel was now lit by the xenons—Carter debated using the zig-zag technique again to make them a more difficult shooting target, but decided that it wouldn't make any difference for a gunner using a truck as a platform, if that's what it was.

"Crossing into Turkey!" Jayden yelled, but his words were drowned out by the most unnatural clatter of automatic weapons fire. Dirt and sand flew up a little behind them and to their right. Carter and Jayden spurred the dromedary, which brayed as it ran a little bit faster into the neighboring country. To Carter, the open spread of brown dirt between them and the vegetation-shrouded foothills of Mt. Ararat seemed like ten miles wide, but it was only about a football field. He wished they had the gun now, for even a small amount of return fire would give their aggressors pause, but he had learned long ago not to dwell on that which could not be changed.

He braced himself for another heavy salvo from what had to be some kind of automatic weapon, even if not a mounted one, when suddenly the engine changed in pitch and they heard angry men's voices shouting in their direction.

"Some Welcome Committee," Jayden said as he white-knuckled the camel's saddle horn while the animal jostled along at what had to be its maximum speed.

"We weren't exactly invited." Carter jerked the camel's reins to the left to avoid a small ditch in their path that had been illuminated by the vehicle's lights. The vehicle—Jayden was saying it was a truck, now—stopped at what Carter figured must be the Iran-Turkey border.

"They won't cross it!" Jayden shouted jubilantly.

"That doesn't mean they won't shoot over it!"

"Watch that rock!"

Carter put his eyes forward in barely enough time to steer the dromedary around the geological obstacle. They cleared the small boulder and kept on going, deeper into the geopolitical safe zone that was Turkey, just as a volley of lead sparked off of the rock behind them.

"Go go go!" Jayden shouted, hunched forward as far as he could in the saddle to flatten himself out and represent a lower profile target. More shouting, and now the flicking on and off of high beam headlights for a strobe effect combined with more shooting—this time from single-shot weapons-- assailed their senses. The lack of auto-weapons fire concerned Carter. On the one hand it meant they were deemed to be out of range for burst fire weapons, but on the other, if they had rifles and knew how to use them, then they were still very much in range. As if to underscore this fact, Carter watched as a section of tree bark disintegrated ten feet in front of them.

It meant they had reached the wooded area at the foothills of Mt. Ararat, though, and at that Jayden was already rejoicing. "Tress! I see trees! Never so happy to see trees in my life. Just a little farther, come on, Camel, you can do it!"

Another shot rang out, echoing off the mountain. A miss. And then they reached a bushy area through which Carter tried to drive their mount but to no avail. The dromedary reared up on its hind legs, bucking Jayden off onto the ground just as a bullet slammed into the leather saddle. Carter meanwhile slid down the animal's neck to just in front of the saddle, which stopped him from sliding all the way off. The sound of the shot spurred him into action, and he took matters into his own hands by throwing himself off of their four-legged ride.

He and Jayden ducked into the foliage and got low to the ground. Carter reached out and hit the camel on its rear quarters, yelling "Yah!" to send it running back into Iran, acting as a temporary decoy until their attackers realized it was rider-less. It galloped away at a normal trot. Carter hoped it would find its tribe again, but he wasn't about to linger long enough to find out its fate.

With Jayden now leading the way, the two mountain trekkers slipped into the foliage and began making their way around the base of Mt. Ararat, deeper into Turkey.

#

Doğubayazıt, Turkey, ten hours later

"Flight's booked," Carter told Jayden, pocketing his smartphone. With tickets purchased in cash, they rode in a public bus that made long distance runs across the country, in this case from Doğubayazıt to Ankara, where they were to board a flight direct to Addis Ababa Bole International Airport in Ethiopia.

"We have to deplane at Addis Ababa International to board a smaller connecting flight to Axum, and they said there may be a short layover, maybe half a day in Addis Ababa, unless we decide to book a charter, but we'll cross that bridge when we get to it."

Jayden let his head loll back on the seat. "Cross that bridge when we get to it…That worked out so well for us in Turkey—I mean, Iran."

Carter shrugged, undeterred. "Hey, it could have been a whole lot worse."

"I just hope our trusty camel steed found its way back home."

"Me too. It was going the right way last we saw, at least. So—" But when he looked over at him, Jayden was asleep. He couldn't blame him. The day had been another long one, especially coming on the heels of the one before that. They had walked from the foothills of Mount Ararat back to the trekker staging area, and from there hitched a ride back into Doğubayazıt with a returning guide group. During this ride they used the same false names they had given their own trekking company with whom they had promised to report back after returning to town to let them know they had returned safely. This tour operator knew the one they had booked with, and promptly called them to let them know their clients were safely on the way back to town. After tipping that driver, they had returned to their hostel and checked out, paying in cash before going directly to the bus depot.

With Jayden asleep, Carter decided to do some research on the town of Axum and where they would focus their hunt for the ark once they got there. He had used the Internet connection at the hostel's café to download numerous articles from the web about the area, and soon, as the old bus wheels rumbled across a vast ag-scape of farmland, pastures and scenic snow-capped mountains in the far-off distance, his mind was occupied and racing to make connections related to the old map that was still tucked safely away in the hidden compartment of his backpack.

#

Ankara, Turkey
Grand Ankara Hotel & Convention Center

"Maid service, sir. Would you like—"

Daedalus yelled at the door without opening it. "I do *not* wish to be disturbed! I will call if I need anything." After the muffled apology that issued from the other side of the door, Daedalus walked back from the entranceway onto the plush carpeting of his main suite, which afforded a beautiful scenic view of majestic mountains in the distance. He jabbed at the remote control button that slid the curtains across the window and stewed in the ensuing dimness.

Glaring at his watch, he saw that it was almost an hour past the time when he should have heard from his brother, that incompetent, overpaid oaf who was still in the field. Meanwhile, his archaeological expert—also vastly overpaid in Daedalus' opinion-- had not yet weighed in with any insights regarding the ultra-high resolution, professional grade scans of the map image he had sent him, going to great lengths to do so over an encrypted, highly secure network. He snatched up his specially encrypted smartphone and dialed the number to the satellite-phone his brother was supposed to be monitoring.

It was answered on the fifth ring. "Phillipo, is that you?"

"Yes, Daedalus. How are you?"

Daedalus let loose a sigh of pure exasperation. "You tell *me* how I am! Do you have the map yet?"

"No."

The black market treasure kingpin closed his eyes in an attempt to remain somewhat calm. "Have you tracked down those two thieves?"

"My dear brother, I am sorry to report that we have failed in that task."

Daedalus' face went beet red. He lost control and shouted at full volume into the phone, which was on speaker mode, while the veins in his neck bulged. "Then what good are you? Why do I employ you? Tell me!"

A few seconds of silence passed during which Daedalus could hear the sounds of birds squawking, like the audio track to a serene nature setting. Then Phillipo's voice came back on.

"I do have some information on their whereabouts."

"Tell me."

"I inquired with the local trekker's network and learned that the two hikers who had separated from the Ararat Trekking group that left from Dogu were picked up by another trekking company's van yesterday, and transported to back to Dogu."

"Dogu! So they could be anywhere now. Why didn't you tell me this yesterday?"

"We just found out now, Daedalus. We are still on the mountain, communication is not so easy."

"You have a sat-phone!"

"Yes, the battery power of which must be conserved for our own use.

Not to mention, of the guides who do carry one, they are used mostly for emergency purposes and not to chat. For that they use the walkie-talkies, which is how I was able to learn of what happened, but that's how long it took. I am sorry, brother, but we have done our best. We are now en route back to Dogu with the timber samples. We should be there later today."

Daedalus took a deep breath. "Well that part is good news. Make sure you follow security protocols to keep them safe."

"As far as anyone knows, they are simply quality old growth lumber pieces for our master craftsman to make luxury furniture pieces with."

"Excellent. You will report back to me when the samples have been transferred in Dogu to my agent."

"Will do. How is the map research coming along? Do—"

But Daedalus had already ended the call.

#

Ankara Esenboğa Airport, Turkey

"Hello duty free shop!" Jayden exclaimed, full of enthusiasm as he entered the store.

"Smaller size bottles, Jayden, that we can use for bartering should the need arise."

"Always the sensible one, Carter. But you're absolutely right. A nice variety of small flasks and even the mini's ought to do us just fine once we're in Africa."

They had a half-hour to kill before their flight left, so they had hit the newsstand for some basic supplies that were small and could be taken on a flight that might come in handy for 'when things got rough', as Carter thought of it—beef jerky, power bars, Tylenol, candy bars. All things that were useful pretty much anywhere but at the same time took up very little space, and that could be hard to find in some of the planet's more remote corners. Jayden even purchased a new backpack to replace the one he'd lost on the mountain. Nothing special, as he put it, but at the same time, they didn't want anything that would stand out too much. Carter also took the opportunity to outfit himself with a new pack, deciding that the jerry-rigged broken strap made his bag stand out a little, and that he also may as well start with something new but innocuous looking. Anything with a tactical or military appearance was out, regardless of the functionality or features it offered.

After checking out with their liquor purchases in the duty free shop, they boarded their flight for Ethiopia. It was a full jet, with what Carter guessed to be an even mix of business commuters, tourists, and people travelling for personal reasons with ties to one or both countries. Flight time would about eight hours, and as soon as it was wheels up, Jayden dozed off for some much needed shut-eye. Carter knew that he should sleep as well, but it wouldn't come as easily. He couldn't stop thinking about the map, and about what Maddy had said about Axum and the Ark of the Covenant. *The other ark*, as Carter thought of it now. Could it be? He had wanted to discuss this further with Maddy, but when he had called from Ankara International, where he had cellular service, her line went to voice mail. He left her a message that they were safely back in Turkey and leaving for Axum, but that was it.

Around the time the "fasten seatbelt" signs blinked off, Carter began reading the research material he'd downloaded to his laptop in Dogu. Flight attendants supplied him with a steady stream of caffeinated beverages and snacks.

He was still reading when the pilot came over the intercom to announce that they were preparing for landing at Addis Ababa.

CHAPTER 30

Axum, Ethiopia

Carter and Jayden deplaned the much smaller prop plane they had transferred to in Addis Ababa after a two-hour flight onto a scorching hot tarmac at Yohannes IV Airport. Carter had learned during the plane ride that the hottest temperatures on Earth had been recorded in Dalol, Ethiopia, a location only about one hundred miles to the east. Situated near Ethiopia's northern border, the town of Axum was home to a population of about 58,000, and lay at an elevation of 7,000 feet. Neighboring countries included Eritrea to the north and east, Sudan to the west, and Kenya to the distant south, far south of Addis Ababa.

The airport was about four miles outside the actual town of Axum, and with ground transportation yet to be arranged, the treasure seeking pair shuffled across the baking tarmac along with their couple of dozen fellow passengers and entered the small terminal. The sign reading "Yohannes IV International Airport" above the entrance was written in both English and Amharic, Ethiopia's official language that used symbols as opposed to any sort of alphabet that would be familiar to westerners. Carter had the feeling that he and Jayden were only two more in a long and storied line of enraptured visitors who had sought the truth about some of humanity's most revered artifacts in this very place, the home of Queen Sheba, the rumored resting place of the Ark of the Covenant.

As they walked through the moderately crowded terminal, Carter couldn't help but keep his eyes peeled for anyone who looked like they might be tailing them. They were using their genuine IDs to travel under, and he knew that Daedalus would likely know what those were because of the fact they were both in the same business. With no luggage to collect, they breezed through and out onto the sidewalk fronting the airport without having noticed anything suspicious. While not as ubiquitous as at a major airport, taxi cabs were not hard to come by, and it wasn't long before Carter and Jayden occupied the back seat of one driven by an Ethiopian septuagenarian.

The man spoke English, and when he asked where they'd like to go, Carter asked him, "What's the most popular church nearby?"

The man nodded as though the request was not unusual whatsoever. "That would be Axum Tsion Saint Mary." He pronounced "Tsion" with a silent *T*. "I will take you there, only a few minutes."

As they rode through the town, Jayden wanted to know why they didn't start with the church that was famous for supposedly housing the Ark of the Covenant, St. Mary's of Zion Church, also in Axum.

"Let's see what an ordinary church looks like first. Pretty much every church in Ethiopia has a replica of the Ark of the Covenant, so let's see what those look like. Also…" Carter nodded to the cab driver, who had turned on the radio to a music station playing reggae. "It's probably best not to let anyone know where we're going if we can help it."

At this Jayden laughed before turning to look Carter dead in the eye. "Are you serious? We came all the way to Ethiopia to go to some tourist trap that the whole world knows about?"

Carter shrugged. "I've been researching this town and its history. As you've no doubt already seen, this place is associated with the Queen of Sheba."

"I picked up on that," Jayden said, pointing out the window to a billboard reading, *Queen of Sheba Authentic Ethiopian Restaurant*. "Was she even real, though?"

"Debatable. She's in the Bible. Anyway, the Queen of Sheba Palace that's here in town is, according to Ethiopians, where Sheba left from to go to Jerusalem."

"And that's where she hooked up with King Solomon, right?" Jayden gazed out the window at a mural of the Ethiopian flag—the bright green, yellow and red bars with an insignia in the middle, a star and rays.

"Right. They hit it off and she had a son with him, that's Menelik, who was born in Ethiopia. He became a king here, and sometime later went to Jerusalem to visit his Dad. He brought the Ark of the Covenant back with him to Ethiopia."

Jayden unwrapped a candy bar and started eating it.

"You're supposed to save those in case we end up out in the field somewhere with no food."

Jayden shot him a sheepish grin. "Gotta be honest. Not sure if my stomach is gonna be down with Ethiopian cuisine."

Carter sighed as the driver pulled up to a complicated-looking intersection to wait his turn to cross. "You were okay with Iranian nomad cuisine, but you're worried about Ethiopia? Anyway…"

"So Sheba's son, the king, brought the ark back here. To this Church of Zion?"

Carter shrugged. "Well this particular chapel didn't exist way back then, of course. But supposedly that's where it ended up."

"So we're just going to waltz in there and ask to see it?"

Before Carter could answer, the cabbie pulled over to the side of the road and informed them that they had arrived at Axum Tsion Saint Mary. Carter paid the driver in local currency, including a decent though not memorable tip, and they exited the cab onto the sidewalk. In front of them lay the church, a large single-story building with a high ceiling. They walked up a short flight of steps and entered the place of worship.

Inside was grandly decorated, with lots of space around the pews. It was quiet, with no conversation taking place or music being played. At the front was a large multi-level stage area, including a music stage with an organ and harp, and a pulpit. Only a few people occupied the pews here and there, maybe a dozen altogether. Carter and Jayden were able to walk freely up to the stage and climb the steps to the top level and highlight of the church, a full-scale replica of the Ark of the Covenant.

"So this is it," Jayden said, unimpressed. "A gold box. A lot bigger than I imagined, though."

"This is one of the many replicas," Carter said, while they stared at the model ark. It was no small container, measuring approximately ten feet by six by six. Two poles were run through two rings on each side of the ark, making it possible to be carried by several men. Two cherubs knelt on top of the rectangular container, their wings touching at the very peak of the piece. The entire work, including the poles, was covered in what was meant to look like gold, but which was plain to see was in fact gold paint, chipping and peeling in some spots to reveal the plaster of Paris and wooden scaffolding beneath.

"So inside it would be the Ten Commandments, right?" Jayden clarified.

"On the two stone tablets, correct."

"You think they're in there?" Jayden raised his eyebrows while gawking at the fake yet nevertheless impressive ark.

"I don't know, but it doesn't matter. This is just a replica. Let's go to the other church now."

Jayden turned and looked out on the rows of pews. "Sure you don't want to stop and pray first?"

#

Ankara, Turkey

Daedalus sat at the coffee table on the balcony of his hotel suite overlooking the capital city's hustle and bustle. He was hoping for a relaxing late morning with time to think and plan, but already the messages and voicemails flooded in—and to his priority phone and email address, not his regular avenues that everyone had. It was an address and smartphone number he only gave out to certain key associates. He had just picked up his cup of black tea when his smartphone chimed to inform him a new email had been received. He set down the tea and picked up his device. Upon seeing that the email was from his lab technician whom he had put in charge of testing the timber samples from the lake, Daedalus eagerly opened the email. Finally, the lab results!

Re: timber sample analysis

Positive results obtained. Wood commensurate from tree species likely to be genus *Acacia*. Specimen dated via peer-reviewed radiocarbon techniques to be 5,000 years old, +/- 250 years.

A rare smile manifested on Daedalus' lips. *5,000 years old, and Noah's Ark was built around 5,000 years ago!* He thought of the lake high up on Mount Ararat, and the rest of the timbers that still lay in its depths, still in the shape of a boat that closely matched the recorded dimensions of Noah's Ark. He threw his head back and laughed. He had done it! Noah's Ark was his! Treasure, Inc. was about to be the irrefutable gold standard for the recovery of priceless antiquities, artifacts and relics. Perhaps this find would be the one that finally catapulted him to his personal dream of becoming a billionaire. Yes, by most people's standards, the tens of millions of dollars he'd already amassed as part of his personal fortune—much of it made from illicit international trade in antiquities-- made him exceedingly wealthy. But he wouldn't feel like he had "made it" until he joined the B-club. Control of Noah's Ark would be the kind of asset that could put him over the top.

Glancing at his smartphone, he saw that a second email message had come in, and this one was from the cartography expert he'd entrusted with (and paid a handsome retainer) to analyze the map in order to determine what other information, if any, it might contain. Daedalus almost didn't bother opening this message. The map had obviously worked, after all. It had led him straight to the ark, so who cares what else there was to know about it, especially since he didn't even have it anymore, thanks to that meddling Carter Hunt. But on second thought, Daedalus had paid his consultant an awfully large amount of money for a single task, as he always did in order to ensure confidentiality. Besides, let's just see how good this guy really is, Daedalus thought. He doesn't yet know that we found the ark, since the timber analysis work was with a different consultant. Daedalus always compartmentalized his project work like this so as to keep any one person from being able to put too much together. *What if he tries to tell me the ark is somewhere other than the Ararat lake? That would mean I can't really trust either him, or the quality of his work.* So he clicked open the message and read what he expected to be a mere confirmation of what he already knew.

And part of it was. In his analysis, his cartographer said essentially that it appears the X-marks-the-spot indicator on the map appears to point to a small lake on the northwestern slope of Mt. Ararat. "Yes," Daedalus said aloud to himself as he read it, "it sure does!" He skimmed over the technical explanation of how the researcher had verified this, something about proprietary satellite imagery and Mercator projection overlays and *blahblahblah...But what's this?*

Daedalus noted with interest a second section of results. An entire second section? This ought to be good, he thought. And then, as he started to read it, he felt himself relax. It didn't seem to be important. Something about Ethiopia, about how this was the only other region on the map with significantly rendered detail—about the same level of detail as imbued to the Mt. Ararat region. Well so what, he thought. Maybe they started to make the whole map with more detail and decided not to, who knows? It led to the ark already and that's all that matters.

He started to tap out an acknowledgement of receipt when his phone's blinking light reminded him that he still had an unopened voicemail. He eyeballed the number, hoping it was something he could put off. But he squinted as he looked at it, not because he couldn't see it clearly, but because it made him think, *I better listen to that.*

Daedalus had learned long ago that it paid to have local eyes and ears on his side, even if that meant outlaying capital for something that most of the time would pay no dividends. But when it did, it tended to be huge. And Turkey was a country he'd done business in before, so it was a relatively simple matter of touching base with an old contact and getting her to reactivate the old human network. Eyes and ears on the street. Hotel maids, store clerks, cab drivers—these people were easy to buy. Tell us if you see two American adult males travelling together—when, where, for a bonus, what they were talking about. That sort of thing. But airport employees, police officers, military personnel, customs officials—those types of positions were considerably more difficult to buy. And yet over the years Daedalus and his Treasure, Inc. inner circle had managed to pocket one or two of that category in the country of Turkey. The richer in archaeological sites a nation was, the more contacts Treasure, Inc. strove to amass. And Turkey was a country known for a rich and varied archaeological history.

Daedalus let the voicemail play. Yes, he'd heard already that Carter and Jayden had made it off the mountain and back into Dogu town with a trekker van. His brother, he of questionable talent, as Daedalus thought of him, had told him that much. After that, though, their trail had gone cold. They could still be in Dogu, perhaps laying low in some off-the-beaten-track hostel. Or they could have left the country, probably back to America with their tails between their legs.

But according to this new message, an airport employee—this was high-level intel for Treasure, Inc., representing an annual expenditure that no doubt registered as a blip on the radar of their chief accountant—reported that the irksome duo had purchased tickets to Addis Ababa International, Ethiopia. Daedalus listened to the message again, to make sure he wasn't hearing anything incorrectly, but he had understood correctly it the first time. Ethiopia, but why? And especially, why directly from Turkey? It troubled him that they had the map, and that is where they chose to go. He didn't know why, but he was aware of Ethiopia being a place steeped in legend and lore—King Solomon, Queen Sheba…It was the kind of place that Treasure, Inc. did well to have on its radar.

Something else bothered him as well. He opened the notes from his cartographer again and re-read them. *Yes, there it is:* the only enhanced detail on the entire map, besides the Mt. Ararat region, was that of Ethiopia. Daedalus found that to be troubling.

He picked up his satellite-phone to call Phillipo, still on the mountain. It was time to set the full-scale salvage operation into motion, to retrieve the rest of Noah's Ark. And then there was the matter of the Omega Team buffoons travelling around with the original map that he now knew for certain led to Noah's Ark. He set the phone back down. He didn't want confirmation of their success to go to their heads and make them complacent. Daedalus relaxed and leaned back in his chair as he sipped his tea.

Let Phillipo stay on the mountain and handle the ark extraction process, Daedalus thought. The old saw popped into his head: *When you want something done right…*

He picked his phone up again, but used it to dial his private charter jet service. Another extravagant recurring expenditure he committed to in order to be ready for world travel at a moment's notice. Although long periods might elapse during which it was not really needed (though still fun), it had already justified itself many times over. After this trip, Daedalus surmised, the private jet charters on standby would seem routine. No, after this, he mused, he'd be able to afford his own *space program*, never mind private jets. He cleared his throat in preparation to speak to his air charter outfit.

I'm going to Ethiopia.

CHAPTER 31

St. Mary's of Zion Church, Axum, Ethiopia

After being dropped off by another taxi about two miles away, at another church, Carter and Jayden had walked here, to the church that Ethiopians claim is the housing place for the Ark of the Covenant.

"Kinda looks like any of the other church in this town," Jayden observed from behind polarized sunglasses. Before them stood a weathered stone edifice, ornately carved with arches and latticework on the windows, with a large dome on top, itself topped with a towering ornate cross. A trickle of people, a mix of tourists and locals, moved in and out through the holy house's entrance.

"It does, and inside, no doubt we'll find the requisite replica of the ark."

"So you already doubt they have the real ark?" Jayden smiled.

Carter shook his head. "Supposedly the real ark is in *there*." He pointed to a smaller concrete building some distance away on the same property that was surrounded by a metal fence painted with the colors of the Ethiopian flag, green, yellow and red. "That's the Chapel of the Tablet."

Jayden glanced over at the other building, which had no people coming or going from it. "The tablet? Meaning, the stone tablets that the Ten Commandments are chiseled on?"

247

"Yep. Thing is, no one's allowed in there."

Jayden laughed softly. "Gee, I wonder why not? Could it be because they don't really have the Ark of the Covenant in there? I mean, has *anyone* ever seen it?"

Carter held his hands up while gazing at the chapel outbuilding. "No. It's guarded by a monk appointed for life who is supposedly trained to kill with his bare hands anyone who tries to enter without permission."

Jayden nodded slowly. "Let me guess. We're going to have to deal with this guy to get in there, aren't we?"

Carter looked back to the main church. "Let's go in there first. See what it's all about, act like tourists, get the feel of the place."

They walked up to the entrance and climbed the few broad, stone steps, milling in with the light foot traffic as they filed through the front doors. Sure enough, the inside of this church, although considerably larger than the other one they had visited, was a lot like it in both décor and interior setup. Rows of long, wooden pews in the middle, spacious aisles on the sides, artwork and historic murals on the walls, with a central stage-like setting up front. This was covered in Persian rugs, and on a pedestal in the middle of it all was another life-sized replica of the Ark of the Covenant.

While they strolled leisurely up to the representative ark, Jayden commented how there were a few curtained-off doorways behind the stage and on either side of the church. Carter nodded, but replied in a low voice that they probably wouldn't find much of interest there. But he knew that as a former SEAL, Jayden had been well-trained to identify and monitor all possible ingress and egress options when inside a building.

They waited their turn among a small gaggle of onlookers to walk up to the ark and stand in front of it. Around them, some people stood in place murmuring words of prayer. Carter and Jayden stayed a respectful amount of time and then strolled away and back into the pews. They took a seat off to the side of one of them near the front.

"It's going to raise our profile a little," Carter began, "but I think it's worth it for us to get a look at the Chapel of the Tablet in daylight."

Jayden nodded. "I saw a few people walking up to the fence that surrounds it and taking pictures from there. Anyone can do that much, at least."

"Yeah. I'd really like to get in there, though."

"How hard can it be?" Jayden wondered. "One guard? Is he even armed? I mean come on, if they were really guarding a priceless treasure, wouldn't it be more like a Fort Knox around here?"

"Only one way to find out," Carter said, standing from the pew.

#

They stood in front of the colorful metal fence topped with razor wire and stared through it at the Chapel of the Tablet. The chapel was an unassuming stone, blocky building but for a small dome on top with an ornate cross atop that. The side they faced featured no doors, only windows overlain with heavy iron grates. There wasn't much to see.

"Let's take a walk around the outside," Carter suggested.

They sauntered around the perimeter as if they were tourists chalking off yet another landmark from their To See list, pausing now and then to point out some architectural feature. But in reality the two operators were taking careful mental notes of the entire structure and property, noting all exits, potential exits and other features of possible strategic or tactical interest.

When they had made their way all the way around, they confirmed that there was only one traditional entry point, a doorway covered with a red tapestry, set at the top of a few narrow stone steps. As they stared at the building, pondering how they would gain entrance, a man, presumably an employee, exited from the front and only door.

Carter looked at Jayden. "Should we just ask him if we can have a look?"

Jayden appeared doubtful. "You know what the answer's going to be, and it would call attention to us. He might remember us later."

"True, but on the other hand, maybe we get lucky, or maybe he could be persuaded."

"Your call."

Carter had a feeling about the man as he observed him, that he was in a congenial mood, whistling as he walked. He turned to Jayden. "Why use brute force when you can just sweet-talk your way in, right? I think it's worth a try."

They walked over to the front of the fence, where the employee—he didn't look like a guard, but more like he performed a custodial or maintenance role, with a large key ring full of keys and a tool belt on. Taking a quick look around, Carter was satisfied that no one else was within earshot of the conversation that was about to take place.

"Excuse me, sir?" he called over to the man through the fence. An African in his fifties, he glanced over at them but did not stop walking as he strode up to the only gate in the fence, which was locked. He removed a key from his ring while Carter and Jayden walked over to him outside the fence.

"I'm sorry, but the Chapel is closed to the public," he said in good English, barely looking up at them. "The church is that building, there."

"Yes, we know," Carter said. "We were just wondering if you could tell us, is the Ark of the Covenant really inside there?"

The man clicked open the gate, apparently in no fear of the strangers whatsoever even though they were inquiring as to off-limits areas. Evidently it was something he was used to from casual visitors. He barely batted an eye as he answered, "Of course it is!"

"Can we please see it, just for a second?" Carter asked.

"No, I'm sorry but it is closed to the public at all times, and under professional guard twenty-four-seven. Only the Guardian of the Ark can decide to let anyone see it."

"Could you introduce us to the Guardian?" Carter asked.

The gatekeeper shook his head, still smiling as if he'd answered all of these questions many times before. "No, he only meets with religious leaders. I myself am forbidden to see it, and I have worked here for years! Perhaps if you were the Pope I might be able to arrange a meeting, otherwise, I am sorry." He pulled open the gate and stepped outside of it, next to Carter and Jayden.

"We are good people, and we respect your country," Jayden said.

"The man smiled and nodded at him. "It is good to hear that."

Jayden began to recite from memory: "*Until the philosophy which holds one race superior and another inferior is finally and permanently discredited and abandoned, everywhere is war. And until there are no longer first-class and second-class citizens of any nation, until the colour of a man's skin is of no more significance than the colour of his eyes.*"

The African's eyes widened and he burst into friendly laughter. "You know Haile Selassie, our great former king! That is from his famous speech!"

Even Carter appeared surprised.

Jayden smiled sheepishly. "I know it from the Bob Marley song. By the way, I love your country's flag and the whole Rastafarian theme everywhere," he said, nodding to the painted fence.

Again, the gatekeeper smiled. "Ah yes, and an excellent song it is! You know that Bob visited our country one time, in 1978, probably before you were born," he finished with another laugh.

"So in the spirit of One Love," Jayden said, "is there any way we could have just a few seconds' look inside, so we can tell our friends back home that we've laid eyes on the true ark?" Jayden did his best to make his gaze as from-the-heart and natural as possible. And the employee did make eye contact with him while continuing to smile. But again he shook his head.

"I am very sorry, but the answer can only be no. No one is allowed in there, not even if you were Bob Marley himself would I be able to let you in there, my friends. I do hope you understand."

At this Jayden could only nod. He had tried. But Carter had one more ace up his sleeve.

He held up some cash bills, blocking any view of them from the church with his body. "Maybe if we could not even actually go inside, but just have a look through the door for five seconds? Five seconds!" Carter pleaded, gesturing with the bills, not a trivial amount.

The smile disappeared from the worker's face as he eyed the money. "Please put that away. We could both get into a lot of trouble. I am sorry but the answer is still no. I will forget I saw that," he said, eyeing the bills as Carter stuffed them back into his pocket. The employee closed the gate and turned the key in the lock until it clicked. "Now please return to the main church. Enjoy the rest of your stay in our country." He glanced down at the pocket where Carter had stashed the bills and frowned one more time before walking away in the direction of the church.

"We better go," Carter admitted in defeat. They walked back out to the front of the main church in full view of everyone, including the employee. From there, they hailed a cab and got in, giving the driver the name of one of the larger hotels they'd seen in town. Carter knew it was within walking distance of others, and they would be booking a room at one of the others so that even the driver wouldn't know where they were staying. It probably made no difference, Carter knew, but at the same time it was a simple enough step to take to provide a modicum of security, and Carter and Jayden had found out the hard way that it was good to stay in the habit of being discreet when in this line of work.

During the cab ride back into town, they avoided any talk of their objectives, but made small talk about where they might eat that night, how hot it was out, the kind that any tourist might make. After being dropped off at the Sheraton and paying the fare with a tip that was generous, but again, not overly memorable, they walked into the lobby and had a drink at the hotel bar. The idea was to stay just long enough to be able to throw off the driver, or anyone else who might be observing them, before relocating to the hotel where they would actually be staying the night.

"Besides, Jayden said, a beer sounds just about perfect right now." But there were a fair number of patrons bellied up, and the soft reggae music playing in the bar didn't leave them with confidence that it would drown out their words, and so again, tactical talk would have to wait. They enjoyed their extra-large St. George Ambers, left cash on the bar and then walked out back onto the sidewalk.

"Hotel Aksum is right up the street," Carter said as they began to walk. Not long after and they were taking an elevator up to the fifth floor after booking a room for the night. Jayden tossed his backpack on the floor and immediately checked the mini-fridge.

"Bummer, not pre-stocked."

"Probably a good thing," Carter said, "Because we're going to have a busy night."

Jayden eyed him suspiciously. "Infiltrate the chapel?"

Carter nodded slowly. "I want to take a look in there. It won't be that hard."

"There will be a guard in there," Jayden said. But they both knew that was no real obstacle for them, two seasoned naval warriors. "To make things as easy as possible, we should pick up a pair of wire cutters at a hardware store."

Carter frowned. Even if they paid cash, they'd be seen doing that.

"Either that or we lug a blanket all the way there," Jayden said, eyeing the beds, "and throw it over the top of the razor wire so we can climb over."

"No, it could be traced back to this hotel after we leave it behind. Even though we're booked on fake names, there's no need to establish any connections."

Jayden perked up. "We could buy one of those general tool kits that has everything, including a wire cutters, so it's not like we're buying only that, which is way more suspicious."

Carter nodded. "Good idea. We'd better get going. We'll pick up some tools, maybe a flashlight or two, get some dinner in town. Then late night tonight…"

"Go time!" Jayden was excited. While he picked up his backpack and took out the things he needed for the trip into town, Carter checked the hotel drawers. It was an old travel habit he'd developed, since one never knew what was left behind, or even had had been left on purpose. The desk drawer had the requisite Holy Bible, and he was about to close the drawer again when he reconsidered. He picked up the book, thinking it could possibly come in handy since the ark stories, both that of the Covenant and of Noah, were biblical in origin.

"Let's go, dude, I'm hungry!" Jayden called from the doorway. Carter put the Bible in his backpack so he wouldn't forget it later and headed for the door.

CHAPTER 32

Midnight in the town of Axum brought a darkness that was not quite as complete as what they had experienced high on Mt. Ararat or in Iran, but still lacking light pollution much more than the typical western city. After being dropped off by a cab at a nearby hotel, they walked a mile or so to the Church of St. Mary of Zion. It was closed at this hour, which Carter and Jayden considered both good and bad. Good, because it meant there would be fewer witnesses around to observe their activities. Bad, because they had no excuse to be here and no one else to blend in with.

They made a beeline for the side of the Chapel of the Tablet that faced away from the main church, since there was no road facing that side. When they reached the fence there, Jayden removed the new clippers he'd purchased in town from his pack while Carter kept a careful watch. The fence had crossbars so that Jayden was able to climb up high enough without a hand from Carter to reach the razor wire with the clippers. These were thick, circular steel coils, not simple barbed wire strands, and it took some doing, and a couple of minor nicks that drew blood from Jayden's hands, even through the pair of work gloves he wore for the task. But he cut through one entire section, and from there they were able to pull it off to the side and tangle it into the fence itself so that there was a razor-free section in the middle.

Over this they climbed, Jayden first, since he was already up there. He dropped with barely a sound to the Chapel grounds and scouted their surroundings while Carter made the climb over. Once inside the fence, they ran to the side of the chapel so that they would at least be partially hidden from view by the building. They made their way slowly around the chapel to the side with the only door. Earlier that day they had noticed it was open behind the red curtain, and the curtain was still there now, but they were about to find out if they locked the door at night.

"You'd think with one of the most precious artifacts of all time that they'd lock the place up at night," Jayden had said earlier, and Carter agreed that seemed to make sense. Except that this was Africa, this was Axum, Ethiopia, the church with the Ark of the Covenant, and here nothing made sense.

"It's open," Carter whispered after pulling the curtain back and poking his head around the corner. He chalked it up to the reality that they had a guard inside at all times, and maybe the fact that as a place reputed to hold the most sacred of religious objects, perhaps they felt people, including criminals, would be inclined to leave it alone, such was the power of the Ark. Or maybe they just forgot? But Carter doubted they got that lucky.

From his brief glimpse inside he couldn't see much, because there was a partition only a few feet in from the doorway that blocked all view of the rest of the interior. He slipped past the curtain, waving for Jayden to follow. Once inside the doorway, they were shielded from outside view by the curtain and from inside view by the partition. Now they faced whatever awaited them inside, namely the Guardian of the Ark.

Where was he? They could hear nothing to indicate the presence of another human. Using hand signals, Carter indicated for Jayden to take the left side while he took the right. Peering around the edges of the partition, they both took in the view of the inside at the same time.

#

After hours of uneventful surveillance, Daedalus almost missed it. He had been staring at his smartphone screen while parked in his rental car, an economy sedan that wouldn't attract much attention on its own, out in front of the Church of St. Mary of Zion when he happened to look up in time to see two dark-clad figures disappearing behind the doorway curtain of the church. How silly to leave the church open all night when it supposedly safeguards such a powerful treasure, Daedalus thought. *Ridiculous!* It must be just another fake, no different than every other church in this town, the Greek antiquities dealer thought. The Ark of the Covenant, hah!

And yet, as someone who had made a fortune off of trading relics, he knew that it was the myth, the lore, the story behind the object that held as much appeal as the physical representation of that thing itself. Ethiopia was a poor nation, and its people took pride in what they did have, which was the legend of Queen Sheba and how the Ark of the Covenant was brought back here from Jerusalem by her son. So they claimed it was down inside this special church outbuilding, safe from prying eyes...*sure it was*...but where was the harm in that? No doubt it made the people feel good, and it even made a lot of the people who visited it feel good. Just not him, because he knew it was all hooey. And yet, the question still nagged at his consciousness: *Why were these two serious treasure hunters here all the way from Mt. Ararat?*

Daedalus was glad he had come here alone. No need to waste the time and resources of his entire team on this silly goose chase. Right now they were preparing the excavation of Noah's Ark from the lake, a task made more difficult since it had to be done in a covert manner. He was not about to apply for a permit and have the Turkish government swoop in and claim the find for their own, as they had done with other archaeological finds on Mt. Ararat in the past. No, Noah's Ark was all his, and the Ark of the Covenant, if it was real, would be his as well.

But he still saw no reason why those two thorns in his side had come to this place, right now. What was the connection? Yes, the *Titanic* map featured enhanced detail for this region, but...so what? It didn't show anything here, no X-marks-the-spot, no text of any kind...how did they conclude that it was worth travelling all the way here, and breaking into a fortified church building in the middle of the night (at least they had cut the razor wire for him).

Daedalus waited another few minutes to make sure they wouldn't be run out of the place by the guard immediately, and also that no one was observing him sitting in his dark car by himself. But they didn't come back out and as far as he could tell he was the only one out here.

Daedalus checked that the magazine on his Heckler & Koch MK 23 large-frame pistol was full, and that the sound-suppressor was fitted properly. He preferred the 1911 he'd had on Mt. Ararat before it was stolen by Carter Hunt, but this would have to do. Then he stepped out of his car and quietly closed the door.

CHAPTER 33

The inside of the place, off-limits to the public, was simpler than they had imagined. Only two rows of small pews occupied the floor, and a dais supported a lectern, with a large cross on the wall behind those. Unlike the main church, this small chapel was set up only for very small, private services. Clearly, it was designed for one purpose, which was to support the reliquary in the center of the room between the dais and the row of short pews.

The Ark of the Covenant?

About the same "true-to-life" size as the other fakes they'd seen, the ark was on plain display at the front of the chapel, the same rectangular box adorned with cherubs and gilded in gold, including the carry poles. It looked the same, but was it? They were about to find out when they heard a noise.

A rasping, sort of a snorting sound coming from up by the pews. Carter recognized it as something produced by either an animal or a human and immediately took a defensive crouch position. His hands went to the fixed blade knife he'd worn in a sheath attached to his belt, concealed beneath his untucked long-sleeved shirt. Jayden also ducked below the pews and listened. After a few seconds it became apparent that they were hearing snoring. Someone was sleeping on the bench. In a normal church, this would be understandable, but this was a private building, moderately secure with the razor wire fence and off-limits to the public.

So who was it?

Carter and Jayden approached the pew from opposite sides, weapons drawn. Each had only a blade, no firearms since they didn't want to raise eyebrows by trying to obtain one in a foreign country. As he reached the end of the short pew and raised his head to just above eye level over the top of the wood, Carter almost had to suppress a laugh.

Laid out on the bench was an elderly man wearing long, flowing robes and ornate headgear. A large cross on a gold necklace hung loosely across his chest as he slept.

Carter and Jayden met again just behind the bench. "Dollars to donuts that's the Guardian of the Ark!" Jayden whispered, laughter in his eyes.

Carter nodded his concurrence. "We need to secure him while we check this place out. You tie him up while I look at the ark. I'll help you if we wakes up."

Jayden agreed and removed the length of rope from his pack he'd brought along for this contingency. They definitely didn't want to hurt the monk, so they had come prepared. While Jayden snuck up on the guardian, Carter moved to the ark.

He considered it for a moment from a security standpoint; he didn't need to trigger any alarms, silent or otherwise, so he scrutinized the assembly carefully, looking for signs of wires or any other electronic components. Seeing none, he then turned his gaze upward, to make sure there were no lasers aiming down, no tripwires or any other exotic apparatus, out of place as it would seem here. Nothing.

He walked right up to the ark and after staring at it closely, slowly shook his head. He could see paint peeling slightly in spots, revealing the plywood beneath. He placed a hand on it and felt the dull, non-metallic surface, definitely not gold gilt.

"It's just another replica."

Jayden looked up from having just trussed up the terrified monk and gagging him with a cloth in case he tried to scream. The old man calmed down somewhat when Jayden told him they were not going to hurt him, and that they would untie him before they left.

Jayden told the guardian, "Excuse me," and walked over to stand next to Carter, who had a sheepish look on his face.

"Why am I not surprised?" Jayden asked.

Carter shook his head. "I'm really sorry. We should have just stayed in Turkey."

"It's cool, bro. Hey, I was wondering how far they take this charade out anyway, you know—like, do they go so far as to have replicas of the stone tablets inside the thing, too? I wanted to find out in the other churches, but somehow I thought it might piss people off to pry the thing open."

Carter shrugged. "Since we've gone to this much trouble, before we leave we might as well find out."

"I'll find something to stand on." The ark was on a raised pedestal that prevented them from being able to reach the top to open it, or see if it even opened.

"It's probably just sealed shut on top, would be my guess," Carter said while Jayden brought a chair back he'd taken from a corner. Standing on that, he was able to get a look at the top of the construction.

"Huh."

"Huh, what?"

"It does look like it has an actual seam that goes all the way around. Let me see if I can lift—" A grating noise was heard as Jayden lifted the lid and slid it a short distance to see whether nor not it was fixed in place. "I'm sure it'd be a lot heavier if this whole thing was really gold plated," he said, pushing it a little farther off center. "Hey Carter, go around the other side and get ready to catch this thing if it slides all the way off, okay? I don't want to make a lot of noise, or break it. Hear that, Guardian—we're being as careful as we can over here. Just a quick look, and we're out of here."

Behind his gag, the monk made vigorous protestations suggesting that he was not at all happy with this turn of events.

Carter trotted around to the opposite side of the replica ark and said that he was ready. Jayden slid the lid, complete with wooden carved cherubic fixtures, further across the top of the container until the edge closest to him dipped into the box. He shoved it further until it started to slide over the far side. "Here it comes!"

"Got it." Carter eased the lid, still heavy even though it was made mostly of plywood, down to the floor. He lay it down flat so as not to damage the intricate carving work on its top, and then called up to Jayden. "So are there fake tablets in there or what?"

Jayden did not reply. Carter looked up to see him staring down into the ark. He saw him aim his small flashlight down into it.

"Jayden?"

"Oh there's something in it, all right, but not stone tablets. You're not going to believe this. Get up here!"

The bound guardian continued to vocalize unintelligibly behind his gag while Carter found another chair and set it next to the one Jayden was using to look into the model ark. Carter stepped up onto the chair, put a hand on the edge of the open ark to steady himself, and then, following the beam of Jayden's flashlight, gazed down into the structure.

Jayden was certainly right. No tablets occupied the inside of the ark. In fact, there was no inside of the ark, not really. The outside, including the stand that the ark rested on, was merely a shell to conceal the floor below. Although it appeared from the outside like the ark was supported by the dais, or stand, in fact the two were part of the same deceptive construction, forming a hollow barrier around this particular section of floor.

"Looks like a combination safe embedded into the floor," Jayden said, shining his flashlight on it.

"Let's check it out." Carter climbed up and over the ark façade, gripping the open edge and then allowing himself to drop straight down for about six feet until he landed on the floor inside the frontage. The bound priest was moaning louder than ever now, and Jayden tried to placate him, saying that they'd be right back, before he, too, dropped into the deceptive "ark."

The floor here was the same as that surrounding the fake ark, except for the combination lock set into it, along with a metal handle. Carter produced his own flashlight and immediately began scanning it, aware that if anyone else were to enter the chapel right now, they would be in very serious trouble. He focused on at first what the lock was set into. It appeared to be part of a cutaway square section of flooring that was two feet on a side.

"It's big for a safe," Carter said, kneeling down to take a closer look at the locking mechanism. "At least this thing is easy enough to understand."

Four dials, each set to zero. The numerals "1" and "2" also visible on the dials. "I assume they're zero through nine," Carter said. Jayden nodded his agreement.

"Four number combo. Let's try pulling the handle. We'd feel pretty stupid if it was already open, right?"

Carter tried pulling the handle, but predictably, it had no effect. "Thing's tight, doesn't budge a millimeter," Carter said. "We need to know that combination." He shone the flashlight around the inside of the fake ark some more, as if it would be scrawled on the wood somewhere, but there were no obvious clues.

"I know who would know what it is." Jayden's eyes widened as he looked up out of the shielded floor safe, toward the monk.

Carter took a deep breath. "We can ask him. But we can't hurt him."

"I don't think there's any point in even asking him. I can't threaten an old priest, anyway. Besides, what do churches keep in their safes? Maybe the donations they collected at the public house of worship next door? C'mon, we're not bank robbers, we're treasure hunters."

But Carter appeared not to even be listening, as he shrugged off his backpack and extracted from it the original map from the *Titanic*. "Do me a favor and hold your flashlight under this, will you?"

Jayden moved his light into position. "I thought we already went through this," he said. "The three invisible lines?"

"Yeah, but I've had more time to think about it with our travelling, and there's something I want to try. Hold on, we might need this." He reached into his pack once again and this time pulled out the Holy Bible he'd taken from their hotel room. "Hold this, too, will you?"

"Sure, I'm not allergic, I don't think." Jayden took the Bible with a smile. "Just don't make me swear on it with my right hand, I've had enough of that already in my life."

"I'll bet. Now hold the light steady, right there…" Carter positioned the map precisely over the light until he could make out the three invisible ink lines.

"One thing about these lines. They're not drawn straight from point A to point B, but curve way out of the way to accomplish the same thing. Why is that?"

Jayden shrugged. "Map maker was no good at drawing straight lines? They didn't have rulers back in those days?"

"Try again."

Jayden stared at the map. "Artistic license? It just looks better that way?"

"Now that could be, but I hope not. Plus, they were done in invisible ink, so aesthetics probably weren't a consideration. Let's look at where these lines go and what they connect."

"Okay sure, no hurry or anything. We've got all night down here, I'm sure." He made a goofy expression that indicated he was being sarcastic.

"So first line, from left to right, goes from the lake on Mt. Ararat to here, Axum."

"Okay. So why were the other two lines even needed?" Jayden asked.

"Let's see. The second, middle line, is from Mt. Ararat to Israel. And the third line goes from Israel to Axum, passing through the Red Sea, the only one of the three lines to cut across any major body of water."

"Still don't get it."

"I know this isn't exactly our private study hall," Carter said, looking over at the bound priest, "But let's unpack this a little."

"Be quick about it."

Carter nodded. "The significance of each line: As you said, the line from Ararat to here is obvious. It's where Noah's Ark was, to a place long rumored to be the final resting place of the Ark of the Covenant."

"Right, so the others?"

Carter traced a fingertip along the map, following one of the invisible contours. "Ararat to Israel. So, real quick: Ararat has two lines leading away from it: one to Axum, and one to Israel."

ARK FOUND

"What happened in Israel?"

Carter thought for a moment before speaking. "We know that Ethiopia is heavily associated with the Queen of Sheba lore."

"Okay, so Sheba who had the kid with King Solomon of Jerusalem, the son who eventually brought the Ark of the Covenant back here to Axum."

"Right, Menelik. And that makes sense because there's also the third line connecting Israel to Axum; that could literally represent Menelik bringing the ark back to Ethiopia. Also, the Red Sea is clearly a Moses reference."

"Because he parted it."

"Yeah. And of course he's the one who brought the Ten Commandments down from Mt. Sinai. So that's what all these invisible line-connected places have in common."

Jayden shook his head. "Those are all great stories, man, but we need some numbers here." He pointed to the combination lock in the floor. "Four of them."

But Carter seemed not to hear him. He was staring at the map, utterly transfixed as if oblivious to the world around him.

"Carter, seriously, if we can't figure this thing out right now, we're just going to have to come back. We know there' something down there. We can—"

"Let's try one thing."

"Numbers, Carter, we need those numbers."

"Right, so how about this: it's weird to me that the lines are curved instead of straight, like we were talking about. So what if the lines are curved so that they have to pass through more countries or distinct regions as dictated by the lines on this map."

"Explain, hurry." Jayden looked over at the trussed monk, who was trying to shout from behind his gag.

"The left line passes through…" His pointer finger parsed the map as he counted. "Six countries or regions."

"Okay, six."

"The middle line passes through only one demarcated region or country."

265

"One, got it. So that's six, one."

"And the third line passes through, let's see here…"a total of nine countries."

"Okay," Jayden said, "That gives us six, one, nine." He made a sour face as he looked down at the floor lock. "But it's a four digit code. Come on, Carter, this is a waste of time!"

But Carter did not panic. He stared some more at the map, lost in deep thought. Jayden was just about to interrupt when he looked up and said, "Queen Sheba, King Solomon…Jayden, it's Kings!"

"Huh?"

"The verse in the Bible." Carter nodded to the book in Jayden's hand. "Look for it. In the Book of Kings, verse 6:19."

Jayden opened the book. "Okay, but there are two Books of Kings: 1 King and 2 King."

Carter hesitated for a second and said, "Maybe there's only one of them with a 6:19?"

Jayden flipped through the pages, running his finger down a particular passage, holding his place and flipping to another section where he did the same. "Sorry, but both of them have a verse 6:19."

"Okay, then just read both of them, starting with the one you're on. What's it say?"

"This is from 2 Kings." Jayden read aloud from the scripture. "This is not the road and this is not the city. Follow me, and I will lead you to the man you are seeking."

Carter chuckled softly. "I think we can rule that one out. So what's verse 6:19 from 1 King say?"

The sound of pages turning was the only noise in the chapel for a few seconds. Then Jayden read aloud: "The inner sanctuary he prepared in the innermost part of the house, to set there the ark of the covenant of the Lord."

"Bingo!" Carter stood up and put the map away back into his backpack.

Jayden's face transformed into a mask of wonder as he still stared at the Bible. "Yeah, now we're talking! Inner sanctuary…innermost part of the house…" He stared at the section of floor with the lock.

"Now I'm thinking this definitely isn't a safe." Carter also stared at the locked section of flooring. "It's a trapdoor."

"That makes good sense, but we still need the combination."

Carter looked up from the Bible and smiled at him. "What did we just do? Think of the verse number: *1 Kings 6:19.*"

Jayden's eyes widened. "Four digits: one, six, one nine! I'll do it!" He quickly knelt and turned the dials until they were positioned to **1 6 1 9** from left to right. "They're lined up. Pull it!" Jayden backed away from the trapdoor and Carter leaned over to grab the handle.

He pulled it upward and the section of floor lifted away with silent ease, on well-oiled hinges. Carter was able to pull the floor piece up and back until it rested in place, exposing the square cut opening in the floor. Jayden moved in with his flashlight and shined it down into the new space.

"There's a ladder. Bare stone floor about ten feet down. That's all I can see from here."

Carter grabbed his backpack off the floor and put it on. "Let's check it out."

"Ladies first," Jayden said, stepping back and aiming his light down the open trapdoor.

"Feels nice and cool down there." And with that, Carter descended the ladder.

CHAPTER 34

Carter swept his flashlight around the space while Jayden climbed down. He could see a bulky object not far away, but a panel on the wall caught his attention first. Walking to it, he found what he was looking for: a light switch. Flipping it up bathed the room in clean fluorescent light from tubes hanging from the ceiling that flickered to life. Next to the switch on the wall was a thermostat. Odd, Carter thought. A climate-controlled room wired for electricity beneath a church out-building in a small Ethiopian town.

"Oh my God!"

Jayden's voice caused him to turn around, and then he laid eyes on it, too.

Another Ark of the Covenant, full size, occupied this subterranean room. On first glance it looked like the other replicas they'd seen, but after gazing at it, subtle differences became apparent. The intricate embellishments, etchings and carvings on the sides and lid, for one thing. Strikingly detailed, a powerful statement of original artistic might, patience, and attention to detail. Another difference was that the light gleamed off of its golden surfaces in a different manner.

Carter couldn't help himself, he seemed to be drawn to the object, this cynosure of the room. He traced his fingertips along the sides of the ark, and instantly recognized the cool, smooth touch of metal, in stark contrast to the wood-covered paint the other replicas had to offer.

"Jayden?"

"Yeah." Jayden slowly made his way from the ladder to the ark.

"If this is a replica, it's not like the others. It's very well made. I think this is gold…." Carter walked around the ark while passing a hand along it. The cherubs on the lid were also golden. The only part of it that was not gilded with gold were the two carry poles, one on each side, each of which passed through two golden rings affixed to the ark.

The ark was set on top of a recessed area of floor such that they were eye level with the top of it when standing in front of it. Jayden reached out a hand and touched the lid. "This is gold. Sure is some fancy replica."

"Why would they have the climate control for a replica?" Carter asked.

"The obvious answer to that is that it's not a replica. We could be looking at the real thing, here, Carter. But, if it is the real thing, why is security so low? A fence and one employee to guard the Ark of the Covenant? Does that seem right to you?"

Carter walked slowly around the ark while he answered. "Maybe people spend so much time openly disbelieving and in some cases mocking the idea that the ark is real, that they don't have to guard it all that well. The easiest way to prevent people from stealing something is to make them think they don't have it, or that it doesn't exist in the first place."

"Well I can think of one way to find out." Jayden put both hands on the lid. "I don't see a hinge, so instead of flipping up, I think it has to be lifted off, so if you go around to the other side, we can—"

"Don't open it! Freeze, put your hands up or I *will* shoot!"

A furious-sounding male voice echoed in the underground chamber. Carter looked up from his position next to the ark to see Daedalus standing high on the ladder, gripping it with one hand while the other aimed a pistol fitted with a sound suppressor at his head.

"Fancy meeting you here, Daedalus," Carter said.

"Stalker," Jayden added.

Daedalus quickly dropped the rest of the way down the ladder without lowering the weapon. "Thieves," he countered. "I believe you have something you stole from me."

"Your sense of humor?" Jayden jabbed.

Daedalus shot him a withering stare.

"You'd think a man with a gun pointed at his head would take things more seriously." Daedalus shifted the barrel of the weapon from Carter to Jayden.

"Here," Carter said, touching one of the straps of his backpack, which he wore over both shoulders. "It's in here. The map, right?"

Daedalus grinned. "The map from the *Titanic* which led us to first Noah's Ark and then the Ark of the Covenant? Yes, you are correct in thinking I want that back."

"And you!" he yelled sharply to Jayden, "get your filthy hands off of this holy object before I shoot them off!"

Jayden lifted his hands from the ark and took a step back while narrowing his eyes at the Treasure, Inc. founder.

"I'm going to take my backpack off and toss it over to you so you can take the map, okay?" Carter asked.

"Do it *very* slowly," Daedalus commanded, now walking away from the ladder a few steps toward the ark. "Any questionable moves and your life is over. It will be difficult enough for me to conjure a scenario where I can allow you to live after this, anyway, so don't give me a reason not to have to figure it out."

Carter employed sloth-like motions to remove the backpack so that he was holding it by the strap with one hand out in front of him. "I'll toss it over to you, a few feet in front of you."

"Got to warn you, though, D-man, we ran outta toilet paper up there on the mountain, and so I might have used the map to wipe my—"

"Silence, you buffoon!" Daedalus waved the gun at Jayden. "You are the farthest thing from worthy of this place."

"We'll see." Jayden remained defiant under gunpoint, arm's length away from the ark.

Daedalus crept up until he stood over the backpack and slowly knelt in front of it. "You can just take the whole bag if it will speed things up. I think that's in both of our best interests, seeing as none of us were actually invited here," Carter said. "Consider it a souvenir."

"Not so fast," Daedalus countered. "Fool me once… as they say. I need to see the map."

"Fine. Inside main compartment, zipper pouch on back, remove the false bottom in that, it's in a Ziploc bag."

"Once you have the map, then what?" Jayden queried. "You plan to steal this giant box by yourself and take on the entire country of Ethiopia to get it out of here?"

"I will have to come back for it, but whatever happens to it from here on is no longer your concern."

"I don't think it's even possible to get it out of here," Carter said. "It looks like this entire chamber was built around the ark after it was in place. Like they never intended for it to be removed again. The trapdoor entrance is far too small for it to fit through, and there are no other exits down here, just four featureless walls and the floor."

"The fake ark up there was only an empty structure that led to a trapdoor," Jayden said. "What if this one is the same? A fancy fake, but still a fake, and maybe, if we open the lid, it's just a hollow structure that leads somewhere below the floor."

"I think this is the genuine article," Carter said, "but there's one surefire way to find out, because we all know what should be inside of it, if it is the real deal."

"True enough," Jayden said. "Think about it, Daedalus. We could all be fighting over nothing. Let's open it!"

Daedalus looked up from unzipping Carter's bag. "The lid does look too heavy for one person to manage. Go ahead, as they say in your country. Make my day!" Daedalus erupted into obnoxious cackling as if what he had said was the funniest thing ever uttered. But when he saw Carter and Jayden standing there watching him, he was quick to anger. "Now!" he yelled, centering the barrel of his pistol on Carter's chest. Carter moved to the opposite side of the ark from Jayden.

"On three, ready?" Jayden said, making eye contact with him. Daedalus moved a step closer, beyond eager to see what the reliquary held.

"One," Jayden began, positioning his two hands on the edge of the ark's lid.

"Two." Carter did the same on his side. Daedalus took one more step closer to the nearest end of the golden spectacle.

Jayden shifted his feet ever so slightly. "Three!"

Jayden and Carter strained with both arms, pushing with their legs, and the lid began to lift away from the gilded container. Daedalus moved yet another step closer to the ark. Carter was exerting nearly his maximum physical strength to do it, but the cherub embellished slab rose from the box.

"Okay, slide it my way, I'll ease it down," Carter breathed. Jayden started to do that, but then he suddenly removed his left hand from the lid. As the heavy lid began to fall back down on the ark, Carter caught the briefest glimpse inside. It was not enough to absorb any serious detail, but sufficient to see that it did in fact have a bottom corresponding to the depth of the box, enough to confirm that it was not a fake façade like the one above.

He saw something inside of it, too. Gray and large, not part of the box itself. And that's all he had time for, because after that, the lid was slamming back down on the top of the ark and Jayden was in motion.

The Asian-American former SEAL's left hand dropped in a flash from the lid to the wooden carry pole beneath. At the same time as the lid slammed down, Jayden slid the pole through its double rings with a whip-like motion of his left arm. The result was to send the carry pole flying through the air toward Daedalus like a spear. The ends of the carry rods were even tapered, lending them a small bit of favorable aerodynamics.

Jayden was in motion toward the Treasure, Inc. crime boss even before the tip of the pole rammed into Daedalus' stomach, doubling him over while Jayden ran to him. Carter saw what was happening and set himself into motion toward their foe a second later.

Still doubled over, Daedalus brought his gun hand up toward Jayden, but Jayden dove, extending his hand in midair to knock the arm down. He was successful, with Daedalus able to squeeze off only a single shot that

missed Jayden, and the ark, lodging harmlessly against the wall behind the
relic. But missing the shot didn't mean the antiquities thief had given up.
On the contrary, he kicked the pole toward Jayden on the floor and then
charged at him, keeping his head down like a battering ram.

Jayden's right foot came down on the pole and it rolled, causing him to
nearly twist his ankle. In fact, he probably would have if it weren't for the
fact that Daedalus' head bashed into his chest, sending him flying
backwards into the ark.

Carter intended to come to Jayden's aid but when he saw the gun fly out
of Daedalus' hand, clatter onto the floor and slide toward the corner, he
went after it instead, seeking the endgame that having control of the
weapon would bring.

When Jayden slammed into the ark, he screamed out in pain as his
shoulder collided with the metal-plated wood. It was stout and stable
enough to wobble slightly, but not tip over. But the lid, which had come
back down askance after they dropped it, now slid off of the ark. Jayden
was on his back and saw it coming in barely enough time to roll out of the
way, avoiding having his skull crushed when the corner of the lid impacted
the floor where his head had been a half-second earlier.

Daedalus scrambled up from the floor and launched himself onto
Jayden, who began throwing short jabs into his assailant's chest and ribcage.
Carter reached the dropped pistol and picked it up. He checked the
magazine and made sure a round was loaded into the chamber, then cocked
the hammer.

"Jayden, just back away from him. I've got the gun, back away!"

Yet Daedalus was proving to be a tenacious fighter. He took the blows
Jayden threw up at him and rained down a couple of his own, his longer
reach compounding his on-feet advantage while Jayden struggled to get off
the floor. The fact that he still wore his backpack back made smooth rolling
on the floor impossible, but he was able to get halfway over onto his side,
then roll away from his back and fling his top leg into a devastating kick
that landed on the side of Daedalus' face.

The treasure magnate grunted as a gob of blood emptied from his mouth and soiled the floor. Jayden crab-walked backwards a couple of feet, onto the ark lid which had landed upside-down.

"Freeze, Daedalus. That's enough!"

Daedalus looked up at Carter with hatred in his eyes, but stopped moving. Jayden backed up a couple of more feet and then rose.

That's when they heard the sirens.

"Someone see you come in?" Carter asked Daedalus.

But the treasure man only laughed softly while blood dribbled from the corner of his mouth.

"Could be that we tripped a silent alarm," Jayden surmised.

"Either way," Carter said, leaning down to scoop up his backpack off the floor, "it's time for us to go."

"Watch him!" Jayden eyed Daedalus, who was in the process of regaining his feet.

"Not yet!" Carter barked at him. "You wait right there on the floor until we're up the ladder. You get up again and I'll shoot."

Daedalus eased back down to the floor while Jayden backed away from him, still not willing to turn his back to the dangerous and power-hungry fighter. Carter kept the gun trained on Daedalus until Jayden had reached the ladder. The sirens were louder now.

"Come on, Carter," Jayden said, a hint of desperation in his voice. "Although from my brief stay here, I think I'd prefer Ethiopian prison to Iranian prison, we do *not* want to try to explain our way out of this if at all possible. Carter? Are you listening, because those aren't exotic birds making that noise out there, they're police sirens."

"I'll never go to jail," Daedalus spat. "My connections are too strong. But you two will rot in hell for this."

Yet Carter ignored him, too. He was transfixed by something he saw on the floor, over by the ark. He handed the pistol to Jayden. "Keep this on him one second." Then he strode over to the ark in a few long steps and knelt. The corner of the ark's lid had broken when it hit the floor, and Carter picked up the broken piece, about the size of his palm. In its fractured state, he could see the thin layer of gold and then the dense, dark wood beneath it.

"Carter, now! I'm heading up the ladder." Jayden bellowed.

Carter pocketed the ark fragment and ran to the ladder, never taking the gun off Daedalus. Jayden was already at the top, pausing to assess the situation in the main chapel. The sirens were very loud now.

"Until we meet again, Daedalus. In the meantime, if the Ten Commandments are in there," Carter said, realizing that he hadn't even looked inside the now completely open ark, "I suggest that you learn a thing or two from them. There are definitely a couple that apply to you."

With that, Carter spidered up the ladder with the gun in one hand. Jayden had already topped over and was standing in the chapel, so he didn't pause at the top but did the same. Once on his feet, he turned around and pointed the gun down at Daedalus. "Come up now. I don't want you messing with the ark or whatever happens to be in it. Get out of there now."

Even with the oncoming police, Carter tried to get a glimpse of the uncovered ark from the top of the trapdoor, but the ark was too far back in the room to be seen from here. Daedalus moved to the ladder. He stared up at Carter, stone-faced, and began to climb.

Outside, the police cars sounded like they were pulling up in front of the main church.

"Got to do one thing," Jayden said, running to the guardian he had tied up. Reaching the pew, he bent down to remove the bonds, when he saw the gunshot wound between his eyes.

"Oh Geez!" He felt the pulse but knew what the outcome would be. "He's dead, Carter!"

Carter now considered the pistol's sound suppressor in a new light. No wonder they hadn't heard the shot that killed the Guardian. He yelled down into the covenant room.

"Daedalus, you scum! You cold-blooded murderer! You killed a bound man! You're a monster. You don't even deserve to be in the presence of that ark down there, genuine or not. None of the beauty or riches that humankind has to offer mean anything to you. Maybe that's why you seek to hoard them, hoping that someday some of it will sink in and erase your ugliness? But it won't. You're too far gone."

"I see flashing lights, Carter!" Jayden called from the partition at the front of the chapel.

Carter ran halfway to the front, then took a left to the wall beneath a window. "Let's not go out the front. This way." He pulled the wooden lattice off the window, then ripped through the screen. He could hear Daedalus climbing up out of the ladder.

"Stay back for sixty seconds after we're gone, Daedalus, or I'll shoot."

Eyeing the outside, he saw it was free of police, so he jumped through. He heard Jayden's feet pounding through the chapel and then landing on the dirt behind him as he ran for the section of fence where they'd cut the razor wire.

The Omega Team pair bolted around the chapel corner and then made a beeline to the cut fence section. They could hear the blare of police radios now, car doors slamming, officers talking. Looking back in that direction, could see the pulsing hues of red lights. Jayden scaled over first, then Carter. Jayden pointed toward a grassy hill with some tree cover, in the opposite direction as the chapel and main church.

"This way, let's go."

"Go, I'll catch up."

Jayden looked at him like he was crazy. Carter pulled a handkerchief from his backpack's outer pocket and used it to wipe down Daedalus' gun. "I don't think we need to get caught with this, do you?"

Jayden shook his head. "Good idea. Toss it. Let's go."

Satisfied he'd wiped the trigger, grip and all parts of the weapon clean, Carter then tossed it over the fence into the chapel grounds.

Then they turned and ran for the hills.

EPILOGUE

One month later
Hidden Hills, California

Carter Hunt was about to get up from his desk when an email notification sounded from his open laptop. A spark lit in his eye on seeing who the sender was, and he sat back down and clicked it open. At last, the lab results he'd waited so patiently for. Confirmation, or at least partial confirmation, of his theories—or—denial—was at hand right now.

Upon arriving back to the states from Ethiopia, he had sent the timber sample from the lake on Mt. Ararat and the ark lid fragment from the Ethiopian chapel to a laboratory he trusted and had worked with before. Without telling them what he thought the samples were, or where they came from, he explained he wanted an analysis of the wood, and carbon dating of each sample to determine their age. The email had a .pdf file attached, but as usual, his lab guru was kind enough to put the "bullet-point take home message," as she called it, in the body of the email. Carter leaned forward and read with rapt attention:

Plant matter (wood) bioanalysis: Both samples are consistent with Acacia wood. Not only that, but DNA testing concludes that both samples are from the exact same "batch" of lumber, or same living forest of trees.

Radiocarbon dating: As expected given (1), both samples are the exact same age, dated to about 4,800 years old.

Carter couldn't help but whisper the word, "Yes!" The wood from Noah's Ark and the Ark of the Covenant was not only the same type of tree consistent with what historians say was used in their construction, but they were the same age with the same plant DNA, meaning they were from the same individual trees. This confirmed his theory that, since Noah's Ark was older than the Ark of the Covenant by about 2,000 years, that the latter had been built using timber from the former. Why else would the map, which had been accurate with respect to its location of Noah's Ark on Mt Ararat, have hidden lines leading to The Ark of the Covenant in Ethiopia?

Because it's the same wood! Carter pounded his fist on his desk as the realization struck him with icy clarity. The map was telling its readers, Noah's Ark is here, X-marks-the-spot, but if you find my hidden lines, you'll find something more. They're hidden because what they lead to isn't Noah's Ark, not exactly, anyway. But it's made from Noah's Ark: The Ark of the Covenant.

Carter thought about the historical connections between the two biblical icons. He knew that both arks were represented in the Bible as powerful symbols of salvation: One for Noah and his family, to repopulate the Earth after God destroyed it during the Great Flood as punishment for humanity behaving badly, as well as the animals of the Earth that humankind depended on for their own survival. But also one ark for the moral code by which humans should live, for their own well-being and to help them avoid the necessity for a second Great Flood. Both constructed from the same batch of timber, two thousand years apart, until God himself summoned Moses from the top of Mt. Sinai in Egypt. Even the basket in which baby Moses floated down the Nile, to escape drowning by order of the Pharaoh, was called a *ta-va,* the Hebrew word for "ark."

Carter shook his head to clear those thoughts. He certainly didn't have all the answers, but he knew one thing: the world now had a much better chance of experiencing its common heritage of treasures, biblical and otherwise, now that they had been wrested from Treasure, Inc.'s control. As soon as he had returned from Ethiopia, Carter had anonymously notified the Turkish Ministry of Culture and Tourism authorities that unauthorized removal of possibly significant archaeological relics was taking place, knowing that this would stonewall Daedalus' operation there. Carter had followed with great interest the Internet news story a week later indicating that Turkey had taken over an archaeological site on Mt. Ararat from non-permitted "archaeologists," who were immediately deported from the country.

There was one treasure that Carter had managed to return home with. The map from the *Titanic*. He had given it to his client, Ms. Ashley Miller, without mentioning the three hidden lines. She was so elated, she paid Carter a bonus, saying she had never expected he would actually be able to recover it from the wreck in the first place, much less get it back after it was stolen. Now that he had, she said she only wanted to hold it in her hands once and see it, to feel the connection to her family's past. After that, given everything Omega Team had gone through to obtain it, and what it would mean to the other families of Titanic passengers, she was happy to donate it to a museum for all the world to see so that the tragedy of that "unsinkable ship," that failed ark, might be remembered by all.

Carter got up from his desk chair and stretched. He and Jayden had both been impacted by all they had seen. It had given them a lot to think about and reflect on. After arriving back home in California, true to Carter's word, they had celebrated surviving the *Titanic* at Neptune's Net, one of their favorite beer and seafood joints on the Southern California coast. While there, Carter presented Jayden with a new G-shock watch to replace the one he'd had to barter for bus fare in Newfoundland. Over fried calamari and Big Wave Ales, Carter told Jayden he was a much better drunken bar customer here than he had been at the pub in St. John's, which reminded Jayden of something he'd wanted to do. He had a friend take his and Carter's picture at a table full of pitchers and food, the Pacific Ocean in the background. Then he looked up the pub online, and saw that it accepted online payments. He electronically sent a large tip, followed by an email with the picture apologizing but hoping this would help make it up to him.

After that, Jayden left for vacation in Hawaii, surfing and scuba diving to cleanse his mind in order to be ready to return to work for Omega again. Carter opened the sliding glass door that led from his office to the back yard. Unlike Jayden, he had preferred to get right back to work, sending in the wood samples, contacting his client, monitoring the news sites for information on the places they had impacted. He knew someone else who he was sure got right back to work after it all, too.

Daedalus, and probably most of his black market company. Getting run out of first Ethiopia and then Turkey wasn't going to stop him. He knew where the Ark of the Covenant was. Carter hoped the Guardians of the Ark would move it and implement stronger security this time. Because Daedalus and Treasure, Inc. wasn't going to give up, he knew that. And yet he had his doubts anything would change. The news stories in Ethiopia, which somehow did not make it beyond the local news cycle, beyond a couple of tabloid-style sites popular with conspiracy theorists ("Church Housing Ark of the Covenant Under Attack by North Korean Special Forces" and such). Police in Axum reported a break-in to the Church of Zion (no mention of the Chapel of the Tablet), where a priest was killed (no mention of the Guardian of the Ark, either). A murder weapon was recovered, but no arrests had yet been made, and the investigation was ongoing. No mention of the underground ark room or that the ark was open and its intricately carved, gilded lid damaged. Perhaps these details were left out for investigative purposes, Carter thought, so that someone who was actually there could be separated out from those who weren't by mentioning certain details.

Carter decided not to tell anyone about finding the Ark of the Covenant. He said only that they went to Axum and visited the famous church, but that the ark there was only another replica. When asked how they thought to go there from Turkey, he explained that he got the idea because the

Titanic map had more detail in Ethiopia than any other place except for Mt. Ararat. He made no mention of the invisible lines. Instead, he put forth the idea that perhaps the Ark of Covenant was built using wood from Noah's Ark, and this notion was promptly disregarded by scholars.

Carter walked out into the yard, down to where a small, babbling brook traversed his property and ran downhill to the city below. It wasn't always running, only after enough rain, but it was now. Smiling, he took the piece of the Ark of the Covenant from his pocket it and turned it over in his hands. So much history, so many people's lives affected by this piece of wood...

Reaching the stream, he held the fragment of the covenant lid in his hands for a moment, turning it over as he contemplated it. Then he tossed it into the water. He watched it drift away, slowly at first, then picking up speed as it left his property and started downhill toward the city, toward humanity, toward the future.

THE END

Sign up for Rick Chesler's mailing list to be informed of new releases: **www.rickchesler.com/contact**

If you enjoyed ARK FOUND, you might also enjoy the following novels by **Rick Chesler:**

ATLANTIS GOLD (Omega Files Book 1)

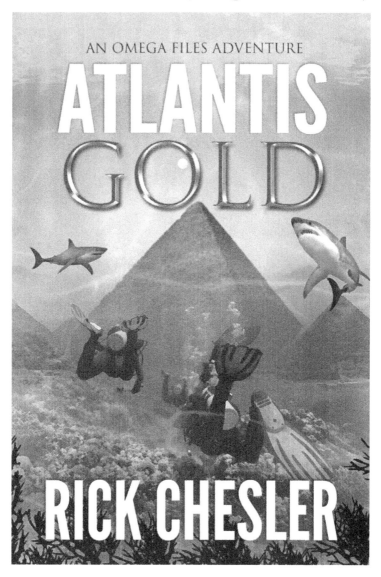

AN OMEGA FILES ADVENTURE

ATLANTIS GOLD

RICK CHESLER

Made in the USA
Middletown, DE
14 August 2021